ASHES TO ASHES

STACEY WILLIS

First Edition.

gentle is *the beast*
of that odd night :

" *stay, stay* amidst the
dying of *the light.* "

OTHER WORKS BY
STACEY WILLIS

THE DAUGHTER OF FIRE SAGA

Daughter of Fire

Son of Death

Mark of Kóri

Heir of Bones

OTHER BOOKS IN THE SERIES

Flake of Snow: A Novella

Reaper of Gods

Tempting of Fate

Crown of Kings

Mother of Pearl

THE KEY HARVESTER

There's a Dagger in Your Back

OTHER BOOKS IN THE SERIES

Dot Dot, Line Line

STAND-ALONE BOOKS AND NOVELLAS

Ear to the Serpent

For those who escape every day
between pages, in search.
Looking for a tale of awe.

Finding a ruination.

PRONUNCIATIONS

Ferream: *Fair-um*

Loid: *L-oy-d (like void)*

Isotton: *Ee-so-ton*

Daemon: *Day-mon*

Takunda: *Tah-koon-dah*

Grande: *Gr-ah-n'd*

Ricci: *Ri-chi*

Excumen: *Ex-koo-m'n*

PRAISE FOR
ASHES TO ASHES

"A breathtaking, twisted tale of love and monsters.
The writing in itself was one of my favourite things. It was poetic, inspiring and addictive, and I stopped almost every chapter with the urge to write a line down because of how good, relatable and real it was. [ ] The queerness of the story only enhanced this aspect, as it was very well-written. The love story was like a light in the dark in the middle of everything and I truly loved how it was both dark and hopeful in a very beautiful way."
Blanche Maze, author of *Darkest of Thrones*

CONTENT WARNING

THE FOLLOWING IS A LIST OF TRIGGERS AND TOPICS OF WHICH THE READER SHOULD BE AWARE:

violence and mild gore
mention of animal death
underage alcohol and substance use
alcohol misuse
mention of psychological abuse
queerphobia and shunning
physical abuse (mentioned & present)
mention of emotional abuse (bullying)
mention of family death
suicide ideation

I

BEFORE

the beast

BEFORE LUCIFER'S COUNCIL

+

THE FALLEN ANGEL'S lulling voice came as a haunting caress to the curve of the demon's ear —nothing but a hissing slither, like a serpent. "Just as you were created, so too can you be destroyed."

Lucifer's detained creation remained silent. It was a muscled yet agile thing; made of iron with giant feathered wings wrought from the depths of the Lowest Ring. Great white horns curved up from atop its head. The long pale tangled tresses clumping over its shoulders were tinted red; the fresh blood soaking and the congealing blood clinging.

It had been about thirty minutes since its apprehension.

The beast recalled the screams and desperate begs for mercy that had accompanied the spilling of the red liquid, and it smiled. The demon had savoured the taste; the smooth finish of it riding down its throat.

It did not think that it had gone against orders. This intervention was clearly and grossly unnecessary.

"Does it not know how to control itself?" asked the adviser and Lord of the Flies, Beelzebub. His compound ruby eyes slitted as he frowned at the beast. The large fissures within its wings splintered further.

The intense heat on the barren planes of the Lower Rings was stifling; the starved ground cracked and bone-dry.

"It appears that I have granted it too much free rein," the king of Hell realised, clicking their tongue in distaste. They roughly gripped the jaw and tilted it upwards so that its turquoise and violet crescent moon eyes met their master's fiery golden suns.

"Haven't I, little one?" Lucifer purred.

They still received no answer. Just wrath and burning hunger in those unholy created irises.

"Hm. It refuses to speak. Does it have no tongue?" Crowley, Lucifer's highly annoyed first general, jeered.

"Oh, he can speak," snarled the Morningstar, jerking the beast's head to the side. "And laugh, too. Do it, Ferream. I command it."

The demon grinned and promptly barked a chortle; causing blood to spill down its neck. The perfect expression of a deprived sadist.

"So this amuses you, my liege," Lord Beelzebub huffed, flicking his sapphire robes and sending up a cloud of red and orange dust. "You have been pardoning this *mistake* for far too long," he went on. "Chance after chance —reality must be faced. It is too volatile."

"Ferream is the most perfect tool for the End Times," Lucifer stated. "Those Heavenly Hosts won't stand against it."

"But the plan and preparations will come to light earlier than we wish if the beast continues," the adviser countered. "Look at what it has done —first a few missing persons, now the decimation of a government office. My king, there is…*talk*."

Lord Beelzebub spoke of it as though it were news to the Council. Of course there was talk —the king knew that. They were not a fool —certain high authorities knew of it too. It had only been a matter of time, really, before Lucifer's secret weapon was to be unveiled in glorious darkness and carnage. The pet was simply getting a little testy.

"The creature does not understand the attention which it has drawn," Crowley then added. "The Archangel Raphael *will* investigate. My king, you will not be able to keep this abomination in the dark forever."

It was too soon —the apocalypse was yet to begin.

"I am aware," the Fallen Angel admitted tightly, turning on their heel before stalking away from the iron beast. The cracked marble wings, just as was the rest of them, unfurled. "Get it out of my sight. I need to think."

The two attending demons at either side of the free-standing door carved from a great oak moved to obey their orders, allowing the officials to leave the copper desert first. The Fallen Angels, burly beings with skin like garnet geodes and wings of black glass, glanced at Ferream.

And they shuddered.

The iron thing then stirred, its large wings rearing in a slow flap. Those crescent eyes locked with theirs of white light and flame. It only stared, toying with their trepidation.

"No resistance?" remarked one demon.

"I thought that it might break those chains," murmured the other. The bloody creature's elven ears flattened against its pale hair, but it did not retaliate in any way. If anything, the Fallen amused it as well.

Would it speak to them, the two guards wondered, even with its master not present?

It was unwise to test the limits of Lucifer's pet.

But the beast opened its mouth, and from it dribbled more thick rivers of crimson. The Fallen Angels saw those canines made for ripping apart flesh and bone. Its predatory teeth were thoroughly stained red.

"Take me," it purred, tilting its head. "The king ordered you to take me away. Why do you hesitate?"

Honesty was an eerily unfamiliar concept to the demons.

They instead exchanged a brief look, before moving to take hold of the captive. The creature was hoisted up, its shoulders gripped by one hold and its ankles by the other. The Fallen ignored the mortal blood, far more concerned with security. The chains seemed delicate.

The only material which could restrain the beast here was salt from the mortal oceans. It burned its iron skin, but it had come to like the pain.

It was not the first time that it had been chained.

It would not be the last.

The created demon did not mind. That was the way Lucifer preferred to see it before them; restrained. The king would fancy themself merciless but when that came in the way of pride, they would waver.

So the monster would suffer for the Morningstar —it would keep that weakness at bay for their sake —and be glad in it.

The small cell was engulfed in rot and sulphur. Lucifer insisted that the foul stench would encourage bitterness and vengeance. As true as that proved, the beast had come to realise that there was a comfort in it.

Familiarity echoed the feeling of belonging.

Though Ferream knew that it had not been made to feel such things — only to take pleasure in destruction. It had an idea of the balance of wicked and good —but it would not accept it. Flattening that office tower had been a scratch on the surface of what it knew to be an intrinsic desire. To see the world fall to its knees, screaming and red.

The creature then shifted slightly at another familiar thing: a presence not like a demon nor its master. There was a particular soul that always drifted in and sat in front of it by the bars, silent.

Watching.

At first, the demon had thought their intention was to mock and pity. The mortal in fact only wished to observe, and keep company.

It unnerved the beast. What sort of mad must the mortal have been, to wilfully remain in its presence after death?

Its crescent eyes met the empty bronze gaze of the naked young soul; skeletal and bereft underneath their warm brown skin, as though the very essence of them had been extracted. The beast wondered if the mortal's living sin had been greed, or gluttony.

The soul did not usually speak. But it would today.

"Who did you kill?" they asked.

Ferream started, the slight sway of hair the only sign of movement. It had imagined a different sort of voice for the soul —perhaps like that of the human men. This voice…was like a mixture, and yet neither.

The beast refrained from speaking in front of anyone but Lucifer. If it did, it was about its master. However…there was a compulsion to speak with the soul that crept and hovered and whispered to the ear.

A compulsion that did not seem to be ignorable.

"…One hundred."

The soul was largely unfazed by the grating, razored voice of the demon —a lesser part which Lucifer had not quite gotten right as of yet —and slowly shook their head.

"*Who*," they repeated.

The Made demon frowned. "All mortals are the same to me. Bits of dirt. I cannot tell them apart."

The soul's gaze wandered.

"How do you always enter here?" Ferream then asked.

The question was ignored. The mortal did seem to be affected by the creature's cold answer, though they could not decipher how. Instead, they posed another, "…I know what you are. Do you recognise me?"

"You have been coming here for a while. I have grown used to your visits, however few and far between they might be."

"So, you've actually seen me all along?"

"Is there a reason for me not to able to?"

The mortal reached to pick at the withering wall. Another question to be left unanswered. "…If I stopped coming to you, would you mourn?"

"No," said the beast.

The soul paused, glancing down at their bare feet. "…I am from the Earth," they contextualised their inquiry. "In each of my dreams, I come here. Then I wake. I always forget in that world. But I remember when I see you. Every time, I am drawn here. To you."

"You yearn for power —but unfortunately I cannot provide it for you. I am already owned."

The mortal shook their head. "I yearn for a closeness. It hurts if I go anywhere else —anywhere but where you stay. Though we had only ever met…here. It is as if a part of me remains behind with you."

"You are a human mortal," Ferream insisted. "It is natural for you to feel those emotions. But…why for me? Have you no righteousness? I am a monster, I know that much. I am Made."

The soul did not respond.

They said nothing further.

The two continued to stare; two tethered things in all of boundless space; until the mortal began to crumble and waft away into a dust. The demon watched, its chest growing strangely heavy, until it was alone again.

It had never before been bothered by the lonely, miserable solitude in the vastness of its holding cell.

Its cage.

Those words had never once crossed the imagination. It was dry and sweltering, adding to the stinging burn of the chains.

Lacking, as though something had been ripped from it.

"Yes," the monster chuckled, too late. "I think I would mourn."

The soul did not stop coming. Not immediately.

Ferream saw them again, after however much time had passed. The progression of time was a difficult concept. It implied life, death and even possibility. Damnation had nothing to do with any of these.

Nothing grew, nothing withered, and nothing flourished. It was a state of stagnant punishment with forever unattainable mercy.

Would you mourn?

It was boring without them.

The question had only been intended to provoke; to garner a reaction. It was a pity that the human had not been permitted to stay long enough to bear witness. What a sight it would have been, to see a beast pause and think about the empty space just outside of its cell. Crestfallen.

Disappointment was a painful, foreign feeling.

But the introduction to the possibility of never seeing that mortal again was in fact what made Ferream fully aware of them. It saw all that they did; listened to all that they said; and it had even begun to anticipate their presence. Even if there were no words exchanged and only looks —even then the loneliness was eased. The wisp of a soul had opened the demon's eyes in a sense, and allowed it to see beyond the binds of whatever held the two together. And the physical ones of its own which seared.

Sorrow then became pointless, and for a moment, Ferream wondered if the mortal's threat had been strategic.

It certainly felt that way with the face they were giving it right then. Total concentration and vague intrigue. A sliver of personality had started to seep into their exchanges. The soul was sitting up directly against the bars, idly clutching them as they stared the monster down.

"Why do you kill?"

Ferream glanced at a damp, crumbling wall. "Why do you breathe?"

The soul's brows rose. "In order to live."

"Then our reasons are the same," said the beast.

A soft disbelieving scoff. "Sometimes I wonder if I want to continue, though," confessed the mortal. Their eyes then lowered. "Breathing."

The demon tilted its head. "Want?"

"Want and need are not the same thing."

The iron beast blinked. They were only some strung words —they did not mean anything. Whatever it was that stirred within it at the utterance had to be one of those terrible miracles of which its master had warned.

But something else roiled inside from that moment on. Confusion and an invasive anger that was not its own; a rage felt on another's behalf. Something that would from then on, forever refuse to be supressed.

It so happened that the monster remained docile within its cage for a noticeably prolonged amount of time. It did not behave as a spoiled child, taunt the Fallen —nor did it boast in its skill to raze.

In fact, it had not killed any living being as of late.

The guards could not account for a lack of destruction. Ferream had kept to itself in contemplation. The only oddity was that occasionally, it would answer questions out loud that no one had asked.

The prospect of putting the Archangels' suspicions to rest was enough not to probe into the slow taming of the beast.

And it was indeed slow —perhaps it had taken whole days and weeks and moons to see and hear the change truly manifest. To Ferream, it had blinked and suddenly known respite.

Blinked and found the innate urge to destroy this mortal diminished. Shifted one inch upon the old, filthy floor and found curiosity swelling alongside a feeling that wasn't hate.

It had come to know four distinct things about the soul.

Their name was withheld.

Names did not matter within the scope of their acquaintance. They knew each other deeper than words —so it seemed. They had felt the texture of skin on occasion; hands on bars and fingers overlapping. Gazes soft and fixed. All of it was cold and a flurry in the heat of the prison. And like a vine curling up along a stone wall, the mortal human had wrapped around the beast and come to occupy its being.

They did not fear death.

Ferream thought it odd that in all of the time it had spent razing, this was the first soul to look upon expiry without cowardice nor embrace. They did not yearn for that end, but they knew it was coming. Though even in the monster's temptation to call it passivity, the human showed a different attitude in small gestures. The lowering of their head; the lidding of their eyes; the tugging downwards of the corners of their mouth —it indicated to the demon that the mortal could not be afraid, yet still dread what came afterwards. It was limp acceptance…and a tiredness, almost.

They had confided in the monster they were sure that when their time came, they would end up right back there —burning and clutching at bars while their lungs drowned in sulphur.

And Ferream had not said anything, because what had needed to be communicated had not been with words. Their vastly different eyes had met, and the creature had offered comfort in that alone. Hell was all that it knew, after all. The two did not share the same fears.

The third thing Ferream knew, was that despite only it being the one in chains, both of them were bound.

By the dreams, and by the hands which guided those. When with the monster, the soul felt free. They could lay down the burdens which came from being alive and pretend for minutes at a time, they were weightless. Untethered. Even if they had to be sitting cross-legged in Hell to achieve that feeling, with only a Made demon for company.

Perhaps the giant iron thing shared in their solace.

Brown eyes caught blue and purple.

Ferream once thought that stare unnerving. It had evoked something which lined its abdominal cavity with a thick, dreadful and sticky residue. It had believed itself to be familiar with all negative emotions, but the one brewing from the cold, dull brown mimicked…malady and unrest.

The eyes were warm now. A beautiful shimmer of anatase, bronze and the sunlight. And it pleased Ferream to stare into them for any unspecified reason; searing the memory into permeance.

Because if there was one thing which was predictable about the human race, it was the inevitability of their deaths. In many ways, mortality was a good thing for them. There was not enough sufficient good within even one to warrant undying lifespans.

But when the monster looked into those brown eyes, time dissipated. Each second was infinite. Had it been that way all along? Maybe the soul was being sent to rip into the expanding spectrum of feeling, and redeem even just one of the wretched human beings.

Though this didn't quite resemble redemption.

It was closer to relief and gratitude.

Whatever charged between them was layered and complex. In fact, it ached and choked and tempted the beast to do away with it. But it could not rid itself of the paradox. The feeling only grew.

What mattered on Earth meant nothing here.

"Do you know what this is called?" the soul murmured, gripping onto Ferream's clasped fist over a bar. It felt like touching fireworks.

"A hand."

They nearly smiled. "No, the heavy feeling inside your chest. The one that weighs you down and stops the breath from going to your lungs. Do you feel it too, dear monster?"

"Yes."

They did not fear the beast. Who was in many ways, death. Perhaps that terror had never been with them. The mortal had always been far too close, far too calm and too inquisitive. They had never approached the creature in any way that indicated they did not want to be there.

Want.

There was a difference between '*want*' and '*need*'.

A selfish part of the demon, still intrinsic, liked to think that their visits were a want *and* a need, even if the mechanics of it all were a mystery.

"What is it called?" Ferream asked, meeting the soul's gaze.

Something glinted in their eyes — like a sadness. "Will you remember if I tell you?"

"…I will try to understand it."

Their fingers moved slightly, caressing its cold metallic ones in idle comfort. "It's called love. Maybe the most contradictory, dual and painful emotion to feel. It can be wonderful, burdensome and ridiculous. But we still feel it. Some of us feel it even if we don't want to. Though all forms differ, love is what drives us. Love is what brings our ruin."

The monster gently stroked their hand in return. "Cool to the touch," it said. "It's boiling in here, yet this refreshes me."

"We must truly feel it then, to be so delusional," the mortal remarked. "I have the heat of blood. Humans are very conductive."

"Is that a…joke?"

"Yes." The skin by their eyes crinkled slightly. "But we are."

Ferream had never heard them laugh. It supposed that it was difficult to find amusement amidst their situation. Amidst a reality so very tangible and harsh in front of them. The most it had gotten was the ghost of a smile; the memory of pleasure and happiness.

"Love," it said. Tasted the word on its tongue.

It did indeed constrict its chest. When had curiosity turned to demand and desperation? Its hand then enclosed the human's tighter. It had been a very gradual, measured decline down a steady slope. Impossible to tell until it was standing at the very bottom of it.

There had been no epiphany; no clap of thunder to alert the two.

Their love had been pulled and tangled by unknown hands, but it was their gravity alone that had let them claim it. The closer they became the more it would hurt and suffocate —but they were sure they knew that.

"Do you want to breathe now?" Ferream asked.

The soul pressed their forehead to the bars. "More so."

The demon smiled. It would smile for them both.

Of course —it knew that the revelation was meant for this space only. It was abnormal for the mortal to be there, and not yet dead. Not suffering. If the guards could see, if they could bear witness to this small thing of great magnitude…everything would return to its original state.

They would be taken from the beast.

And it would not feel; not because it would lose the ability to do so as soon as they were absent, but due to the very fact that Ferream would no longer have anyone with whom *to* feel those emotions.

Love meant nothing without the one who had taught it such.

Love meant nothing without the one who did not fear.

"Stay," pleaded the monster. "Keep coming, or I will mourn."

The mortal's lips parted as if to give an answer, but the crunch of dirt at the end of the hallway abruptly turned their attention. They had never paid mind to the surrounds. Whatever alerted them had to be a true threat. But Ferream didn't understand. It shouldn't matter.

Brown fingers pulled away —too quickly and without enough of that thick, sticky feeling it still had not named.

It barely blinked, and the human had begun to disappear.

Ferream's ears flattened against its hair. Someone was approaching. Rhythmic footsteps strode towards them. The created demon then tensed. It knew those feet. It had kissed them in reverence.

Lucifer's robes came into view.

They crouched down, the wings blocking all light so all Ferream could see were the wells of flickering fire which formed their gaze. "Have you yet learned something, little monster?"

Their voice was not affectionate when they said that word.

"Come," the king commanded. "There is work to be done on you."

For the first time, the beast hesitated in its obedience. Had the Fallen Angel always been so irksome? It wondered if calling them '*master*' was still viable after learning all which it had. Ferream had grown into its own entity —separate from its purpose. It could feel other things now.

It could feel love.

And whatever the king had given all along, was not such.

Its gaze slid to the empty space to the side of Lucifer, where a young mortal had sat just moments prior. Its hand was too warm and there was no trace of the soul. Not even a disturbance to the sand and dust.

It had to be the fault of the Morningstar if the soul was gone. They'd never come to the cell since giving the order to place the beast there, and the moment that they had, the human had gone. Had felt *fear*.

Something exploded within the iron demon.

Something red and screaming.

Following the regular and unhinged alterations to the monster's function, it was to recuperate within its cell. But it was far darker without the light; stifling without the cool breeze. Initially Ferream worried that the mortal had been so terrified by the king of Hell themself that their subconscious would not allow them to visit. Though they had never established that the dreams were in fact within their control. So if they were, and the soul was staying away of their own volution, where did that leave the pair and their bewildering, secretive bond? For a while the beast dared not think of it.

Each thought and speculation was a pick to chip away the iron at the place where a heart would be in its chest. There had to be a reason as to why the human was biding time.

So it waited.

It waited until the dirt that tracked inside had piled an inch higher, and the temperatures had increased a few degrees. It waited for the time it thought the Earthly moon would take to wax and wane.

But the soul did not return.

And deprived of answers and touch; with the collective experience of a child, the beast became inconsolably angry.

the town

IN THE WAKE OF CRISIS

+

HUMANS HAD WAGED plenty of wars on the whims of emotion.

The Made demon could not understand that complex stupidity of the mortals —the apparent favourites of Lucifer's own former Master.

But it could fathom their urge to destroy.

It coursed through it constantly.

Nothing was lovely; nothing was good; nothing was kind. Ferream's vision returned to the world with which it was familiar: broken, doomed and bloodied. It knew that it was necessary for misery and judgement, but there had been no limit. The beast had known of no end to terror, and no rules that might be attached to rein in instinct.

It might have been made entirely of it; that involuntary tendency.

And that drove it to wreak havoc.

There was a small, insignificant riverine town in a country so riddled with foolishness and corruption that it seemed to beg Ferream to rid it of its very existence. It noted no redeeming citizens —though that still didn't stop it. All humans appeared the same; were of the same nature and had the same potential. There was no time to be wasted upon educating their wilful minds —like barren lands no longer suited for growing crops, there was no real chance of salvation.

Only death, and cleansing.

In the absence of the one lone beam of all which could be good, the monster reverted.

Ferream had marked out every inch of the forest lining the small town of Pine Creek. It had spent a year long ago, on and off, documenting and assessing the most favourable routes in order to carry out a plan. It knew of every living species within; every sort of tree, each bird, arachnid and insect which migrated or was deeply rooted.

Despite its reputation, the beast was a calculating creature. All that it did was thought out and never truly on a whim. Each savage slice and rip had been measured. The only variable aside from those beyond even its control, was how much blood would spray on and within its skin and hair, and how much of it the monster would hold on its tongue.

Blood tasted of pride and guilt.

It ripened with age.

The demon raked a hand down the bark of a tree as it descended into the forestry beside the town. The wood curled, falling in thick ribbons. It did not want to raise alarm, but the feeling at its fingertips distracted from the still rising agitation. It was sharp but inconsequential, since no splinters could pierce its impenetrable skin.

It pictured the tree as a human being instead; imagined the screaming; and it knew that was the only way its rage could be satiated. The piercing sound reminded Ferream of the fact that it was conscious, and that basic delight came from rendering others not so.

The void left by the lack of one happiness demanded to be filled.

The sky was a washed out grey —the sun was there…somewhere, and the mass of colourlessness was an off-white not dark enough to warn of rain. The clouds had all merged together in a spiteful shield, though the only thing they blocked was the sensation of heat. Light still penetrated through the cover even if it was soft and muted.

Leaves which still clung to their tree and those that had lost their grip were deep red, canary and amber flame; vibrant and bursting with the mid of Fall.

The colouring was different in Spring or deep Winter. But the monster favoured the season of deterioration and haunting. Red likened blood and the orange was like fire. Quite like the setting sun at the end of the day.

Ferream signalled an end, too.

As it strode for the town through the wood and by the Youngs River; so leisurely without hastened steps, the grey was smothered and doused in a dark ash. Now not only did the sun not shine but the hope in the dull light withered. The shadows rained down very slowly —almost in way of a taunt. Great streaks of ink seeped and bled as if running down a canvas. All light was swallowed up if it didn't escape, and the only thing on which to focus by the time Ferream had made it to the town centre were its sharp and unforgiving eyes.

The cyan mesmerised the baffled residents as they stumbled from their homes and places of work. The violet crescents frightened.

The screaming was not immediate this time —that was the benefit of the demon's altered voice. Instead, it lulled. Almost like…like a miracle.

Unlike Lucifer, Ferream had no desire to be worshipped as God.

It knew of subordinacy and the merit of acting as a part of something larger than itself. The weight of Supreme appeared too hefty to bear.

"Love has abandoned me," declared the beast, unfurling its wings to the sky. "And now, so has your God. Only my wrath lies before you."

It could not confirm that, but reason had left long ago.

Someone screamed then. An elderly woman called Ferream the Devil. The unnatural parts of its form; the iron and long fissures, sporadically came in and out of view as ash darkened the horizon. Those curved horns were an afterthought, since the Made demon was not red.

Yet.

The monster snarled, revealing its canines. "I am the messenger. And I have no master."

Confusion still hung thick in the air, even after sight had been stolen. No one would be able to see the hand in front of their face —no one but the predator as it slaughtered each prey.

Ferream gathered all of the loneliness and betrayal it was certain it felt as if into its fist, before swooping down to the closest victim.

The first shriek put it all into perspective.

This was the town's abrupt, unsought end.

The crunch of bone alleviated a bit of frustration tensing the demon's joints. Watching the life vanish so effortlessly from a mortal body twisted the sensations of pain and rage; blurred them together until it was almost numb, and ripping through the rest was a task done in a lucid state.

Ferream wondered for a dangerous moment if the town's destruction would actually appease its knotted indecipherable agony —a moment that did not last long enough to stop the creature.

It tore through the next person —a mother, perhaps, and then her child lingering in the hallway, in some small semblance of mercy.

The screams were beginning to rise as the monster stood over its pile of corpses. Its iron wings reared, opening slightly as it assessed the dark. The residents had clamoured into their houses or cars, desperate to escape. But they would not be spared. Ferream's eyes pulsed with a more vibrant purple, and all the power died.

No car would start.

No call would go through.

No signal would travel.

In the blink of an eye, Pine Creek was dead to the world. The beast made sure that they would all be forgotten —a disposable speck in the middle of nowhere solely for it to vent out its anguish. These filthy mortals could be of some use and contribute that much.

They paid in insolence and sacrifice, as all retribution demanded.

Ferream wasn't sure who it was it pictured as it strangled a neck. Was it the soul? Was it Lucifer? Or was it abstract: its own emotion it wished to crush and take life from?

By the time the creature had gotten to the thick wooded outskirts, the screams were dying. It could now be mistaken for a demon made of ruby. Not only blood coloured its grey skin; bits of clothes and hair clung to the mess. It all trailed behind its strides, leaving inky prints, but it was too preoccupied to care about such things. Evidence would not matter.

Consequences were irrelevant.

The burn of abandonment screamed.

Branches and stone alike broke beneath its feet as it stormed the forest in search of stragglers. It sniffed the air for the telling scent of mortality but the waft was disappearing. Ferream had killed almost every resident of the small, pitiful town. There had hardly been anyone out amongst the trees. But there was a concentration —heading northeast, towards the city.

It wasn't gladness…the burst of motivation which came from locking in on the remains of Pine Creek was simply the catharsis of annihilating so many people at once. Instead of it being cruel and glorious as the beast might have described before, the carnage was *righteous*. Deserving.

Ferream could hear the light scamper of their feet striking the ground as they bound through the wood. It could hear their waning breath. Each insufficient gulp more desperate than the last.

It licked its teeth. There was no issue.

The monster liked the chase.

With one flap, it shot to the sky.

It wondered what the human could see as it ran. Had they no fear of the river? It did not seem as though they were aimless, but Ferream knew that their vision was not clear. Not enough to run without stumbling.

Their foot suddenly caught on a protruding root.

The beast immediately dove towards the panic, swerving between the pines and cypresses as it heard the rapid hyperventilating more clearly.

The scent of fear was always overpowering. It rose up and thickened among the other smells of species and age. What the demon picked up on was a mixture of that terror, and the fresh grassy tell of youth. So it was a human on the cusp of adulthood. Ferream did not feel remorse for taking the future away from them.

By unfortunate chance, the prey then found themself at the edge of a gorge, where the river split to carve out more earth. It was not too deep, but the jump was wide and it was enough to make them hesitate. Weigh their options. The water flowed below, cold and hardly less frightening in the dark than the monster chasing them.

Ferream landed a few paces behind.

It swept its wings along the forest floor before tucking them shut and straightening. It did not savour this hunt. None of what had happened was a feat of enjoyment and satisfaction. It had been a painkiller; a numbing solution. Just as quick and unpleasant as it was to swallow a pill, the beast lunged for the mortal with no thought, only urgency.

Claws and fangs snagged at whatever clothing was tightly wrapped around a torso. It quickly ripped apart, providing access to skin. Ferream was blinded by the pungent swirl of shock and innocence, and only sought to silence the cries and pleas which would turn out to be short-lived.

The moon peered through a tear in the ink.

It wasn't the beast who had called for the shadows' retreat. Just a small spotlight, coned and specific to let the beam through the gap onto the kill. Suddenly, the monster could see very clearly.

There were tears streaking down a narrow brown face contorted with agony and horror. Though even through the blur, something flickered in those eyes. Something with which Ferream was well acquainted.

"Ye —*argh*. De…Wha —"

Their words were choked garble.

Every memory came rushing against the hurt. The softness of a hand; the comforting lilt of a voice. The respite of company. Even the steadiness of hastened breath. The soul from the cell reappeared within Ferream's mind with all of the loveliness onto which it had come to clutch.

And then the dying human had a name.

But it was too late.

The demon saw the very life flash and drain from their eyes, as the blood continued to splatter out towards it despite its sharp withdrawal.

This was a variable for which it had not accounted.

The mortal collapsed —and it was not like the crumple of a paper bag or the gentle sway of a leaf. The body hit the ground with such a deafening thud like its bones were tungsten. The death was swift.

Though cruel and unceremonious.

Those glistening brown eyes were still open wide.

No. Not those eyes it loved. They *couldn't* be.

The monster paused, leaning over. None of its wishes were granted. The body before it…it was staring at that soul. That wonderful, traitorous soul. It had found the mortal on Earth, in the very place it was certain it knew like the back of its hand —yet of course the first thing it had ended up doing was killing them. Its source of life.

How disgustingly poetic.

It scrambled to gather the body in its arms. The warmth was seeping almost as fast as the blood. Yet the beast pulled their head to its iron chest and parted the curls of dark hair with an unfortunate bloody hand. That familiar face threatened to seem no longer so.

They were a child —quite like itself, but not. Ferream might be twice their size and physically fully formed, but in the ways that mattered, the soul had lived just as it had. Loved just as it had. Feared just as it had.

The demon reached to close their eyes.

Blood and slaughter separated their experiences…or at least, that had been the case before today. Right then, they had been the closest to each other as they had ever been. Even now —as they were both dead.

Only the beast should experience the horrors of damnation.

"*No*," Ferream forced out, as if making the denial audible would cause things to right themselves. "No, no, *no*." It turned broken. "No…"

The word had the weight and consistency of mud.

Even so; even with that sensation —there was no one else to blame. It was all the creature's doing. The dreaded stickiness lining its insides also intensified, and for a moment, Ferream was on the precipice of what it might be called. It hurt far worse than discomfort.

This was what love had had a part in.

A tightness encased its chest as though it could not breathe. It did not need such a thing, but the quick prohibition of it was truly alarming. There was an urge to grab at its throat and gasp; an uncontrollable shake in its wrists; and a weakness in its knees. Love did indeed ruin; that had been a truth.

It would never get the soul's expression out of its head —for centuries to come. Recognition and betrayal. Though this agony in the aftermath was tenfold compared to what had splintered inside of the created demon when the soul had stopped coming. Simply *knowing* that their exchanges would never happen again; caused directly by its own hand…that was the truest torture. The most ruthless fate.

Ferream swore right there that it would never '*feel*' again.

Only one thing remained: the soul did not know the beast when awake. But in that moment; at death, it had.

the toll

BEFORE HELL'S COURT

+

THIS NUMBNESS WAS different.

After the height of anger, instead of satiation, all that the monster felt was hollow. There was absolutely nothing —within nor without it. Now that Ferream had had a taste of vibrant emotion, there was no way to go back. It wouldn't settle for its previous existence. There was in fact, not much of an existence at all without that soul.

Without all they had brought with them.

"The abomination has truly done it this time," the attending demon to the beast's left side remarked, leaning against their spear.

The one on Ferream's right needlessly tightened the salt chains again. "I think this will be the final straw. No one will see it for a long while."

"Perhaps even until the End Times."

"I hope so. I cannot take much more of this babysitting."

Oh how the beast wished for an end. But for it to last forever.

The chains were pulled, and the creature was pulled along with them. It had not put up a fight when apprehended. It never had, but the incidents from before were something of which to be proud. Now there was simply no need to resist. No need to want.

The demons led Ferream towards the main hall, where the Council was waiting for the trial. Of course there would be no true procedure. It was all for show in an effort to allow all of Hell to witness the crime and punishment. Yet the monster couldn't bring itself to play its part; to worm around in its restraints and be a warning to the Fallen.

It was an untamed creation.

That was what Lucifer had insisted. And fear was the best tool to keep subordinates in check and themself on the throne. Clearly only being the instigator of the millennia old war was not sufficient in garnering respect and eternal command. The other demons may have fallen with them, but that did not guarantee that they would all always follow.

So the expression that the Morningstar had on their face as Ferream walked unled and nonchalantly into the hall before the court was rather satisfying. It was the smallest way of displaying its spite and resolve.

"Most prized of the Morningstar," Lord Beelzebub spoke first; acting as prosecutor in his king's stead. Lucifer shifted atop an egregious golden throne in the centre of the hall, elevated multiple storeys in the air so that they could always look down upon their subjects.

The loosely draped marble wings which extended from their straight back were poised to glide —stiff and outstretched.

Ferream thought that they looked like a peacock asserting its value.

"You have done something reprehensible which cannot be ignored by high Archangel Raphael himself. Thus, you have made a mockery of the Brightest Throne. Your king and our leader never intended for you to have the free rein to slaughter as you please without order. We believe you to be undisciplined and…crude," bit the Lord of the Flies. He met the beast's vacant gaze and glared. "Unfinished."

Those words did not pierce any deeper than the others had —Ferream hoped that its expression reflected its lack of focus. And will.

It would not truly matter if the Made demon was perfect and obedient. Polished. It all fell on Lucifer's cracked shoulders. The monster imagined them crumbling away beneath the weight.

"The consequences of the crime committed will be more severe than any previous," the adviser continued, striding back and forth in front of the iron thing importantly. "You wittingly wiped the existence of an entire town off of the Earth. Responsibility *must* be taken for every life disrupted by your little tantrum."

Ferream didn't like that word. Tantrum.

It made its actions childish and irrational. What it had longed for was unhinged and unreasonable —not the whiny selfishness of an infant. Why could it not be seen as an equal with the Fallen? Why was it not permitted to be righteously scornful with an insatiable appetite for revenge?

"Why did you do it, Ferream?" asked the Morningstar.

They finally leaned over to peer down at their creation —though their face twisted in disgust rather than usual disappointment.

The beast had always been honest.

"Love," it grumbled.

The dark hall fell still and silent. Numerous Fallen Angels looked between themselves and the sound of tinkling glass echoed through the chasm.

"...What?" Lucifer quipped. Their brows furrowed together.

"Love was taken from me," the monster said quite clearly. It was still not used to its siren voice. Hell likely wasn't, either.

"*What* is it talking about?" Lord Beelzebub hissed, his head whipping towards the stands. He glowered at the crystalline demons, as if silently urging them to shut it. He looked up to his king, but they did not have the intention of divulging any information.

They looked down on Ferream as if they knew several things which it did not. And several things which should be kept hidden.

"So you felt the absence of something that you eventually learned the name of?" Lucifer mused.

"The love for its master?" Lord Beelzebub frowned. "It *was* detained for a long time. But it was docile in its cell."

Flashes of brown and ice replayed within its mind again. It flinched, as though the memories were tangible, slicing blades.

The Morningstar did not clarify. Those gold flames stayed trained to the iron demon knelt before the court. Then they rose, leisurely, pushing off of the throne. "I have determined the punishment, little one," they said loud enough to reach the furthest corner of the hall. "Evidently, solitude is not what teaches you. And the lack of the '*love*' which you feel is to be your tutor. You must come to understand that emotion which is felt by those who are left behind. But it will only be *you*, of course." The Fallen Angel landed beside Ferream, rearranged their long robes, before leaning down close enough to murmur into its pointed ear.

"You will be taught with a curse," continued Lucifer, still putting on airs. Even though their gaze was on the beast, they projected for everyone to hear. "To dwell among your victims and to relive every atrocity."

Then their voice became the serpentine whisper which now sent a chill up Ferream's spine. Cold, displeased lips brushed along its ear. "…Only to wait each cycle for the love you will *always* destroy."

The monster's ears twitched as it tugged against the salt chains.

They couldn't know.

Shock panged through the creature. It could not move. There had to be a reason that that was the only sentence the king had decided to hide from the rest of the court. One for Ferream alone.

Lucifer was not amused. Their face was hard and cold and still —quite like the marble from which they were made. This was not a punishment. This was a warning. A test. They needed to see how the little beast would fare in a torture of its own making.

It was not about establishing their position; not entirely.

If the Morningstar knew of the visits and of that soul, then this was a challenge. They might not have addressed it directly but there was enough in the twist of their words for the threat to sink its teeth in. While Lucifer might not know of the soul's death, they could make Ferream live through it all. Forever. It would be its own personal Hell.

Its skin grew cold and its ears fell, low and shameful.

So this was fear.

The demon struggled not to let it show. Its nerves were so fresh with the agony of a mere hour ago. It wondered if this was justice —perhaps it deserved to be plagued with it all until it learned of hate and self-control. Because love had been the undoing of all for which it cared.

It could stay away from the mortal each time; never chase after it in the woods and never bring that end to fruition.

Lucifer tilted their head, lips curving ever so slightly with icy spite as though they could read all of Ferream's thoughts at a glance. "…There is nothing that you will be able to do to escape the destruction."

The beast's eyes widened.

Its first mistake in a swift fall out of favour.

Pine Creek then became a phantom trapped between realms.

Memories of people who lived there from the land of the living were simply…suspended. And the victims bound to the king of Hell's selfish retribution had no desire to escape. That did not surprise Ferream in the slightest. It had already established that not an innocent soul was among them.

Ferream fit like something with body wedged between the folds of a piece of paper. No matter the hoops of logic through any mind would have to leap, it was evident that something was horribly amiss in the small town outside of time.

The beast joined the family he had ripped into as the elder brother of that child it had not spared. That boy had seen death engulf his home. He had stared into its flaring eyes of blue and purple. It was a special sort of madness to force that child to call Ferream '*family*'.

Over and over and over.

All for the sake of a monster experiencing searing loss. At least, the humans seemed to be granted the mercy of not remembering. Lucifer had not lied —Ferream truly couldn't avoid the destruction.

Against its will, at the end of every cycle, it would take on its demonic form and kill every resident all over again. Sometimes the deaths changed slightly from that dreaded day, but most remained identical. To the point where it could anticipate the sound of blood and cracking bone, and block it all out; mindlessly going through the motions while slipping further and further inward into the darkness at its centre.

The repetition was a sharp descent.

It still chased that human through the woods.

Ferream had the choice of replaying everything as it had happened, or attempting to prevent their demise by confessing everything directly. And *only* in regards to them, as it seemed. No one else was a variable.

Each choice still brought death.

Telling the soul of the future drove them further away, and deeper into hatred and despair. Not telling them still forced the beast to rip them apart.

The only difference was that they had no reasons why.

Each cycle, a cherished sensation would whittle away. A newly built revelation would splinter and wither. A bit of life would die. The demon had no choice, nor was there a way to stop it. The soul had taught it many lessons —but none so cruel as what would happen in a Hell on Earth.

Towards the last tapering of sanity, Ferream wondered if its numbness was enough to feign regret and repentance.

Until the time for breaking would come to an end, and the Morningstar would be left with a passive husk to mould once more.

The only difference was that they had no reason why.

Each cycle a cherished sensation would whittle away. A newly built revelation would splinter and wither. A bit of life would die. The demon had no choice, nor was there a way to stop it. The soulbird taught Terran this lesson—but none so grim as what would happen in a Hell on Earth.

Towards the last tatters of sanity, Terran wondered if its numbness was enough to fuel regret and repentance.

Until the time for breathing would come to an end, and the Morningstar would be left with a petulant hush to endure once more.

II

NOW

the long haul

ALEXANDER

EN ROUTE TO OREGON

+

I KNEW THAT that my mother was dead, but the way my father was clutching her urn to his side as he drove made it seem as though her ashes might suddenly smoulder and ignite —fulminating into some sort of wild, reincarnated phoenix. And that his grip would never relent, and he would try his hardest to cage her.

She still wouldn't *be* there; Hugh Grahams would have to handle the fantastical situation and come to terms with the fact that the remains of my mother would have found a new purpose.

Without him. She had often done things without him.

They hadn't spoken much during her last month alive. Not even on her deathbed. He had never said it, but anyone would've been able to tell that he wanted to be anywhere but that hospital ward.

"Hey, son," he spoke for the first time since we had started driving. His voice was strained, choked with unwept tears. "This'll be like a reset. Just to reorientate ourselves —you know?"

I glanced at the urn, then back at the window.

No. It will be the same as it's always been: playing pretend. Whether Leilah Grahams was there or not, nothing would make my father kick his old habits. He was stuck on a loop, and the record machine was breaking. He didn't want to accept her death and its fissure —even though he had not exactly tried to prevent it.

Though acceptance was a relative term. I acknowledged that she was no longer with us, but that break was too fresh and tender. I might fall inside of it. While I could accept the fact that I would never hold her again, I still saw her; still felt her ghost.

I was usually good with death, but now I wasn't so sure.

I had not said that much two weeks ago either. But it had not been because I hadn't wanted to be there —I just hadn't been able to put my thoughts into words. I had simply knelt beside my mother and cried.

I had cried for an entire week; unable to get out of my bed or sleep or eat —until my father couldn't handle it; the sight of a face that resembled Leilah's, in that old rickety house any longer. He had packed our suitcases and then we were bound for Pine Creek, Oregon.

1,453.4 miles away from Albuquerque, New Mexico.

No tears were falling now.

It was difficult to be in despair while sandwiched between a cooler and the bag-lined car door. It was difficult to do *anything*. So I sat. And stared at the road for twenty-two and three quarters of an hour.

I could hardly sleep, and my father had not been willing to buy a room in a motel halfway through the journey. He had pulled aside and parked, before dozing off. I gawked at him in disbelief, but was ultimately forced to go along with it. The morning and a McDonald's breakfast muffin with coffee had not come fast enough.

"Nearly there, son," my father now murmured.

Hugh was not actually that much of a conversationalist —he was working through an online workshop about how to talk to your reclusive teenager. Most of his attempts went ignored, but it made my skin crawl every time he uttered the word '*son*'.

He added it like a pet name to the end or the beginning of absolutely everything. I could not blame him entirely —it was likely to positively reinforce his care for me, not to drill in a gender identity.

However, my patience was finally reaching its limit —but I knew it wasn't wise to suddenly erupt and tell him that he didn't *have* a son. Nor a daughter. Just an offspring named Alexander.

I knew that bringing it up would cause more problems than it was worth. It was the very reason that we had left Pine Creek in the first place —though only one of my parents had known about it.

Sometimes when I closed my eyes and drifted between being dead and awake, I was back in the elementary school; with paint dripping down the back of my collar and black marker burned onto my arms.

My mother had whisked me away at the end of sixth grade; as soon as she had noticed the ink and bruises. I had refused to talk about it, but that in itself hadn't rung too many alarm bells back then.

Just kids being kids.

That saying made me sick. I tried to start afresh in that new year, but they had poisoned me —the scrawled words. The ink itself had long since been scrubbed away but the letters of *b o y* still lingered in my stubborn sight. They had sunk in and were wriggling about.

Occasionally the phantom words swirled beyond recognition, fooling me into thinking that I could ignore it all. Because the words were always there. Them and the faces of those who had written them.

It got better when we moved to New Mexico.

I could hide everything there and be someone else.

I was also working through my own online workshop: therapy. It had been my mother's idea. It was at my own pace, and not in person. Being quicker witted than my father, she realised that the torment had not been because I was shy or maybe underdeveloped for my age. She hadn't asked questions, nor tried to make me see some lame excuse for reason.

Now the burn for vengeance was a candle flame. Now I could pretend that going back to our home town did not bother me. I could pretend that seeing the faces of those who had destroyed me did not cause me to retch.

Thank God it was still the dregs of Summer break.

That meant no school for a while.

No obligatory socialising.

If only I was just a year older, I could leave my father and go to a college on the other side of the world. Never to look back.

But I would do this for my mother; for her memory.

Because Leilah Grahams had adored that small town.

I obviously did not share in the sentiment. If I had been smart as a kid, chills wouldn't crawl along my spine. Sweat wouldn't cling to my brow. Dread wouldn't bury itself underneath the surface of my skin. I wouldn't be biting my nails at the prospect.

Hugh Grahams did not know his child was on the verge of an anxiety attack, let alone why.

And he likely never would.

It was the dead of night when I felt the car come to a gentle halt. The blanket draped over my curled form was insufficient for keeping warm, but my body had become used to it at some point.

I hoped that my old oak double bed would still be decent.

My shoulder was gently shaken and I stirred, shifting to sit upright.

"Hey, Alex. I've made it through the second leg. We've arrived, son. Are you hungry?" my father quipped.

Only he called me that —'*Alex*'. A part of me liked to think that maybe if he had not been the one to start it, I could have claimed it for myself. It was neutral and simple, and would have made existence a bit easier. But I had little to no dysphoria about my birth name. Amidst the chaos, it felt like the one thing that I could control.

The one thing that was real.

I did not try to hide my scowl, and thankfully the little frustration went out with it. "Dad, we talked about this. It's *Alexander*. Full or nothing."

He sighed, nodding dejectedly in agreement though I saw how his grip tightened on the steering wheel. He did not know the real reason, but he liked to pretend that I actually told him things sometimes. "…I know — you don't like it when I shorten your name. I apologise. I will continue to try to respect your feelings."

My nails slowly dented my palms. He always said that, but he didn't really mean it.

I dug my cellphone out of my pocket and blinked at the screen as it lit up. It was early morning —just after midnight.

Then my brows knitted.

"That's weird."

"What's weird, son?"

I ground my teeth together. "There's no signal."

My father sighed and offered a lazy shrug. "Maybe the towers are just malfunctioning. Wouldn't surprise me if they haven't been replaced since we moved away."

"…I guess."

I then glanced outside to see where we had parked by. *Little Hatchet*. "Oh God, food." I practically leapt out of the seat.

"Wait, you don't know what I want to order."

"Not the usual?" I frowned.

He smirked. "You still remember what that is?"

Oh, I certainly did: a large chilli dog with a mountain of cheesy fries and a cold medium soda. My mother had appropriately dubbed it *o Ataque Cardíaco Pendente* —the Pending Heart Attack.

"Don't forget about the extra ice, son!" he hollered as I jumped out of the weathered yellow Chevy. My shoulders tensed.

"I got it," I called back.

It was the first week of Fall, but the night air was already biting. My teeth chattered and I shivered as I climbed the short steps, briefly glancing at the *open twenty-four hours* sign which was thankfully still applicable after so many years, and then pushing the swinging doors open.

The lights were warm and dim. Though it offered takeout, it really did have the musky ambiance of a bar.

I readjusted my glasses as I sauntered over towards the front counter. It was super early morning, but somehow eerily quiet for a place that was supposed to be open. Where were all of the employees?

I was scoping the menu when I glanced up to see someone in front me. Not in the way that strangers near-silently creep up on you—no…this felt as though they had burst into existence.

In the blink of an eye.

I noticed the writhing darkness first. Behind the waitress, as though extra parts of her shadow, were long black tendrils snaking and whipping through the air. I started, stumbling backwards into a stool. I wondered if I was hallucinating, or if I was half asleep. But I had never felt more jarred awake, and the darkness seemed real —tangible.

I then noticed the waitress's choppy blonde hair —as though she had hacked it with a pair of scissors. My gaze narrowed, however, as I took in the colour of her eyes and the shape of her face.

My blood turned to ice in my veins. *No. No way.*

There was no way that Louise Barnes was the possessed addict going through withdrawal —rather, the girl standing in front of me.

My heart rate spiked as if solely from being in her presence. Flashes of hurling rocky snow balls and the stabbing of marker pens deep and hard enough to draw blood flickered in my mind.

I dropped her gaze to dispel the thoughts.

She didn't seem to recognise me, though. Not that I could blame her —there were probably loads of people in the world who looked like me. Many people who could have passed through in all of these years.

"Can I get you anything?"

I couldn't bring myself to find the words with which to answer. My gaze snagged to the twisted shadows —on that living, hungry thing. And as I stared at the leftover stains of tear-ruined makeup and the strained smile on her face, I wondered if she knew what had its claws in her.

The thin wispy arms clawed at the waitress's uniform, and her bare arms. The action left no scratches nor indents, but the girl flinched slightly in time to every slow, deadly caress. As though she could feel it, and was trying to suppress the pain.

I was not just seeing things. That darkness was truly there.

"Should I…call an ambulance, or something?" I asked uncertainly as I put more distance between us, glancing back at the exit.

But when I turned and blinked, the shadows had melted away. It was just an ordinary silhouette in the shape of her. Just a shadow. I frowned, my temples pounding with dull confusion.

"Can I get you anything?" the waitress repeated.

"I…I just…"

I struggled to form coherent thoughts. Had the car ride really messed with my head that much? Had I truly hallucinated those shadowy arms?

Her makeup was still ruined, though; her hair still chopped. Her eyes still lifeless. I subtly pinched the skin just above my left wrist. The sharp familiar pain told me that I was conscious. It made my muscles tense, so they were alert to danger. It made me calm down.

"…A large chilli dog," I whispered. "Large cheesy fries and a medium soda. Double the ice."

She looked me up and down, with her eyes lazily lidded. "You've got the space for that?" she snorted.

"It's not for me," I cut back, frowning in offence.

A flicker of a personality I wanted to forget came out in her dead eyes; a frigid light blinked very briefly in that icy blue. And it shook me.

Then she sighed, reverting to the struggling demeanour she had now, while she pulled out a little notebook and pencil. "And for you, paying customer who braved this especially chilly night?"

"A Dagwood burger. And a coke —no ice."

She sucked on her teeth like my request had been for her to move a mountain, before turning to the timber partition doors fashioned like those of a saloon rightward and behind her.

"Earl!" she hollered. "We've got a hungry customer. Get your butt to the grill!"

A gruff and tired voice answered her with equal spite and impatience. A towering, lanky middle aged man sauntered into view, donned with a questionably stained apron and frankly useless hair net.

He eyed me briefly with a sneer that sent a shiver down my spine and clicked his tongue as the waitress handed him my order.

I didn't know him.

It had been years —it didn't surprise me to see a new face. Though he already looked plenty seasoned with the joys of the small town.

His shadow did not grow extra arms, but it still appeared disjointed. As though it wasn't his own.

The girl then turned back to me, and narrowed her eyes. I handed over some of the cash that I kept in my pockets in case of emergencies. After ringing the order up and handing me my change, her expression remained sceptical. Deciphering.

"So are you just passing through?" she asked, a hand on one hip.

"We're…actually moving here," I mumbled.

My social skills had not improved that much over the years. I was still wary of the smallest things, and terrified that with just one look a stranger could simply figure out everything about me as if I had no armour.

The girl's blonde brows rose. "Moving here?" she echoed. "We don't get a lot of visitors, let alone new residents."

I offered a weak grimace. "It was my Dad's idea. My parents had lived here for a while, before."

"Ah," she sighed like she understood. "Did they move when you were little? Do you remember being here?"

I visibly stiffened and my glasses slid down my nose.

Her question didn't sound like coincidence. Darkness gathered in the corners of my vision, devouring the sparce light. I clenched my nails into my palms, desperate not to have an attack right there.

Not in public. And not in front of her —the girl who felt too familiar, and too cruel.

I pushed my glasses back up and shook my head. "…No."

It was better to pretend to know nothing about Pine Creek.

"Well it's a small town," she huffed. She appeared to believe me, for now. "Everyone knows everyone. And your business is our business."

I struggled to swallow. "We have no secrets."

Another lie. It was becoming easier.

The girl smirked, and it was hollow. "Then you'll be fine." Something told me that was a lie too.

"So," she sighed and moved towards the bar with a stack of takeaway cups. She made filling them up seem like a meticulous task. "Aren't you getting your Mom anything?"

A chill shot up along my spine. But my throat was a parched desert. "She…isn't alive," I whispered. I forced myself to meet the waitress's widened gaze. Whether or not she really was Louise Barnes did not matter for a moment. I couldn't allow the torment to be held over me forever. I couldn't let it show. "…That's why we came back."

She didn't say anything for a long pause. An abnormally long pause. Usually when you tell people that your mother is dead they quickly gush out apologies and shower you with excessive sympathy —which was not to be confused with empathy. Or they were quiet and solemn.

The unnerving girl on the other side of the counter did not look like she was thinking about the right words to use. She didn't even bow her head in understanding and pity. She just stared at me.

Directly into my eyes. As if *I* owed her an apology.

As if she felt nothing.

A brass bell sounded.

The waitress did not start at its shrill. She simply turned, still burning a hole into my skull, and opened the wooden doors to the kitchen.

My suspiciously fast order was then placed in front of me in a brown paper bag with a patch of staining oil at the bottom. The food's familiar greasy pungency almost made me rethink my appetite.

"Thanks," I said anyway, reaching over.

She watched on silently as I backed away. I made it to the door before she said anything after I had mentioned the death of my mother.

"…I'm sorry about your Mom. But you really shouldn't be here. You shouldn't have come back, Alexander."

My feet stalled on their own, and my stomach churned. *Fuck.* It *was* Louise —even with the hacked off hair and dripping makeup. I wondered what had she done to herself. I remembered her caring a lot more about her appearance. And when exactly had she realised that it was me?

Was it my lingering fear?

Maybe it was when I had mentioned my mother. Her death sentence had been a secret that many had been privy to even after we left.

Or maybe it was my naïve, hopeful lies.

I had likely laid it on too thick; been too stiff; and allowed her to catch a glimpse of seven years ago. My panic sharing hadn't helped.

Regardless, I would be lying if I denied that something within me felt glad to see Louise this way. Vacant. So far from my memories. Perhaps the universe had avenged my misfortune, and subjected the fallen queen to her own mistreatment. It was a selfish wish, and maybe I hadn't healed as much as I ought to, but in the moment it made me feel better.

I remembered everything that I had learned from therapy —counting to ten and ensuring myself that I was awake, and that the people who had tormented me were just people. Weak, wavering human beings.

I didn't have to forgive them, but I didn't have to show how they had damaged me either. I could cut them out of my past, and build something better for myself. Eventually.

Keep it together. She can't hurt you in that state even if she tries. She's one mistake away from disappearing.

…I wished Louise Barnes would disappear.

I remembered etching that into one of the bathroom stall walls back in school. I had sat crying, shaking, and scratching at flaking paint with my copy of the house keys. In the end, it had looked murderous.

I hoped that she had seen it.

I swallowed down the nausea and squared my shoulders as I continued to leave. I didn't want to hear what Louise might say next. I didn't want to look at her again. But I left with the last word.

"…You think that I wanted to, Louise?"

the regression

ALEXANDER

OUR HOUSE SEEMED to fit like a too-small old jacket.

I could barely breathe.

And it wasn't what it had been.

Even when the lights had been switched on, the shadows stretched behind the furniture —large pieces too new to be truly old, but fashioned to be authentic and vintage. The darkness was like a wet thing I might fall into and drown; while I knew by the creak of the floorboards that I could not call the house '*home*' ever again. As if it knew we were in it.

"It's just a tad dusty," Hugh admitted, hauling in a couple of suitcases. "But I had Sue check in from time to time for the past few years."

The image that I had of Sue Loid was grainy but there. As my mother's best friend, I could imagine she had felt some sort of obligation to tend to an empty house indefinitely for the sake of memory. I *didn't* like the idea of my parents having planned to move back at some point, though.

Every sound echoed.

We were meant to be alone in these wooden halls, but phantom breath warmed the back of my neck. A breeze chilled my unwisely bare ankles, and I could not figure out from where it was coming.

My ceiling was the exact same shade of cream.

That was the first thing I had noticed when I walked in, dragging my bags behind me. The bedframe sat passively against the far wall, with a dresser, wardrobe, wooden bookcase and painted desk flanking the sides. The semi-circle of furniture resembled some sort of ritualistic setup.

If I laid down on the purple, yellow and grey rug I'd gotten for my last birthday in the middle of the floor, would that make me a sacrifice?

A heavy thud drew my gaze to the closest wall.

I held my breath, needing complete silence to decipher the sound. It seemed to have come from inside of the walls and yet…downstairs.

Instinct was to call out and assume the worst. "Dad…?"

My breath shallowed as the echo went unanswered.

"…It's fine!" my father finally assured, a little bit winded. "I just lost grip…of a suitcase while going up the stairs."

I sighed and rolled my eyes before making my way to the desk. There was nothing I could do to make it feel familiar. We were strangers in this house. My fingers ran over the wood, expecting splinters, but there was only a thin layer of dust. Sue must have not been over in at least a week.

But she *had* been here.

From what I remembered, my mother had tried to get me to befriend Sue's daughter, Lily-Mae. All that relayed in my head were awkward play dates with her dolls and kitchen set or in the Loids' sandpit —nothing else from months later, when the bullying had gotten worse. Lily-Mae might have been self-centred and whiny, but she hadn't joined in with the other kids at school. She had just stood there, dithering.

I tried not to blame children whose ages had been in the single digits, but that was difficult as the target. It was difficult not to have some faith in people and hope that even at that age they had a shred of empathy.

Years later, though the hurt had scarred over, the memories and stress lingered. My body remembered that pain and couldn't completely let go. For me, the prospect of facing those kids was far worse than letting them see that I was still alive. Breathing.

Would they start again?

Would they even still…care?

I could deal with it if they had forgotten all about me. Louise Barnes was the exception, because nothing ever happened without her knowing about it. The teenage Louise I had met did not look like she could pin me down. If anything, I could now hold my own.

That didn't mean that I was in any way okay with finishing my senior year here. It was going to be fundamentally different from the anonymity of New Mexico. Age soured certain people like milk.

I hated that I couldn't control the past.

I hated that I'd had to come back.

And I hated that I couldn't explain to Hugh *why*.

He was not a '*sit down and talk for hours*' sort of parent. As soon as the designated person for that role was no more, my father had retreated inwards and could barely hold a conversation longer than a question and answer with me. Usually I didn't mind—I appreciated the increase in free time. But for the things that needed more than a nod or a shake, I felt the weight of loneliness.

It was *lonely* without my mother.

Seeing her echo everywhere only served as a reminder. In the wake of her death I wasn't angry, I wasn't in denial, I wasn't any *more* depressed and I wasn't itching to exchange someone else's life for hers. Those Five Stages of Grief seemed to be bullshit to me.

I was in a hollow, uncertain limbo.

And there didn't seem to be a stage for that.

My online therapist suggested that grief was not so linear —the stages most people knew were generalised abstract categories used to understand rather in which to wallow. So it didn't invalidate whatever I felt or didn't feel, and I shouldn't feel strange for not reacting…normally.

It almost had me up until that word crawled back from the hole I had buried it within. I hate, hate *hated* that there was some sort of standard expectation for every single little thing.

It was the reason that I hadn't managed to log in for the last few days despite my semi strict schedule. I wondered if it was even noticeable. I knew that I tended to become irritable and shut off whenever I slumped and started brooding. Without a way to untangle the knots of emotion and a lack thereof, the threads only tightened.

And I couldn't breathe.

I reached for instinctual comfort.

A box stuffed with my small collection of books —not very wide nor tall, but enough to make me strain as I lifted it onto the bed. I was infinitely grateful that I wouldn't need to assemble anything to house them. I took each novel one by one and slotted them on the old shelves after vigorously wiping the dust off with the first thing I could find: a white t-shirt.

Nothing was more important than getting my books out of their box. After the shelves had been lined, I admired the pastel and vibrant spines in the attempt of a rainbow coloured order.

I didn't read all too widely. My interest pooled in romance. If that was the main focus, then I *had* to read it. It could be a light fantasy, mystery, contemporary or comedy —I simply did not want to suffer through long passages of exposition and be dragged into complex world building. The more predictable and shallow, the better.

I picked one at random and thumbed through it.

In the wild turmoil of things going wrong, simple and wishful stories calmed me down. Many people read to escape the mundane, but my life had always felt the opposite. Reality was horrors unconfrontational, and I read to picture the world that the rest of the world seemed to live in.

I had never been afforded the luxury of being ordinary and enjoying it. Loving myself was a feat I had not yet accomplished, even if I was in a better place. Freedom was still dangling just out of my reach but in the coverage of oversized clothes I could express *something*. Of course there were things I wanted to do beyond Hugh's sharp gaze —piercing my ears, trying on heeled shoes, or simply growing out my hair.

For now I would bide my time.

It was one thing I had become good at.

Dinner, or the semblance of it, was spent in silence. Or rather *I* was silent and my father ranted about a sports team's loss in whatever match he had watched last week. A small part of me was glad that my food had gotten cold enough to put me off, though I still picked at it between sips of coke.

"…Do you think Mom would've been happy to be back here?" I then plucked up the nerve to ask.

My father paused, his mouth open and a fry halfway inside.

He set it down. Slowly.

"She…she's in our hearts, Alexander," he sighed. His hands had balled up but I could still see the trembling of each muscle. "She's with us. And this…uh…this is what she *wanted*. You…you know that."

I wished that I didn't.

It was clear that Hugh, for some reason, didn't understand it. It was not that she would have wanted to come back, but rather she would have wanted us to move on in a healthier way.

She wasn't forcing us to live here.

He was.

Dinner had never been a loud or warm affair. But it had never been quiet, and it had never been uncomfortable. It felt as though if I moved just an inch, the shards of ice poking me would suddenly impale.

I wondered if it would be like that with other people I knew.

The thought had never crossed my mind before, but now it was all that I could hear in my head. Leilah Grahams had been the voice in the silence. The song on the wind.

This unroused breeze was deafening.

I set down my coke and rose from the rickety dining room chair. "…I think I'm going to go to bed," I murmured, frowning. "I'll buy some food in the morning from the grocery store."

My father sighed but did not stop me.

After fighting with my bedding, I eventually curled up on the sheets and pulled the comforter over my head. In the dark, there was some little assurance that I was safe if I couldn't see. If I didn't dare to look.

It did not stop my mind from whirring and the seeds of my dreams to form. I never seemed to remember any of them when I woke, yet I knew that in the moment, they had always felt real. And feelings would linger instead of images: stifling heat and a hunger that food wouldn't satisfy.

There would also be streams of tears.

A crushing weight in my chest as though I had not wanted to leave.

I turned over so that my back was to the ceiling.

The rustling of cotton sounded too much like branches scraping at the windows. I couldn't understand why it felt like I wasn't alone. It had been that way for many years, but I was far more aware of it in this house. Even as I counted steadily and curled my fingernails into my palms I could not discern whether any of it was real.

Everything was deceptive in the dark.

Another thump rattled up the wall.

I paused, straightening out under the covers as I tried to place it again. My father didn't call out this time. There was not a lot of heaviness in it. It did not have the thud of wood, or the clang of metal. Instead, it was airy and hollow and did not quite reach my ears. The sound wasn't followed, but it unsettled the defensive posture I had adopted. The night air abruptly chilled as I burrowed further. The house fell so quiet that I could not bear the sound of my own heart and breath.

Had Hugh gotten the television downstairs to work yet? I wished that it would drown out the silence.

I wished it wasn't cold.

I wished I could fall asleep as soon as I closed my eyes.

the birds of prey

ALEXANDER

+

DEAR DIARY,

I LIED AGAIN. I THINK I WANT TO REMEMBER MY DREAMS.

SINCERELY,
YOUR SCRIBE.

MY ONLINE THERAPIST suggested that keeping a diary or a journal would help with healing and identifying certain feelings.

I didn't want to feel my feelings.

Though I wasn't yet at the stage where I could be numb to it all either. Journals felt like homework, but diaries were raw and personal. When I looked back on what I had scratched onto that paper in the heat of raging emotion, I was forced to see myself in the most vulnerable state.

It was jarring, at times. But most confrontations were.

I think a small part of me wanted to be rescued. I wanted someone to offer their hand and lift me out.

Because I didn't believe that I could crawl out by myself.

As the sun cut through the dark, I hauled myself upright and blinked at the curtains billowing. The window was slightly open.

I hadn't even touched the latch.

My gaze wandered.

There was a book on the floor —the only one to slip off the shelf as though it hadn't upset the others. I reached for my glasses before making out the small title on dark blue.

They Both Die At The End by Adam Silvera.

The surface of my skin chilled. The breeze outside was picking up. I climbed out of bed and trudged to the bookshelf. My books were so tightly packed that I couldn't understand how any of them could fall, especially due to the wind. I carefully slotted it back in its place and tried not to think about its plot. Of the death and inevitability.

After tugging the sheets and comforter into place, I slunk towards the bathroom. The wooden floorboards were cold under my feet.

The water wasn't heating up.

I was used to this sort of bad luck.

One shitty thing after another formed a string of reality. Good things only happened to the deserving. At least, thinking so made me feel better.

The enormous house was still unsettlingly quiet as I padded back to my room. I had no doubt that my father was still asleep, regardless of the time. My phone said that it was thirty minutes past eleven. And there were still no bars. I sighed and pulled on my trousers and a knitted sweater over a long collared shirt, before stepping into worn maroon Docs.

I caught sight of myself in the mirror and shivered at the urge to tug and pull. The trousers seemed too tight, and the sweater wouldn't sit right.

IT'S WRONG. YOU LOOK WRONG.

No, reason growled back. *It's just a costume. For a few more months.*

Something I had kept saying for several months of my life.

It hadn't always been this bad.

As I had grown, the desire to break the mould of what was acceptable in society —in *our* society —due to the binary it clung to so tightly, had only grown. There was no place for someone who didn't fit at each end.

Not for the middle, off to one side, or off of the spectrum entirely.

And I still didn't really know where I lay. My teeth ground. I wanted to talk to the friends I'd left behind. Only two, but more supportive in my life than the family I had been born into: Sebastian and Anne. They would be worried that I hadn't at least messaged them; if only to complain about how terribly I was adjusting. Last night refused to shake off.

My sleep paralysis demon had looked different last night. Instead of a looming horned beast made of audible buzzing flies, it had been a long shadow against the wall. But the gaps like eyes had stared directly at me.

It was a different sort of awareness. The beast was almost curious. The uninvited shadow had been confused. Frustrated.

"Dad, I'm off," I called down the hall, and didn't bother to wait for a response as I descended the stairs, tote bag flying.

I planned to stop by another place apart from the grocers, so I wouldn't be back until the afternoon. I didn't *want* to be back until then.

The clouds were stingily hoarding the sky, and not enough sunlight peeked through to warm my face. Summer here had always had a bit of an identity crisis. It would go through spells of heat, and almost equally dip to Fall temperatures. A heavy shroud of grey would wash over the icy blue, and a chill swept the streets.

But this was the weather I liked the most: not too warm; not too happy. When things were beginning to die.

So that everyone could be miserable together.

My gaze caught on something in an unwashed grey. A wooden sign swinging in the gentle breeze that needed oiling.

The Honeysuckle was a small burst of flavour in the blandness of Pine Creek. A hole-in-the-wall plant shop in the middle of the main strip mall, owned by a woman who seemed too kind for her own good. We had never had a conversation, just the odd hello whenever I had found myself inside of her shop. I could still picture her working with her aunt; long skirt and crocheted bolero over a slim fitting vest, decked in long, silver handmade jewellery and braided leather.

The twists of ivy creeping along the surrounding brickwork were fiery orange and yellow. I stared for a moment longer, before the bell sounded and out stepped an older Kay Isotton. Her golden brown hair was a much shorter pixie cut, and it suited her slim face —along with a large pair of funky glasses. She had multiple studs all up and down her ears that caught the sparce sunlight, glinting in the dullness.

But that tentative smile was still there; warm and hopeful.

Something that had not been there back in my memories darkened the doorway. Something that should be her shadow.

She waved, eager despite the gloom.

"Little Alexander, is that you?" she called.

I cringed and considered bolting even though I had very clearly seen her and maintained eye contact too long to be a coincidence. Guilt seeped into the fear. I had no reason not to greet her. She was the only person on the street. And the way she stood, welcoming and curious even with the dying of her plants and the lethargy that seemed to cling to the town itself. I couldn't just walk by like a jerk.

"…Miss Isotton?" I grimaced.

"Just Kay, silly. So it really is you," she breathed, straightening up as I approached. Even though I was nearly eighteen and giving up hope for a growth spurt, she still stood over me. "Did you come to visit?"

"No," I clipped. Then drew a breath. "I mean, Hugh and I just moved back. Leilah…my mother passed away."

Kay's eyes welled with sympathy. "Aw, my condolences to you both. Would you like some lilies? They symbolise a peaceful departure and rest at memorials. On the house, rest assured. Leilah was a friend."

My mouth twisted in a shape. It was just the sort of people she and her aunt had been, but realistically it wasn't a good business practice.

"It's okay," I lied. "We're…uh, coping."

Maybe that last part was more wishful than delusional.

Kay was sceptical. It was as if she was staring into my soul. She was a decade older than me —had just finished high school when I had been a little kid. I doubted she'd known what was happening; too young to join the adults' conversation and too old to meddle in nine-year-olds' scuffles. Though I could remember lingering glances when I would trudge past the door, sniffing and wiping blood.

Those cool green eyes were pitying.

My throat closed and my rib cage tightened around my lungs.

"…Anyway," I rasped, turning back to the sidewalk, "I need to go buy some groceries and unpack, so —bye."

She didn't need to know that I was planning to live out of my suitcases for the next week.

Her disappointment was not well hidden. There was a hesitation in her wave; the awkward indecisive forwardness of not knowing how friendly to be with a familiar stranger. "Oh. I guess I'll see you around, then. Don't be afraid to stop by for anything at all," encouraged Kay.

I nodded and offered the smallest smile.

She couldn't get it.

Kay Isotton was so beaming and carefree.

Reality had apparently not slapped her in the face yet.

No cars were being driven as I attempted to cross the road. I thought it only a little bit odd, since there was still a scattering of parked ones. In the mornings, only a handful of people were up and about, and those who opened early had long since come to work. But it felt desolate all the same —utterly empty, like a hole in the world.

There was no one else at the grocery store besides the cashier. I didn't recognise them at first glance, but it was not as if I was looking for another awkward conversation.

I gathered the essentials —leaving out things that needed to go into a refrigerator —into a metal basket before wandering to the front counter. The cashier was tall. Too tall for the ceiling. A drooping tree; immobile and topped with a spraying of brown freckles and a knot of ginger hair. Someone new. He sighed and started ringing up, occasionally glancing at me with furrowed brows. I looked at the wall behind him —at his shadow. It was elongated in places, unlinking in others.

Like someone had pinned some fabric on a mannequin for sewing but both things had kept moving around.

"That'll be fifteen dollars fifty-three."

"What?" My gaze snapped back before I plucked my debit card from my trouser pocket. "…Right."

"I'll need cash, unfortunately," he drawled, gesturing to the till. "Card machine's still busted."

I uncertainly dug into my tote bag.

"Just enough," I murmured in relief.

After stuffing everything into my bag, he handed me the change. But his hand did not then withdraw like a normal person's. His eyes narrowed accusingly. "…Are you Alexander Grahams by any chance?"

I started. Then frowned.

How the fuck could he know?

My hands balled tightly. "Who's asking," I bit, returning the judging expression while reading his nametag. "…Donatello?" I scoffed.

"Donny," he cringed. "And I was just curious. Geez."

"None of your business, though," I quipped.

I was thoroughly pissed off.

So even total strangers who had only heard about what happened many years later, knew who I was and wanted to put a face to the name.

"How long have you…been here?" he ignored my dismissal.

The question was strange, though. He didn't ask me when I had come back, or if I was settling in well. What he asked sounded…careful. Almost paranoid. And I could excuse it because when I looked into his faded dark hazel eyes, my body did not curl away in pain.

"Since last night," I said through my teeth, then whirled for the exit.

A violent shiver ran down my spine as the outside hit me once more. In the absence of fear, there was anger. Since when did I owe anyone from this town anything? Not every resident had been responsible, but that did not translate to obscure entitlement.

I wanted to lay low here —as low as I possibly could.

Yet at each turn the past reared; demanded to be seen. I clutched the strained, thin handles of my bag and didn't bother checking either end of the street as I stomped across it.

"Whoa, check out the balls on that kid."

My head turned. Foolishly.

A group of teenagers were leaning against an alleyway by the barber's shop. Some smoked cigarettes while the others sucked on *Jolly Rancher* lollipops; but they all wore leather, cargo and plaid several sizes too big. Though their shadows shouldn't have been visible at this angle.

My shoulders squared. I remembered all of them.

"...Alex Grahams?" Lincoln Keller quipped, his eyes widening as he popped the candy out of his mouth. "What're you doing here?"

I breathed hard through my nose. If there was one thing I hated more than Hugh calling me that, it was other people doing it.

THEY CALL YOU THAT BECAUSE YOU LOOK WRONG.

"Holy shit," Jesse Milburn cackled, nudging Lincoln's side. "It's been years. I thought you'd now be like, a girl or something."

I gritted my teeth. "That...that's not what I —"

"Shut it, assholes," Aspen Roland snapped. She raised an eyebrow in amusement as she stood, flicking ash at her side. "Little Grahams. I can't imagine why you're back. Were those other pastures not greener?" Her smile wasn't wide, and there was no glint in those brown irises, but my muscles still locked with a defensive steps backwards. Aspen's gaze then narrowed. "How'd you get that scar on your lip?"

My throat dried.

"You're scaring him," Maggie Elwoods —from the family of the town founder's entitled descendants —sighed, pulling Aspen's shoulder back. "He's not a little child anymore. And neither are we."

THOSE WORDS ARE WRONG.

STOP HER.

Can't help it if they say what they see, was the limp insistence.

Maggie was not a nice person.

She just didn't want to be seen as a completely shitty one.

Aspen huffed, then spat on the ground by my shoes.

None of it surprised me. These were the kids that even back then had been given up on by their parents. The kids who shot gum in people's hair and brought lighters to school just to set the toilet paper on fire. Yet these troublemakers hadn't been my biggest bullies. Not by a long shot.

"But…is Grahams still confused, is the question," Lincoln sniggered, feeling invincible from the meter distance between himself and Maggie.

What a gross and insensitive accusation. And I could guarantee that he had heard that phrasing first from Mr and Mrs Keller.

The anger moved to my fists. "Wouldn't you like to know."

Jesse burst out laughing, and his shadow didn't move with him.

"Well, you don't *look* like much changed," Lincoln continued. "Did you go to a camp after all?"

I started. "Excuse me?"

"That's what the rumours said," Aspen agreed, nodding.

What pierced deep into my soul was not the fact that there had been rumours. It was that no one wondered why; no one might recall why I left so abruptly. The poison from the marker ink and the irrevocable damage that wasn't as visible.

What if everything repeated itself?

The edges of my vision were darkening. This could *not* be happening. Not again. And I didn't have my lifeline this time.

"…I have to get back and unpack things," I muttered bitterly, moving in that direction. They did not let me get far.

"Aw, let us help," Aspen smirked, roughly hooking an arm around my neck. "We should be good neighbours and greet your parents."

"No need," I insisted, wriggling.

"What, you don't want your friends to come over?" Jesse joined in.

Lincoln glared in my general direction, irritated by his failure to rattle me. Maggie just stood there overseeing, as she had always done.

"I have never had any friends in Pine Creek," I bit, grabbing hold of Aspen's wrist and twisting it. She was taller, with more muscle on me, so I managed to surprise her more than anything.

Each of their gazes grew cold. It wasn't funny anymore, and I needed to get out of there. Aspen opened her mouth to say something more, but her head turned to blink at the approaching figure powering towards us.

It was weird to see Louise Barnes in anything that was not a mini skirt or heels. If she was anyone else, she might have been laughed at for the stockings underneath her studded shorts and fraying sweater. But here, no matter what personality she donned, Louise seemed to be God.

"What do you want, Barnes? A smoke?" Aspen quipped.

Louise glanced at her sideways, before taking me by the shoulder. She refused to dignify the taunt. "Come on, Grahams," she huffed, nose rising. "You do *not* want to be hanging around with these losers."

They only scoffed and clicked their tongues dejectedly.

Then came the quick muttering under Jesse's breath. "…Just wait 'til Hyde gets a whiff of this."

The hair at the neck of my neck stood. There was no one from all those years ago I remembered with that name. Yet I felt dread burrowing.

I looked at Louise as I wrenched free of her. "Who's Hyde?"

She didn't hesitate nor look at me. "Not important. Tell him Milburn, and you're dead." Her thumb then motioned a harsh slit across her throat for emphasis. That bloodthirsty look on her face…

Flashes of pitch darkness momentarily took my vision. The darkness of a small stale locker; a locked classroom; a dusty cellar —even my own bedroom. At least I had been safe in that house, once.

My breath shallowed.

"Oh I won't have to," Jesse assured. "Ain't nowhere to hide in Pine Creek, you of all people should know that, Barnes."

Louise ground her teeth together and glared at her sneakers. Even the others shuffled around uneasily. Who could exist who was so terrible that even Aspen Roland shut up and glanced aside?

That even Louise Barnes dared not provoke him?

I didn't want to care.

If it was someone who I could steer clear of if I was careful, then I would. Because if he struck fear into the most feared, that meant he was potential new bully number one. An obstacle to my plans.

Hide and seek had not been a part of those.

You'll be found soon enough. That was what Jesse meant.

The only question was when and for what reason.

But I still hoped that he was wrong.

the sleuth

ALEXANDER

LOUISE BARNES WAS almost as bad at lying as my mother. Her eyebrows furrowed and she looked straight ahead —any direction but your face. And there was something clearly *big* that she was hiding about whoever this Hyde was. Clearly he had taken over in the void of incident.

His name was cold, like ice water pouring over my back. It wasn't the same as terror. It was visceral recoil. But Louise was afraid. And she was not afraid of many things.

Now she was tailing me. She might have been unsure of where I was going, but her attempt to keep pace was clear. She followed me along the main street, past the windows and bleached wood eager to redecorate for Fall and Halloween. Every elaborate building was old, and every one of them was empty. No owner in sight, or even a sweeping part-timer.

My senses then returned.

"Just what are you doing here, Louise?" I grumbled, whipping around to address her. "Thanks for getting me away from those guys, but I really don't want you to act like you know me."

"But I *do* know you," she pointed out, blinking rapidly. Then her eyes scanned my person.

"What," I hedged.

"…Did anything seem off to you last night?" she asked cautiously. "A series of strange noises or strange shadows on the walls?"

I stiffened, holding my bag handles tighter. "Why do you ask?"

She drew a breath. "I need you to come with me somewhere. There's something you should know. Especially since you don't seem to have one, strangely." She looked me up and down again.

"Have what?"

"I'll explain on the way."

"What makes you think I'd go *anywhere* with you?" I demanded. "I have plans. Don't you have anyone else to stalk?"

"I'm not stalking you if you know I'm there."

"That's not how it works."

"Okay," she surrendered. "If you want to talk in a public space first, that's fine. *Straws & Fries* should be a good compromise."

"You're missing the point," I insisted, folding my arms. I tried to look her in the face. Her makeup streaked; her eyes glazed; her lips pale and chapped as if she was ill. "I *hate* you, Louise Barnes. Everything keeps circling back to you and your psychotic need for control. And you cannot just come talk to me as if none of it ever happened."

She dithered.

It felt good for a brief moment, to see that guilt.

But it couldn't last.

"I…I know," she murmured, dropping my glare. "I know that those girls and I were awful to you. The whole school, in fact. It's just that…things are different now. Something is wrong with this town, and I need —"

"Unbelievable," I cut her off, swivelling on my heel. "I can't even get a basic apology from you. Maybe I expected too much."

"W-wait, Alex!"

I didn't stop but my steps faltered.

"Do. Not. Call. Me. That."

"But isn't it your name?"

"Stop following me," I warned, my strides lengthening. "And no, my birth certificate actually says Alexander —don't shorten it."

"But Keller —"

"*Fuck* Keller," I barked. "At least he's not following me!"

"Please! At least hear me out. Haven't you noticed that no one can use a phone, car, or that the shadows have minds of their own?"

I made a mistake.

I stopped.

Louise ran into my back, before losing her balance and falling backwards onto the sidewalk. My head tilted to the side so I glanced at her from the corner of my eye. There was an expression on her face that I had never seen before, but with which I was intimately familiar.

Desperation.

The begging kind.

"…You're pathetic," I said flatly. Coldly. She blinked. "You must be such a disappointment to your parents. You know, you don't deserve a family. I hope that God forgives you for the confused little freak you are."

Louise's eyes widened at each sentence.

By the way her face reddened she definitely recognised the words that had come directly from her prepubescent mouth. Pain finally hit her.

But sure, kids never know what they're doing.

"I've never forgotten the things you said to me," I assured. "All scars linger. So until you even *consider* apologising, do not approach me. You don't get to be nice to me now because you're going through something.

Next time you think it's a good idea to interfere, I want you to remember all the shit you put me through, and stay the hell away."

Her head hung as keeping my gaze became unbearable. I wondered if this was how I had always looked to her. On the ground, petrified and on the verge of tears. My therapist was wrong. The sight of Louise Barnes in a mirrored position to mine didn't feel complicated and unsatisfying.

I was very simply *ecstatic*.

Revenge did not taste the least bit bitter.

Undeservedly, I left it at that and turned away.

My feet only paused on the front steps of the library.

Pine Creek was not the most well-read town. The books that lined the shelves were practical and academic —save for the collection of fiction requested and donated by the more…open minded members of society: its respite. Despite Oregon being a liberal state, the sleepy river town was comprised of a majority of conservatives. My parents —or rather mostly my father, had those views. And they had consequently contributed to the suffocated experience of my reconciliation with who I was.

From a young age the idea of anything that went against your parents' demands and those in the bible —absolutely in that order —being sin was shoved down every throat. At first I had not realised that not wanting to wear '*socially acceptable*' attire and wanting long hair was an automatic ticket to Hell. I still didn't think that, but that was thanks to my mother.

She had told me continuously that there was nothing wrong with me. Not with my discomfort with my assigned gender, and not with the desire to remedy it. To have others perceive it, on the outside.

To not be trapped in a box manufactured by people long dead.

I was *um filho amado de Deus* —a beloved child of God like all human beings, and that meant I had been made precisely as intended. Non-binary and all. Because God did not make mistakes, or something.

It was different from being a whole stranger in someone else's body. When I thought too deeply about it, it was like wearing the slightly wrong sized clothing for your entire life because everyone told you that was what you were supposed to wear —then discovering that other clothes exist and that the material doesn't have a gender anyway.

Except I couldn't change those old clothes yet, and so was disastrously parading around in certain things that were unnoticeably not mine.

But in the library, I could almost forget what it was that I was wearing. Tucked away within a musty corner, on a beanbag that was unstitching at its seams where no one could see nor care.

Those who did, would never set foot in a library.

The weathered floorboards gave me away as I stepped past the heavy wooden doors, glancing at the librarian briefly on my way to the back. No face to be seen, because they were deeply absorbed in a dark fantasy. A sign on an identical door indicated the restricted section was right beside the large table designated for studying students. The fiction bookcase was as sparce as it had been when I was last there, though it did have a few new titles. But I wouldn't be reading those.

I produced a paperback from my tote bag and settled in what was now the *only* beanbag.

My lungs expanded as I looked out of the curved window before me. It streamed in the intermittent sunlight in precise thin slices; making the otherwise invisible dust in the air seen for a few moments at a time. Like some sort of magic.

This was better.

Nothing could intrude here.

And then I saw *Strange the Dreamer* by Laini Taylor on the shelf. It was then my thoughts which intruded; dragging me into my own dreams that I could not remember. Clearly they were the sort that made people believe dreams had real life meanings. But instead of scoffing at that notion, now I wanted any answer at all.

The last dream I remembered was just from a year ago. It held no real significance aside from its permanence within my head. It had not been interesting or logical or even an amalgamation of memories —it was just a dream, in unfamiliarly familiar setting and driven by whatever my brain could conjure. Mundane. But even that strangeness was welcome.

The uncertain static of my head had grown monotonous.

A gust of wind burst through an open panel I was sure had been closed in the window before. I curled into the wall, fending off the chill.

A pair of shoes were standing in front of me when I opened my eyes. They were short heels the colour nude, and in them were the same shade of nylon stockings. My neck craned to look up at the person who owned them. Thankfully, it was a stranger.

She was something out of a book.

Her blazer was a pristine off-white, and her blouse black silk. Her skirt ended just below her knees, pleated in a material like thin tartan. The only thing out of place was her wavering but stern expression —the want to be angry was there yet she couldn't muster enough malice.

"…Please keep the windows closed close to the Fall."

Her voice was hardly more audible than a murmur.

"I didn't open it," I protested.

She reached over to redo the latch. I then noticed something else that was out of place. The librarian was missing a shadow.

Her head turned back to me, strands of her light coppery hair fluttering on a breeze that was no longer there. "You are the first patron of the week. If you're not here to do any work, please keep the quiet rule."

Her finger slowly rose to point at a poster tacked to the noticeboard.

I found myself only capable of nodding.

She let out an odd nervous breath as she returned the gesture curtly, before turning towards the scratched up half-moon front desk.

Like the slithers of light and dust, her shadow came in and out of view. But the arms were long and bony, with claws at the end of each hand and a spine that bent more so like rubber. It was only misting flashes, but my heart stuttered in warning that it was as aware of me as I was of it.

Louise's words repeated in my ears.

'*...The shadows have minds of their own*'.

I frowned and straightened up, then set my book aside. I did not want to believe a single thing she said, but for some reason I doubted that she had looked aside even as she had desperately shouted after me.

And I trusted my own sight over anything else.

Those phantom monsters had proven themselves able to be sensed and hostile. Some only latched, while others invaded the very anatomy of their hosts. There was something frightening about the chosen residency being in the invisible second shape of a person.

As if they were more of an extension than a parasite.

I got to my feet, dusted off my trousers, then wandered off to the case labelled '*Religion*'. It was, as always, decently stocked —which could be seen as more of insulting disinterest than a sign of a devout town.

Not to my surprise most of the books were various editions of the bible and respected collections of essays on it. I wasn't certain about what I was looking for, but the wonders of Heaven and the wrath of God did not seem to be it. My hand shakily gravitated to the only book which felt purposely obscured. I then discovered why. It was black, with a title in blood red.

Modern Demonology: A Comprehensive Guide to the Figures of Hell in the Major Denominations of Christianity. By Anonymous.

My eyes widened behind my slipping glasses.

Though my taught faith had never been concrete or passionate, even I was wary of demons and anything to do with '*punishable*' sin. That was why I had such a hard time going against what had been indoctrinated — against all I believed my parents cared for.

But *I* believed that I had no other starting point for understanding what might be happening in Pine Creek. So I lifted the heavy hardback cover and skimmed over the table of contents. Each of the denominations had its own complete section or part —one through ten. The last section was for the other denominations; a shorter set of common demons' names and descriptions in accordance with their overlapping beliefs.

So it still left out what each of those many other branches believed in detail. How comprehensive could it really be?

"I've read that one already. Nothing helpful."

"*Jesus Christ*!" I hissed; jumping and then stumbling backwards into the bookshelf as I attempted to catch my breath while clutching my chest. My shock was immediately overshadowed.

"You again," I growled, snapping the book shut with a loud thud.

Louise Barnes didn't even crack a guilty smile.

My gaze then focused on the shadow hand on her shoulder, squeezing. Her expression winced in response. I blinked rapidly. Could it be that the creature was coaxing her in whatever had remodelled her personality? I was yet to see another shadow with that much influence. The others only seemed to drain people of their general energy.

"Alex…ander," she said disjointedly. "You never have to forgive me. I did and let things happen to you that I can't fathom, but know still haunt you. I'd like to say I was a different person then —maybe I was, but that doesn't excuse the actions —*my* actions," she breathed, and the hand then loosened its grip only slightly. "…I've been such a hateful person, when my faith isn't even supposed to be about that. It wasn't my place to think I had any right to lecture or berate or harm you. It *isn't* my place. It isn't anyone's in all the world."

My anger wavered into a frown. My response would serve as a guide on proper remorse. If I said I accepted, she would be relieved. If I stayed infuriated, she would conclude I couldn't heal. Not that she had any say in that matter. So I took the neutral option.

I stared at her and said nothing at all.

Louise had applied more makeup, but it had run very obviously. What could she be hoping it would achieve? A show of stubborn perseverance?

"I'm sorry." Her voice broke halfway.

It was such a simple phrase; one that was often said for the sake of it, just to smooth things over. And the way she said it didn't smooth over a single thing, but I didn't get the impression that she didn't mean it.

The hand on her arm moved to snag the ends of her hair. She flinched, though not from any visible pain. Then it disappeared into the dark.

I didn't give a response to her apology. Not verbally, and not with my eyes either. I wanted her to agonise over it. Trust was not something to be easily given. Especially when there had been nothing holding it together in the first place.

I sidestepped her and walked to the large table. I dropped the demon book onto the bleached wood. It was enough to drive in my point, while allowing her to realise that I hadn't told her to get lost.

After a beat of hesitation she followed me, choosing to sit in the chair across as I opened to the table of contents again.

"Is there…a problem here?"

Our heads turned to the librarian who had once again appeared out of nowhere. Her book was clutched to her chest defensively and there was a slight flush to her cheek. There was that self-conscious firmness again.

"No," Louise mumbled, shaking her head. "We're just…working."

The librarian looked in my direction to confirm, but my concentration was firmly back on the book.

"…Please keep quiet then."

I listened to her quick, retreating footsteps while flicking through the main denominations. These differed from one another the most; adding or removing certain demons, classifications and sub species depending on their theological and regional origin.

I lingered on Catholicism, simply because it had been followed by my parents. It was just what I remembered from church, however. There was nothing new that could fit the description of the sentient darkness.

"I, uh…I've read it several times now," Louise spoke up after a while. "Even the more obscure denominations didn't give real clues."

My eye instinctively twitched. "You could have missed something," I clipped, flicking over a page.

"Oh. Um…right."

Fury was replaced with annoyance. I sighed, removed my glasses and pinched the bridge of my nose in exasperation. "What is it you want?" I asked. "Clearly you didn't follow me just to apologise."

Louise squirmed, avoiding my sharp gaze. It felt a little strange to be the person with the upper hand after everything she put me through. But it didn't mean that I didn't like it. It was gratifying to see her hesitate for fear of my reaction. I could *almost* understand if that feeling had been her driving force in her climb up the social hierarchy.

"I…meant what I said back there," she whispered, leaning over. "The part about minds of their own. Have you noticed that some things aren't working, and that everyone's shadow…seems wrong?"

"An understatement," I hedged, sliding my glasses back on.

"I know that you've barely even been here for a night, but…something happened several weeks ago —and according to the trend, everyone who comes to Pine Creek or is living in it should have that darkness over their shoulder. I call them Daemons, because that's what they remind me of," she said, pointing to the book. "It's happened to those who set foot in for at least a few of hours. Not to the handful of brief visitors, though."

"But nothing has happened to me or my Dad," I pointed out. "And it's already been *several* hours. Plus, we moved in."

Louise fidgeted nervously. "Are you certain?"

I hated that I paused.

I hated that my mind arrowed to the noises I had heard in the night, the open window and the book on the floor. Even my sleep paralysis demon. Nothing felt amiss with me, but what if the same couldn't be said about Hugh? I hadn't even checked on him on my way out.

"Why are you so worried about the timeline?" I demanded, my brows knitting. "Surely we'll become miserable like you in no time."

"I'm serious, Alexander."

She did look grave.

"Does this have something to do with that guy —Hyde?" I pressed. "Why does it seem like you're all afraid of him?"

"*Shh*," pleaded Louise, bringing a finger to her lips. She glanced about as if he might be in the library, listening.

My eyes lidded. "Well, does it?"

She took her bottom lip between her teeth until it turned red. "…Shane Hyde," she breathed. "That's his name. He likes to keep to himself, so it's unlikely that you'll run into him. And yes, this does have something to do with him. A lot, actually. At least I should think so."

"Why?"

She dared to meet my gaze then, resolute and pleading. "Because he's the only person in this town without a Daemon. It's just…he's been here for years. Since a few months after you left."

I swallowed, but the lump in my throat only solidified. And that cold sensation washed over me again —mingling with the quickening crush of anxiety. It wasn't the coldness of wind. It was the void of warmth.

Louise's bravery lasted only a moment, as she hurriedly looked back down at her hands. She fiddled with the ends of her sleeves, pulling them down over her blanched knuckles as though she could feel the cold too. "If one doesn't claim you soon, you'll be just like him."

"As in…feared?"

She shook her head. "No. An anomaly. A challenge."

I couldn't run fast enough. The tips of my boots kept catching the edges of the shoddy brickwork. I had to get home to my father. Even if he wasn't my favourite person in the world, I didn't *want* him to fall to whatever it was Louise Barnes was referring to as largely unavoidable.

Tears stung the corners of my eyes as my pace hastened —cutting in the brutal wind. I told myself the watering was because of that cold.

Soon each bound was accompanied by a hissed wince; a determination to push onwards. Faster. All that Louise had told me was yet to process, but I couldn't allow a single inch in the margin of possible error.

I somehow managed to whip out my cellphone in the blur, glancing at the screen with fierce hope.

But God did not see my situation as good enough miracle fodder. The symbol for four bars was completely greyed out.

"*Merda*," I cursed, rounding a corner.

Then I swore again —I ran straight into something hard and tall. After adjusting my glasses my head rose to look upon a boy. His face contorted with frustration, but as soon as his eyes focused and met mine, that look turned to stunned surprise. Mine probably appeared the same.

Even though I was out of breath I still managed to draw a sharp one. I had never seen eyes that shade of turquoise. Platinum blond hair settled in waves skimming his forehead —dyed, perhaps, given a contrast in the brown of his eyebrows. A silver piercing hooked over the left.

I didn't want to admit to so thoroughly appreciating his visage. But he seemed to be doing the same to me.

His lips parted. Those brows pulled together.

Our staring lasted several seconds too long before I managed to snap out of it. "I…I'm sorry," I stumbled through, before taking several steps backwards. "I have to get back…I have to get home."

My feet bolted despite the flaming of my face.

And I didn't dare to glance back.

the vicious cycle

SHANE

THOSE BROWN EYES.

Bronze. That brown skin. *Tiger's Eye*. That brown hair. *So thick and dark it appears closer to obsidian.*

The soul was early this time.

Home, they had called it.

They had never…moved back to Pine Creek. They had never come so far ahead of the massacre.

Shane had never had the opportunity to know them again. *Truly* know them; from a time long lost. He did not know how to behave. How could he approach someone he had spent years killing and mourning over in any way that could be perceived as normal?

And entangled within the confusion and frustration remained that love that had made him so vengeful in the first place.

Every single time he saw them —alive and breathing —every time, it undid him. There was no question of the ruin and destruction that would follow behind each encounter; each reliving of the tragedy. Each misery. Yet even knowing that devastation, the monster could not help harbouring that selfish need to stay close. To feel the cool sensation of skin.

True to the Morningstar's threat, he had tried many times to stay away to no avail. No amount of mortal self-control had been enough to keep his true form from bursting through his fragile skin and ripping through the town. From tearing into the soul.

He'd screamed and cursed. By the thirty-seventh cycle, he had run out of sounds to hurl. His throat had torn itself apart. It was on the inside that the burn of devastation had seared. No more screams were then ever heard from the forest.

Alexander.

The name that haunted his dreams and terrors.

He had only managed to say it aloud very few times, due to some sort of reverence. He had never dared to call them by their name in person at all —convinced that he neither had the right nor the courage.

Alexander.

In a few cycles, the soul had hated him on the spot. That had hurt more furiously than any wound; any pain; so much so that he had then spent a good amount of the following repeating seasons wallowing in darkness attempting to rid himself of his own breath…without success.

To receive hatred was to be expected.

Without warrant or explanation was puzzling. That face they made at death had even distorted with contempt.

So for entire shards of them; scattered piece by piece; to turn and find their love no longer worth trial and their affection misguided…it was just enough to make the beast spiral. Rooted deep within them, Alexander had developed cause for resentment.

Though rightly so.

Would the beast come to a point in the cycles when the human felt no love for him ever again? He couldn't think for a moment on how to cope.

All of that existential dread had pushed to the furthest recesses of his mind when he had once more he looked upon their face.

No measure of time would be sufficient to replicate it perfectly, yet he knew every part blind. He knew how it felt to graze his knuckles against their cheek; how their breath hitched when he neared; and he knew what it was like to kiss them. The tremble in their confidence, and the eagerness of their lips. It had been an unforgettable memory —because as if the king of Hell was watching, it had not really happened since.

The world had stopped when Alexander crashed into him.

It took Shane a moment, just a second or two, to realise who the person staring back at him was. That narrow face; those inquisitive eyes behind a pair of falling glasses —even that little scar along their bottom lip which had always found a way to reoccur. And the Portuguese swear in surprise, which was just so like them.

Everything had halted, and arrowed to that infinite moment.

Then he had thought properly about what it might mean to see the soul there at a time unprecedented. Why had the set gears of the curse changed and why had Alexander stared back with that gleaming gaze —as if they had nearly recognised him?

It could not be related to anything good.

That look as they'd left…the mixture of apprehension and unease, was playing over and over in his mind as he leisurely sat on a park bench and exhaled smoke towards the clouded sky.

Shane sat up slowly as he heard the familiar jostling of Lincoln Keller and Jesse Milburn, with the girls trailing. He eyed them with little interest, but for the sake of appearances he would acknowledge and interact with these teenagers. Especially figurehead ringleader, Maggie Elwoods.

"Hyde, you'll never guess who we just saw in town —" Jesse started, before being promptly shut up by Aspen, who slapped her hand over his mouth. He wriggled, trying to shove her off.

"Christ, don't you have any fear?" she hissed.

"I ain't scared of Barnes," he scoffed. "What's she going to do —ban me from *Little Hatchet*? Her old man would never agree."

Shane then took a deliberate drag, thoroughly unamused. "Think very carefully before you involve me in your bullshit," he warned.

"It's worth hearing, we swear," Lincoln insisted.

"Not only does the town have a new —*returning* resident, apparently the shadow things haven't affected them yet," Maggie chipped in.

Aspen rolled her eyes. "It's only been a couple of hours, dumbasses. No reason to worry. You'll see the life fade from him soon enough."

Shane frowned, bouncing the cigarette between his lips. "See the life fade from who?" he demanded.

"Alexander Grahams," Jesse loudly volunteered the answer so that no one had the chance to hesitate. "You remember those stories about the kid who left before you came? They called him the End of Pine Creek."

Shane scoffed. *I am its end*, he corrected. *And they're not a* 'him'. It was a conflicting pride and punishment. Case and point, these idiots.

He tried to keep his expression neutral. "…I see."

The humans looked between each other, at a loss.

"That's it?" Lincoln muttered.

"I thought you would be at least a bit intrigued," Aspen quipped. Her chin stuck upwards as she stared Shane down.

"Why?" he questioned. His head did not raise to grant her the honour of attention. Only those frigid blue eyes set upon her; shining through his darker lashes. Even with the difference in angle Aspen wavered, as if his gaze inflicted something physical.

Jesse pouted. "You don't want to figure out why that little fa —"

"—You're not allowed to say that word, Milburn," Shane cut him off. He pointed his cigarette at him importantly. "*Unless…*"

"I'm not," he immediately denied it. The tips of his ears reddened self-consciously even as he glared in adamant denial.

"Then shut your mouth," Shane clipped.

Maggie put her hands on her hips, through two of the holes in the grey top she'd thrown over a black collared shirt. "What if Alexander doesn't get one?" she pressed. "Wouldn't that be suspicious?"

"Not my business," Shane grunted, before inhaling dismissively.

He did care —a little.

The shadow entities were a new thing, but in the past cycles Alexander had received one whenever they had entered the town for more than a day. Each previous circumstance had been them and their parents only visiting, so there had not been a lot of deviating instances to work with.

What the Made demon truthfully felt, was unconcerned.

This cycle would correct itself without his interference.

Aspen Roland clicked her tongue. Evidently, a lack of a reaction from Shane Hyde pissed *her* off. "No fun," she hissed. She turned on her heel, linking an arm through Maggie's as she then stomped away. Her shadow wafted up off of the ground in wisps, trembling in the tell-tale sign that it was about to devour some bad decisions. "…Come on guys," she ordered. "Maybe we can bother Barnes instead."

"You're buying," Jesse insisted, slinking after them with Lincoln.

"You wish," she chuckled.

Shane leaned back on the bench as he watched the group leave. None of them glanced backwards over their shoulders, but he knew that they knew he hadn't yet looked away.

He sighed up towards the expanse of washed grey again, wishing that it would rain. Smoke curled away. If he squinted a little, it looked like the dark grey rose to add to the clouds.

Flashes of inky black flickered in the forefront of his mind. When the sky had gone. It made him wince. Had he not yet suffered enough?

He did not like reverting back to that monster against his will. It had become painful —physically and mentally. Knowing that the iron beast was always below his human guise was so disgustingly uncomfortable he wanted to tear it off. Tear off *something*.

But another memory pushed through the darkness.

The soul discouraging the hatred he had come to feel towards that part of himself. Wanting to be rid of it was not only a bad response, but it was impractical. It *was* him. The demon had been made that way. All that he could do was either learn to exist with it, or to twist it into something more tolerable. Something less cruel.

A raindrop broke on the bridge of his nose.

"…Fuck."

He hadn't mean *that* soon. Now he had to go back to that little house, with those innocent strangers he'd been forced to call family.

Shane trudged through the front door of number fifteen Cypress Circle a sodden mess. A little boy of seven years old wobbled across the foyer to plod up the stairs; the thudding echoing as the structure rattled.

"Ken, don't go through the house in those roller-skates," warned the boy's mother, shaking her head at the answering giggles.

Shane watched it happen like it was a movie. Like he wasn't there.

The mother turned to him. Her expression upon seeing him softened; a softness that carried through her light eyes and loose mousey bun. And she gave him a smile he didn't deserve, and never would.

"Aw, honey did you get caught in the rain?" She reached for his cheek, and he instinctively flinched. If she noticed, Samantha Hyde had stopped reacting many years ago; in that hurt, crumpling way that mothers did. But her smile did not slip. "…Wash up before dinner, okay?"

"Mm."

Her second husband emerged from the living room, tired and irritable. He eyed Shane as though he almost knew that he was a monster invading his home. There was nothing the beast could do to appease Jeffery Hyde, and hanging around Maggie Elwoods did not aid his case.

"You listen to your mother, now," he added, needing to insert himself into the conversation. His nostrils flared. The drenching of rain could not hide the scent of nicotine. "…And cut that crap out if you know what's good for you," was the quiet threat out of earshot from Samantha.

He didn't know what was good for him.

Surely that much was obvious.

The man's shadow whipped back and forth, hoping for a fight. Shane should have felt bad for the family having to deal with the monstrosities when they had done nothing to deserve it.

But he didn't.

Shane gave no response and drifted for the stairs. The less difficult he was, the better. The less of their faces he saw: the best.

He couldn't do it today —pretend.

Pretend that he hadn't killed that mother without thought, and her son. Pretend like he was supposed to care about them. He had learned that the man had been one of the last to die. All that they shared was a last name, and some mortal blood. Cycle after cycle, betrayal after betrayal.

Every part of it was a horrid joke.

Footsteps padded up and down the hallway, but he certainly couldn't pretend to entertain the little boy either. He had a peculiar shadow too — they did not discriminate in age —it matured at the same pace that he did, tantrums and childish naïveté alike. It latched onto his every mistake and white lie, but did not ever touch him.

In fact, none of them usually clawed at their victims. If they did, that was entirely the fault of the human's innermost guilt.

Kendall Robert Hyde had no concept of the word.

"Why didn't you take an umbrella?" he asked Shane as he rocked back and forth on the skirting board, clutching the handrail.

"Forgot," Shane hedged. He shook out his hair and sent water droplets flying. The little boy snorted before jumping down. He looked a lot like Shane; honey blond hair and easily tanned. He had his mother's eyes and father's height though, in a grassy green and at three feet. Thankfully. It was for that reason that Shane bleached his hair —to other himself.

"Dummy."

"Yeah."

Shane then took the opportunity to disappear into the bathroom. Of all of them, Kendall was the most oblivious to the beast's distancing. He could not comprehend the resentment that hung thick in the air of the house; the pain carried by his parents, though unbeknownst to them.

Even in death that child always had a look of the greatest shock.

After all, there was no way his older brother could hate him.

Not for real.

Shane was almost certain that even when the monster took over Kendall still fully believed that his brother did not mean any of it.

It baffled the demon: to think that such unconditional love and hope could exist even when they were not a real family and even when Shane had never shown much reciprocation. It was one of those questions he had asked the soul once, in his belief that nothing was given for free.

And the soul had replied that in most humans there was an instinct to believe that all that they felt was true, despite their surrounds. So hatred could be faced with a love holding out for change; and despair could be endured with a constant trickle of aid.

He still thought it all ridiculous.

But everything just sounded so absolutely true coming from them.

Shane had to wonder what he was going to do in the current cycle. He didn't think he had the strength to stay away so obviously, but neither did he have the audacity to involve himself in Alexander's life now. Not with the possibility of several constants being misaligned. Keeping close might result in…complications.

And he couldn't pretend to be able to deal with those.

"…Do you think that it's noble to give your life for someone else's?" the soul asked. Their forehead pressed to the cell bars; knees bent up to their chest and held together by spindly arms.

"Why would anyone do that?" asked the demon with a little snark.

"I am not quite sure," they admitted. "But I think that 'someone else' *has to mean something to you. To mean everything."*

"I suppose," Ferream huffed. "However…if they mean everything to you, then were you not already giving up your life for them?"

The soul stared at the beast; their bronze eyes glinting in the low light from the scorching torches. It stared back, aiming to devour but coming to the conclusion that the mortal had already wholly consumed it.

Shane stumbled out of the shower in as much of a haze as the vapour steaming up the glass. It was not his hand which reached for a towel and those were not his feet that stomped back across the hall to his bedroom. A middle aged black cat trailed after him from downstairs.

"Oh to be you, Omen," sighed the created demon —slowly running a hand over its arcing back. "An oblivious cat amidst the inevitable."

Omen's nose twitched as its ears flicked back and forth. Its amber eyes slitted before it turned to prance all over the bed.

A bird had landed on a branch by the window.

Shane leaned back on his hands and sucked on his teeth. He had run out of chewing gum. Smoking was a new, recent habit. A new distraction.

Nothing was entirely his own, and the human vessel was the worst of it. He considered himself fortunate that he had not been forced to take over a life that already existed —to replace someone once loved. It was simpler to be an alien than a changeling.

But there was no desire to rid himself of anyone before the massacre. There was no point, after all.

They would keep dying no matter what the motive.

Whether they meant everything to him, or not.

the encounter

ALEXANDER

IT HAD BEEN a while since I had seen Hugh Grahams curled up on the floor. When had he turned into the child, and when had I grown up? I didn't like that my first thought after running back was so removed from the situation, but as I stood in the doorway to the living room panting, all I could see was my father in the corner beside the sofa, head against the wall and a couple of empty cider bottles at his feet.

I didn't know if I should approach or stay away.

I didn't even know if I *wanted* to step closer.

And it was not because of the gathering dark behind him. Or the mass by the window, staring at me.

I knew by those hollow eyes that it was the thing that had replaced my sleep paralysis demon. They were carved out spaces of nothingness; more void than the shadows that made it.

"Alexander?" my father rasped.

My gaze stayed on the Daemon furthest away as I answered. "…Dad, what happened?"

"…You were gone for so long," he murmured, also not looking at me. His eyes looked glazed over. "I…I couldn't…There was a knock on the door. But…there was no…no one there…"

The darkness writhed, picking at his t-shirt. I jumped to conclusions. It was a Daemon, here to claim my father. I looked closer at the one still keeping its distance. There was nothing stopping it. Yet an invisible mesh of wire seemed to bind it back.

"…So it got you," I said tightly. My hands balled into fierce fists, and I flinched at the cut of my nails. "This cannot be happening."

I had arrived too late, finding my reality aligning with Louise's theory. It had now been a sufficient number of hours since we had set foot in Pine Creek so we had to conform. But was I then meant to step back and allow it all to happen? Even though I didn't care for a majority of the residents, it surely wasn't right to leave them the way that they were.

All I knew for certain was that Louise had had a point. Something *was* wrong with the town. And it was more than just its people.

My father didn't say anything.

The Daemon at the window moved.

My attention shifted and my feet slid in the opposite direction —towards the front door. It still struggled to move freely; the wires pulling back its very advance; but its movements were desperate. Its dark eyes slitted with a rising anger as several wires seemed to snap. It lunged for me, clumsily and uncoordinated but with enough presence for me to run.

Or rather, I attempted to.

Wires tugged back my limbs too.

I called out for my father but he was in no state to hear.

Panic set in quickly, and the breath I had found was snatched away in an instant. It was another blur —now I was running away from something I was unsure about how much damage it could truly do. No mark lingered from its claws but people clearly felt the sensation of pain. And that was enough for me to consider flight.

I had no weapon. Nothing sat in the holder by the fireplace where tools were meant to be, but I doubted they could fend off smoke. That thought triggered another: what if it could touch me but I could not touch it?

The Daemon was looming now that I had given it the opportunity with my hesitation. I looked up, meeting those eyes again.

This time I saw all absence of life and light within them. Like black holes; they pulled in every stray ray until all that was left was the darkest emptiness. It was like seeing the end —the sheer oblivion in the aftermath of everything disappearing.

I didn't know what Hugh was doing.

His head still rest to the side, defeated.

"Dad, please! *Do* something!"

There was that foolish hope once more, spurring on the delusion that he might snap out of it. It all turned into furious despair when I realised that I was on my own. He was already being consumed by whatever tore him up inside, and that had to extend to me too.

My body refused to move in the way that I wanted.

The wires pulled tighter and all I could manage was whimpering and curling away against the wall as the elongated shadow stopped within an inch of my boots. Yet the tendrils would not get near enough —they went around and hovered, as if second guessing their path.

The breath escaping my lips was quick and shallow.

Its hand creaked —towards my face. I could clearly *feel* the darkness encroaching. And I didn't want to brace myself for what it might feel like to have those claws sink into my skin.

NO. STOP IT. FIGHT. FIGHT.

For the first time in my life, I did not argue with the louder voice in my head. I gritted my teeth and mustered all of the will slipping from me in that moment. My hand twitched. In the weakest response, my fingers then slowly unfurled; my arm rising from my side in time; until it was all one large push and I reached out in protest.

"*No*!" I cried.

My hand shot through the Daemon's torso —displacing large streaks of shadow as my fingers grabbed at nothing. The only sensation was cold. It felt as though I had run my hand underneath a faucet made for ice water.

It was a feeling that did not last because in the moment of tearing that hole, the entity froze. Its joints jerked at sickeningly unnatural angles and those eyes flared like they were crying blots of ink.

A high pitched ringing sound pierced the inside of my ears. The flash of a heat so unbearable washed over me —then bursts of fire in my mind, and the smell of burning.

The cool broke through the flame.

A harsh voice soothed the sear.

Though I couldn't make out any words, nor see beyond a staining of red. Then it all flickered into obscurity while I lost the grip on it. My sight returned first before the rest of me was jarred alert.

I blinked away beads of tears. I was still half risen on one knee, in the same moment that the shadows shattered outwards like glass behind the Daemon. Those shards slowly dissolved into the stale air until all that was left were tiny shimmers in the filtering moonlight. I finally lowered to my haunches; numb and draining of adrenaline.

Hugh turned.

He might have been taking everything in, but the action was so blank and vacant he appeared vaguely annoyed instead.

"…Were there…two? Where is…yours?" he whispered.

Mine? It sure as hell didn't belong to me if I didn't want it.

"Got rid of it," I told him. I was sure I'd killed it.

He frowned. "How?"

"I don't know." I shakily rose to my feet, leaning into the doorway to catch myself as I nearly fell. "But it's gone and I don't have one."

You don't have one.

YOU DON'T HAVE ONE.

Was it the truth now setting in, or was my mind struggling to comprehend what had just happened? My breath was in no hurry to return to normal. I turned my hands over and back, watching them tremble, before beginning to count softly and pinching above my wrist.

What on Earth had I done?

Had I unintentionally ruptured procedure?

I reached the number fourteen before I looked at my father. His focus nor conscious were still not all there, but that failed to supress my anger. I debated on whether or not I should leave him alone. At least, before I remembered he had done nothing when I had called to him. I readjusted my glasses and turned towards the front door. I had to get out of there, away from the house; I had to breathe air; I had to get out of Pine Creek, even though I couldn't yet drive; I had to…I had to talk to Louise Barnes. I had to know what turning into an anomaly really meant.

It wasn't the first time I had found myself at Louise's doorstep. The times prior consisted of stealth observations and non-confrontational wishful vengeance. Kicking at the grass along the curb, or yanking off the head of a rose from Mrs Barnes' neat little flower garden. Now those pink and white blooms were wilted and I didn't think that anyone could tell if it was because of the season, or something more sinister.

The door went unanswered for several minutes. I thought about going back, but the idea of trying to sleep under the same suffocating old house as my father in his now unpredictable state was not at all appealing in that moment. I had to process. I had to decipher.

The biting night air served its purpose partly. My curls bounced in the howl whistling through the dying leaves, and the coolness to my skin was a welcome balm. Suddenly I could think a little clearer, and replay those last moments without effort.

I could still feel the freezing shadow along my fingers. The hollowed eyes wouldn't leave my head even when I closed my own; the bottomless pools of the most frightening *nothing*.

For once, I was grateful that I couldn't remember my dreams.

Henry Barnes was the one to see who it was at such an hour; though he might have just finished dinner, his shirt and pyjama pants were draped in a warm dressing gown. Hazel eyes I had once feared studied me. I tried not to look away. I was the last person who should feel ashamed. He was a stocky man; about twice my height with a thinning sweep of grey and brown hair. The sort of man who was deemed '*sensible*': with a gruelling office job and picture perfect family and a sail boat.

And his Daemon —or perhaps the signs of it —seemed to share in the delusion. It rippled with the breeze, but looked as solid as ice.

His eyes slowly widened, then he blinked in realisation. "…Alexander Grahams? What are you doing here?"

"I need to talk to Louise," I got to the point. "Sir."

"What? Right now?"

"It's urgent," I assured.

He stood there at a loss for another second before Louise herself came to a standstill beside him. She looked between the two of us, then moved to step outside. "I'll just be a minute," she promised.

"I didn't know the two of you were…friends," said Henry, very flatly.

"We're not," we answered in unison.

Her tone was half disheartened. Mine was brisk.

Her father didn't like it. But he was tired, and we were tired. He could see it in both of our faces that whatever this was, it was more important.

"Keep it short, all right?" Henry sighed. Then he glanced at me; brows folding together in an uneasy discomfort that was close to guilt. "…And, welcome back, Alex."

"Alexander," I immediately blurted. Before adding '*please*' as a total afterthought in response to Mr Barnes sceptically narrowing his gaze. He looked back to his daughter who, to my surprise, nodded encouragingly.

The frown morphed into a twist of the mouth. "Yeah, sure."

I only breathed again when the door closed behind him.

Louise's surprise finally showed itself when we then stood alone in the driveway. "Who's the stalker now?" she breathed shakily, and I saw it waft into the air. It sounded like it was meant to be a joke, but her tone was off and she struggled to look me in the eye.

"Still you," I deadpanned. "Everyone knows where you live, Barnes. Besides —I rang the doorbell."

She huffed, accepting her unmoved position. "Fine. What could be so pressing that you had to show up at night?"

"…It happened," I said tightly.

"What did?"

I had the suspicion that she already had an idea.

"Hugh got one," I clarified. "A *Daemon*. But I…I didn't."

Her eyes widened comically slowly. With that, I felt like a freak of nature once again; that child in me viscerally shrinking away.

"Holy shit," whispered Louise. "So did yours just not show up at the same time?"

"It did," I hissed. "Look —something else happened when they came. Something you need to tell me whether or not is normal."

She crossed her arms and leaned into one hip. "Yeah?"

That stance —it was well ingrained in my memories. Cool, confident and impatient. I had come to associate it with power. Because she had had all of it, and stripped me of mine. Even there, somehow, it felt as though all my recovery might be futile and unimportant. What was meant to be a monumental feat for me was in danger of being reduced to fuck all at the drop of a hat. How could it all still be *her* story?

And for a split second, my entire body recalled the terror it had been put through. I was shaking again, boarding on an attack if I failed to calm down and to say all that I needed. My feet took a step back.

I wasn't sure of how much to tell Louise. As we had agreed —we were not friends. The circumstances surrounding even this conversation boiled down to a mutual desire to unravel and undo all the knots into which Pine Creek seemed to have tied itself.

I had to remind myself that she was the only other one seeking answers —even if I wanted to turn at every glimpse of her silhouette.

"…I tore through it," I rasped. "With my hand. It felt cold."

"You what," exclaimed Louise, her arms dropping to her sides. "How did you manage that? I've never been able to touch my Daemon."

"I don't know," I insisted through clenched teeth.

But at least I had my answer. What I had done wasn't normal.

What I *was*, wasn't normal.

"I need to figure out if this can happen to others," Louise quipped. "I might not be able to physically interact with mine, but that doesn't mean that applies to everyone else."

I could almost see the gears in her head grinding.

"Right. Well, that was it," I said. "Bye."

It was unceremonious and curt, and Louise looked a little bit hurt.

"Oh —okay. Bye, then."

My feet moved of their own accord. Having accomplished my mission I had no reason to remain on her property. The sleep would be difficult if I was even to fall asleep at all. And I had only been left with more questions than answers. Then I paused at the memory of turquoise blue.

I turned back, self-consciously rubbing my arm. "…Out of curiosity, what does Shane Hyde, uh…look like?"

I hoped that the question wasn't too obvious. Ever since I had ran into that boy I couldn't help but wonder if I might have already met the person I was supposed to avoid. It had only been for a few seconds, and it hadn't seemed as though he knew who I was.

But I had to know if I knew his face. It would certainly make staying out of his way all the easier.

"Why do you ask?" Louise matched her father's previous expression while she lingered at the white wooden front door.

"So I can avoid him."

Louise huffed, but relented. She probably saw sense in my rationale. "He's blond —but he's bleached his hair nearly white. And his eyes…the most vibrant shade of tropical sea blue I've ever seen."

"Oh," I said.

Oh.

We *had* met —and I had slammed into him like a brick wall.

From Maggie and her friends' reactions, I had imagined someone who looked closer to a Halloween costume. Instead, he was just some teenager. And I tried not to think about his unordinary good looks or that piercing gaze. I could conclude that meeting those eyes had been similar to looking into a Daemon's, except *I* was the infinite, unfathomable emptiness.

Something told me that I should be as frightened of him as everyone else. After all —he was associated with some of the people who had made my life Hell; even in a limited capacity. However, his instinctual reaction to our run-in hadn't been vexed or unreasonable.

So my first thought…was that he was sort of beautiful.

My father was no longer on the floor when I snuck back inside.

It was dark and quiet —as it had been when we had first set foot inside the night before. In fact, I couldn't be certain that Hugh was in the house at all. Until I heard a thump from upstairs, which caused me to jump and crash into the glass topped console table where I had left the groceries.

Muttering curses, I began the monumental task of putting all the food away in the likely unwiped kitchen cupboards.

In the past, my father would have come flying down the stairs at any oddly timed disturbance, with improvised weapon in hand. It felt ominous not to witness that now. He didn't know that it was only me, and I dreaded what might happen if I had been an intruder.

I dreaded what was to come of all of this —what would his Daemon do to him, and would I be able to deal with being in close proximity to it?

The answer on the tip of my tongue was '*no*'.

And the longer, painful one was betrayingly conflicted. My father was not and had never been an alcoholic —but I always feared him becoming one because he had a vibrant history with substances. He was a different person after enough beers; enough straight spirits. And it wasn't violent —just different. Pitiful. Like you couldn't let him be alone.

Town-wide depression seemed like the perfect opportunity for the fear to turn into a reality.

So I couldn't just leave Pine Creek.

I couldn't leave him.

Being the only other person in town without a Daemon, for whatever reason, had to mean something.

The stairs squeaked under my boots in a way that was guaranteed to wake most sleeping souls. And the familiar flop of my bed was a welcome but odd comfort. Those unholy eyes still watched from somewhere.

I groaned at the ceiling and smothered the sound with my pillow.

What was pissing me off the most was that I hadn't managed to draw a single thing all day. Not that many of my plans ever really fell through. Despite the feelings attached to this place, the woods were beautiful and I thought I could stay there drawing for hours.

Maybe that was where I would disappear to tomorrow.

I rolled over and reached for my bedside, where I had vehemently laid out my priorities: my diary, stationery and reading lamp.

Uncapping my prized fountain pen —an unironically pastel rainbow wrapped and cloud bobble topped thing of two years old —I sat up and curled inwards with the small leather bound book before writing.

I wondered if writing it out would actually help me to process it. My hand hovered over the page, uncertain as to where to start. Even though the diary was my property and no one would ever read it, divulging every detail felt…vulnerable and exposing.

As if I couldn't dare to spill the words even to myself.

I kept it short.

Removed.

Like I was writing someone else's story.

But I would remember the sensations and the feelings; and the things I was a bit too shy to name. And the things that would haunt —if I was still susceptible to nightmares. My head might not remember whenever I gasped awake, but my heart certainly would.

I still had to prepare myself for a night with no sleep.

DEAR DIARY,

I RAN INTO A BOY.

AND I ALMOST GOT CLAIMED BY A DAEMON.

BUT I DIDN'T.

ALSO, I THINK I MIGHT'VE KILLED IT. SOMEHOW.

FEARFULLY,

YOUR SCRIBE.

the game

ALEXANDER

IT HAD RAINED overnight and everything was blissfully dismal in its aftermath. I pressed my cheek to the chilled glass panes and watched the fattening droplets race down the window; some in heated competition and others utterly unbothered.

The weather would not stop me.

Nature looked unmatched after a shower. To be able to sketch a bud freshly watered against the background of its fellow plants and not within a shop simply did not compare.

I had left a brief note on the console table after seeing myself out and thinking better of not informing my father of where I was going. I couldn't be around him, but I would be lying if I said that my worries didn't rule.

It'd be difficult to live with myself afterwards if he really succumbed to an unescapable pit and I could have helped to prevent it, somehow.

So I marched briskly through the streets, tote slung over one shoulder and my umbrella in hand, ferociously deceiving myself into believing that there was a semblance of normalcy within each step.

On the main street the stores were appropriately hesitant in opening their canopies and doors. With each visible beam of sunlight another chair was put out; another table lain —all with the hope that the rain would not come again. Without an internet connection and weather forecast app, it was impossible to tell; and ultimately blind faith.

All piles of yellow and orange leaves were soggy heaps getting swept down the slope. I wondered what it might like to be a leaf. To live a much shorter life, and still serve some small kind of purpose.

The glint of a suncatcher then caught my eye by the thrift store. The Halloween decorations were also being hung and strung; tiny pumpkin lanterns and felt ghosts; plastic skeletons and woollen spider's web.

Of course, it was just for fun. No one looked into the holiday's history and real traditions. It was all going to be about the costumes and candy.

I was too old to dress up seriously.

A part of me stared wistfully at the makeshift witch's costume in the display window. There was a gothic corset over a plain black frock, with a pair of ripped stockings —and a very out of place blue and white plastic broom from *Walmart*. The hat was the pièce de résistance: the brim edged in a decorative purple lace and a point going up for a good twelve inches.

"Um, excuse me, you're blocking the path."

I turned to find myself before a trio of girls in pleated skirts with shiny golden crosses, holding fresh spiced lattes. My delusional want was gone in an instant. The shadows behind and between them had large, crooked wafting partings where faces might be, that resembled grins.

"Alex?" Laura Takunda quipped. "Alex Grahams?"

"No. Way," Carley Vasquez chipped in.

I wanted to scream.

Everything in me cringed —though the paralysis only lasted a second and I rediscovered my spine in time to take a defensive stance.

"...Alexander."

It came out as a fucking mumble.

It took a lot of mustered up courage to say one word in front of these girls and yet once more my persistent terror swallowed it all up. They had been the accessories to Louise Barnes' bidding; the followers of orders and the doers of despicable things. The true demons of my torture.

"What?" Georgia Grande said, cupping her ear.

My fingers curled into my palms and the action reminded me just how little power they had. And the fact that I wasn't suffering from whatever their Daemons were doing was giving me a wisp of superiority.

"Alexander," I said a little more clearly.

I lifted my head.

I towered over all three of them.

Something had clearly been kind, to compensate me with height. They had to look up at me now and I was as sure as hell about to relish it.

"My name is Alexander," I bit. They blinked rapidly at the change in my demeanour. "Do you know why? Because once upon a time, you took my name from me —took the choice. But not anymore." I swivelled on my heel to glare back at them. "...Either say my damn name or don't say anything at all."

I was not sure what reaction I had expected, but the clicking of tongues and sucking of teeth had not been it.

Some people did not change —it was an unfortunate fact I had had the displeasure of learning, though only second-handily up to that point. After tactical monitoring on social media it had become apparent that certain personality traits developed at that young age and stayed; forever shaping a person. And it was not my fault.

I was sure that I could walk away quickly enough to avoid hearing any retaliation, but I had only gotten a few feet along when I caught the end of a snide remark.

"...The gall. Doesn't he care about going to Hell?"

My pace momentarily faltered.

I *really* wanted to have the last word.

"As if you haven't touched a dick, Grande."

The consequent smile on my face had no business being there. Half of me still hoped that the joke had gone over their heads; that I had implied something about my own bedroom activities.

A confession in the heat of the moment, of course.

I wasn't ready to parade *all* of me just yet.

For the sake of safety as well as the fact that I was actively grappling with the reconciliation of it and faith; even though I had known for a while the sort of people to whom I was attracted; I had not yet dared to make a single move beyond the bounds of the closet doors.

I could picture how Hugh would react. Not only was I genderqueer — my sexuality wasn't heteronormative either.

And though I owed him nothing, I knew he would be iffy about having no blood related grandchildren from his only child. Maybe he would have an easier time accepting my identity if I was into cisgender women. I had never truly gravitated to anyone in particular, but I knew who I liked.

Androsexuality —referring to a person of any gender attracted to men or masculinity. And for me, my preferences included specimens I deemed to be the '*epitome*' of a man or non-woman.

A perfectly secure standard not yet redefined.

Somebody not only comfortable within themself, but who also made me feel just as comfortable to appear outwardly as I felt within.

I still hadn't found a person to fulfil all of that criteria.

I could call them silly little crushes —the kind where you watch them from afar, or write sappy anonymous notes. It was not simple no matter where I was, be it Albuquerque or the moon. But that equally silly part of me believed in love, which was why I still poured over all of those books. I wanted that sweeping romance. I wanted my own story.

The forest of conifer trees so tall they blocked out the sky was eerie and beckoning. The perfect place to be alone for many hours. I had packed up a paperback, a thermos of instant coffee and a lunchbox crammed with crustless peanut butter and jelly sandwiches cut into triangles.

Anywhere but home.

At least until I had sifted through my thoughts.

Despair; Daemons; darkness.

Bullies; bitterness; blood.

Though it all trailed behind me with every step through the town, I still had hope that time would play a part in helping me exist here for however long I needed to. To help keep me from actually breaking.

Those girls were a slap to the face. As if I could waltz back, like it was all over. Ideals were thoroughly ingrained —for most rather than some. My fingers clenched around my tote bag handles. I would need to keep a more discreet profile.

I shook out my umbrella and walked through the little wooden gate at the side of Mr Ian O'Finley's farm, which sat by an old watermill. Even in the blue-washed rows of grains and wildflowers it had the whimsy and foreboding of woodland folklore. It was so removed from the modernity behind me that it felt like stepping into another world. One where no one had ever heard of Alexander Grahams.

One where anything seemed possible; and where neither the darkness nor the light could not reach, beyond the slither of sunrise and sunset.

My childish fancy was quite fixated on some kind of fate and clung to the idea that my soulmate was out there, waiting.

"…Come and find me, then," I told the wind.

I had forgotten a pencil sharpener.

Fortunately, I had brought multiple pencils for such a situation. I had laid out a mat on a patch of mossy dirt and perched on a dead tree stump. The view from there was of the misty distant mountains. The sea was not visible, but I liked to imagine the shoreline from the tops of the trees. It was a sea in itself; the large waves of pine and oak rising and falling but forever frozen and never crashing.

Although looking up and over their expanse, it certainly felt like they would engulf the shallow valley.

The tip of the pencil scratched back and forth along the same curve of an imaginary surf. I was struggling to capture the sharp, steep slope of the peaks on the horizon down to the perspective of the pines beside me. Most of the A4 landscape was from memory, but the muffled rush of the river and its scent made me think of the ocean when I closed my eyes.

I couldn't remember the last time I'd sat and drawn in the woods.

I couldn't remember the last time I'd needed to draw.

All those years ago, when I'd failed to bring a pencil to paper or paint to a canvas, only inescapable dread had clutched me. And the possibility of never being able to draw again had consumed my thoughts.

Those children had taken away something so fundamental to the fabric of my being that to this day I could not etch a line without shaking first.

Something snapped some distance to the left of me and every hair at the base of my neck stood on end. My rhythmic scratching stopped. The only sound was the whistling through the trees and gurgling of water.

Yet I could not disregard the feeling.

It was less about the disturbance and more so about the echo of a fear too real and buried. The sort of sensation that made me flinch at the mere suggestion of threat and suspense.

And although the sound did not repeat, I found myself unable to relax and uncurl. The risen goosebumps along my exposed skin did not fade. The something hadn't left—I could feel it. It was as if being in the dense forest alone made my senses soar past their parameters.

I slowly rose; gathering up my art supplies in my stiffened arms.

If I called out, would my murder happen faster?

"…So it's you," a level, velvet voice affirmed my mounting terror. It was coming from above. "Heh. I hear you repel the shadows."

I glanced upwards —in time to witness someone jumping down from the branches to land squarely in front of me. I gasped and started violently as they straightened up, dusting off their dark jeans.

My glasses slid down my nose as I regained my footing and held my sketchbook closer to my chest. I fumbled to adjust with one hand, before another breath hitched in my throat when I saw more clearly.

It was the boy.

Shane Hyde stared at me coolly. My gaze did not know where to settle, and so nervously flittered across his face as I dithered. Should I scream? Should I ask what he had been doing up in the trees? Or, the most pressing option: should I ask what he knew about me breaking the norm?

I chose the former-most.

He blinked in surprise at my odd, mid-pitch exclaim —but ultimately he waited for me to start hyperventilating instead.

"You —"

"I was not aware that there were people who didn't get…infected," he cut me off. He had to lower his head while I cowered; and though I may have imagined what he looked like when he smiled, there was not a trace of amusement. His eyes slitted, assessing me and determining worth. He did not appear scary. I could simply *feel* the urge to be terrified exuding.

Yet, there was another feeling there.

Something a little more crackling and a little more frightening.

"…Shane Hyde?" I whispered, backtracking along path. "Right? I'm sorry for running right into you yesterday."

"Huh —you already know my name," he mused.

It wasn't a question.

His gaze flicked down to my arms. "…It's dangerous to be out here alone, Mr Grahams. Especially when it gets dark."

My eyebrows lowered as the initial shock began to wear. "That's what people call my father," I mumbled. "My name…um, my name is —"

"—I know your name."

Oh.

I pressed my lips into a line.

He moved closer. His heavy boots crunched dirt and sodden leaves as he consequently backed me against a tree trunk. In the moment, my heart was racing with an onslaught of fear. I gasped when my spine hit the bark, before dropping my pencil. It snapped in half beneath his sole.

I tried my best to return the glare he had adopted.

"Everyone knows your name," he said in a lower tone. I could feel his cold breath on my skin. "And I know what they did to you."

I didn't know what face I then made, but it seemed to adequately show the pain that tore through my insides. I hated that he already knew of my past; that he knew my name; that he knew I was now as much of an outcast as I had been before. I hated that my vision stung and blurred while I bit the insides of my cheeks. He didn't soften. I saw the streaks of blue that made up his irises, and the unapologetic indifference in them.

He wouldn't care if I started crying.

But I didn't want to do that in front of a stranger.

"I'm…not supposed to talk to you," I spoke up —before immediately cursing in Portuguese because of how lame it had sounded.

Shane Hyde blinked once, then twice, before a smile cracked through the stone. It wasn't because he had found it funny. The smile was slight, uncertain and mischievous. He lifted one hand up to press against the tree, right by my cheek. My shoulders went rigid. There was a waft of cigarette smoke under the sharpness of spearmint chewing gum.

"I wonder why that might be," he murmured.

Several strands of his platinum blond hair fell over his forehead, just skimming his dark eyebrows. At a million miles a minute, I recalled every scene in my romance books that resembled the position in which I found myself. He was very close. In a way that made me unsure as to whether I was about to become a missing person or the victim of something wildly inappropriate. And this boy seemed quite capable of causing both.

I swallowed.

The tension remained, but I forced myself to remember how to breathe and make eye contact. He kept it with a look of expectation. It was clear who was in control of the conversation. I straightened, holding my things more securely and attempting to stand my ground.

He acknowledged that. For the first time, I noticed a strain. It was not limited to the way his eyebrows then came together in a frown. I saw it in the visible veins along his neck and hands. In the way he was making this into an intimidating interrogation, but the only answers he could produce were frustrating or plain irrelevant.

I then racked up the nerve to ask my own question. "…What happened to your Daemon? Did you…get rid of it?"

His head tilted to the side, in some sort of disbelief. I couldn't imagine that no one had ever asked him that before.

"Who's calling them that?" he deflected.

I didn't hesitate. Especially because I suspected that she had had a big hand in passing on information about me.

"Louise Barnes."

Though judging by the irritation which flooded his face, someone else had mentioned my situation —perhaps one of Maggie's friends. I hefted my sketchbook and shifted my weight onto my other leg. The hand beside me lowered slowly. "…What do *you* call them?" I rasped.

Shane Hyde turned frigid once more. "Mercy."

A chill shot up my spine in a violent shiver. "That's a pretty twisted and ironically unsympathetic outlook."

He sneered. "It's reality."

So why was he still in Pine Creek? If he was so bitter about the strange goings-on, surely he could just leave. My mouth twisted into a shape even as he finally leaned away. I let out a soft sigh and tactfully moved towards my stump. I didn't want him pinning me again.

But I underestimated the weight of his presence, because my feet still obediently planted upon his return. He did not back me into a corner, yet I certainly *felt* cornered. Though my heart stuttered and that frightening thing fizzled in the little distance between us.

My tongue acted on impulse. "You're not going kill me, are you?"

Caralho, damnit!

I could have very well sealed my fate.

Shane Hyde stared at me but it wasn't with that disbelief, or surprise. There was a sense of unease and…anger. As if to say, where had I gotten the audacity to ask. I could accept the offence taken at my sudden blurt.

But I didn't like that he didn't answer.

"You and I are going to play a game," he said instead. He unclenched his jaw and tried a more playful tone. His eyes did not cooperate with the smirk; that slitted, freezing blue swallowed up all the light. "Let's see for how long you can stay away from me."

That sounded like it should have been the other way around.

It also sounded like a threat, not a wager.

My eyebrows knitted together. "Why would you want me to do that? Am *I* something to avoid?"

He leaned in again; his expression then hardening to mirror mine. But I could see a guilty glint in his gaze. For a moment, any trace of vexation was replaced with a sadness embroiled in…longing.

"It's so that I don't feel anything by doing the same."

Those words didn't help.

A sharp stab pierced my gut and I could not place it. If he didn't like me, along with many other residents in the town, then he had no obligation to interact with me. I wouldn't force any of it.

"Wait, don't you want to know why I don't have a Daemon?"

He actually hesitated. Only for a second. Then he straightened his grey denim jacket and tugged a hand through his hair. Shane Hyde looked me up and down for the last time before he turned to start walking back along an unfamiliar path. "…I shouldn't."

the losers

ALEXANDER

THE GAME HAD no set rules.

I only realised that by the time I had gotten back home.

I wrote it all down in my diary immediately —not for the sake of being a diligent patient despite the inaccessibility of the internet, but for my own sake. It had been so bizarre that I wanted to remember every second of it. Even the part when Shane Hyde had suggested that we keep our distance.

It bothered me —gratingly so.

Of course, I recalled my own resolve quite clearly.

It had been my plan to avoid him first.

But there was something about turning whatever had occurred in those woods into a challenge that brought out my pettiest traits.

I wanted to spite him.

"Alexander."

I looked up from my diary to see my father sitting on the sofa, hugging a cushion against his chest. His dark circles were growing darker. My gaze flicked upwards to the shadows over his shoulder. The Daemon smiled at me; the gap of its mouth a wide crescent.

"Dad," I returned.

He dithered, parting and pressing his lips together every few seconds until an eventual sigh. His eyes appeared clearer, but he had not had more than the energy it took to descend the stairs.

Hugh's face contorted as he reached the verge of tears.

"…I keep seeing your mother," he said.

I snapped my diary shut. "So do I."

"She…looks like a stranger."

I frowned and leaned against the doorframe. "Are you feeling guilty about how it all happened? How you'd refused to see her at the end?"

He could not find the words.

It was possible that while I saw Leilah Grahams' ghost as how she had walked the Earth, her face was slipping from my father's mind. Maybe it was because he had forgotten by the time she had passed away; or maybe it was a form of self-punishment for not wanting to visit her after she had been hospitalised.

Now his Daemon was feeding off of the guilt of whatever was the root cause. I refused to think about what the same creature that had come for me could have done with my trauma. I looked at the shadows again.

And I stumbled, reaching for the wall as my diary and pen clattered to the floor. The mass of darkness had changed its shape. It was willowy; up to the top of a window and as precise as a real shadow.

It was Leilah. It was the silhouette of my mother, cast behind the sofa as if she was standing there in the living room. Her head turned slightly —towards Hugh. Nothing else. She simply stared without eyes.

I couldn't scream.

It felt specifically for me; this show that I would have chalked up to my imagination last week. But not now. It was real…the shadow was real and my fears were being played to it.

Even if I didn't have a tormentor of my own.

Then its grip on me loosened like pulled string and I slid to the wooden boards, trembling. I clapped my hands over my mouth to contain unsteady breath as I shut my eyes. I saw her shadow on the wall even then.

They opened to a blurry room and Hugh knelt in front of me.

My glasses had fallen.

"Alexander —what happened, son? Are you all right?"

He almost looked as though he cared again.

But I was disoriented and shaken. I curled away from him and shook my head, not permitting the tears welled within my eyes to fall.

"…I hate it here," I choked out. "I hate this *house*."

My words were a blow to his already crumbling reality. Still, he took me by the shoulders and drew me in; his unsteady grip like a vice.

I jolted from sleep.

The first few seconds of consciousness were heady, but as my mind began to clear one thing became very apparent.

A dream lingered.

It was unravelling quickly, but I managed to catch bits and pieces as I rubbed my eyes. I scrambled for my diary —and crashed onto the floor in the process, pulling down the comforter and pillow.

FIRE. TORCHES. FLIES.

LOTS OF BRICKS AND GOLD AND RED SAND.

I CAN SMELL SOMETHING LIKE ~~THE SEA~~ SALT.

MY HAND HURTS LIKE IT WAS CUT WITH A KNIFE, AND I CAN FEEL THE BLOOD SEEPING FROM THE MIDDLE OF MY PALM.

AND THAT'S IT. I CAN'T REMEMBER THE DREAM ANYMORE. BUT, I THINK I WAS SCARED IN IT.

CONFUSED AND HALF ASLEEP,
YOUR SCRIBE.

My heartbeat hammered and my breathing was shallow, but my eyes were dry. I hadn't cried. The heaviness in my chest still throbbed, though. What I had experienced last night had not been sadness, or even fear.

I could not pinpoint any lasting emotion in particular, yet I was certain that I had had a nightmare.

And though it was impossible to get a message to my therapist, I got my cellphone and typed it out before hitting send.

After pouring over what I had written in detail, I decided to go to the library again. The things I remembered from the dream were not much to go on but maybe I could gain a better understanding of what the Daemons were and their capabilities based on what had happened yesterday.

Perhaps they did not belong to a singular folklore.

I breezed through my morning routine and left another note for Hugh before leaving for the main street. My skin tightened over my bones as I thought about what his Daemon had done to me. It wasn't as if I wanted my father to suffer through that *instead* —I was just a fierce advocate for my own self-preservation.

Some would call it being selfish.

I chose to see it as safely avoiding a trigger.

Besides, I couldn't readily help without documented information on what I had taken to calling '*The Haunting of Pine Creek*.'

That title made it a little less…real.

The sun had poked through more of the clouds and it glinted off of the raindrops scattered over brickwork and wood.

Kay Isotton was hauling out potted plants outside of *The Honeysuckle* for a natural light sprinkle when I walked past.

"Alexander!" she called out. "Good morning."

I paused and mumbled through a greeting. Seeing her Daemon caused me to flinch, but hers did not appear too hostile. At least not like the others I had seen. Whatever afflicted her, it was a struggle with which I was not familiar. She offered a small wave, which I stiffly returned, before turning away. I didn't hear her call again.

Maggie Elwoods and Company were not by the alleyway —and I had to count my blessings for it. I had no capacity to deal with any of them. I did however, spot a long black bomber jacket and plaid button down shirt —and cigarette smoke over the shine of silver chains.

A normal looking shadow: soft, accurate and without extra arms.

My eyes strayed there for too long, because suddenly I was staring at cold turquoise blue —with matching furrowed dark eyebrows.

I looked away rather conspicuously.

Shane Hyde did not call out to me either.

At least that was understandable. Apparently making eye contact did not violate unspoken rules. We could spot each other from opposite sides of the street, but that distance was to be kept.

My head turned back for a moment to betray me.

From the flash of blue and fumbling through his coat I realised that he had also been staring. And the possibility of curiosity being mutual made the tips of my ears warm and my heart beat thunderously inside them.

PUTA MERDA, *GET OVER YOURSELF*.

He wants to stay as far away from you as he can, remember?

HA! HE HATES YOU.

Maybe he's allergic to people who are nothing.

I bit the inside of my cheeks and picked up my pace, shaking my head. I hated it when the voices that battled within me were in any type of sync. I.e., whenever I used either complete and rational logic, or complete and utter nonsensical delusion.

There was unfortunately no in between.

A humid air had settled in the library. Compared to the coolness of the outside, it was like stepping into a sauna. I figured that it was as a result of not opening the windows —a stupid rule that seemed to put the books themselves in jeopardy. But I shouldn't judge the librarian. Maybe when no one cared to pay attention, she inspected and dusted them all down. I couldn't be sure how she prevented mould, however.

She, too, stared at me as I walked in; bundled in a shirt, sweater and long cardigan. I shrugged off the lattermost as I settled at the study table. I then produced my diary and a tattered copy of *The Last Wish* by Andrzej Sapkowski. Up to that point, I had never read it too closely. After all, the romance made up only a small element of the storyline.

But this session would not be about romance.

I wanted to study every mentioned monster written in the pages, and compare them to the Daemons. It wasn't my only source material —I also picked out various novels from the bookshelves and laid them out in front of me. They ranged from Greek and Roman to Chinese —even Egyptian and Māori mythology. Not every one of them spoke of demons, though.

Not in the sense that I needed them to.

And if they did, it was in relation to ghosts —which didn't perfectly relate to what the shadows were doing. It was as if they'd been fabricated with bits and pieces of different folklore; a haunting technique from here, but an entirely opposing appearance and origin from there.

Nothing really aligned.

I yanked my fingers through my curls and cleaned my glasses before scribbling down in a notebook what I thought I already knew.

ABOUT THE DAEMONS:

- THEY LIVE IN PEOPLE'S SHADOWS
- THEY ARE *MADE* OF SHADOW AND/OR SOME SORT OF SMOKE
- THEY CAN SHAPESHIFT (MAYBE BASED ON MEMORIES. SADLY AND SOMEHOW NOT LIMITED TO THE ~~POSSESSED~~ HOST)?
- THEY *CAN* DIRECTLY TOUCH THEIR HOST
- THEY FEED OFF OF THE HOST'S ~~GUILT~~ *EMOTIONS??*
- THEY ARE LIMITED TO PINE CREEK
- I THINK THEY'RE A FORM OF PUNISHMENT. THERE ARE THOSE WHO HAVE IT WORSE THAN OTHERS (AKA LOUISE BARNES)
- NOT EVERYONE GETS A DAEMON (ONLY KNOW ABOUT ME + SHANE HYDE). REASON UNKNOWN; UNCLEAR CRITERIA/IMMUNITY ASIDE FROM RESIDENCY.

Looking at all of the properties together didn't get my mind any more or less going. Whatever had a hold of the town, it was unlike anything the world had ever seen nor conjured.

My forehead hit the table and I let out a frustrated groan.

"Whoa, you've been busy."

I tensed; every muscle reacting to the voice, before I glanced upwards and readjusted my glasses. A girl in a pair of wide-leg jeans, a cropped t-shirt and an unzipped hooded jersey that reached her thighs looked down at me, with her arms loosely crossed.

She took the liberty of sliding onto the chair opposite and flinging her sling bag beside the books. "I had a feeling I would find you here."

"*...Barnes*," I said her name like a swearword.

She flinched —her Daemon relishing the reproach and curling a little more snuggly over her shoulders. Her mascara, liner and gloss had turned into an art piece. It was just as messy and running, and it seemed as though there was nothing that she could do about it. It was now a part of her.

I pictured her standing in front of a mirror every morning, wiping off the streaks and reapplying as if to fool others into thinking she was fine. But then she would break down crying —either because of her Daemon or because she *wasn't* fine. Or both.

I scoffed.

"I found out that I can't touch mine," she murmured. "Nor my parents'."

"Christ," I hissed. "So...is that all, then? I need to continue."

She fidgeted like a reprimanded toddler. "Well, you're the only one I can talk to about this curse nonsense," she confessed, slipping back into that very familiar quippy attitude. "No one else will hear me out. It's like it's...normal. Like having a Daemon is normal. Nothing I say gets taken seriously. My Dad's convinced I've just gotten...more down."

My eyes lidded. "I can't *possibly* imagine why. Now I must ask, what is it you want me to do about any of it?"

Even though I wanted to be very obvious in the display of my disdain, I mentally added her comments to my list.

"I literally just said," she sighed. "*You* talk. You can hate me as much as you want and I deserve, but it's you and me in the know." Louise leaned forward, folding her arms atop the table. "…Apart from Shane Hyde."

"Why don't you try bothering him?"

Her eyebrows knitted like I was an idiot. "He, uh…doesn't like talking to me. I did see him a couple of blocks from here on my way, though. So be sure to avoid going by the barber's later."

"*Another* surprise…" I breathed, closing the book I had been reading. Then I realised that I hadn't told her that I had already met him. I slumped. I wouldn't tell her. It was a secret thing between him and me.

Louise got angry instead of crumpling. "*Hey* —"

"Look, Barnes," I cut her off, levelling at her a straight look over the top of my glasses. "It's not just the fact that I hate you. Once upon a time I would've killed for the opportunity to get revenge on you. But actually seeing you again like this —it's forced me to acknowledge certain things. One: the effects of being terrified of you haven't gone. I'm not sure that they ever will. I don't *want* to be scared of you again, but my body refuses cooperate with me." I then pointed at her accusingly. "Two: I need you to understand that you fucked up —and if you want to have civil exchanges with me, you have to give me space. And time. Please don't come looking for me constantly."

She blinked, glanced at her hands, then tilted her head to the side. For a moment I wondered how she would protest. But she gave a nod, pressed her lips together tightly, and rose from her chair while grabbing her bag. She was quietly walking away when she then paused, glancing back out of the corner of her gaze. "When can I talk to you about it, then?"

I *really* wanted to say '*never*'.

But my selfishness needed to know a few bounds. It wasn't that I was caving to her —I was adamant about healing from what she'd done to me.

Certain matters took precedence over manageable strife.

"My Dad's Daemon tormented me," I reluctantly offered. There were little bobbles on my sleeve, that I started picking at. "It changed into the shape of my mother, and what it did was meant specifically for me to see —he sounded like nothing had happened to him, afterwards."

Louise audibly drew a breath. "…Noted."

I pressed my cheek flat to the table and stared at the flecks of dust that filtered through the beams of sunlight. Point: Alexander —for having the last word. Even if the victory suddenly felt ominous.

I spitefully loitered by the barber's.

And it wasn't because I chased the satisfaction of going against every little thing Louise Barnes said like some kind of child. A small and foolish and morbid part of me wanted to be there.

I had no doubt that I looked expectant and pathetic. It surely wasn't worth standing under an insufficient bit of canopy, in the spitting drizzle. Indefinitely. Yet I stayed, considering closing my umbrella. After a few minutes though, I had to ask myself for what it was actually, that I was waiting. Perhaps I just wanted a distraction.

The sight of Carley Vasquez sauntering along the opposite sidewalk, though, brought me back to my senses.

I pivoted sharply in the other direction —only to stumble back at the appearance of Shane Hyde. My breath caught before I pouted indignantly with the realisation of what our '*chance*' meeting meant for the game.

"You're really bad at this, Grahams," he scoffed, putting his hands on his hips. "It hasn't even been forty-eight hours."

I didn't have the time for the ensuing embarrassment.

"Excuse me, I was just leaving —"

I managed exactly one step past him.

"*Ha*," he spat, leaning over to block my advance. "Bullshit. You were waiting around for a good ten minutes."

My pout returned at full, mortified and stubborn force. Then I thought about his taunting claim. I gave him a sceptical look. "Wait —how would you know that unless you…were you watching me?"

He had no shame. He simply shrugged, and glanced a little ways past me. My head turned. Carley had stopped beneath her pale pink umbrella. It was not a question of whether or not she had seen us —those dark eyes were darting between me and Shane Hyde. And then her face grew more and more intrigued.

"Damnit," I hissed, whipping back around. "This is your fault."

He raised an eyebrow. "How so?"

"You *could've* avoided me."

The corners of his mouth twitched slightly, as if he was tempted to smile. "Yeah," he surprisingly agreed. "I guess I could have."

"Fix it," I demanded.

He did a double take. "You're scared of Vasquez?"

I couldn't admit nor deny, so I hoped that my expression was answer enough. Desperate and unashamed of it. It seemed to do the trick, because something resembling sympathy flickered across his face.

"…Hand me your umbrella," Shane Hyde suggested.

"Why? What are you going to do?"

"Fix it," he reassured, taking hold of the handle. He held it up between us and then leaned in. "My guess is that you would rather everyone in this town leave you alone. *I* can help," he quipped, meeting my bewildered gaze. The raindrops made the clear turquoise refract light —his irises two precious jewels. They were somehow the only inviting thing about him. Even where my covered arm brushed up against his was icy. "No one will dare to bother you if you're seen with me."

I started; the hypnotic spell of his stare shattering. We were standing in the middle of the sidewalk on the very public main street, pressed side by side under one umbrella.

"You can't be serious," I clipped. "Being seen anywhere *near* you will have the exact opposite effect! And may I remind you that it was you who voiced the idea of staying away from each other."

He didn't move an inch.

"Would you rather have everyone stare at you because they remember your past, or because you're with the guy they all fear?"

"Hey, I am not *with* you," I firmly insisted.

Shane Hyde offered a stiff smirk. "…My mistake."

I glanced across the road. "Oh, look —she's already gone," I snapped, before yanking back the umbrella from him. "No doubt to tell everyone who's anyone about the bizarre apparition of Shane Hyde and Alexander Grahams sharing a goddamn umbrella."

"Don't be pessimistic," he sighed, flicking a cigarette over the lighter he had just taken from the inside of his jacket. "Oh ye of little faith."

He glanced at me without lifting his head, drawing all of the focus to his dangerous, calculating eyes. I shivered.

"That was not the way I wanted you to help."

"Then maybe you should have been more specific," he huffed, before nodding importantly. He blew smoke towards the road, away from me.

My mouth twisted into a shape. "You didn't…*scare* your Daemon off or anything like that, did you?" The questioned wavered on my tongue. It did sound a little ridiculous. As if a mere human being could instil enough of that fear to frighten a supernatural entity.

What I had done was not the same —even in my peril the creature had still approached, and had only been stopped quite literally by my hand.

Shane Hyde bounced the cigarette between his lips, still staring at me from beneath the wisps of his hair.

"…What if maybe I did?" he murmured. "Would your perception of me change. Would you treat me like everyone else does?"

I could tell that his tone was teasing, yet the worry in his hypothetical rang so loudly —at least to me. How exactly *did* the other kids treat him? Arguably not what could be described as positively, since he was sourcing the most basic of social interactions from *me* of all people.

"I'm not afraid of you," I told him.

His eyebrows lifted in surprise. But he surely couldn't be that easy to convince. His lips twitched again, and it was suddenly clear that he was perfectly capable of smiling —for some reason, he repressed the reaction. He flicked ash onto the tar. "Well, then you might be the only one."

I didn't know what to make of that. After all —we were still supposed to be playing a game. Though we were both irrefutably losing.

I turned on my heel. "I, uh…I should get going now."

He didn't stop me, but he did call out. "Hey Grahams."

"What?"

Now he was amused. "Minus ten points for round one."

My eyes narrowed in disbelief. "Minus fifteen for you."

the bone crush

SHANE

SHANE WAS WELL aware of the fact that he had not even fucking tried. That stupid game had been the best ruse with which he could come up on the spot. He had not planned to adhere to it perfectly.

But by the Morningstar, could he have shown some restraint.

The *tiniest* slither of effort.

He had, quite predictably, weakened at the slightest hint of rebellion. That hesitancy —the glance back and slight step over the line Alexander had taken; the very one that Shane had drawn himself; had been enough to throw the undefined rules to the wind.

He wanted to think that their every unauthorised conversation counted as the greatest penalty, while a lingering stare was worth the loss of five points. Of course the numbers meant nothing at all —he needed an excuse to keep running into them.

Love was something that could never be gotten rid of.

It could morph into hatred or diminish to the point of insignificance, but the layered emotion could not just be erased. Every time the object of it came into view the mind could be tricked into believing that no feeling was attached to it. But something lingered. Even the very thought.

If the heart no longer raced and breath did not hitch, then had it ever been love in the first place? It was easy to fool yourself into thinking that infatuation was love, too. The only way to be certain was to be thrust into a dire situation where everything was on the line.

If nothing else mattered —in the most violent way, it was love.

If something held you back, even the slightest tug…

Shane still cursed at his line of sight instinctively following Alexander whenever he saw them. The entire world simply gravitated to that soul — revolved around them completely.

In the few days that followed, Shane had established a pattern.

Near to mid-morning, Alexander would make their way to the library or to thc woods. And they would return just before dark. They always had a weighted tote bag at their side with art supplies and food, as if they were ready to escape at any moment.

A fog had settled in Pine Creek. It carpeted it so low and thick that it was difficult to see the ground when walking. He imagined it made the soul's journey harder to navigate and more susceptible to a cold —but at least he had noticed a new red and black tartan decorated flask giving off steam. At first the beast had wondered if there was something in there, by the forest, that made Alexander want to frequent it. But he had come to realise that through time, they had always found solace in solitude.

In the firs and pines.

It was the only place they were free from judgement.

And they deserved every minute of that freedom.

Shane hadn't stopped himself from chuckling under his breath when he spotted Alexander kicking up the fog and absentmindedly watching it disperse. In fact, he had almost been caught.

It was a forlorn sort of exhilarating to find himself turning to hide in an alcove to evade suspicion. Was he still a child? Maybe being on Earth had influenced him a bit more than he cared to admit. His heart had started beating faster than it had in many cycles.

He had not permitted himself to interfere, for a while prior.

He had not had the opportunity to know them this way.

He had never harboured the hope.

Alexander not being claimed by the shadow was opening the beast up to the possibility that this cycle could be different. If he dared to test those waters. The issue was that it truly would be uncharted.

Each cycle before had left barely a three week window to get to know the soul as a human. Having the extra time —the extra time to fool about with this game —was not something for which he was prepared.

But he wanted to try.

It did not help that they never remembered the conversations in their dreams; the lives the two had led. The monster would not have the cushion of that foundation and he was definitely feeling its effect.

There was one comfort: they did not seem to hate him.

He smiled in thought of that declaration —that they were not afraid of him, either. Partial bullshit, but it had been nice to hear.

"What the hell?" Aspen Roland snapped, gaping at Shane. "Why are you making that face, Hyde?"

It immediately slipped as a result, before the beast sighed and popped a piece of chewing gum into his mouth. He'd momentarily forgotten that he had been relaxing on a bench, when the people others called his friends had descended upon him like vultures to a carcass.

"I didn't know you *knew* how to smile," Jesse Milburn quipped. "Like, properly. I've literally only seen you sneer and frown."

Shane's eyebrows furrowed in irritation.

"Like that," said Jesse.

"Okay, now that it's been established you're a real human being," Maggie Elwoods cut in, lowering onto the bench right beside Shane, "tell us about the rumour going around. Is Vasquez lying?"

The demon visibly leaned away in time as if he and Maggie were the same poles of a pair of magnets.

"Yeah, you weren't talking to Alex Grahams all friendly or some shit, right?" Jesse asked, one foot up on the armrest. "Does he have something on you? Where would he even get the audacity, though?"

"Alexander," Shane hedged without thought.

The three of them paused as they shared tentative looks.

"What's it matter?" Aspen scoffed.

He offered her the closest thing to a glare he allowed and crossed one leg over the other before shrugging. "It doesn't. Asp."

Her face scrunched. "*Oi* —"

"Oh sorry, did that offend you?" he drawled. "When I said something you didn't want to be called by? Weird."

He knew that she wanted to argue. But contrary to her appearance, she actually had a working head on those shoulders. And she knew how much of a mistake it was to push something with Shane Hyde.

He wouldn't be surprised if the scar along her back had not faded.

Aspen snarled in his general direction. Her Daemon lifted its hand and dragged the long claws right across her neck, with meticulous cruelty. She coughed, clutching along the faint lines streaking her pale skin before they slowly disappeared.

"...Keller said Carley's serious," Maggie spoke up in an effort to shift the subject. "But we don't just want to take his word for it."

"Yeah," Jesse chimed, surprisingly picking up on the unease. "When a guy starts dating, he can never be completely trusted again. They all side with their girlfriends no matter what."

The monster was certain Jesse only had that opinion because Lincoln and Carley had been MIA as of late. Besides —it wasn't as if Lincoln had ever been that trustworthy prior.

"Guess we can always rely on you, Milburn," Maggie laughed. "Since you'll *never* be biased; 'cause a girlfriend will never exist."

Jesse started. "Hey, uncalled for."

Shane tuned them out and glanced across the street. His fingers tapped the top of the backrest as he saw Alexander marching into *Straws & Fries*. Going in there would guarantee a loss of points.

Yet all of a sudden, he was hungry.

"I'm going to eat," he announced, rising after meticulously counting fifteen minutes. It wasn't an invitation but the three would tag along.

They all wandered into the diner and received an appropriate amount of hard stares from the few patrons seated. Maggie Elwoods and her posse were the infamous signal of trouble. It followed them whether they carted it with them or not —though consequences never stuck. They were not violent delinquents. Well, Shane Hyde was. But they had found a kinship in perpetually busy, neglectful parents and talking shit.

The soul was seated towards the back in a small booth, tucked under the gold ambient lighting and nestled in a Chiltern Edition of *Jane Eyre*. A picked-at platter of French fries sat on the polished table, beside a tall glass of caramel swirled milkshake with a paper straw.

Shane couldn't hear the nonsense beside him as he stared across the room. They were ordering something, probably, but all in which the beast was interested was the beauty rolling up their sweater sleeves.

Alexander glanced upwards.

Beneath the opalescent bell shaped light fixtures and amidst the brown leather, their eyes were a dark shade of honey. Their glasses then tipped. It made them look like a scowling librarian.

The soul didn't look away. They held Shane's gaze with an expression difficult to decipher; blank and cool. A mimic of his.

They then discreetly raised one hand above the line of the booth, and wrote something out in the air. Shane scoffed. *Minus five*.

If there was one thing that he enjoyed the most about them, it was the limitless pettiness and sarcasm they brought to any situation.

Jesse Milburn glanced at Shane and then in the direction he was facing instead of their own table. A curly head was buried in a flowery book.

"…Oh look," he quipped. "The wimp is also here."

The Made demon turned back at those words. "What wimp?"

"Who else?" Jesse sighed, vaguely gesturing. Aspen and Maggie then craned their necks.

"Caramel?" Maggie remarked in disgust. "Sickly choice."

Shane rolled his eyes.

The regret of allowing these humans to stick to him was swiftly nearing its threshold. He did not want them there. He wanted to be on the other end of the diner, listening to the prattling of how problematic it was that Edward Rochester should keep his supposedly dead but mad wife locked up in secret, and hide it from Jane as he falls in love with her.

It then occurred to the beast that he could in fact do whatever the fuck he wanted. So he stood, slid out from their booth and strode directly for that little table. Their hushed murmurs and chuckles followed him.

"Has the fire happened yet?" Shane smirked, hands in his denim jacket pockets. Alexander paused, lifting their head and adjusting their glasses.

There was no way they could not have seen the other table. It was too loud to miss. But Alexander courageously chose to keep their composure and focus solely on the person in front of them.

Their eyes widened as the question finally registered. "Wait. I'm sorry —you've read *Jane Eyre*? And no, not yet."

"Watched," he corrected. *With you,* he wanted to add.

Always with you.

"...Still a feat," they muttered —then watched him unapologetically settle onto the seat opposite. They set the heavy book down, marking the page with the ribbon. Those brown eyes creased at their corners. "Oh?"

"I needed to get away from them," Shane explained.

"*Oh.*"

Alexander briefly glanced at Maggie, Aspen and Jesse. And the look had a flicker of envy. The trio's amusement had faded, turning into pissed off bewilderment. They couldn't comprehend why Shane would entertain the idea of having a normal conversation with Alexander Grahams.

Why he would even look at them at all.

"Why caramel?" asked the demon. He already knew the answer —he just wanted to hear them talk. And the soul then seemed to brighten at the unwitting gesture, like they were willing to indulge him.

"So how many points have we each lost now?"

Shane Hyde rounded a tree, leaning over before tapping his chin in mock thought. "...Would you believe me if I said that I'd lost track?"

Alexander levelled a look at him from where they were idly sketching. "Actually, yes I would."

He hadn't lost track.

He was sitting on minus thirty-five, and they were on minus fifteen. It had all occurred within the following few days —a near constant stream of '*accidental*' meetings and even less inconspicuous stares. The soul was by far better at following the rules than the beast, but at least, they had stopped considering bolting at the sight of him. They would now meet his eye and hold it there like they were drowning. And although he could not clearly recall if they had reacted that way in the cycles before, he knew that it was something deeper and older that tugged within them.

That tugged between them.

"Oh you wound me, Grahams," Shane sighed dramatically; the back of his hand over his forehead and all.

Alexander generously offered him a soft chuckle. It was followed by a pause. "When will you tell me why you wanted to avoid me in the first place?" they asked. He had their undivided attention; they had laid down their sketchbook beside them on the boulder they were perched upon like a lopsided chair. They crossed one leg over the other, putting their face in one hand. That expectant expression was unnerving.

Shane hesitated.

Predictably, the other kids had started talking. He had no doubts about who was saying what *and* from where it had started, but he was well aware that his ability to shield Alexander from it was limited. Especially when they were not with him. His harsh reputation alone would not be a fool-proof deterrent. And the stickiness of guilt coated his stomach once again.

"I'm not that much of an idiot," began the demon. "Despite my initial surprise at the fact you didn't have a…shadow," he said tactfully, "I had this idea that it would just sort itself out. Up until you moved back, I was the only person without one. And I thought that it would remain that way.

But when it became clear that you were as much of an anomaly as me, I took an interest in you. Which hasn't exactly been working out much, I'm sure you've noticed. That was not my intention —I never wanted you to become the centre of attention again." His face contorted in anger. "*Some* people can't seem to mind their own fucking business."

Alexander blinked and rubbed the side of their arm as they stiffened at the reference to the past. "That's why you said you shouldn't care?"

"Well," Shane smirked, "that part was…something else."

"Oh. Tell me," they quipped, uncertainly shifting forward.

"I…" he started but couldn't finish.

The soul huffed, glancing down at the brown leaves trodden in mud. "Did you hate me? *Do* you?" Their face fell with apprehension.

"You think I hate you?" questioned the beast.

Alexander wouldn't meet his gaze. "Maybe…you wanted to, then?"

A gust of wind rustled the needles and drying leaves. The fog was a blanket over the low growing flora and fungal undergrowth; almost giving the impression that the rain had not really left. It swirled around Shane's ankles and up to the flaps of his boots. Mrs Hyde was going to give him another earful about hanging around the woods and damp socks.

The soul shivered, unprepared in thin, loose corduroy trousers and one brown woollen sweater over a stiff black shirt.

In all these years, Shane had never hated them. Not once. He would resent the situation and take out his wrath on them, sure, but he had never done it based on pure targeted maliciousness. It had never been their fault after all. The curse was in essence, his own torture to which to succumb.

"…I've lost more than double the points that you have," he eventually admitted, fishing for a cigarette in his inner pockets to steady his nerves. He hoped that his statement would serve as a roundabout implication of his feelings towards them.

"What, you can't stay away from me, Hyde?" Alexander then scoffed —clearly joking, but it so visibly startled Shane that they stared at him in disbelief when he frowned uncomfortably and fumbled trying to light his cigarette. He inhaled and blew out towards the denser cluster of trees. It had never been that difficult to regulate the temperature of his face. And he had never worn his affection so close to his sleeve.

"Uh…great, so you don't hate —"

"Ever smoked?" the monster interrupted, turning his head to glance at them from the corner of his vision.

"What," the soul frowned. "No."

He grinned, showing his teeth. "Want to try?"

Shane wanted to be the bad guy again. He had revealed too much in a stumble of deluded safety, while being even that marginally vulnerable.

Alexander hesitated. "I shouldn't."

Precisely. They…they were *good*.

"Probably not." He reached into another pocket to produce a different small, cylindrical object. "How about something without nicotine?"

He was despicable.

Their gaze narrowed. "Marijuana?"

"You don't have to if you don't want," Shane assured, swiftly putting out the barely smoked cigarette. He ensured that its ashes wouldn't cause a forest fire. "I just…want to feel something else right now."

They didn't question what exactly that might mean, even though they looked like they wanted to. And they said nothing about the weed, either. So Shane leaned against a trunk of bark and set to work further tangling the endless threads constricting his chest.

Alexander tried to get back to their sketchbook, but their pencil would not move. They stared blankly at the fog, drowning. Every now and again their eyes would snag to the smoke curling on Shane's breath.

The beast was well aware of the soul's habits. Each cycle had been a little different but they were fundamentally the same. Of all of them, they had only smoked twice; with polarising intentions and bases for doing so. So it had never been beyond the realm of possibility.

He simply wondered if this iteration of Alexander had been raised as strictly and watchfully as the others. Their level of caution reflected their level of parental obedience and respect.

Apparently, this Alexander Grahams too, did not have much.

They stood, slotting the sketchbook and pencil into their tote bag, then strode over with something to prove. The look was of raw determination, but Shane could have sworn there was also a deep agony. It then clicked that the soul was a mere inch away from him.

And no God would have mercy.

"Want to feel something else?" he stiffly offered.

"I…I'm supposed to feel really bad about this, right?" they murmured. "I know better. Yet, I can't bring myself to think of the consequences."

"Sounds like you're attempting to be rather rebellious, Grahams." He held out the joint. "Can't say it'll be good for you," he made sure to add, not wanting to be entirely blamed. "What will your poor parents say when you get home smelling like grass and pacific northwest mist?"

What were the parents in *his* house going to say, was another issue he wanted to push to the back of his mind.

"My Dad won't notice," Alexander said flatly. They plucked the joint from his fingers. "And my Mom's dead."

That made him blink. Their mother had never died before.

They coughed horrendously —which was something that Shane really should have been watching out for. They had told him that they had never smoked before. Yes, he was despicable. But he didn't want them to choke. Instead of dissuading them from taking another hit, he thought on his feet in a regrettable state that was not quite sober.

"Here, we can try shotgunning. It's easier."

"Wha…what's…shotgunning?" Alexander wheezed while peering up at him from their low recovery position of hands on knees.

Shane audibly swallowed as they straightened and neared, one hand on the bark —reminiscent of when he had pinned them to a tree. He now considered jumping into the Youngs River.

"…It's like this. Open your mouth."

He took a long drag. Then slowly —carefully and unsure, he reached out towards their face. They flinched slightly and sucked in a light breath, but did not retreat. Those eyes swallowed the expanse of the sky. For a moment, he completely forgot about what he was doing. There was this; only this. In that moment, the soul knew him again and was uttering that word while holding his hand in a dungeon. *Love*. There was the briefest spark of something utterly dangerous and it pushed forward past the fear. They let Shane gently cup either side of their jaw, before understandably tensing as he leaned in. He clearly saw an alarm in their eyes. The natural urge to repel that which was foreign and strange —the urge to reject *him*. At least, that was how he selfishly took it.

But for the sake of his pride he kept his expression cold and unfeeling as he measuredly blew out smoke towards Alexander's mouth; their lips still parted out of sheer surprise. Their eyes refocused as they were then forced to concentrate on breathing it in.

Somehow the awkwardness lessened with each administration —even with the increasing awareness that the miniscule distance between relative innocence and a sinful graze kept wavering.

Shane's next mistake was direct, tremulous eye contact.

The two froze, as though it had all become clear right then. The smoke escaped past the soul's curls to the trees behind them.

The demon struggled for words in the uncomfortable silence.

"Wow that's so weird," Alexander eventually laughed softly, pressing a hand to their mouth as quickly and slick as they believed possible.

It wasn't fast and discreet enough.

"Yeah," Shane muttered, turning away to inhale far more than he had before. He desperately needed the effects to set in so he wouldn't be aware if he found himself doing something even more stupid. "It's meant to be a method for incompetent first-timers such as yourself."

"*Incompetent*?" they spluttered.

There was something hilarious about the English language.

"Glad that it worked quickly for you," Shane sneered, mildly jealous. Though he couldn't deny that he was kind of enjoying the sight of a high Alexander. But he did wish that they would laugh without influence. That was too rare an occurrence.

It was that thought which grounded him as it finally fully hit.

It was a mellow, existential sort of lull. At some point, the two of them ended up sitting on the forest floor knee to knee, staring up through a haze at the dots of stars. The moon was there somewhere but it came and went in ribbons of cream between the swimming branches.

"I don't think I deserve to be spared," Alexander murmured. "I'm not better than *everyone* here. I should have been possessed."

"Possessed?" echoed the monster, trying to grasp the conversation. "I don't think the shadows possess you. They're not ghosts."

"Right. You called them '*mercy*'. Maybe not ghosts."

"They're mercy 'cause people die nice and slow."

Alexander glanced at him blankly. "That makes no fucking sense."

Shane chuckled. "Sudden, violent death is mercy, then?"

They frowned in deliberation. "…Yeah," they decided, nodding. "If it comes without like, *any* warning, I think we should be…grateful." Their hands flailed out in front of them in exaggeration.

The soul had never looked upon him at death with gratitude.

"Not mercy," said Shane.

"Not mercy. Suffering."

The beast paused, vaguely recalling scorching rage as he stared at the tops of the pines. "Hm. Maybe they *should* suffer. All, for the sake of one."

"What did they do to deserve it?" Alexander giggled.

He shrugged. "Jack shit. Does there have to be reason?"

"Yes!" they insisted, feebly nudging his side. "Did they…did they kill somebody?" Alexander's eyes narrowed as they clumsily raised a finger to their lips. "Steal something worth too much?"

Shane made a face that gave away all of his pain. It was as if the soul were talking about a different town—a place that hadn't caused them any grief. And he couldn't explain any of it. His fogged mind did not have the capacity to dissect it. Not to mention, it was unlikely either of them would remember the conversation. "Greed," he said limply. "We all get greedy."

"But…not you and me?"

Back in Pine Creek it was.

"No. I think we're the greediest."

the onset

ALEXANDER

I WASN'T CAREFULLY picking out clothes and glaring at a mirror for a particular reason. There should be no excuse not to curate a perfect ensemble when going out in public.

Especially now that I was so central to it. People hadn't started saying things to my face —likely thanks to Shane Hyde —but I had barely been a few steps away when I had overheard the first comments. They'd mostly been expressions of confusion over our sudden association; which I could understand, because it didn't make sense to me either.

It was enough that he was interested in why I didn't have a Daemon. It was another matter when he started joking around; teasing and hovering as though he wanted to befriend me.

I still had reservations about that part. I didn't want to relive the past. These consequences were just a fragment —just a glimpse into a possible future that was struggling to stay buried. It could become a lot worse.

Yet for some reason, I decided that the pros outweighed the cons every time I caught sight of his face. Of those eyes, which still frightened me. Of the strain in the muscles in his face when I spotted the slightest slither of a smile. As if he was *trying*.

Quite like a moth to a flame; except I was very aware of the danger of a burn, while the fire bent and beckoned to receive me.

That had been my first thought when I woke up the morning after our debauchery in the woods. Part of me couldn't believe that I had done that. It was as much of surprise to me as it would have been to my parents — but it had been a build-up of frustration and helplessness that had finally culminated in the burst of a reckless decision. And though I didn't recall exactly what had happened after it hit, I didn't feel regret.

For once, I hadn't made a choice thinking about tomorrow.

My father was on his feet when I descended the stairs.

And I tensed. I had chosen clothes usually folded away at the back of my wardrobe: a cream silky bolero and brown low-cut V-neck sweater — still over a shirt, of course —with a large golden angel pendant. Hugh had never seen the necklace, but the bolero had belonged to my mother.

I really hoped that he didn't remember.

"Morning, son," he said with a little more life than a sigh. He was bent over the sink, doing something with an old coffee mug. The jar of instant cappuccino sat on the counter beside him.

"*Dad*," I drawled, momentarily forgetting about my apprehension.

"*What*?" he mocked, to my surprise. Then he turned around.

It all came rushing back in that second —the shame beneath the silent judgement like they were better than you. That look in their eyes —it said absolutely everything without a single word.

And I felt so small, yet so enormous; as if I were a new zoo attraction.

Hugh Grahams raised the kind of eyebrow that did not allude to shock and I saw his Daemon ripple with gross anticipation. I harboured no hope that the creature would demonstrate any mercy towards me.

"Are you sure you want to go out like that?" my father muttered. "The other kids won't…you know, poke fun?"

My fingernails dug a little harder into my palm.

I should be used to this.

I shouldn't crumble at every instance; every snarky suggestion; every cruel piece of advice. I should let it flow through me. Like a sieve, even.

But I felt it all and was dragged beneath the current of it.

"…No one cares," I eventually rasped, my voice a little shakier than I had expected. "And I don't really bump into any old classmates."

Someone else's classmates, not mine.

"Yeah, but my old friends are out there, Alex," he sighed heavily. His brows furrowed in the telling sign of rising vexation. "They're going to ask questions that I don't want to answer."

Like I was embarrassing.

BUT IT'S NOT YOUR DAMN PROBLEM.

…Right?

"I'm going to dress however I want," I told him, though still not as firmly as I wanted. "*You're* not going anywhere, and I'm not going to be talking to your friends. So nothing to worry about."

My father's gaze narrowed. I steeled myself for a raise of voice; or for something he had never done before. He grumbled, took a teaspoon from the drawer and wiped it down. My lungs did not dare to expand as he then unsteadily scooped in granules and turned to the microwave for water.

It was the loudest, longest nine seconds of my life.

Only when the spoon grated along the sides of the mug did I draw air. Hugh's hand paused as if I'd done it without permission.

"I worry about you all the time," he said.

That was simply what he told himself.

His Daemon grinned at me again, looming over his shoulder. My face contorted. I knew it then. Just as much as that creature tortured him, so too did it latch onto my misery. Instead of having my own, I shared one with the only person holding me down in the town.

I whirled towards the door. "I…I won't be back for dinner."

"Like hell you won't," clipped my father, clumsily stirring. "You had better be back just before dark or I'll come hunting for you."

I wouldn't have put it past him —last month.

I was about to say something bad and I didn't want to see the look on his face. "…*Oh meu Deus*, as if you can set one foot outside of that door," I forced —and it was still wobbly. It still revealed my fear.

But I got out.

I got out.

Kay Isotton's morning greeting was as friendly and indignant as always.

We were dressed similarly today. She was the first to notice. I tried to gauge her reaction, prepared to make a swift exit if she gave me a funny look. Only, her eyes brightened slightly and she *complimented* me.

"You have such a sophisticated sense of fashion," she beamed. "Very academia. Any reason you're looking a little more…formal?"

I blinked, absentmindedly fingering the handles of my tote bag.

"No reason," I blurted.

She folded her arms as the corners of her mouth tugged upwards. "Sure. You know, I remember what it was to be a teenager."

"God, you sound so old right now," I gasped. But despite the terrible morning my face broke out in a small smile.

"I'm still '*connected with the kids*'," she joked, making air quotes. "In all seriousness, Alexander, it's okay to enjoy life as you know it. No one knows how long we each get of it. It'll slip through your fingers and then you're suddenly halfway done. Or, the end finds you unprepared. So get out there —live. And do it with whoever you damn well feel like."

It wasn't just her personality. Kay was warm and down to Earth, and her advice usually made me cringe a little, but this time I stood there in dumb awe like I had been meant to hear it. My mouth twisted into a shape and my shoulders slumped as pressing issues speared for the forefront of my distracted thoughts.

"Is…is there something on your mind?" she tactfully asked. I kept my lip buttoned. "It's all right if you don't want to talk about it," she assured. "Just be sure to acknowledge that it's there, bothering you."

I glanced at her shadow. Tendrils of it shifted with the breeze, and did not display any additional or disjointed limbs. It sported no vicious claws but I could not be certain that it had never hurt her.

Something was definitely bothering her, too.

"Have you ever fought with your parents, Kay?" I murmured.

She blinked, not expecting a response or a seemingly topic changing veer. Her face then softened. "I'm sure everybody has, at least once."

I had to draw a deep breath. "…Did you ever feel like…they wouldn't accept who you really are?" I went on in an even smaller voice.

Her smile was tentative as she reached into a giant pot and plucked a stubbornly flowering marigold before holding it out to me. "Sometimes in our quest for validation, we seek out the people who either surprise us or don't. Those who do can either turn into friends and family, or be put away with those who define us only by what they see on the outside. I've had my fair share of people who care based on the way I live my life, and know

I know how valuable it is to have the ones who see underneath the layers of masquerade and love it still.

"This flower represents the value within you, Alexander," Kay went on with that winning enthusiasm. "The purity of the soul at its very base. Uninterrupted by life or death. I hope you remember there is a place for you, even if it's not what you once called home."

My fingers reached out for the marigold and twirled it briefly.

"Do you always get like this with customers?" I chuckled.

Her smile then reached her eyes. "Sometimes."

I caught sight of Shane Hyde by the next alleyway. He was difficult to miss —a dark mass amidst the greying green, dust and vermillion.

"Oh, I need to get going," I announced in a rush, tucking the blossom into my tote bag. I reminded myself to pause before my feet got the better of me. "…Thanks. For talking."

"Anytime," Kay returned. "Oh, and have *fun*," she sang.

I determinedly marched to the boy with the too blue eyes. He stuffed his hands into the pockets of his outmost jacket and smirked down at me.

"Grahams," he greeted. His voice irritated me for some reason.

"Hyde," I quipped, eyes lidded. "Minus fifteen."

It became apparent that aside from not having any shadows over us, Shane Hyde and I should not share a lot in common. We were close to opposites in many aspects —our personalities were types that wouldn't intertwine ordinarily and yet, there we were. I had never spent so much of my time with one person before. And while I didn't go out of my way to seek him,

I had never stopped him from staying. The game had allowed us to edge around and discover things about each other in a way that retained airs of mystery. Retained reasons to chase.

Intimidation had turned into mocking banter —with flat stares turning into troubling and forlorn. There was so much in his eyes; stories and odd devastation. I didn't understand it.

But I think that I wanted to.

The circumstances around our first meeting were unbelievably taking a backseat. It was less so that we were unaffected, and now that we had just become friends by default. Although, I wasn't sure if I could call us '*friends*'. It was different from me and my friends in New Mexico. There was something violent between me and Shane Hyde —it had been there from the start. It charged with a pull unignorable.

"I think Daemons can affect other people," I hissed, scribbling in one of my many notebooks. We were sat at the small bar section of *Straws & Fries*; hungry and shivering by the early afternoon. The forest was a bad idea in the wet wind. "Not just their hosts," I added.

"What makes you say that?" he murmured as he picked out something from my hair. I flinched before narrowing my gaze at him.

"Please don't do that where people could…see us. I'll start penalising physical contact," I warned. "Minus a whole twenty points."

Shane only heard the first sentence.

"So I can take leaves out of your hair when we're alone?"

I froze. It wasn't his words —his *tone* was off. Instead of sarcastic, it was a playfully teasing. It made my skin crawl. My gut reaction was panic and annoyance. And I was sure that he knew of the effect it had, because he started smiling. I had never seen him smile…normally. It always had an edge of slyness and cunning.

"No," I answered firmly.

"Aw," he chuckled.

"Stop joking around," I hedged, instinctively slapping at his arm. Before immediately gasping at my own potential hypocrisy.

He raised a brow, catching on. "Minus twenty, Grahams."

"*Vá se foder*," I muttered.

"What does that mean?"

"I swore at you," I put it plainly.

He let out a defeated sigh. "Yeah, no —I figured."

I tapped the open notebook. "Now comment on my discovery, Hyde," was my order. He obediently leaned in close —the little distance between his face and mine so unnecessary in their proximity. My breath shallowed and I wondered if he could hear it.

"Malicious bastards," whistled Shane, before his head turned slightly to meet my eye. "…Did someone's do something to you?"

"My Dad's," I whispered, subtly leaning away. "I don't know why or how, but it knows I'm there. It knows what I fear."

He looked a bit taken aback.

The concern settling on his face confirmed my terror. If this surprised even Shane Hyde then the floor might as well fall out from beneath my feet. There was nothing to reassure me. I wanted answers —and although he was not the expert on *The Haunting of Pine Creek*, I had hoped that he could offer definitive insight. Not a wordless look of damnation.

"You don't share the same fear as your father, do you?" he murmured.

My denial was iron-clad. "Not a chance."

"Hm," Shane hummed, swirling a tall coffee. "I've never heard of this before," he admitted. "Barnes hasn't encountered anything like that."

My eyebrows knitted with my grave, "Maybe because she's never had to. No one has."

He mirrored my dejection and my fear grew. It was the first time I had seen his exterior truly fracture. Perhaps he was not made entirely of stone, ice and self-importance.

"…I wanted to leave town today," I then admitted, feeling as though I had nothing left to cling onto. "I don't…want to say why, but I seriously considered hitchhiking all the way to Albuquerque."

Shane did not offer me a reason not to. I preferred that response. It felt weighted with respect. Though his jaw clenched so hard that it blanched and he would not look at my face. Instead he glanced down at my hand. His little finger slid over, hesitantly tapped the side of mine and lingered in the briefest brush. I stared at the gesture, not breathing —and analysed its effect. But I could not name the answer.

Then he whispered, "…Glad you're still here, Grahams."

My chest grew warm.

I drew a breath. "You can call me by my first name."

There were a couple of seconds of shock on that cold, pale face. Then it wasn't so pale anymore. His lips parted as his hand jerked back.

"Wait, what am I seeing here?"

We simultaneously swivelled inward to face Louise Barnes. She stood there with folded arms, sporting sweatpants under a giant varsity bomber jacket. Her expression was not one of disgust but of genuine surprise.

"This isn't what it looks like," Shane Hyde blurted.

I scoffed, then lightly punched his arm. "Dude."

"That's another twenty." He flashed a grin.

"You have *some* nerve —"

"Since when were the two of you…friends?" asked Louise, in an offhand manner. "Last time I checked, neither of you wanted anything to do with the other. So much for '*staying away*', you liars."

"Times change," I clipped, fiddling with my straw. Then my lips lifted at the corners. "We all have our demons. This one's mine."

"…You can't introduce me like that," Shane frowned, flushing.

"You might as well be my own *persistent* shadow," I clarified.

"Now I'm a little offended."

Louise blinked between us as we both took sips from our drinks and shared a knowing look. Then she cleared her throat, reminding us of her presence. "Well," she huffed, "I suppose this will make all our discussions easier. Now I can find you in the same place."

"*Our*?" I questioned.

"You haven't forgotten about the Daemons, have you? How about the fact that you two don't have them? Or the other weird shit in Pine Creek."

Shane sneered. "Do you have to call them that? It's such a dumb name. Just say demons if you must."

I nudged his side, subtly shaking my head.

"See, but they're not '*demons*' are they?" hissed Louise, wagging her finger importantly. "Not in any sense I've read up on so far."

"You keep reading religious texts and books on mythology from the library," he deadpanned. "Eventually, everything blurs."

"Actually, she has a point," I sighed. "We haven't found anything. So I don't think that we should classify them by something they're not."

Shane Hyde sucked on his teeth and did not offer a refuting word.

Louise shifted her weight onto her other hip. "…Have you…have you ever *spoken* to other Daemons?"

I started. "Spoken? When did we get there? Making eye contact with them and touching the things is bad enough."

"Yeah," Shane agreed. "What are you talking about, Barnes?"

She stiffened, lowered her gaze and appeared a lot softer. That razored edge I had known so well went brittle and useless as a fear set in. She had come searching for answers too, yet all that we could offer were the same damning stares.

"Sometimes I can hear it breathing," Louise whispered, glancing from left and right as if she could feel the few pairs of eyes on her. "Sometimes it feels like if I say something, there'll be a reply."

No shadows visibly slithered over her shoulder, despite clear distress. "*Have* you ever said something?" I asked.

"I don't dare," she rasped. "It already reads my every thought."

"Got to add that to the list," Shane muttered.

I obediently flicked to that page and wrote it down.

Louise bit her nails, then tugged a hand through her hacked, tangling hair. She looked directly to me. Her eyes were an empty ice blue and her lips were pale and chapped. It was turning her into a ghost. "…Have the interactions between you and your Dad's Daemon…changed in any way? Anything more than darkness on the wall?"

"I am not about to try talking to it, too," I quickly shot down the idea. My hand snagged the side of my bolero; my fingers digging in as I tried to keep my senses sharp. "I don't even want to go back to that house."

Shane gave me a sidelong frown.

"But it hasn't touched you, right?" Louise Barnes was almost worried.

I managed to shake my head.

I did not want to elaborate nor explain myself. It would be a prodding of a gaping wound; one long used to being picked at as a scar. It had never had the chance to heal enough never to bleed again. Telling someone else the words that had sliced at it this time…that would be excruciating. How did people do it every day? How could they stand to exist and evolve and not rip apart? For the most part, I didn't understand those who had learned to smile through it all. It must take such immense strength.

Strength that I did not yet possess.

The honorary bartender then rounded the corner from the staff room, so we all went quiet. I glanced at Shane out of the corner of my eye, then at Louise. I was not about to turn her away out loud, but I didn't want her to stay. He seemed to pick up on the hint, and turned to give her a subtle look. Though to our surprise, she read the room and excused herself as if all she had come for was to say hello.

Shane and I took simultaneous sips again.

"Should we be…concerned about her?" I whispered.

His brows knitted in thought. "Not beyond basic courtesy," he clipped with absolute certainty. "She hasn't earned any more than that."

It was nice that he wouldn't accept excuses for her either.

But as true as that was, I could not shake the tremble in her voice that had not been there before. The terror that most of me was glad she was finally experiencing for herself; but still churned my stomach because of my own relationship with it.

And I was no longer sure if I wholeheartedly wished it upon her.

"Everyone in Pine Creek is haunted, Grahams," Shane reminded me. "The severity may vary from sin to sin, but essentially they're all dying."

I lingered on that for a moment, before drinking my hot chocolate. If it was a question of sin, did we not all deserve it? If anything had stuck with me from Sunday School, it was the concept that no one was without sin. No one could be exempt from punishment —unless they believed that a holy man had taken it for them. Even then, it did not bar the trials of the life you had to live on Earth. While you were mortal, all of the darkness would flock without fail.

"…Have I not sinned?" I then asked, half rhetorically and half directly to Shane. "Why was I allowed to reject one of those creatures and no one else? Unless…did you manage to do the same?"

"I don't know," he sighed. He seemed sincere. "And that's starting to worry me. No, your experience was different from mine. You might have been able to fight off yours, but I…" he struggled, and I could almost see the beads of sweat on his brow. "I never even came into contact with it or chased it away. It was there…right in front of me, and it…it flinched and cowered like it was afraid of me."

I blinked. "So you didn't scare it off—on purpose?"

"Likely not with the way I looked," he murmured. "Maybe it took one glance at the core of me where a soul should be, and saw…kin."

My head turned to gape at him. "Don't say that. You can't really think of yourself like that. You're not like them."

Shane's face asked me how I knew that. "…What if I'm worse?"

I ignored the chill to the back of my neck. "Not possible."

I was mostly saying words. I didn't know if I entirely believed that he wasn't capable of that sort of torment—not necessarily physical but much like the people who had bullied me. But I did not want him to call himself evil and have that broken look, like the world was crumbling around him.

Despite my pleading, I did not miss the cold dimming of his eyes that turned the turquoise into teal. He stared back at me with the most hollow, consumed and defeated resolve I had ever seen. And though the light was faded, I still felt the tug. The sparks. More so.

"I haven't told anyone about this, Grahams," he then hissed. The hard frown returned, masking all of the feeling. I heard the warning of those words clearly.

"I won't tell anyone."

My hand inched between us, and my little finger nudged his in an echo of comfort.

"Twenty," he deadpanned, eyes glued there when I didn't move away.

I bit my bottom lip and brushed against his hand a little more boldly. His gaze flicked to mine. Another fracture split through the stone.

I couldn't really breathe when he looked at me so…ferociously. Like he wanted to know every single thing about me.

"How about…we stop playing the game?" I then murmured, glancing downwards at his lips. I did not have the confidence to keep talking if he was going to stare like that. "I don't think that either of us were taking it very seriously, anyway."

His mischievous smirk returned suddenly; as though he had flipped a switch. "Are you saying that because of all the points you've now lost?"

"No," I frowned. "And I'm pretty sure you lost the most."

He leaned over, as close as he had been before, and held his cheek in one hand. I dared to look back up. The light had not returned, but I could have sworn that I saw the smallest twinkle. "I don't doubt that."

the cat

ALEXANDER

FOR THE FIRST time in my life, I had snuck back into a house past midnight and then left just a few hours past the crack of dawn.

My father hadn't come hounding and I didn't see nor hear him when I was leaving. But I saw several bottles of beer on the kitchen counter. It made me pause, but in that moment and light of what had happened it was not enough to stop me. Though it did mean that he was going outside.

If my footsteps were loud enough, he made no moves.

He seemingly let me go.

I had to ask myself very seriously if I wouldn't mind coming back to a body on the floor. I didn't want to think about it, but our relationship was nearing that point where I had to choose between my own sanity versus the faith he wouldn't slip past the point of no return. Truthfully, there was only so much that I could do. So much I could take.

Not everything to do with him was my responsibility, and I shouldn't feel bad for needing to wedge space between my sense of heroism and his judgemental self-righteousness. It was *my* life.

If I managed to save him, I would still be moving away. And if I could not save anyone at all, that was not ultimately my burden either.

In the instance relevant to me, I could find a way to save Hugh without coming into direct contact. I didn't want to hear his voice; see his sneer; and certainly didn't feel like buckling, challenging his Daemon.

Sometimes I saw it when I closed my eyes.

I began to wonder if it would have been better to have my own.

The fog was creeping higher and denser. I couldn't see past my knees and had to take each step with caution. There was no doubt in my mind that I would find myself face down on the tar if I went at my normal pace towards the library. I did not dare venture towards the woods at this hour.

Despite that, the air was heavy with stagnant rain. There was a breeze rippling the fog, swirling it around the grated tree trunks and pushing off dead and dying leaves into the murky depths.

The sun was once again behind the solid mass of grey and blue. It was the kind of atmosphere where a storm would be expected; where people would stay indoors and the wind howling through the gaps of structure sounded an awful lot like prowling creatures.

I felt it on the back of my neck.

I felt it on the back of my ankles.

It was cold and damp, yet the dryness was so thin and whipping that the tip of my nose drained of all warmth —then feeling.

It was too dark to be daytime.

But I made it to the threshold of the library. Washed over in the gloom of outside so the overall brown colour had drained. All that mattered was that it was a little warmer inside.

And that Shane Hyde was already there.

He jerked out of his chair when he caught sight of me. He was all dark and dangerous again —a far cry from the vulnerability he had shown me the day before. His gaze had returned to its bright piercing blue. He smiled at me, only with his mouth, and stopped within a foot.

"I was worried about where you'd slept, Grahams."

"I did go to the house," I clarified.

"And you were okay?"

"Yeah," I breathed. "I didn't see him, so…"

"You could've come to my house," he offered. It felt uncharacteristic, given what I knew about him. He wasn't generous and he certainly wasn't the kind of person to worry about others. His earlier comment could have been a taunt. Yet…he looked genuine —despite his hands in his pockets and furrowing of his brows.

My own eyebrows raised. "I would rather sleep in the woods."

"Would you really?" he playfully prodded as we settled down at the study table. "Surely there are worse things than a sleepover."

"With you? It's possible," I hedged.

He mimed being shot with an arrow —which, against my will, made me laugh just a little. Perhaps I didn't fully believe my own words. There certainly could be worse things than spending the night at Shane Hyde's house. Sharing air in the same room.

And we needed to orchestrate a solution to one of those worse things.

"I couldn't find out anything new yesterday," I sighed, taking out my notebook from my tote bag. "Given the resolve not to run into my Dad, I didn't even catch a glimpse of his Daemon."

"Given what it put you through, that doesn't surprise me."

"So um," I murmured, folding my arms over the table. "If you can say, how do your family's Daemons behave around, or react to you? It's just I've been wondering if it's a case of us not having our own punishment, or if my Dad's one being aware of me is an isolated thing."

I saw the muscles in his arms tense as his jaw clenched. He dropped my gaze and definitely considered it. I was aware of his unease since the day before, which was why I had offered a choice. He didn't have to force it, just as I knew he would extend the same courtesy to me.

Shane gripped the edge of the table in a fist before clearing his throat. He couldn't meet my eye, but that was all right. As long as he managed to say something if that was what he wanted.

"...They can see us," he rasped. "All human beings. Even those who pass by and don't stay long enough to be latched onto. However...I don't think they should be able to affect other people —especially you and me. It's weird that it happened to you."

"Of *course* I'm more of an anomaly than you," I hissed, lowering my forehead to the wood. "Ugh, maybe I'm being punished after all."

"No," Shane said firmly. "I don't believe that. There has to be another reason. There has to be a factor we haven't seen."

I straightened. "Speaking of —you and Barnes mentioned that visitors don't get Daemons. But I noticed that there isn't any signal, let alone cars driving on the roads. So...are we...are *we* even able to leave?"

His face told me all that I needed to know.

We couldn't.

Then he drew a breath. "It'd be easier to show you than to explain. In one of the woods that form the perimeter."

I swallowed, processing what that meant. We *couldn't leave*. So even if I had wanted to —even if I could drive, or even if I had had the courage to hitchhike...I wouldn't have gotten anywhere.

"Do the Daemons stop people from leaving?" I asked.

"I believe so," Shane mused. "But that would not explain you and I, who also can't leave. Well. *I* can't. Have you tried?"

I shook my head.

Though if I was hypothetically the only person who could leave Pine Creek, what would it change? I still didn't want to abandon the situation. I didn't think of myself as that selfish.

"…If you had one, what would it feed on?"

The question caught me off guard. I had never contemplated anything specific. It was simply an overarching awareness of everything that I had likely done wrong in all my life. I tried to be a fair person. I tried not to be too self-centred. But if it was a case of a large sin that had altered the course of my life…maybe I could have been there more for my mother. Maybe I could have not snapped back at my parents so much.

Maybe it was my habit of lying.

"I have no idea," I said. "What about you?"

His lips pressed together in a line. "…Too many to count."

I clasped my hands, intertwining my fingers. "Could this be '*mercy*'?"

"Suffering," corrected Shane, after a thoughtful pause. "Even without the trailing darkness, is anyone really okay?"

My mouth refused to open in order to answer. Everything was too big to voice. Because I knew that we were not.

I seriously had to ask myself why I had come along.

We were stalking through the woods that afternoon and Shane had an old shovel balanced over his broad shoulder. It thudded —in a way which looked painful —with every bounce in his step. I tried not to think about the slenderness of the trees like skeletal bodies or the smell of damp wood that resembled rot as the breeze picked up.

The pines were tall beyond; the nearer larches were dry and shedding; and the fog had thinned a little, reduced to a fluffed up rug. The coverage was impressive —no one would know we were there.

My eyes were glued to the path marked out only by the lack of grass and shrubbery. He hadn't told me what we would be doing. The one hint I had was that shovel —weathered, rusty, and recently dunked with water to wash off the collecting dust.

Then Shane yanked me aside, and I stumbled away from a tree.

"Watch it," he barked.

I squirmed and grabbed his arm as my sneaker hooked underneath a protruding root. His body was hard and cold, like a reptile. After finding my footing I gasped, glancing up in utter embarrassment.

His face relaxed, before he smirked in smug observation.

"…You're looking a little nervous, Grahams," Shane remarked, tilting his head slightly. "Only *you* would agree to accompany a shovel-wielding teenager into the woods and not ask any questions."

I cracked an uneasy frown and clutched my sketchbook tighter against my chest. "Is it far-fetched to think that you could have brought me here to be an accomplice to murder?"

His smile was genuine. "If I had wanted anyone dead, I would've tried to make them disappear a long time ago."

I didn't doubt him.

And I didn't pick at the layers of the statement either.

Shane Hyde had been to me initially, a potential tormentor. There had been no insults beyond teasing and that tentative instinct to solve conflict with violence and intimidation.

He didn't instil the same fear that had gripped me when I was younger. It was a different trepidation. It was borderline cartoonish.

Yes, while murder was likely, I actually worried about us being alone in Kindling Acre even more. It wasn't as though there had been incidents in the past —not with humans, anyway. Ever since I'd been old enough to remember, animals smaller than a large dog had found their way to the outskirts of our patch of Astoria's national forests…mauled and torn as if a coyote or even grey wolf had done it.

I didn't want to encounter the creatures responsible.

We finally stopped at a clearing; a little stretch of sparse brown grass and weeds. A tree —maybe a year or two old —jutted out in the centre, lopsided and indignant. Come rain or shine, it seemed determined to stay rooted. I glanced at the shovel as Shane lowered it.

Would he dig it up?

"We're here to bury my cat," he said.

I flinched.

He got started immediately —striking the earth and then angling to scoop. It wasn't difficult. The soil was mildly soaked and loose.

I kept my head down as I sketched a patch of forest; the scratch of the pencil so loud and hard in the silence.

I had not planned on attending another funeral.

My mother's cremation service was still fresh in my head. It had been a cold, quiet affair. Cold because of the unavoidable air conditioning, and because the hall had been so uncomfortably silent. Sobbing was minimal and contained —that included mine, due to Hugh pinching the side of my arm so that the person on the podium could actually finish their sentences.

So I had learned to bottle everything up until I was in the privacy of my own bedroom —not house. Though that clearly hadn't worked for my father, either.

I still didn't dare to cry properly in front of him.

He wouldn't say something inappropriate if I did —the crying itself was not the issue. It was the fact that I would be mourning Leilah, and he had not resolved his guilt. That alone would be sufficient in making him think that I was healing from it.

He didn't know that I hadn't stopped leaving nail marks in my palms or staring unblinking at the ceiling, wondering if I could join her early. I had never done that before. Not when my aunt Nera passed away when I was eight and we had to drive into the city; not when my pet hamster died when I was thirteen; and not when my maternal grandmother Paula had gone in her sleep around a year later.

Those deaths, I had understood.

My mother's hadn't made sense.

A cat's was putting me in a strange in-between because even though I had not known the poor creature, I felt bad for Shane Hyde.

I wondered where the body was.

I got my answer when he then wandered to the outer ring of trees and reached behind a cluster. He produced a bundle of jerseys and sheets — which were not conducive to neutralising odours. It was dark with blood, and tufts of black fur poked out from between the wraps of material.

"What happened?" I asked as I left the drawing and sidled over.

"Found him at the end of the backyard by the fence last night," he said tightly. "Well, Ken found him first. I heard him screaming."

"Ken?"

"My…little half-brother."

"Why isn't he here?"

"He didn't want to see."

I nodded slowly. I hadn't wanted to see my mother's body in the casket. Not because it would be unbearable to see her so icy and pale, but because

I had wanted to preserve her warm, living memory. I knew if I had taken a single glance, I would be seeing her ghost as my father was: as a stranger and a nightmare.

The hole by the little tree was shallower than it probably should have been, but this wasn't a formal funeral.

Shane lowered the cat into it, then hesitated over the shovel, before he decided to stand and prepare to say a few words.

"I always told you that curiosity would get you, Omen," he murmured, his voice thin and crisp. I tried to imagine what it would sound like if he was choked with tears. It seemed too foreign of a concept.

He looked at me.

I started. "Do you want me to say something too?"

He didn't answer, and I figured that was him giving me the choice. I fidgeted, racking my brain for appropriate sympathies. After all, there was no one out here but the two of us and a corpse. Shane didn't look like he would cry, but I didn't think I would know what to do if he started.

"I'm sure Omen was well loved," I settled for. "Whatever did this…it was undeserved, and we're allowed to feel that way no matter what '*laws*' nature has in place. We're allowed to miss anything —and any being, that was close to our hearts."

There was not even the sound of breath.

The heavy solemnity would be ruined by it.

"…Even though I am the one who named Omen," Shane then mused, "we weren't particularly close. Many cats just come and go, so I laid back most of the time. I didn't think that this might happen."

"Death can happen anytime," I whispered. "It's not your fault."

He didn't have a response to that.

I wondered if it would be strange if I reached for his hand and held it. It wouldn't be strange to me, but that didn't mean his masculinity wasn't so fragile that he couldn't accept blatant physical contact and comfort like that from someone who wasn't a girl.

"…I should be accustomed to death," he eventually sighed. "I've seen plenty of it. And somehow, it's this cat that's making me…*feel* things."

I frowned. "Don't you *want* to feel things?"

"Not…this."

I let out a long breath. "It's terrible, isn't it?" I offered. "Grief."

"I want to crawl into the hole."

"I wanted to be set on fire."

Shane glanced at me. "Was your Mom cremated?"

"Yeah. My Dad keeps her ashes on his nightstand."

"Kind of grim."

"Right?"

There was then that silence where someone might say that they were sorry for your loss. But neither of us could articulate such flimsy words; words that would not balm the hurt, and instead roll right over it.

"I'm going to see Omen everywhere," he scoffed, fishing in his pocket for a cigarette before lighting it. "Like my own shad —Daemon. Except, there wouldn't need to be any contact to drain the life from me."

A light went off in my mind. Like a phantom, Omen would linger in Shane's life. Just as my mother remained in mine. And I hadn't had any physical contact with her —she had simply been there in the corner of my eye, still and humming the lullaby she had written for me as a baby. My father's Daemon was twisting that into something absolutely horrifying. Not into a monster, but it was sinister. Details shifted. Proportions were distorted, like a bad memory. My vision blurred. The creature was taking my mother away from me, which had been the consequence I had feared by seeing her dead body in the first place.

Something spilled down along my cheeks. My lips parted in shock but nothing went in or came out. The air was solid to block my throat.

"Grahams?" said Shane, exhaling smoke. "Are you…crying?"

I turned to meet his gaze. It wasn't hard —he was genuinely surprised to see tears dripping down my face. He dithered, unsure of how to react. There was nothing that he could do, though.

My hand went to my chest and then my neck.

I had cried last night. This felt different. Raw, almost. There were far more tears now than there had been —maybe akin to after the funeral. I could hear my heartbeat echoing inside of my ears; between my temples and right at the front of my forehead. Right away I knew that I was in for a killer of a headache.

"Grahams," Shane whispered. His free hand then slowly raised, like he might place it on my shoulder. He flinched when I sobbed —loud and violent. My crying abruptly became audible; real and guttural, as if I had never expressed such an emotion before.

"Alexander."

I whipped around again to face him completely. He had not called me by my first name before. And it was soft in a way that was telling of how long he had been deliberating over letting it pass his lips.

There was a sudden flood of everything about which I had ever wanted to cry. "…*Shane*," I finally choked out.

I darted forward and tightly wrapped my arms around his neck. I clung viciously; gripping his jacket like it was a lifebuoy; and too caught up in the desperation and impulsiveness of it all. I would be lying if I said that I wasn't scared that he would then push me away. But he didn't. I felt him stiffen and stagger, second guess himself…before his free arm carefully wrapped around my torso. But he held me just as fiercely, and let me bawl over the back of his jacket.

I could breathe.

Sort of —I gulped lungfuls of air in between. In the furthest recesses of my mind I worried about the aftermath and how I would have to explain this, but in the moment nothing mattered beyond purging a few weeks' worth of fear and turmoil —finally following my therapist's longstanding advice. '*Let it out and let them deal.*'

Hugh Grahams wasn't there to stop me.

No bully was there to berate me.

I could breathe, and I could cry.

the boundary

ALEXANDER

IT ONLY REGISTERED that I had hugged Shane Hyde a number of minutes after the fact. I wanted to be casual about it, but we both skirted around the incident. Clearly it meant more than the brush of a hand.

We squatted beside the little tree marking Omen's grave —the clear tape-wrapped cardboard headstone my handiwork, while he had scrawled the name in permanent marker —in more of that unforgiving silence.

"…I don't think this is going to hold up against the rain," I murmured. I was growing tired of the whistle of the wind and flicking of ash.

"Yeah," he sighed. "It seemed like a good idea at the time."

I tapped my fingers on my knees.

"Hey Grahams," Shane then quipped. "Are you…okay?"

"I don't think so."

I was very aware of the turn of his head and the stare of his piercing eyes. My own moved to return the look. A dull pain throbbed in my left temple. He was trying to rationalise what had happened. I couldn't know for what purpose, but it was clear that he was thinking about it deeply.

"…You cried as if you had never been allowed to."

I swallowed and looked back to the leaning headstone. What could I even say to that? I bit the inside of my cheeks and curled my fingers into my freezing palms. They were always cold —for as long as I could recall the skin of my hands had never retained heat, even in the Summer.

I liked to think that it was a reflection of my soul.

"I cry all the time," I eventually blurted. I could feel him frowning in confusion. "...*Caralho*," I added under my breath, glaring at nothing.

"I saw the look on your face," was his counter. "The pain in your eyes. It was...it was a lot. There was too much in there for someone your age."

"What?" I chuckled uneasily. "I've lived a good few years. I've seen shit. I...I should be used to death too."

I rubbed the side of my arm uncertainly.

Shane exhaled upwards to where the impenetrable clouds had begun to part for slithers of golden sun. The dried, shrivelled leaves that the light touched turned a shining gold, too.

"Do you ever think, perhaps you don't '*get used to*' death but rather stop feeling anything when it happens?" Shane thought out loud.

"I think...that I still feel something," I admitted. "Maybe I tried telling myself otherwise during all the deaths before, but when my mother..." I winced, curling inward on my already precarious posture. "I felt it then. I felt too much."

"Would it be the same for those who kill?"

I frowned. "I think there are two types of people who might go through with premeditated murder: those who don't know how to control what it is they feel, and those who've mastered it —to the point where it appears as though they have nothing to show."

Shane clamped the cigarette tightly between his lips.

"...Why do you ask?" I prompted.

He shrugged. "...I've wanted to know if a monster is ever created so, or made to be that way later on —for some time now. If there is a way for someone to change or be redeemed."

It was an age old question. I wasn't really into philosophy as much as my diary ravings would suggest. Questions like that would have led me down a path that I dared not tread —dangerous and engraining. I might have grown to think one extreme or the other. Reality simply wasn't black and white. People were too complex for any box.

"What's your hypothesis?" I asked.

He didn't hesitate. "I think they're made."

"Why?"

"I said made —I didn't add '*later on*'."

"What's the difference?"

He inhaled deeply as he then glanced down at his shoes. "I cannot speak for every case," he acknowledged, "but I think that since the dawn of time, the concept of a monster has always felt too much and then acted without forethought —consequences be damned. It is my belief, that all monsters are made: both influenced to be, and created so. That maybe both notions can be true at once."

"So, there is no correct answer?" I murmured.

"It was never about the '*correct*' answer," Shane clarified. "Just what was and what wasn't. After all, it's not black and white."

"You don't think that we all have the potential to be awful?" My voice came out as a trembling whisper. I had never been too good at hiding my emotions. Not like Shane Hyde.

"Humans do," he breathed; with the fragility of my own fear and soft tone of my dread. "But most of them do not succumb to it." Then he asked me a horrible question that set my stomach swirling. "…Do you think that those who tormented you are indeed monsters?"

I wanted to say '*yes*'.

All of those years ago, in the thick and brunt of it, I believed that they were all irredeemable and monstrous.

According to Shane's revelation, that could be true. Their homes and parents had moulded their ways of thinking. They had been taught to hate and be intolerant through observation or direct teaching. Some of it had worn off now that they were growing into their own people, but I could not pretend to be brave and say that I bore no ill intent towards them.

Religion and political views should not be excuses to harm.

The older version of me could be cautious and rational, but the child had never heard the sound of an apology. They were still there, innocent and naïve, with too much pain curling them into a tight fist.

"You can't ask me that," I grumbled, clutching my midsection. "You weren't there, and most importantly, you weren't *me*."

"No, I wasn't there," he agreed. "But I know what they did. I had to ask around because no one person could give me a straight answer, but eventually, Barnes told me everything. I mean, I did corner and threaten her. She still told me. A lot." His brows narrowed. "…Too much."

I went still. I had to close my eyes. I had to be conscious of my every breath so that I wouldn't stop drawing them. It had been quite a few years since my body relived what happened. I no longer felt the burns along my arms, or the sharp stinging across my scalp.

"Do you know what started it?" I muttered, opening my eyes again to the dead, twisting trees and browning grass. "It's kind of stupid."

"Yeah?"

"Show and Tell. A ballet character skirt."

I had decided to raid my mother's wardrobe that morning and change into one of her old adjustable ballet skirts in the bathrooms when it was my turn. Even though I had been four and the garment had been made for a three-year-old girl, the hem had swept the floor like a gown.

"The whole class gasped and stared when I strutted in, before twirling and holding an arabesque," I explained. "I declared that I was going to be a ballerina, just like my mother had wanted to be when she was younger. I distinctly remembered someone blurting out '*isn't ballet for girls?*'. The teacher corrected them and then gently informed me that while boys could do ballet, they were not referred to as ballerinas.

"In my naïveté, I had said that I didn't care. I *liked* the skirt. My ankles were going to be strong enough for pointe —or so I told myself."

I had never spoken about something with such enthusiasm, to this day. I hadn't pursued ballet that far either. I could no longer tell whether it was because of perception or if I had simply grown out of a hobby.

"The kids hadn't done anything immediately after the lesson," I then continued. "They had waited until recess to bombard me with questions. I had changed back into my trousers but the deed had already been done. The other children had never heard of someone who wasn't a girl wearing something that only girls typically wore, and they wanted an explanation.

"To their credit, I suppose they attempted to comprehend the concept of '*non-binary*' in their own terms at first. The mistake had been asking their parents for a second opinion." I then struggled to say the next thing. "...I became the advocate for wrongness after that." My voice had waned considerably. These were things that I had already told my therapist yet it felt as though I were saying it for the first time.

"I...I was shunned, cornered and shoved into. I...hadn't minded the solitude too much —I had not had that many friends in the first place. But then...then the bullying turned properly physical."

Shane had been listening patiently. He looked...offended, as he then put out the diminished cigarette. "That's not stupid, Alexander."

I pressed my lips into a tight line.

He didn't say that he was sorry.

Of course, there was no need for him to. But it was then that I realised I had grown accustomed to hearing it from people. For nearly everything. When it wasn't said, it did not mean that they were guilty or felt nothing. Those words were simply a default.

"…I think that as human beings we want to believe that monsters can be born," I said into the quiet. "It makes it easier to stomach certain things and behaviours. It makes us feel better about ourselves." I reached down to draw into the crumbling dirt. "We all have free will, and it scares most of us to think that people could *choose* to be a monster."

Shane shuffled a little closer towards me, leading me to lift my head to meet his gaze. The turquoise gleamed in the sunlight —then I could've sworn a ring of violet shimmered around both of his pupils. It was hard to tell in the reflection of light, but his eyes definitely appeared brighter.

I didn't move.

I was falling into that gaze, slowly and steadily, from a great height. Not because it was mesmerizing and foreign, but because I had the faint image in my mind of the same pair of eyes, though somewhere else. Somewhere far harsher. And where they were the only anchor.

"Would you think I chose to be bad?" he asked, and I had to glance at his mouth to realise that he was speaking. My gaze almost immediately flicked back upwards.

"Are you a monster?" I asked softly. Far too softly for the little space between us and the infinite vastness of the world.

The intensity in his irises lessened. "It's possible."

"And yet…I don't think it would bother me."

His focus on my face wavered slightly. “Because you have no fear?”

My lips were dry. I quickly ran my tongue over them. Shane suddenly drew a sharp breath and turned away to rise to his feet. I blinked up at him before following suit. I didn’t have the chance to dwell on those seconds, nor on the wild racing of my heartbeat.

“Come on,” he said dryly, nodding toward the path we had taken. “Let me show you what happens when you wander too far to the boundary of Pine Creek. It’s not dangerous —just strange.”

“Okay.”

I gathered my things and trekked after him; the shovel wobbling and balancing on top of his shoulders.

The Kindling Acre was one of the furthest parts of town and the farm land surrounding it. There was a metal border along the reserve owned by the city of Astoria, for which I assumed we were looking. But something was immediately amiss when after walking in a what we thought to be a straight line westward, there was only more eerie forest.

“I swear that we’ve passed this tree already,” I quipped, pointing to a leaning, knobbly young oak.

“Exactly.”

I met his serious frown with one of confusion.

“It’s just a theory,” Shane elaborated, “but for some reason, no matter how close you get to the edge, even those desperate enough to hike here —you always find yourself circling back inward.”

“What? How is that possible? There has to be an explanation.”

I fumbled through my tote bag for my cellphone. Thankfully, I didn't need any sort of connection in order to use the compass. I lifted it up and orientated myself with the West, towards the border fencing.

Shane flanked me with an indecipherable look and luminous eyes.

I made sure to watch the compass.

Yet somehow, that oak came into view once again. I glanced down at my screen. The line representing the needle still pointed West —despite us being on the opposite end of the tree as we approached.

I shook the cellphone. "*Merda, o que está acontecendo*?"

"Hm?" Shane hummed from behind me.

After a calming breath I turned in his direction. "I was just wondering what is going on," I translated. "…Angrily."

"Yeah —I know enough curse words in Portuguese now," he smirked, bouncing the shovel. "From you saying them so often."

I sneered half-heartedly. I swivelled, and the line spun back and forth without my influence before settling eastward as it was meant to. A chill ran down my spine. My teeth ground in apprehension.

"Is it like this with every part of town?" I asked.

"Believe me," he sighed. "I've been to every curve and corner. I can't run into the fence, and I can't cross very far past the river. I even went up the highway —and kept looping back to the same stretch by the welcome sign until I couldn't walk anymore."

I yanked a hand through my tangling hair and groaned at the treetops. "So we really can't leave. Including me."

Shane shifted his weight to one foot. "I'm starting to think that us not having those Daemons over our shoulders is the only thing that makes us different from the other residents."

I didn't want to believe that, but it seemed as though I had no choice.

As grateful as I was that I didn't have phantom claws digging into me, I only came up with more questions than answers. If we truly were only set apart by that one factor, then what was the point?

What would be the plan?

Could I…did I even have the means to do anything?

My resolve to save Pine Creek began to show its cracks.

the stranger

ALEXANDER

"I'M TELLING YOU —the Caesar Bacon is one of the best burgers on the menu," I insisted. "After the Dagwood, of course."

"What? That's *completely* biased," Shane Hyde exclaimed in a fluster, slamming his hands down onto the counter. "You've never even tried the Barbeque Chicken."

"Obviously," I scoffed. "Why would I deviate from perfection?"

"*Perfection*?" he gasped, clutching at his chest. "That is some nerve." He then turned to Louise Barnes —who was vigorously wiping down the bar section and attempting to remain calm even as her eye twitched.

We were the only ones in *Little Hatchet*. Earl was out for a smoke.

It was the cool of evening, before most people would have dinner. We had been invited over for a makeshift meeting and the promise of drinks on the house. Shane would not minimise his malice either, and sided with me in making Louise work to earn any trust. She was meeker than usual, which put me less on edge, and appeared to accept her standing within a very unlikely trio. The process was, however, slow.

"Would you two take your incessant dumbassary elsewhere?" Louise huffed, flinging a tea towel over her back. "There's no use in you coming here if you're just going to goof off."

"You're the one who wanted us here, Barnes," Shane pointed out. "So badly that you had to bribe us. You can't complain now."

"I wouldn't have had to bribe you if you had been so courteous as to include me in your debriefing."

I folded my arms over the varnished wood, only half satisfied with her frustration. "It's not our fault that you hadn't been there."

Though I was glad she had not.

Her shadow almost looked like it was laughing.

She sighed and made her way around to the other side where we sat. Her uniform was a little stained and the hem was fraying at the side, but I didn't think that she actually took notice. I wondered how she'd react if she was more alert —if the creature of roiling smoke wasn't there and she wasn't slowly dying.

I hadn't decided whether to take it literally yet —outward appearance seemed to suggest that that was exactly what was happening; and that she could disintegrate into dust if anyone away long enough. But her cheeks were not sunken and she hadn't become any thinner. Even the marks that should run up and down her forearms with her every scratch and grip did not last. Of course, I could not take those observations at face value. I of people was aware of masking problems for the outside world. Hiding the parts deemed too horrible to witness.

I glanced aside and pretended not to see.

"…We can't go past the outer limits," Shane finally caved. "Even if we walk straight into the woods towards Astoria we circle right back."

Louise blinked. "That's freaky."

"We thought that shadows were doing it, but now we know that's not the case," I added. "Though it does mean that essentially, no resident of

Pine Creek can leave."

"But you just came back," countered Louise. "You could've classified as a visitor."

"The house was still here," I deadpanned. "Dark and maintained, like it had been waiting for us."

"So maybe *that's* the criteria to be cursed," she speculated, her hollow gaze narrowing. "All residents, and those who lived here and came back. Great timing by the way, Grahams."

I rolled my eyes. "Tell me about it."

"That doesn't really help in understanding the curse, though," Shane spoke up. "Sure, we know a bit more about the conditions, but what about actually *breaking* it?"

"We know what the Daemons do," I confirmed. "So let's start there. Any ideas on how to counter the effects?"

Shane snorted. "Duh —be a better person."

"…That feels targeted," Louise murmured.

"Because it is," he hedged.

I pretended not to hear.

The bell on the door sounded.

Our heads turned towards a tall, well-built figure. Adorned in a lightly rained on three piece suit the colour of fresh blood from a finger prick and sporting a matching fedora, with impeccable caramel blond hair combed in a neat sweep over one side. Completely blocking out any eyes, were a pair of dark aviator sunglasses. They wore no smile nor scowl.

Every hair on my body prickled.

It was a stranger.

They waltzed in with their hands in their trousers' pockets, head turning this way and that in assessment. Their nose wrinkled before they sucked on their too white teeth.

Louise wasn't having any. "Who's this rich, frigid ass —?"

Shane elbowed her, interrupting her not quiet enough hiss, and visibly stiffened. I met his gaze, which was icy and alert. That only rendered the shudder that rattled through me so chillingly appropriate. I had never seen him react that way to anyone.

Louise, unfazed, sidled back to her station. "Can I *help* you, sir?"

The stranger didn't answer immediately. They stalked over to the bar —uncomfortably close to me and Shane, and clenched their jaw. At first glance, they appeared normal. But I then noticed something that made my heartbeat thump in my ears, and hold my breath.

The overhead light cast them no shadow.

"…Whiskey on the rocks."

Shane's hand suddenly shot out to grip mine.

The stranger's voice was one of the most beautiful that I had heard. If Shane's fingers hadn't been so tightly clasping my own, I wouldn't have remembered that I was in *Little Hatchet*. I wouldn't have remembered my name, and my lungs would not have remembered to expand.

My eyes darted to Louise dreamily drifting from the cabinet of glasses to the one of spirits, then to the refrigerator.

"Don't you get tired of a small town?" drawled the stranger.

My lips parted but no answer made it out. Shane pointedly squeezed my hand, spreading a bit of life in through the action. I took a long breath and glanced at him. His eyes had the little crescents of purple light again —brighter and more vivid. And they held me there, in reality.

Louise presented the drink. "I want to get out of here," she stated.

Something was wrong. And it wasn't Louise's honesty.

The stranger clicked their tongue but offered her a small smirk. "Do you really? Why haven't you tried?"

Something was very, *very* wrong.

Louise's eyes appeared a pale, glazed grey. "I'm really terrible," she said candidly. Her expression was slack but her voice came out as a clear statement, like a drill sergeant. "I don't deserve to leave."

They smiled a bit wider, revealing a set of canines too sharp and long to be normal. "Who told you that?" they purred —deep and low like a cat. "I could get you out of here. All you have to do is ask."

Her mouth obediently opened.

Shane let out a low growl, but the stranger barely paid any mind. They leaned back and took a sip of the whiskey. Louise stood motionless as if waiting for a cue. Only then did they turn their head towards us. Although we could not see their eyes behind the dark glass, I no longer had a doubt that they were not human.

"You must not have any fear to show up here," Shane hissed.

My eyes widened. *He knows them.*

"Mm. And you must not have any either, to be so blatantly obvious in your relentless pursuit of a happy ending. But I am sure you know that no such thing exists for unruly beasts, don't you?"

Their grin only widened at his strained silence. He held my hand even tighter; so desperately that feared he might break my bones. But I didn't dare to let go. Whatever was happening to Louise, I didn't want the same happening to me. The contact between us was clearly a counter to it, even though I could do nothing but breathe.

"Why are you here," demanded Shane. "What have I done?"

The stranger shrugged nonchalantly. "I was merely sent to check that things are unfolding in the way they are supposed to. Morningstar knows you would not ensure it."

"I have not deviated."

"Oh I know," they chuckled. "But see…this isn't just about you, beast. You may be holding it together, but there has been a detection of improper use of resources." Their head tilted slightly.

I knew that they were looking at me, then.

I was sure my face reflected my fear.

The stranger then stood; flawless and professional in their movement, and left a bank note on top of the counter beside a barely touched short glass of amber. They tipped the rim of their hat and flashed those sharp teeth, before making for the door. The last trace of them was the echo of the bell ringing well into the quiet.

My throat opened and I stumbled from my stool —caught by Shane's hand still fast in mine. I had a million questions on the tip of my tongue.

But Louise thudded to the floor.

"*Jesus*!" I cried, forcefully ripping away and clambering up over the counter. I landed next to her. "Is she okay?"

"She'll be fine," Shane sighed, leaning forward. His eyes had reverted to their usual, unnatural state. A chill crept up my spine at the sight. "But she won't remember when she wakes up."

I wished that I wouldn't remember.

I moved to my haunches and stared up at him, pleadingly. My fingers dug into the sides of my arms to remind myself that I was awake. "What the hell is going on?" I asked. "And who *was* that?"

His gaze narrowed into that piercing icy glare. All that it did was fill me with trepidation. No crackling held our staring. Nothing but cold pain and distrust. He winced like the pain was physical.

"I didn't want this to come up," he admitted. "I…I wanted to believe that I could ignore it until the end, like normal."

"What is *normal* about any of this, Hyde!" I snapped. "And what are you not telling me?"

Shane dithered, pushing back from the counter. His jaw looked like it might crack. "I know a lot more about this town than it seems."

"Clearly," I hedged.

"And I've been here for longer than you think."

My brows furrowed. "How long?"

"I…I've lost the concept of time."

Frustration clouded my sense of patience. "*Pelo amor de Deus, isso é uma loucura. Eu vou ficar louco,*" I ground out, scrambling to my feet. I grabbed my tote bag but went still when he took hold of my wrist. It was loose. It was a request.

"Alexander," he said, voice clear and serious.

I cringed. The way my name sounded on his tongue still set off giddy butterflies in my stomach. Even in this situation. I gritted my teeth. "Don't lie to me," I warned. "Don't do that, at least."

"Okay."

His hand moved. Very slowly —with the intent to allow me pull away. But I watched his fingers uncurl and lower to mine. *This* did not feel like friendship. They didn't dare to get greedy and lace. It set off dangerous flickers, which caused my hand to twitch. He paused. My eyes roved from between us to his own. They burned with a desperation.

It was only then, after that person in red had made my mind wander, that an idea finally settled: Shane Hyde was not entirely human.

The prospect, however, did not scare me as much as it should.

"You have to know something," he began. It was very matter-of-fact. "There is a world in the shadows and light of yours. I come from it. And in every story, there is a hero and a villain."

My breath hitched. I wasn't sure about where this was going.

"*You* are the hero," Shane declared. His head nodded earnestly like he was trying his hardest to convince not just me but also himself. Then his eyes broke contact for a split second. "And I am your villain."

"What?"

At first, I thought it a delusion. It sounded ridiculous —we didn't live in some sort of fairytale. Life was not formulaic and wildly idyllic. But I recalled the creatures that lurked in shadows and the barrier around Pine Creek, and the other little things that I could no longer explain.

And the stranger.

Suddenly it was not far-fetched. I had been thrust into something that was not normal from the very start and it was only startling me now.

"…Are you a monster?" I asked again. Just as softly.

He couldn't even answer this time.

He loosened the grip he had on my hand. "I have done bad things," he confessed. "And I can't ask if you might be okay with that. *I'm* the terrible one who does not deserve to leave. That was why I told you to stay away from me." He met my gaze then. "I can only bring misery. And that person in red…that was another reason."

"What were they?"

"A demon," he stiffly offered. "A real one."

I shivered. Whatever dark forces they had used lingered in the cold of the air. *A real one*. Did that mean it was all real —sin, Hell…God? And Their wrath. It did trigger another question. How exactly did Shane Hyde know a demon? My gaze narrowed. Was he—?

"I'm just as trapped here as you are," he assured. "More so."

That stifled my suspicion. If he was being punished along with the rest of us, then he couldn't be a malicious demon. And who was he to decide what he was good for? If anything, he had been the unlikely replacement to quell a loneliness I had been repressing. And I didn't want to lose that.

"I must ask you something," I murmured, briefly glancing down.

"Anything."

My heart skipped a beat but I frowned deeply to stop myself from giving the feeling away. "Do you…do you want to keep being a villain?"

His smile was tired and sad. "I, uh, don't have the choice. I am not the writer of the book on your life."

I opened my mouth to say something else, when Louise groaned from behind the counter. After a beat of deliberation and the careful retreat of my hand to my chest, I moved to help her up. Shane was right —she didn't remember a thing; she just had the thought that she had slipped and briefly knocked herself out from the impact.

I tried to act normal.

I didn't mention anything about the demon, nor Shane's revelation. I wasn't sure if she *should* know. It felt…personal. Not the drop-by demon, but the internal torture. The notion that he was a bad person —and worse than Louise. I watched him light a cigarette; watched the turquoise of his eyes fluctuate between luminescent and dull; and I watched the hope die within them. I walked away with my head turning back every few seconds in a way which was likely irritating, but one which I couldn't help.

I stared at my ceiling for a very long time after curling up in bed. The past two days were only beginning to process. My mind was attempting to wrap around a few incomprehensible issues. The most pressing: Shane

Hyde was more of a mystery than I had previously thought. There was no question that he had wholeheartedly meant his warning to stay away. He had kept information to himself. He'd admitted to wanting to keep it that way before the demon had quite literally forced his hand.

And it implied that he was minacious.

But what of the things he done to actively watch out for me? I tried to align those with some kind of agenda but it would not fit perfectly.

His metaphor was stuck in my head and wouldn't budge. At face value it could simply be the way in which he saw himself in my life —a terrible influence and the voice of recklessness.

He was no angel.

He wasn't wrong in that regard.

But the more that I thought about it, the more literally I considered the meaning. What if it wasn't a book, and we truly were a pair of adversaries locked in some kind of stalemate?

Though those looks and the touch of his fingers did not feel like hate. Quite the opposite. That led to the other issue.

That frightening, violent thing had taken hold —reacting accordingly when he got too close. It had to be wrong, then. It had to be a reprehensible crime if all that I saw in his gaze when he spoke of what we were, was a devastation so sharp and unhealing.

I had to bury it. Though, the shameless and naïve reader in me wanted to spite the notion of outside forces dictating anything in life.

I turned over and stared at the wall.

It would be easier to disregard it all and believe only what I could see. It was difficult to swallow everything otherwise. Difficult to be defiant.

Because the hero was not meant to fall in love with the villain.

There was a searing and gaping agony resonating throughout my body. It concentrated in the middle of my chest.

I was aimless and very aware of one foot going in front of the other, following only the inviting sensation of ice.

It was scorching like there were coals beneath my bare feet.

Blood streamed from the middle of my palm; through the gaps of my fingers and down to the floor. A long, purposeful cut from the base of my forefinger to the opposite end of my wrist stung in the humid air.

Every few feet, a torch burned and a buzzing fly landed.

The light illuminated rows and rows of cells barred with impervious, unreal metal. Alongside the ice, the smell of salt led me along corridors and passages with which I was unfamiliar. The soothing was my guide; the chance to alleviate the hissing heat was my motivation.

I stopped when the scent was overwhelming.

It was different from the other cells. The bars were the reason. They were a gritty off-white; stained brown with age…and handprints.

I stopped at the viewing side. The burning had ceased.

A great figure the colour of silver sat in the middle, chained. Its large wings were unfolded behind it. I took a step closer; yearning for more of that cold. Then the creature lifted its head, and I was met with turquoise blue eyes with pupils half-ringed in flaring purple.

The sound of my own gasp drove me from deep sleep.

It was the dead of night —not even birdsong pierced the silence. I kept panting even as the shock eased, drenched in a strangely odd cold sweat. It hadn't been near hot enough for that to happen. My eyelids blinked out tears left unwept, feeling them slide down both cheeks…before I finally realised something alarming.

I remembered the dream I had just had.

In detail, like I had lived it.

And it wasn't fading.

the lost girl

LOUISE

THREE DAYS LATER

+

IT HAD BEEN stupid to think that life would always remain a certain kind of…easy. That people easily forgave, and that time easily healed all of the disaster she had very easily left in her wake.

But Louise Barnes had finally seen that instead of scraping away the broken path and relaying each brick, she had smothered hot tar over the pieces in the hopes that it would smooth itself.

That had inadvertently created two messes to rectify.

She was living through it now —upending the hardened tar to expose the initial damage. Alexander Grahams had been the sheer knife to shatter and slice up the debris, and Shane Hyde had bulldozed his way before and after. Mostly after.

He sided with Alexander.

For whatever reason, they were the only person to whom he paid any attention. The only one he would look at for longer than a few seconds.

Louise couldn't tell if it was with warmth or with hunger. She couldn't question their connection, nor Shane's razored shunning. Even she knew that it was treatment that she deserved.

But she didn't like trailing alone behind them.

Louise Barnes was a stranger to solitude. The concept was persistent and didn't possess a filter; all while offering her no sympathy. It wanted to be her favourite friend —she could tell. In numerous situations, such as yesterday, solitude had squeezed between her and confidence —prying the wedge between normalcy and much crueller *reality* wider and pushing her further from others.

Solitude was not inherently a bad person.

Louise had simply been so attached to its twin and opposite. Viciously so, that when that friend had left she was sure that life itself was over. If anything, solitude was the only one who had been real with her.

She had learned some very hard truths as soon as everyone around her had grown and moved on. For a long time, she had been stuck at twelve as if existence peaked there. It had taken her too long to realise even after seventeen that there was more to the world than what she saw directly in front of her face.

Ruth Barnes had taught her daughter that in life, there were those who led and those who followed. Of course, all should follow God foremost. Then women followed their husbands. But thereafter it was a free for all. Young Louise had figured that since she had been born a woman and that within her household she had the last say, she would lead elsewhere.

'*Lead*' had been misconstrued. She knew that now.

She had been a bully. There was no excuse.

Solitude and her Daemon would not stop whispering to her that this was what she needed. A sudden and unforgiving reality check. She wasn't the centre of attention; she didn't command respect for the sole reason of '*because I said so*', like her mother —and she certainly didn't have any friends. The girls she had once referred to as such had grown up to be the daughters her mother would have wanted. Louise had undoubtably fallen short —quite literally in her opinion, since she took after Ruth's height.

But even though she didn't like pumpkin spiced lattes and *Mary Janes* and four by four SUVs, she had the feeling that she could still be a better person than any of them. Even in the identity limbo she found herself.

Ruth Barnes did not like Louise's new friend, solitude.

She blamed it for all of her daughter's new grunge fashion, metallic taste and reclusive behaviour. She blamed her Daemon too —though that actually held more truth. But since the entire town had been cursed with the creatures, Ruth had laid off of her a little.

She was now too preoccupied with the exposed disintegration of her own marriage.

Louise had first learned that her mother was a regular human being —and not the mouth of God —when she had turned fifteen years old.

It was the last birthday party she had ever had or wanted. Everything had been planned meticulously; exactly in the way that Ruth had dictated a budding queen of school should host an event; and initially it was going off without a hitch. That snag, had been Carley Vasquez waltzing into the party in a cocktail dress far too similar to Louise's. And it was without a doubt that it better suited Carley's equally distributed height.

Ruth hadn't hesitated to scream as much.

Beyond the burn of humiliation and ruination of the idolisation of her mother, Louise could not forget the sight of the girl with cinnamon hair, crying. The audible sobs that she knew had been fake, because Carley was a clinical psychopath. It was not as if she was incapable of crying, but in that moment Louise was sure that she had not felt anything in reaction to the commotion. Rather, she would have sooner laughed than blubbered in shock and remorse as everyone believed she had.

Revenge was a funny thing.

Louise had had the opportunity to reveal Carley to be the person she truly was, regardless of her condition. But frankly, it wasn't her business. And another memory of her lingered: of an emotionally scarce, desperate girl who had decided that she trusted her friends enough to tell them about her diagnosis. Of her asking them to take it to the grave if she never told anyone herself, and simply to treat her as any other person.

Louise couldn't ruin her life over something like that.

That first taste of friendship had been precious to her —someone who up until that point had thought of her mother's hierarchy as her on top of her whole school. She had savoured and clung to that trust.

Which was what had made it hurt all the more when that foundation of glass had broken beneath her.

"Louise," her mother's poisonous voice said from the doorway. "Are you not going to ballet class?"

"No," said the teenager, removing one earphone and setting down her book. "I don't go anymore —we've already talked about this. Besides, I doubt Madam Claire can even get out of bed."

"Well, do something about that hair at least," Ruth huffed. She shook her head in disapproval. "It's an absolute rat's nest."

"Can you please just leave me alone?" Louise snapped, anger welling at the reference to her hair. "If you have nothing useful to say, go back to arguing with Dad over the custody of your succulents."

"*Louise Margret Esther Barnes*."

She cringed. She absolutely hated her full name.

"Where did my sweet, obedient girl go?" her mother asked. "You used to thrive. Then you stopped being friends with those lovely girls. It's all this time alone, in the dark. It's changed you, and now you look like you belong with…*Maggie Elwoods* and those hooligans. Who even are you?"

"What, do you only ask because I'm not like you anymore?" Louise scoffed. "But don't worry, I'm trying to figure that out."

"At least breathe some fresh air, for God's sake!"

"Ugh, *fine*!"

The slam of the door was both satisfying and not.

Ruth had some nerve saying that, perpetually in her Winter dressing gown. Her parents didn't leave the house anymore, and they were running out of physical money quickly. With Louise as the involuntary designated housekeeper, it was her duty to buy groceries and other errands. It might not have been all that bad if her parents weren't driving her up the wall.

Louise's Daemon pressed a ghostly hand to her shoulder.

A chill ran down her spine as if someone dropped ice cubes right down the back of her shirt.

She heard the breath again.

It was shallow and steady and directly in her ear, like some disgusting creep. And she swore that she heard laughter, too. She knew why it was reprimanding her. Many years ago, she might have cared that she yelled at her mother and cut back so disrespectfully.

But she wasn't having it now. The status of '*mother*' was not going to be abused any longer.

Louise pushed off her spitefully unmade bed and trudged over to the mirror. She was still in her long pyjamas at two o'clock in the afternoon. Solitude expressed its concern over putting on presentable clothes while her Daemon countered it with horrible thoughts of self-loathing.

She had never seen herself as less than pretty.

It was difficult to see now with her tear-stained puffy face and running makeup. Especially with her hair; a length of honey blonde at which she had been ceremoniously hacking with the kitchen scissors for a couple of months. It trailed just over her shoulders now, coiling and matting without proper care. And proper scissors.

Louise pinched a clump between her thumb and forefinger, wondering how bad it might look if she cut it again.

What's the point, said solitude. *No one really cares. About you or your hair. They're too busy dealing with their own crumbling lives.*

Her Daemon fed on her hesitation and consideration; it tugged on the arm holding her hair so that she felt it at the root, on her scalp. She winced, letting go. She would not cut it today.

"I'll curl it," she announced to no one but the concepts in her head — and the shadow wafting over the back of her neck.

It was easier said than done.

Louise was promptly bombarded with snark and snide with each flick of her wrist. It was very possible that she would burn herself. She knew that her Daemon would love nothing more. But she urged her hand to stay steady and away from the last row of hair at the back and around her ears —which left it uneven and haphazard, but more visually tolerable.

Another great compromise was one thin sweater over another, and a pair of flared jazz pants. If she couldn't see her body, nobody else would. She stuffed her feet into ankle boots and shrugged on a tan furred jacket.

Imagine if you died, mused solitude.

"Wouldn't that be something," she mumbled, turning away from her reflection.

She could think of five people who would be quite relieved.

Mostly, Louise Barnes just wanted to stop feeling shitty.

That's why she crossed the street to stomp along the opposite sidewalk after she spotted Donatello Ricci on his day off.

He was sauntering towards his house with a steaming hot drink in his hands; loose bun bouncing with each step. At first, he was too distracted by his own feet to notice her. But his eye caught the end of her movement and Louise frowned at the realisation that he had seen her.

She dithered. It was too late to run outright.

Maybe if she just kept walking…

"Barnes?"

Louise started as Alexander Grahams suddenly rounded one corner at the intersection and stumbled to a halt in front of her.

"Alexander," she breathed.

From the edge of her vision, she saw that Donatello had stopped in his tracks, too. The expression on his face was a mixture of confusion and an emotion Louise would rather not name. She didn't need the reminder.

"What are you doing here?" Alexander asked.

They were dressed in a way she was still getting used to —a shirt and tie tucked into an argyle sweater, all under a leather jacket —but she had to admit that it suited them. It was the type of style that could be altered to better reflect who they were and how they were slowly growing to be more comfortable in their skin. It wasn't as customised as they wanted, but that was due to their far less understanding father.

Alexander had since explained their predicament to an extent that they thought necessary. Louise was resolved to give them the respect owed.

"Help me," she hissed without too much thought; subtly referring to Donatello by darting her eyes back and forth in his direction. He was now marching towards them, determined yet still not all that confident.

"Come on, Alexander," she said ostentatiously —loud and wobbly. "I have that…that thing to show you, remember?"

They blinked at her, then glanced at the quickly approaching boy, and finally caught on. "…Right," they deadpanned, readjusting their glasses. "In the woods, you said?"

She turned sharply to lead the way. "That's right!"

"Louise," Donatello quipped. "You look well."

He'd *just* caught them.

Solitude swore and her Daemon started laughing. In fact, she felt its claws caress her shoulders like a proud parent.

Louise slowly turned back around. She didn't know what face she was making, but given Donatello visibly flinching at her reception, it wasn't friendly. Which was a little ridiculous, given the entire fifteen inches he had on her. His Daemon towered too —just as mocking as her own. But his eagerness did not diminish in her unease. He straightened, cleared his throat and shot Alexander a brief assessing glare —which they returned without hesitation.

"There's no need to lie," Louise clipped, offering him the same.

Donatello shuffled a bit from foot to foot, deliberating on what to say with the little time that she was granting him. He fiddled with the handle of his messenger bag, which for some reason, annoyed her.

"I…I like your hair."

Her face pinched in disappointment. "*Ugh.*"

She'd give up —unable to deal with one-sided small talk. She wordlessly took Alexander by the arm and turned them away with her.

They left Donatello scowling there alone, free to jump to all and any conclusions he wished.

Alexander edged away as soon as they were out of sight.

Fighting the sense of rejection, Louise then paused to remind herself of who they were, and more importantly, what she was to them. *Nothing*. She didn't deserve their quiet tolerance or cooperation.

"...Thanks," she mumbled.

They simply stared. It was their default response to anything that she said, and it still unnerved her. Alexander had the kind of gaze that seemed to stare right into you; to pick you apart and reveal all of your wickedness.

Solitude told her that it was karma.

Her Daemon told her it was mercy.

"That was bad," Alexander stated after several seconds of judgement and condescension. "Can't you even talk to human beings anymore?"

Louise simply groaned.

Despite the spur of the moment panic, there indeed *was* something that Louise wanted to show Alexander. Their playing along had reminded her of a makeshift treehouse within Riverbend Wood —the closest patch of forest around the back of her yard.

"You don't need to meet up with Hyde?" she asked.

"No."

The answer was immediate and awkward. Maybe the two of them had had a fight. Louise scratched the back of her head.

"Want to come to my clubhouse? It *is* actually in the woods."

Alexander frowned. “That’s profoundly sad.”

“It’s got a few notes on the curse.”

“…Fine.”

Louise hadn’t been there in a week, but she could remember the last time she had used it for its original purpose. At six, she had begged her father for a proper treehouse instead of her mother’s idea of a Wendy House on the front lawn. Since six years old had been insignificant to her parents and Ruth had hoped that she would grow bored of it, they had caved and built a small hutch on stilts in the branches of a sturdy oak. It had a rung ladder hanging off the side for when Louise felt adventurous, otherwise she heaved up the slats up along the tree trunk instead.

Decorations had been natural and simple: moss and ivy draped from corner to corner and down the support beams, and shelves lining one wall —adjacent to the other door that led out to a small balcony. Louise would drag out a beanbag during Summer but it had long since rotted after she had left it out accidently in multiple rain storms.

Alexander ducked below the angled roof and took in the hodgepodge of an interior. While it was minimalistic, Louise had added little trinkets to hang from hooks and catch the sun. A large collage of band posters and memorabilia were nailed by the door.

She didn’t care what they thought of it. That wasn’t why they had both come. But she found her Daemon chuckling softly at Alexander’s pursed lips and raised eyebrows in focused assessment.

Mercy.

What about any of this was merciful?

Her parents would faint at the mention but Louise was beginning to doubt all she had ever known to be truth. That included her faith, which had not ever been on the rocks before.

Alexander fiddled with a dreamcatcher by the window pane, made of rope and sticks. "I keep dreaming of an iron beast," they murmured.

"Oh?"

The amount of times they had initiated any conversation with her was few and far between. She didn't want to seem too eager, but she offered her ear by leaning a little closer. Her Daemon nudged her further.

"…It's all chained and bloody, but not with its own blood," they went on. "I don't think it can bleed."

"Any idea what its significance could be?" she asked as she motioned for the balcony. She sat down cross-legged on one side, and offered them the other. They both stuck their legs through the gaps in the metal railing.

"Not really. It's…like a living statue," said Alexander, their shoulders slumping. They stared out at the trees. "I also learned its name."

"Chained…uh, is it some kind of prisoner?"

They nodded. "I think so. It's always in a dungeon made of salt."

Louise followed their line of sight, exhaling slowly. "Well. I've been told that sometimes, dreams have meanings."

"You have no idea," Alexander frowned at their left palm. "But they don't feel like messages. They feel like memories. Like I was…*there*."

Her gaze narrowed. "Is there anything familiar about this…beast?"

They looked at her —and for a moment she wondered why, before she saw the blatant fear written there. "Its eyes."

"Hey, why do you look so scared?"

"Because it looked like some sort of demon," breathed Alexander.

the hurricane

ALEXANDER

WHATEVER WALL I had previously managed to break down was adamantly rising back up between me and Shane Hyde.

All of that time that we had spent together was suddenly under threat to mean nothing at all. And I didn't know what to make of it.

I hadn't left the house in three days in an effort to both avoid him and get over the roil of feelings tangled within me. All of that time only served as a distraction —because my father had only cracked down on his frigid disapproval whenever he had gotten the rare chance of seeing me, and the only person I could talk to was *Louise Barnes*, of all people.

It had not changed anything between us though —I still recoiled at the close proximity of her and she politely shuffled away; darkness bubbling over her back. But I no longer felt like she should disappear.

Not necessarily because she deserved another chance. I was sure that there was someone else who did. And if they might be who I thought they were, then maybe Louise could have a stab at it too.

After telling her about the dreams I had started to remember I felt torn and conflicted about their contents as well as Shane's mentioned goings-on. With each time I fell asleep my senses were tossed about and thrown.

I hadn't thought that remembering would have such a side effect. As I had told Louise: it didn't feel like something yet to come, or a warning.

The brick beneath my fingers had been real; the smell of salt had been too strong to be conjured; and those eyes *knew* me.

That notion was as terrifying as falling for someone I shouldn't. Deep down, I had a feeling that the imprisoned beast deserved its punishment. Just as Shane had implied about his. I had not yet spoken to the beast but I was worried about what it might say.

That I knew it, too.

And that was horrifying because every time I met its searing gaze my heart would flood with an onslaught of vengeful anger and a painful love. There was a wall even between it and me. But I hated the idea of looking at someone and feeling things without reason or prior meeting.

Though how in the world could I have fallen in love with a demon?

I wondered if it had anything to do the blood dripping down my hand. As much as I could not stop thinking of the iron beast in a salt dungeon, I could not stop thinking about Shane Hyde either. My eyes kept looking for him at every hint of smoke and glimpse of black cloth.

And it was dangerous.

So I kept my head down when I walked to the grocery store the next day, and waded as quickly as I could through the fog. It had receded to my shins and the rain had lightened.

I didn't expect to see Louise there.

She looked like she had just woken up. She wore a large shirt and pair of board shorts, and boots that were definitely not made for the outdoors. I did a double take as we nearly ran into each other in one of the aisles. Her eyes grew just as wide. She glanced down at her shorts and then back at me, and almost appeared to be blushing.

"Whoa," I breathed, swapping my basket over to my other arm. "Was it an emergency? Didn't you have time to get dressed?"

"No," she said through her teeth, fists tightening over the sides of her own basket. "I just…I wasn't planning on running into anyone."

I frowned. "In this little town?"

Her cheeks got a bit redder.

"I can pretend I didn't see you," I offered coolly. "For old time's sake."

She guiltily dropped my gaze.

I sidled off with the temptation of a smile playing on my lips, and left her to stew in her own choices. Personally, I didn't care. I had gotten used to seeing certain residents wandering around in pyjamas and gowns and seeing her at the grocery store in hers wasn't a big deal.

Some people's Daemons were simply draining faster and deeper.

Perhaps that was from where some envy had come whenever someone eyed me in completely ordinary clothing —me, and anyone who had their general shit together.

I didn't run into Louise again until we approached the front counter to check out. Donatello Ricci was leaning back against an '*over twenty-ones only*' sign, arms folded and dark circles visible. The picture of death. His curly hair was knotted in a painful looking ponytail, with his brown eyes unfocused and his Daemon looking ravenous.

Until Louise dumped her basket onto the counter, vaguely sneering.

Donatello obediently rang up her items and occasionally stole a glance at her face. The dead expression refused to go as she stared directly back at him. She wasn't so nervous and skittish now.

"Uh…that'll be eleven thirty-four," he murmured.

She fished down the front of her t-shirt and produced a twenty.

Their hands brushed ever so slightly in the exchange. I saw the flinch in the cashier's fingers. Louise had no reaction whatsoever.

"I…I hope you have a nice day, Louise," he tried.

Her brown brows shot up in surprise, and wisps of her Daemon began to flicker over her back.

I slapped a hand over my mouth and coughed to disguise a consequent burst of laughter; my eyes widening comically.

Donatello flushed, turning a very clashing pink. "Uh, I mean both of you —both of you I guess, er…have a nice day."

I looked between the two of them, momentarily regretting not having a bag of popcorn on hand.

Louise scoffed, narrowing her icy eyes in disbelief. "Don't talk to me, Donny." Then she turned on her heel and stomped towards the exit.

His expression of defeat morphed lightning fast into a scowl as I then placed my basket before him.

"Don't take it personally," I offered. "She doesn't like *anyone*."

Donatello bared his teeth. "She seems to tolerate you."

"*I* tolerate *her*."

"Doesn't really look like it from where I'm standing."

I scoffed at his frustration. "Even if I didn't hate her as much as I did, you know what she did to me, asshole. How can you dare to entertain the idea of me being a '*threat*' to whatever weird crush you seem to have on her? What a sick joke."

Colour tinged his cheeks again even through a snarl. "I…I didn't…"

I slammed the exact change onto the counter and stuffed the items into my tote bag. I didn't wait around for him to finish his sentence, and left without a further word. The audacity was disgusting.

I was so busy seething, that I didn't realise that I had started walking in the direction of *Straws & Fries*.

My head turned to the windows —and my heart stopped. Shane Hyde was hunched there at the bar section, deep in thought over a tall glass of chocolate milkshake. I was sure my breath audibly snagged in my throat too, before his gaze roved…and landed on me.

I had wanted to forget.

I really had.

But as soon as I saw the blue through the glass I remembered it all at once; everything at full force. And it hurt and exhilarated in a vast whirlwind of contradiction. Like a blizzard in the heat of Hell.

His lips moved.

Minus five.

I blinked in disbelief. I should move. I should walk away and go back to the house I hated so much, just so that I didn't give in to temptation. So I didn't give in to him.

My feet betrayed me and followed the beckon Shane never gestured; walking straight into the diner and stopping in front of him. I had expected his face to reflect a sense of hurt or anger. But I couldn't read it at all.

"Grahams," he said.

"Hyde."

"…I see you heeded my warning."

I slid onto the stool beside him. "I tried to. But I…couldn't."

His eyebrows knitted together as if I had stabbed him. It wasn't easy to understand his reaction. Though I supposed that if he had wanted me to stay away from him and failed, he had reason to be upset. However, it didn't look like he was mad. It looked like my admittance broke him.

"Why," he asked.

I shrugged. "Maybe I want to see all that you are, and like it still."

Shane almost seemed surprised. Then he drooped once more, his gaze dulling and his expression hardening. He didn't answer. He glanced down at his milkshake and swirled the paper straw.

The diner was empty this morning.

That was not what drew my attention. It was the quiet patience of the air; the softness of the lighting. The fact was, we were all alone. Not even the honorary bartender was in sight.

"…I've never had chocolate," I said offhandedly.

He paused. "Want to try?"

I started. "What."

He slowly slid the glass over, his eyes on mine. "Have a sip."

He had clearly been drinking it already. It wouldn't be as if I was the first to put my mouth to that straw. However, the fact that no one would be watching gave me all the nerve.

There were no words to describe how I felt in that forbidden moment. In the entire motion of me reaching for the straw, then taking it between my lips. In the slow sip. I could feel him staring as I withdrew.

"…How is it?"

He had to repeat the question for it to register.

"Um, it's nice."

And I was pathetic.

His gaze held me there for a moment longer, before the door opened. My body automatically flinched. A couple of grown-ups walked in. Even my head lowered —if anything, for the sake of not being recognised.

Shane's fingers nudged mine, startling me. "Let's go somewhere else and talk."

I swallowed. "Okay. But I should drop off my groceries first."

"I'll come with you," he offered.

"Are you sure that's a good idea?"

"Just to make sure you come back out again."

I drew my lips into a line. "*Esse garoto*…"

"I wouldn't call me that if I were you," he hedged, the hint of a spark coming back to his eye as we settled the bill and prepared to leave.

"What? Wait, when did you find out what it meant?"

"A while back," he admitted. "Looked in a dictionary. I'm not a '*boy*'. Maybe you'll come to learn that, Grahams."

My brows shot upwards.

His smirk widened into a smile. "What thought popped into your head just now? I was referring to my age. I'm half a year older than you."

"Uh…just, do you speak that way to everyone?"

"No, it's just part of my natural charm."

I braced myself as I pushed and turned the front door's knob. I knew that my father would most likely be moping in the living room, staring blankly at a television that didn't work. I found reassurance in Shane standing by the porch, not to come inside unless he heard something amiss.

I walked in calmly and casually, heading straight for the kitchen. I was not going to reveal that I had still been sleeping here unless forced to.

"…I see you came slinking back eventually."

I tensed —but I didn't let it stop me from putting the food away, even as my hands shook. "I'm only dropping off all the stuff I bought. I have somewhere to be."

"Where on Earth do you keep disappearing to, Alex?" Hugh sneered.

That hurts.

HE WANTS TO HURT YOU.

Get out.

SCREAM.

You need to leave.

SCREAM.

Go before it becomes too late.

FIGHT.

No. He can't be aware of what he's doing.

This instance felt spiteful with intention.

But…he had never done that to me before. Even through the begging for parental love and acceptance of the smallest things, he had had that much decency. Was his Daemon bringing out…the true harshness of him?

I felt the blood boil too close to the surface of my skin.

"I've been investigating how to get rid of your damn curse," I hissed. "Not that I expected you to be too grateful."

"Curse?" my father only scoffed. "Hm. I suppose it is."

"That, and I can't stand hearing your opinion on everything."

"Then live appropriately."

My lips ripped back in a low growl.

Get out.

SCREAM.

He did not sound angry. His head was not even turned to address me. That tone was cold and flat, as if he could no longer be bothered.

I didn't care. I couldn't care if his Daemon was responsible —I wasn't about to tolerate it. I marched back towards the front door. "I don't have the patience for this. I'm leaving."

"Do you only know how to run, Alex?"

"*Esse não é meu nome*!" It came out as a scream; like the sudden cork out of a bottle. "That's not my damn name," I repeated, remembering how he was not fluent. "And you know it."

Hugh slowly tilted his head. "…Your mother really screwed me over by teaching you Portuguese and leaving me out of it."

"You didn't even want to try! How can you *say* that?"

I was almost certain that Shane Hyde could hear all of it from outside. It didn't stop me. I wasn't about to hold back. Not when I had the chance. The rage consumed me beyond the notion of self-control.

Hugh would not respond.

My hands balled into fists after flinging open the door. "*Oh meu Deus, eu te odeio, seu burro crítico*," I ranted, before slamming it behind me.

I had to stumble back as Shane ran forward.

He'd heard it. I could tell by the look on his face. Searing sympathy. I wasn't sure if I would appreciate his pity —usually I would want to be alone in these situations. I had never told my father I hated him, or called him an ass. And for some reason, I didn't mind that Shane had glimpsed that part of me. I hoped with every foolish fibre of my being that he would come to like it still.

"Grahams," he whispered. His voice was hardly ever so soft.

I knew that unending tears were falling down my face. I was tempted to furiously wipe them away. "…Fuck," I rasped, desperate for air.

He raised a hand, and beckoned me.

I was pulled by that bit of rope.

We fell in step and veered off back towards the main street as fast as my pace dictated. For a long while, Shane did not utter a single mention of it. It was not that he was trying to figure out what to say. Rather, he gave me the opportunity to feel everything. To cry.

And he didn't walk away.

It was only when my eyes were dry and I had stopped sniffling that he even looked at me at all. I then realised why though. If he had given me that face any earlier I would have pushed him away in a red, blind rage of mortification and shame. But now…it was understanding. That turquoise wasn't aglow with ferocity and intrigue. It was plain and clear and real.

He *got* it. In some capacity.

"It would seem that both our houses suck," he offered.

"Yeah." I tried a tired smile.

It didn't work.

"You…don't have to try to seem more okay than you really are," he added delicately. "Especially not in front of…*ahem*. I can see how bad it is. Last time you cried for nearly fifteen minutes."

I pressed my lips together to stop them from trembling. When we had stepped into thick forestry from the brick and tar of civilisation, I had still been crying. Now, as we ambled through the maze of trees, could he see the pain that prickled there? Had I always been so transparent to him?

"Maybe *you* should be my new therapist —you sound just like them," I joked. The lightness of it didn't last. "You know, anyone else would be awkwardly backing away, heading for the hills at this point."

Shane took my self-deprecation personally.

"I'm not anyone else."

My feet faltered, but he caught my arm. Only for a moment. His hand retreated as our gazes aligned. I let out a soft sigh and readjusted my long cardigan. "…What's your house like?" I asked. "Any better?"

We didn't drift to widen the distance between us.

"My Mom thinks I hate her," he began. "My adorable, naïve and self-centred little brother is nosy; and my stepfather thinks I'm a monster."

"Oh."

"But I do," he said through clenched teeth. "I hate my Mom. I hate my little brother, and I hate his Dad. I hate them…because they should hate me more. And I can't pretend that I belong there; that they have no reason to hate me; as if they deserve what I…"

"I don't hate you."

The words tumbled out of my mouth before I could think about what I was saying. But I believed them. I wasn't yet sure of what he had done to deserve that strong of a response, but I didn't want to be another name on a list. I wanted to be the someone he knew wouldn't leave. But I was slightly frightened at the prospect of listening to his reasons.

What if I couldn't maintain my resolve?

Despite my selfish determination, there was a chance that I would not be able to look past whatever it was that he had done. However…there was that horned, winged iron beast in a cell made of salt; dripping blood that wasn't its own. And for some reason, I didn't hate *it*.

Shane gave me a grave, knowing look. "You will, when we're finished with this conversation."

"*Why*?" I genuinely asked. "Have you done reprehensible things? Let me hear them anyway. I'll be the judge of whether or not I hate you after."

He drew a sharp breath and rolled his head —frustration pushing out through the apprehension. "I think we should sit down."

We found a pile of boulders and rocks sufficiently free of wet slippery moss and unidentified fungi. I sat right beside him, turned inwards so that I could read his face as he spoke. Because I had the feeling that he would try his best to turn away at every opportunity.

I wanted him to think that he could face it.

I wanted him to think that he could face me.

He didn't, for a good few seconds —and collected his thoughts while frowning at his sneakers. Then he started to speak, and I let him.

"You know how you want to save Pine Creek?" he murmured. "I think it's brave. I think…given the time you have this round, it makes a lot of sense for you to reach that decision. But I have to be realistic with you. It will not be possible. Now, I…I know that I've been somewhat helpful to you, but I made a promise that I wouldn't lie to you, Grahams. I intend to keep it." He turned his head to look at me, then. Dared to see if I was still there, still listening. I was.

"You may not believe me at first," he warned. "I will not blame you. But you need to know, so you can understand. The curse is more involved than it appears. No one else can tell, but I always know. We're trapped in this time loop —a series of events that can't be avoided. And it's all my fault. I'm the reason —I'm the monster. This is why I hate my…'*family*'. It's because we're not a family. We're all strangers. I'm an intruder. And I have to watch them die, over and over again. And there is nothing that I can do to stop it."

Traces of emotion had billowed away with each sentence. And though his eyes remained a flat blue, that icy, stony façade returned and hardened there. Maybe to be the last line of defence against judgement.

I really wanted to hold his hand.

It was difficult to comprehend what he was saying fully. It all sounded like science fiction, but I had evidence before me that we were alive, and that things weren't right. I felt the darkness; I'd seen the evil.

"What…what did you do?" I whispered. "It's okay, you can tell me."

He really didn't want to.

But he forced his lips to part, and his throat to work. "…I killed them." It was barely audible but I heard it under the small, darkening sky. "I kill everyone, at the end of each cycle. In a vicious blur of blood and claws. It keeps repeating and I keep turning into this…beast that feels too much."

I swallowed uneasily. I could picture it, maybe. I didn't know what a monstrous version of him resembled, but it seemed far removed from the too perfect face I saw before me now.

"Every…*everyone*?" I murmured.

He flinched slightly. He knew exactly what I meant.

"Everyone. But one…one is an accident."

The confirmation was a gasp.

Like it was a fresh pain, each time. I fiddled with my glasses. It hit me then —that my instinctual question had been justified. That was why he had not answered. It had not been a matter of *if* he was going to kill me, but when.

"Shit," I breathed.

That was all that I could say. I had failed to give him the reaction that he had expected. I could see the furrow of his brows. I wasn't screaming, I wasn't running, and I wasn't turning away to retch. I was right there on the rocks, at his side. Listening. My reaction was quiet and uncertain. It was trepidation in and of itself —not knowing if I was thinking of revenge or just the right words to say.

Shane decided to fill the silence.

"I call the Daemons mercy because then the death isn't so sudden. So the humans see it coming, and think that they deserve it."

I raised an eyebrow. "Do they deserve it?"

"I used to think so. I still do for some."

"…Fair enough."

He folded his arms, but held himself like a child desperate for warmth. "I can't be a fucking saviour of this town, Alexander. I am its executioner," he declared flatly. He wanted to appear detached but I could see the years of anguish engrained in his eyes. "Always have been."

My hand tentatively rose, my fingers flexing as I reached for his arm. His eyes followed the gesture. All the way until I had made contact. He was stiff and freezing. "Why did you do it in the first place?"

The teal of his eyes flickered a little.

"All, for the sake of one," he told me. "The most important person in my existence had been taken from me, and I turned to blame everyone but myself. I took out my misguided rage on a small, forgettable town. Now it is what I know as punishment. I'm supposed to learn some '*lesson*', but I haven't. Not if I'm still here."

"Wait, you…you killed an entire town because you got *dumped*?"

Shane did a double take.

His expression flipped from nothing to utter offence, and the dullness shone with newfound intensity. My fingers flinched back from his jacket.

"Dumped?" he clipped, showing his teeth. "What the hell, you ass. I wasn't dumped. We were prevented from seeing each other."

I leaned back in surrender. "Oh. Okay, sorry."

"Why?" he then followed up. "Do you think…do you think they really could have just left me? Like it all meant…nothing?"

"I don't know."

It'd hurt, of that I was sure.

"…I hope that their love did not change," Shane then sighed. "For the brief time before this curse. I hope that they kept loving me back then, even after seeing all of which I was capable."

"Well, did you keep loving them?" I pressed. "After being imprisoned in a hopeless town with hopeless people?"

"You're not hopeless."

"We're not talking about me, Hyde."

He frowned, his piercing glinting in the light. "…Right."

"So. Do you love them?" I leaned in a little, genuinely curious.

Shane glanced aside but it didn't look as if it was to think it over. His irises were back to an unsettling luminous state. And I was almost certain that he already knew the answer.

The ghost of a smile haunted his lips. Like he should not be permitted to recall such happiness.

"…Yes," he admitted. "I'm still in love."

My heart lurched.

Stop it. You have no right to feel jealous.

YOU'RE SUPPOSED TO BE FORGETTING.

I must have sunk in quite snuggly to delusion. I thought I might have a chance given our little exchanges; given every electric charge between us and every hitch of breath. But perhaps he was actually caught in a web of feelings: for the one he loved, and for the possibility of someone new.

How presumptuous that person might be me.

My vision stung and blurred —for a second before I blinked away the hurt. *No fair*. That was all that my selfish heart was wailing.

Above the revelation; above the development of Shane Hyde actually being a convicted murderer —in a supernatural capacity, no less —above all of the winds of that hurricane, blared the very torrential tragedy of my infatuation. I was unbearably falling for him.

How unforgivable and violent.

I was no angel, either.

"Do you still not hate me, Grahams?" Shane then asked. "Are you still not afraid?" He had leaned in closer, too. I could feel his shallow breath.

The rings of purple had come back. It was like fire on water —a dance of light over a torrential ocean. I drowned in it as I always did, and didn't mind. And it wasn't fair.

Then there were flickers of flame, and the clink of chains. In the back of my mind, I saw two sets of eyes —both blue and purple, in a way that I had never connected before. Shane was not made of iron. And the beast was drenched in ruby. Yet…was the inescapable and irrational affection that I had for the one, the same for the other?

I didn't know what answer I was going to give when my mouth finally opened. But I was myself, and it was going to be honest.

"Ferream," I whispered.

The air stilled.

That was not what Shane thought I would say. Emotion flashed across his face once more: shock and horror. The violet crescents flared. "…You're not supposed to know that name."

My mouth opened to say something else.

Several twigs snapped a few feet away. Shane's head turned towards the noise, instinctively alert.

I assumed that it was just a small animal, but his face said otherwise. Then three figures came into view between the silhouettes of trees. My breath caught in my throat as I tried to gasp. More of those red suits like blood. Ethereally sculpted visages without a hair out of place.

And black eyes; wells of depthless oblivion.

the library

ALEXANDER

WE WERE RUNNING too fast but all I could think about besides a fear of being caught was the fact that Shane Hyde was gripping my hand so tightly, as if I'd disappear entirely if our fingers slipped.

I couldn't pinpoint it in that moment but it gave me disgusting, awful hope. And I clung to it —just like his hand.

He did not get to say why we were running, though I knew the answer if they had anything to do with the stranger. They were most likely, more demons —with the same excuse of observation and maintenance to roam the town. Like prison wardens.

We bound and stumbled over roots and bushes; more concerned about how fast we needed to get out of the woods versus the thudding of earth and crunch of branches and leaves.

I was quickly running out of breath but the urgency pushed me on.

Shane pushed me on.

It should be terrifying —I should be petrified and possibly fearing for my life, and yet…I could not feel any of that because his hand was holding mine. Everything was real and anything only mattered because of it.

Of course the novelty and sentiment abruptly wore off when his head turned back to me and I caught glimpses between the dark trees of an odd anger rippling through the muscles on his face; carving out hard veins and deepening frown lines.

Shane Hyde was not afraid.

He was furious.

I could not name the reason as to why.

We dove behind a row of bushes off the side by Mr O'Finley's farm fencing, panting and top-heavy in our outer layers. My hand got scratched up but that pain was absolutely dulled by the rush of adrenaline and sound of my pounding heart drowning my awful thoughts.

The strangers marched right past; their footsteps striking the ground too solidly as if they were made of lead. Their suits were too pristine; too neat and averse to the muck of the outdoors. No dirt caught onto the silk and even the mud slid off of their shoes as they lifted and treaded.

"Who are they?" I whispered.

"Barons," Shane hedged. "Barons of Hell. The lowest rank, actually. But definitely the most *self-absorbed*. Same as the stranger."

"Are they…what are they looking for?"

"Don't know," he hissed. "Like I said before, I haven't…" He trailed off, gaze narrowing at me. I sceptically mirrored the expression. His eyes widened. "You. You can't get taken. I won't let that happen."

My head tilted.

"Don't give me that look."

"What look?" I murmured, eyes momentarily straying to the barons.

Shane gave me a look too —the one that made it feel as though he saw the perfect, naked soul beneath the inadequate flesh.

"The look you give me like you don't see all the bad I've done."

I searched for something in his eyes that I could fathom but not name.

He was not wrong. I didn't see a monster —not by the standards we had discussed. I saw a creature unfamiliar with the intensity of love and how it had led it to destroy. But it itself was not destroyed. The corners of my lips then lifted insignificantly with a strange boldness.

"…Do I give you that look often?"

He softened considerably. "You have for a long time."

The soft stare held for a few seconds more —in which I realised how close our faces were and froze like a deer in headlights —before Shane's head turned again at the rustling of dry leaves too near to our hiding place.

"We need to go," he said, tugging on my hand. He had been holding it the entire time.

"Let's go into the town centre," I suggested.

"Humans won't deter them."

"No —but it's gotten dark and they might not expect to find anyone in a place that's closed. Maybe they'll check our houses if they're hunting for *us* specifically."

"Hm. Not a bad idea, Grahams."

We took off in the opposite direction that the barons were searching, ripping through a barely established path. Branches snagged at our clothes but stray threads or even holes were the least of our concerns.

We hesitated when the tall buildings came into view; the large strokes of visible grey cloud looming as if they were solid masses that could fall at any moment. The diner and bar would be open but not necessarily full of patrons. We had to pick somewhere completely empty and dark.

I gasped.

"What? Have they caught up?"

"No —we can head to the library," I hissed.

We veered off and didn't slow down to glance back and check if the demons were close. But the echoing of heavy footsteps followed us.

I only considered the possibility of taking a deep breath of relief when we spilled in through the doors. It wasn't surprising to find it open —even the uptight, organised librarian could have forgotten to lock.

Shane let go of my hand and I grew cold once again.

I slid to the floor, barely breathing.

My legs had never worked so hard in my life —the only time that was remotely close was years ago, having being late for school. I clutched my chest, feeling my heartbeat racing throughout my entire body.

"Are they still after us?" I rasped, crawling forward on my knees.

Shane peered out of the window. "…It looks like they're moving on and heading to the suburbs. Let's go further in."

I shakily rose to my feet and followed him through the library. It was eerie at night. The whimsy of bookshelves disappeared into the shadows.

We opened another door marked as *staff only*, and closed it behind us. This space was even darker. A waxing gibbous of moon shone in through one window too close to the ceiling.

I gasped. "We're in the supply room."

"Hm?" Shane frowned.

I could realistically make out little more than the silhouette of him and his irises —aside from a few clean strips of his face where the light hit. That part of his hair was white and glowing.

"You've never snuck into the supply room?" he smirked.

"I…I've never had reason," I defended myself, scratching at my arm. "Why would I, when I don't work here?"

"You've never been curious? There's even some stock back here. This is your chance, Grahams. What do you usually read?"

"Romance. Fairytales."

Shane walked over to a shelf. "Whoa, that shit can have tons of smut," he quipped, flipping through a book.

It dropped onto the floor with a painful thud. I cringed before reaching for and slotting it back as I then hissed, "Just because you prefer it doesn't mean you have to ruin it for everyone else who doesn't."

"Oh?" he murmured. He levelled at me a challenging glare.

His turquoise eyes gleamed in the dimness. He took two strides to get there, before leaning in. I had to angle my chin slightly to meet his gaze. It happened again. All of that feeling thundered there.

"Happily-ever-afters, huh?" he asked. "Kind of delusional."

My blood heated, and I could no longer look him in the eye. "…That's not exactly what I meant, Hyde."

"But apparently that's what you read," he continued, sliding a hand up along the wall to rest beside my head. I stiffened as his fingers began to tap in an irritating, slow and rhythmic pattern.

"Why don't you tell me why you find it so appealing, and maybe then I will understand," he suggested, his voice a caressing whisper.

This felt like a seasoned move. As though Shane Hyde knew how to unnerve people; how to bring them to their knees.

I refused to show how easily I could concede.

"Fine." The strained word was out of my mouth before I could pause to plan a proper way of escape.

The silence was trickery.

Suddenly the demons didn't matter. We weren't being monitored and possibly going to be killed. I was no longer in danger, and Shane didn't need to protect me. Or this was all an elaborate distraction from the reality of just outside. Though I could not blame him for attempting that.

I turned and reached out for a title —and to add to my nerves, it looked like a horrendously tropey and formulaic one. I checked the age restriction just in case.

Thankfully it was on the lower end.

Shane's brows rose slightly and he inclined his head as if he knew. He refused to move, so I had to lower down to the floor, legs crossed. I stared at his shins for a second before he sank down beside me. Close enough that his shoulder pressed against mine, and his knee jabbed me every time he fidgeted.

Ironically, I tried to concentrate on the book.

The words were initially mumbles; my mind reminding me that I was far too ashamed to say some of the miserably sappy words at which I was looking out loud. It *was* embarrassing. I could admit that much.

But Shane treated the situation with surprising seriousness. He stayed silent and attentive, his focus on the sound of my voice.

"…And Nicola knew, even as his rough calloused fingers caressed her cheek in the sweetest promise of patience, that she was his. And always would be."

A pleased smile tugged at my lips.

"I think Nicola is something of a fool," Shane then commented for the first time since I had begun reading.

"What? No, she's a woman in love," I corrected.

"I doubt she cares much for Ludwig apart from his giant —"

"Seriously, what's your problem?" I snapped. "Why are you being so crude? I…I thought you'd believed in love."

Shane's expression flickered from surprised to shrouded in the matter of a second. He glared at me, and then at his shoes.

It was clear that he was fighting with some part of himself, and neither winning nor losing. He seemed enraged and frustrated —though directed inward. I could understand on that level.

"...I wasn't actually made to feel that kind of emotion, Grahams," he eventually confessed. "I learned it from someone."

"What are you talking about? Everyone *feels*. Or...is it...has it got to do with what you really are?" I asked delicately.

"Yeah," he breathed. "I literally wasn't made to feel anything but rage and bloodlust."

I scoffed. "What, like some kind of genetic experiment?"

It had been a joke but I immediately got the sense that it was in awful taste as Shane did not respond —and I noticed the way his fists tightened while his jaw clenched so hard that the skin turned bone white.

Could that really be what he was?

Daemons existed and were draining the life out from our neighbours. Nothing seemed to be out of the realm of possibility.

"...Even if you are some experiment, Hyde, I don't think that feeling things is so beyond you. Remember that improvised funeral? You had a rather human reaction. That has to do with this current form. It's possible that you might not be able to understand these feelings, but that doesn't mean they're not there."

Shane drew a sharp breath. Then he slid his gaze to mine.

"Then tell me what I'm feeling right now," he whispered.

My mouth went dry. "Okay. What are the symptoms?"

"My heartbeat speeds up and I say all the wrong words —I know what I want to come out in my head, but it's like there's a disconnect in signals. But that's not even the worst of it."

"What...what else happens?" I rasped, vaguely aware of him moving closer and my back pressing against the wall.

He levelled a highly straight look at me, before stating, "I keep getting hard after I think about every time they got too close, and it takes ages go away, no matter how many times I rub —"

"Okay, that's enough!" I gasped, clapping my hands over his mouth. I did not need him planting images in my head. He then paused, frowning as he realised that I was in no state to talk so casually about his bedroom habits. I slowly withdrew, trying not to think about how his lips had felt against my skin. "Jesus, Hyde —I didn't need to know that."

Shane snorted at my use of the Lord's name and his in the same breath. Then he clicked his tongue, anger welling up within him again. "So what does it mean?" he pressed. "It's not like what I felt before."

My lips parted, but nothing came out for a moment. It was obvious — at least to me. Shane was attracted to whoever the person was. But part of me was hesitant to reveal that. What if he acted upon the feelings? Would he become completely smitten with them and leave me all alone? Having Louise for a friend was laughable.

Not to mention the one he was still in love with, outside of the curse. Though I supposed if he had resigned himself to exist in a horrid loop and never to see that love again…then exploring and pursuing whatever a new one could be, was rather understandable.

But I didn't want to voice why it all bothered me. It would open up a can of worms I wasn't prepared to gather back up. However, it didn't stop my mind from racing to figure out who it was he might be talking about. Shane Hyde had plenty of friends, unlike me.

"…Grahams?" Shane prompted, tilting his head. "Come back to Earth and answer the question."

I couldn't think fast enough.

"You probably hate them," I quipped.

His brown brows furrowed in disbelief. "Are you sure? I know what hate feels like. It doesn't feel like I'm standing on the edge of a cliff, one step from falling. Then I do, because someone pushed me."

Puta Merda. He was in deeper than it seemed.

"Let me elaborate," I sighed in defeat, finding no other way around it. If he knew what negative emotions felt like, then I couldn't convince him that his developing crush was murderous intent.

I couldn't be that selfish.

I took a deep breath. "…You like someone, Shane Hyde. As in, you've fallen for them. And you hate it."

"Oh. What's, uh…what's your cure?" he inquired.

An answer tumbled out of me against my will. "Confession. Closure."

Shane tensed as he glanced ahead at the shelves. I looked down at my sneakers, fiddling with my thumbs.

His voice spoke again. "Okay."

My shoulders shot upwards.

"Listen up," he murmured. I frowned in confusion, my gaze still glued to my shoelaces. Then he began, as though he were praying. "Forgive me, Master, for I have sinned. This is my first confession. I have fallen prey to the one for whom I was the predator."

I turned my head, and so did he. The air was too stagnant and heavy. There was that familiar crushing feeling which being near Shane always triggered; deep and suffocating. Why had he said all of that to me? And why was his confession so…religious?

My mind was in too much of a disarray to think about it logically.

I could no longer do anything logically.

I didn't speak after that.

There was this desire in my fingertips to skim over certain features I was seeing in detail for the first time. His hair, his jaw, and that piercing over his eyebrow. Those eyes drew me in and indulged my curiosity.

I could no longer repress the urge to reach for his face.

I felt the sharpness of his cheekbones. The roughness of his skin. He didn't even flinch at the brush of my fingers nearing his mouth. But I drew a sharp breath at the self-conscious tightening of his jaw and retreated just a little. My immediate first thought was that I had ruined everything.

What the hell did you just do?

THIS *TAKES THE CAKE.*

He'll never talk to you again!

Shane's eyes locked on mine. "…Ever kissed someone?"

My hand withdrew further as my head shook on its own.

The cogs within my brain ground and shuddered and whirred. There could only be two possible reasons why he would ask me that. Either he wanted to practise —for some very absurd reason —or, the person whom he had been talking about was…

But, it couldn't be.

Shane's brows narrowed as he then took hold of my glasses. I was too confused to protest when he removed them.

He then inclined his head to the side. He leaned in —second guessing each inch. The kiss was soft. Cautious. His parted lips hooked onto mine and lingered long enough for my heart to lurch. He dragged out the parting too; the warmth of him reluctant to disappear.

My eyes widened.

That turquoise was unreadable —something I could see even without my glasses. The only sounds were the shallow breaths we let out into the quickening darkness.

I couldn't possibly deny it now, let alone continue to doubt.

"…Why did you do that?" I whispered.

There was not a single shred of emotion in his face, let alone remorse or regret. "Did you hate it?"

I bit the inside of my cheek. "That's not the point."

His fingers reached for the action; grazed my mouth and its little scar, before unsteadily tracing along my lips. A shiver shot up my spine.

"I should have asked," he acknowledged.

I glanced aside. "Yeah."

Shane balled his hands into fists at his sides. He seemed angrier than *I* should be. "Why didn't you push me away? Or tell me to stop."

"Should I have?"

Shane growled in irritation. "Yes."

His expression was one of pain. I frowned in response. Then we stared at each other for another moment, unsure of what to do next. The library felt infinite with no one but the two of us in it —knee to knee and elbow to elbow while huddled in the shadows.

It wasn't a good idea to be with him in this way. I knew that.

But…there was nowhere else I wanted to be. It had not registered that he might actually share my stupid feelings, and that his '*charm*' had been something close to flirting. He made me into the kind nervous wreck who instinctively felt they should run away. Yet I couldn't.

I didn't want to.

"I'm not afraid of you," I told him. And I knew that it was something that he needed to hear again, since I wholeheartedly meant it.

I had been, once —for what felt like a brief second. Now, because I'd learned more about him and not turned away, my opinion had less room for that fear. It had been pushed aside for something just as frightening.

Shane's expression did not soften. "…You should be."

He didn't invalidate it. He didn't gaslight me into thinking that I was.

It was limp acceptance that he offered me, along with a warning. I *should* be afraid. Maybe he thought he should push *me* away.

But, he didn't.

My hand shuffled along the floor, inching towards him. His eyes followed the movement, and he didn't move when our fingertips met.

My breathing grew heavy. I was then getting ahead of myself. I didn't want to stop, though. I had just been offered my current darkest desire and I wasn't about to let the voices in my head battle it out on how to handle the development. Shane Hyde had just kissed me and damnit, I was going to deal with the fallout *later*.

"…Can I?" I whispered, and it sounded too loud.

Before I knew what I was doing, my free hand had cupped his jaw and turned his head towards me. Now his expression showed conflict. Maybe even his own form of fear. His brows knitted in a frown, but his eyes were steady. Fully taking everything in. Then he bowed his head.

It was as though he had never done this before.

Suddenly I was the expert —the flirt, leading a novice through a guise of tuition. But it wasn't that. Not this time.

"Yeah." His voice was too big for the space as well.

We were both in uncharted territory. Not in the action —anymore — but with these wants which were welling within us. I let him feel precisely how terrified I was, through our clasped hands.

And he let me kiss him. Clumsily and uncertainly and likely too hard, but with a fragile feeling that wasn't hate.

the way down

SHANE

AMIDST THE EXQUISITE reminiscence of yet another selfish and worthwhile first kiss and the succeeding ones, there was the more pressing matter of Alexander knowing the most forbidden thing that a demon could ever give away or have stolen from them.

Their *Excumen* —their True Name.

In all ways that mattered, the soul could bind him and have him belong to them for eternity. Though not in any way that was…appealing. He had no fear of that specifically —Alexander was clearly into him. It was both a dangerous and joyful turn of events. Thankful for it not turning into hate, but well aware of the issues which arose from being involved with them.

The monster was theirs; always and forever.

But the fact remained that he *was* a monster, and that the curse would still loom over whatever momentary happiness he'd deluded himself into thinking was possible. Over the shoulder of every embrace, would be that seeping ink and the blood on his hands.

Selfishness had burrowed deep beneath the surface of his being and it had turned him into a creature slavishly devoted to his own gratification. Although it did stem from his own nature, instead of drowning in carnage and destruction he had become fiercely obsessed with love.

It had been too many cycles since Alexander had entertained the idea. Granted, all of those times had been short flings given the limited time. The two had been granted a little longer this time —time to fall a little more naturally in love and not just act upon attraction. Shane savoured it. The organic feel that had been there in his cell when they had first fallen. It made it feel a little more real.

So them suddenly saying his *Excumen* aloud…that was a hammer to their stained glass mural.

How had they uncovered it? The beast was sure that he had careful — that those stupid *barons* had been careful, and that no mortal; resident of Pine Creek or otherwise; could be granted access in any capacity to the materials that contained demon names.

The disaster which would ensue was catastrophic.

He remembered watching the foolish demons with amusement —who had somehow given their *Excumen* to a human —when they would sink to their knees in despair at the predictability of betrayal at the prospect of being bound by the mortal…until their death.

It was different in the case of the soul, since they would never remain dead after every massacre. If they wished, through losing and regaining memories, Shane would still belong to them for any whim. Forever.

Of course, he wouldn't mind it for a far different purpose.

"*Focus*," he scolded himself, taking a slap to the face. He stared at his reflection in the bathroom mirror with nothing but a towel knotted around his waist. Wet hair flopped over his forehead, each blond strand swaying past the soft glow of his eyes.

This fragile vessel was strange, but it was growing on him. Quite like the glow-in-the-dark mushrooms Alexander had compared him to. It did help that they seemed partial to its visage —the look of nothing good and a heart of stone. And although they didn't recall seeing '*Ferream*' before —and a stupid part of him hoped that they wouldn't for longer than a few seconds; akin to the undifferent cycles —he had the irrational belief that Alexander might not take off running at the sight.

That they might stay and like him still.

A small fist banged on the bathroom door.

"Shane! You've been in there ages already! I heard the water stopping in the shower…uh…fifteen minutes ago!"

The demon groaned at the early morning complaints of Kendall Hyde. It was *too* early. For his shrill voice, and for other people in general.

"I'm not done," Shane lied, tightly gripping the edges of the sink. "In fact, come back in half an hour."

"No fair!" cried his brother, "I'm telling!"

Thumping footsteps receded down the hallway.

Kendall wouldn't get it.

Shane was having a crisis, and no one could possibly get it.

But the small annoyance was right —the beast could not stay in there all morning. The bathroom was impractical for venting out every emotion whirling through him; familiar and alarming.

Feeling merciful, he swiftly dried his hair and then ventured out within plenty of time before Samantha would make the trek over down to their floor. She wouldn't appreciate Shane walking around in just a towel.

He disappeared into his bedroom and flopped over onto his bed. No one in the house had said anything about perfect strangers in red suits and sunglasses —and though he had anticipated that lapse in memory, he had been curious as to whether anyone else was able to elude demons' enthral. So far, no human being at all. Even the soul was not exempt. Thankfully the monster had the power to keep them awake. He did not want to keep much from them, and it was simpler if they were in the loop —for events like that. Although, he was also opening up an avenue for questions.

He was unsure about how many he could truly answer.

The library popped back into his head.

Despite the disarray and haste of the circumstances, he could not hold off a smile. Though it was not the first time, the sensation was something entirely apart each time, which was why he wondered how he could have stood to do away with it in his previous resolve. He reached up and grazed his own lips. Alexander was not a good kisser.

For now.

They had had no practice in this iteration —yet he wanted to kiss them again, just to feel it. To feel them.

Everything was different.

The soul remembered and did not fear.

The beast was tamed and…and…

Everything was different.

"Holy shit," Shane exclaimed, sitting bolt upright. "Shit, shit, shit."

He knew precisely why he had not thought about all of the anomalies occurring in the current cycle. He could forget about not interfering so it could correct itself—it was clear the events were distinctly wandering off of the path set by the curse.

Alexander's mother dying, leading them to come back sooner.

Them not receiving a Daemon.

Shane's *cat* dying.

Alexander remembering things that they shouldn't.

It had all started the moment the soul had directly ran into him weeks ahead of the downward spiral. Just that one encounter had toppled a line of dominos leading to where they were now. For once, the created demon did not have an answer. He did not have a plan and he did not know what the end might have in store for him and the soul.

For the whole town.

Now he looked at the future with as much obstructive seeping shadow as every other resident.

And it was terrifying.

Not knowing was *awful* —how did people just live like that?

Shane got to his feet and trailed to the wardrobe for clothes. He needed to get out of there. He had put on hand-ripped grey jeans and had an arm through another shirt over a jacket when a knock pounded on the door.

"Honey, did you really tell your brother that you'd be half an hour in the bathroom this morning?" Samantha sighed.

"I was joking," he answered flatly, buttoning up. Then he grumbled at the far-off sound of pelting water. "Isn't Ken already in there now?"

"That's besides the point, Shaney —you know how literally he takes what you tell him."

"Please stop calling me that," he groaned as he finally opened the door to her. Her hand was clasped by her chest as if she had thought to knock again, and her eyes were big and hopeful.

Disgusting.

She offered him a smile.

"Don't do that, either," he clipped. He couldn't bear to watch her face crumple, so he sidestepped her and popped a collar. "I'll be back late."

"Shane…"

"Yeah, yeah —I'll watch what I say and set a good example, I swear. Bye." He was down the stairs and out of the front door before Samantha's husband could corner and lecture him too.

He paused in the driveway. And he remembered how the paved brick had felt beneath iron feet. How the sensation had in fact barely registered in a blinded storm of haste and ruthlessness.

He truly was a demon.

There was a love in his gaze as the beast looked at the beauty through the glass windows of *Straws & Fries*. He was sure of it.

Alexander Grahams was pouring over a new heavy Chiltern hardback —*Emma*. The floral design; which resembled peonies; were pink, purple and maroon against the gold accents and shiny edges. Almost as thick as *Jane Eyre*, and they had already gotten through about half of it.

Shane stared at the way the soul held their chin in one hand, eyes going back and forth rhythmically as they idly twirled a few curls at the back of their head. As if they did not have a single care in the world —or perhaps every plausible one, all at once.

But when they looked up, that focused gaze turned uncertain before it lowered. As if the demon had had no expression on his face at all —with the turquoise of his irises cold and foreboding.

He prodded the glass, consciously frowning.

Alexander flinched but lifted their head again —their eyes roved and took in the amount of patrons. It was sparce, but it did mean that the two teenagers would be in public; visible if they did anything…obvious.

Shane wandered inside with a bravado he had learned to perfect —the kind that radiated respect and frigid reverence. The kind that ensured that people didn't simply walk up to him without reason.

"Grahams."

He was very aware of his hand in his jeans' left pocket as he came to a standstill. They were bundled up today —a turtleneck, sweater vest and shacket folded over the spare chair. And the look he offered the soul: a straight, softened frown. Like they'd met a distant relative's funeral.

He slid onto the chair opposite them, elbows on the table.

"Hyde."

Alexander marked the page with ribbon and then set the classic down. Their expression gave little away. Evidently, they were not hung up about the events of the night before. They'd even gathered the nerve to meet his eye now. That brown caught the sunlight and Shane found himself staring a little longer than he should have.

"So…have you seen them?" they cleared their throat and asked their plate of gingerbread cookies below. "The strangers in red."

"…They didn't come by. I think they left town. For now."

"Oh."

Silence wedged between them like a loud estranged friend. At first the beast could not decipher why their conversation wasn't flowing naturally. Then he thought about the library…and it all fit together in an unsettling puzzle. But he didn't know what to say. Where to start.

And Alexander wasn't looking at him with stars in their eyes. Those were jagged shards of glinting glass.

He wanted to blame their location, but truthfully, he could not bear to consider the possibility that even if the two should find themselves alone, the atmosphere would not change.

Everything was different now.

So maybe he had been entirely foolish to think that things might stay uncomplicated after they had kissed. Consequences had been the furthest thing on his mind and in the excitement of being with the soul again, he had forgotten about the very real struggles of *this* Alexander and how they would handle the development.

While some aspects of their life were constants, details like who they found attractive and how they were perceived for it varied. On occasion, they had even had difficulty reconciling their interest in the beast with all they had been taught about God and the Morningstar.

Maybe those kisses had been the worst thing to happen.

Shane clenched his jaw and slowly withdrew the hand that had been absentmindedly inching across toward Alexander's, which was balled up with their other one in their long sleeves. "Uh…you remember the name you said in the woods yesterday?" he asked.

Their dark brows furrowed. "Ferream —?"

"—Don't *say* it," Shane clipped.

"*Jesus*, okay."

They retreated further inward.

It was not with dejection. It felt like…anger. They were mad —likely at him. The monster stuck up his nose as he ran his tongue along his top lip. They had every right to be. He then sighed, letting the uneasy tension pull taut again but now for a different reason.

"How do you know that name, Grahams."

He didn't say it like a question.

Alexander took the hint.

"I just…do," they murmured. And then dithered when Shane raised a tired eyebrow. "…Look, I've been having really weird dreams," they admitted. "I just heard it in one of them. Is it a dangerous curse, or something? I've been having issues recalling them even a bit since I was younger, but all of a sudden I'm dreaming and…I can remember."

Shane was sure that he had gone slightly pink. "It's…it's not a curse. Just not something to throw around."

"Oh. Right…"

He wanted to tell them it was his name —he really did. He wanted to hear them say it, knowing exactly what it was and what it meant. But the library swirled in the back of his mind and fogged up that desire. Instead he erected an iron wall and buried a deep rooted cacophony of feeling.

"So. What are you dreaming about?"

The soul hesitated rather violently. Their eyes widened and every one of their muscles stiffened. Shane had never seen them so shaken before. And then that offended shock turned into betrayed accusation.

Alexander's mouth opened and spoke no words, while their eyes saw what was not there. "A monster I loved."

"Loved?" he echoed.

"Yes, past tense. I…I don't understand why yet, and I don't know if I love them now. In this life, or something."

"Oh."

Shane Hyde tried hard not to take it personally. Right now, to the soul, the beast and the mortal adolescent vessel were two separate beings split between affection that didn't make sense either way.

Alexander then leaned forward slightly and uncurled. "Tell me about your existence before Pine Creek. Before the curse. The death…*then*."

He flinched. "It's not a happily-ever-after fairytale."

"I know," they admitted, shrugging. "But I want to try and understand the depth of your eyes."

the bonfire

ALEXANDER

I STILL WASN'T sure how Louise Barnes had talked me into it, but by the time we were approaching the sound of music and fire it was a bit too late. It had been nearly thirty-two hours since I had seen Shane Hyde. In that time I had tossed and turned in bed; bumped into Louise at *Straws & Fries*; and spoken with Kay Isotton —keeping it as vague as possible.

But I suspected she easily caught on about who we were talking. I had been careful to omit details like gender, location and time, but something told me that she actually knew that it had been the town's most infamous delinquent who had corrupted every part of my life.

She did not judge and she did not pry.

She offered me a pat on the back and gave me a begonia. My stomach had turned when she explained what it meant: caution. A warning.

I wasn't stupid often, but I had certainly felt that way this morning.

Even someone as optimistic as her had the sense to keep distance. If all I wanted was to press closer, then surely I had lost those senses. Now, as I trudged through to the outskirts of the forest towards a bonfire being held to celebrate the last week of freedom before the start of a school year, I knew that I would rather be staring into two pools of tropical blue. Senior year was the last thing I wanted to stress over.

The year that we wouldn't be starting —and never would.

I found it odd to wrestle with the fact that I would always be seventeen within the curse; cycle after cycle, no matter each duration. I didn't want to think about for how long I had already *been* seventeen.

The roar of teen spirit became louder than the sea of my thoughts.

Louise sauntered over at my left; decked in denim shorts, tights and a curiously crocheted sweater. Her long chains swung and clanged with her every movement. She had curled her hair again —or tried to, and was now compulsively tucking loose curls behind her ears.

"Stop doing that," I deadpanned.

She started, maybe having forgotten that I was even there, and looked away sheepishly. "Just trying to be a little presentable for society."

"Well it's making me a little nauseous," I stated.

"That's why we're out here, breathing fresh air."

"I wish I was in bed."

She tilted her head to the side and smiled. "Do you really?"

I scowled. "…I hate you."

"There's no need to worry. I'll be right there."

"*That's* reassuring."

My sarcasm rolled right off of her back. "Trust me, everyone is going to get too drunk to even think about what happened back then," she quipped.

I wished that the notion actually comforted me. Because although that situation was inevitable, there would still be the minimum hour before — where they could still be sober assholes.

"I'll just have to get as wasted," I sighed; hands firmly planted in my pockets. "Then I really *can* be numb."

Louise brightened a little. "That's the spirit!"

"Actually, not a bad start. Vodka could work."

"See, we'll make you a wild young adult yet."

"Mm."

My conclusion was that I simply didn't want to be at the house, with that man. And that an unsupervised and illegal party with people I hated was somehow better. But it wasn't as if any of the adults could —or would — actually do anything. The town didn't exist, as far as the world could tell.

A sizable tepee blaze of definitely stolen, professionally carved logs; amateurly broken branches; old books and notes from the past year; and bits of wooden furniture, finally came into view in a clearing that seemed too small for the intended purpose. Several scattered teenagers loitered by it with red plastic cups and bottles in hand.

It was, however, a small comfort to see writhing darkness slipping in and out between them. The entire event was a festering of bad ideas.

A blond boy in a bomber jacket waddled over immediately.

"*Por favor me mate, Deus*..." I muttered.

"Where've you been, Lu?" cried the boy, hands flying —and beer. He was wearing a Pine Creek Stags sweatshirt underneath the black, yellow and orange school jacket. Ah. A football player.

God was mean.

God did not kill me.

And I was allowed to be angry, now knowing They were real.

Louise scoffed and pulled her sleeves over her hands before balling them into fists. She knew this football player. But she tried to make it look like she didn't. And in spite of that resolution, her Daemon wasn't letting up. "Avoiding *you* specifically, Jack."

They chuckled like it was funny.

My gaze narrowed and averted, burning with scorn.

You shouldn't be here.

I hated how easily Louise Barnes seemed to slip back into life as she had previously led it; cracking jokes and attending an underage party in the godforsaken woods —even amidst her crisis and fall from the high school throne. As though she'd learned some damned lesson, and people still cared to be her friend.

My eyes scanned the early night, hoping for platinum blond. They did not find the right head of it.

I then became aware of many people staring at us.

I knew many of their names. From the perpetrators to the bystanders. There were a few faces I couldn't recognise. It only made me more self-conscious. Though I praised myself for not squirming in my jewellery and corduroy jacket, wanting to bolt for a safer and emptier place.

People raised their eyebrows, but there was less malice in their stares. I went still beneath their assessment. It was possible that their manners could have been due to Louise's mere presence. I could understand how seeing the two of us within a few inches and carrying a conversation was a confusing sign. We were still not friends —she had kept tailing me for her own personal agenda, and I had become used to the lack of silence.

"…Why'd you drag Hamilton here?" Jack then demanded rather than asked. It didn't look like he was the only one who wanted to say it.

I couldn't help stiffening as I forced at least my body to turn back. His blurry judgement took in my tall stature; my slightly out of place clothes; and generally who I had become. He wasn't sober enough to be a dick.

"I invited Alexander because this thing has always been more fun with a lot of people," Louise huffed. "It's been years, Branner; get over it."

My teeth ground together.

I knew she didn't mean it in the way the louder voice in my head was screaming. I knew that she was warning him about saying anything out of line, not that it was trivial. I *knew* that —but the voice raged still.

"Well…the more the merrier, then," said Jack. "Here's to a killer year, bud." And it wasn't with a smirk. Though I was tempted to, myself.

Killer indeed.

The tension in my shoulders eased slightly. Was it possible that a lot of the fear was in my head? Maybe time and age really did have an effect on most people.

I gave the scene another onceover and rocked on my heels. "Is, um…is Shane Hyde…going to be here?"

Louise gave me a look, which I quickly glared at her for. The football player looked askance. "Elwoods and her little gang were banned a couple of semesters back, but I guess…nothing would stop him."

My chest lightened. "Right."

"Why?" asked Jack.

"Why what?"

"Why do you want to know…if Hyde will show?"

Hopefully he was too drunk to remember what I was about to say.

"We're friends."

His eyes popped out of his head. "*Really*? So Carley was —"

"Branner," Louise barked, grabbing his sleeve. "Drop it."

He tried to protest but for once I appreciated her doing me a favour as she started dragging him away, back to his cluster of teammates.

"I need to sit down," I announced or muttered, heading for the fire.

"Oh, sure," Jack slurred, whirling around and splashing more beer on the grass. "Keg's over on the picnic table —along with wine, spirits, some mixers and whatever's left of the chips, ha."

"Yeah…thanks."

My feet obediently moved for said table. Half of it, horizontally —the half that wasn't supporting the keg —had been scrapped for bonfire fuel. I sighed and grabbed a plastic cup, then reached for a nearly empty bottle of vodka. I definitely poured in more than one shot and then barely diluted it with coke from a spilling bottle. Then I lifted it to my lips.

Wait a minute. What are you doing? That's alcohol.

IT'S ONE THING TO TRY WEED, BUT NOW YOU'RE GOING TO BE JUST LIKE *YOUR FATHER?*

I froze in my tracks, before jerking the cup away from me.

The voices knew how to hurt me too.

Yeah, but you're not drinking beer. You're not a football player.

WHO WOULD CARRY YOU HOME IF YOU HAVE ONE OF THOSE EPISODES, LIKE HUGH?

You can't rely on anyone like that.

I wanted to scream.

My hand opened, and the cup free fell to the ground. I felt it splash on the ankles of my trousers. No. No, no, *no* —I had to be a special type of mad to even consider touching the stuff. However…it was not as if it affected my father and me in similar ways. I didn't curl away from the world under the influence. And it was spirits, not beer.

Therefore I was technically drinking less.

BECAUSE YOU'RE TECHNICALLY DRINKING MORE ALCOHOL CONTENT, YOU ABSOLUTE IDIOT.

Fuck.

I backtracked, retreating from the half-of-a-table as quickly as I could. My mind tried to think of something else. Anything else.

I lowered onto one of the unoccupied logs placed hexagonally around the tepee, leaning into the heat to fight off the chill. No one approached me, and that was just fine. No one knew of the mild panic and cup spilling vodka coke into the root system.

My mind drifted to the conversation Shane Hyde and I had yesterday. Inside I was still a nervous wreck about what it was I wanted and expected from whatever we would become. If it had even meant that much. I could not help worrying that my '*coping*' had come across as a rejection of some kind. I hadn't meant to be cold. I was just…confused.

But when I saw his face —when I met those eyes, sound logic escaped me and I drowned in every single one of my feelings. They switched from gentle lapping waves to great winds and hail.

And I just…stopped.

Stopped moving, breathing, and even being. I became all and nothing —a paradox of perfectly captured infinity. Frequently feeling that much at once caused states of shock and withdrawal.

It was as equally addictive as it was terrifying.

Especially when I realised from Shane's account that this was not the first time we had met. Not even from the curse. He had spoken of ice and fire and red sand. Of duty and loyalty. Of a war beyond comprehension. Of prisons and chains of salt. And a monster without doubt or reason.

The monster I knew.

One I apparently loved.

I had seen the iron beast's eyes last night, and heard its voice for the first time. The same luminous blue as Shane but void of life, and a very grating sound coming from its throat. Yet its words comforted me.

I had also heard my own voice and was crushed beneath a heavy love that I was only beginning to understand with the memory of exchanges I hadn't recalled before. And I wasn't sure if I was entirely the same soul.

But it was me. I was my own problem. I was the love that Shane Hyde couldn't get over, and the love I thought he wanted to explore.

In spite of that revelation, I hadn't seen him in thirty-two hours, twelve minutes and thirty seconds. Thirty-one seconds. Thirty-two seconds. And if I saw him right then, I wouldn't know what to say.

My gaze gravitated to the fire.

Its smoke curled high and dissipated well above the treetops, and the way the sparking embers whirled in the air only intensified that stinging in the eyes.

For a moment, I wasn't quite there.

Everyone blurred around me —chatty and boisterous. It moved like a scene out of a movie where colours ran into each other and people turned into lines like thick paint slashed across a canvas. And I thought, what if my whole life had been like that: a freeze frame where the subject was at a standstill and realising that they had never really been a part of the fast paced, out-of-focus world.

And there was a moon up above, also unmoving.

"*Eu sou uma pessoa morta,*" I breathed, holding my chin in my hands. God couldn't kill me because I was clearly dead already.

"Alexander!"

I glanced upwards to see an arguably mellow Louise; her pale skin flushed with a bit of colour. She didn't have a little red cup in her hand. An entire wine bottle swung back and forth in her wrist.

I sucked on my teeth. "You left for ten goddamn minutes, Barnes."

"Live a little, Grahams," she scolded, pausing in front of me. "Did you not find the vodka? You still look very sad."

"What, I can't be drunk *and* sad?" I quipped.

Jack Branner laughed beside her, while she frowned down at me and tilted her head to the side in something that resembled concern.

"…I'm not drinking," I sighed. "It turns out that's *not* the way I want to forget all about this bonfire nightmare. Do not ask me why."

"I wasn't —"

"Eddie's got some weed if you want," Jack chimed in, pointing across the tepee. There sat a familiar, yet slightly altered sight. Under the age of thirteen, it had been fun and games and fluorescent safety gear. On the cusp of legality, neon had darkened to black and neutrals and beanies.

What was that thing Shane had said —wanting to feel something else?

"Actually you know what," I started, rising to my feet and dusting off my trousers, "that'll be perfect. Thanks, Jack."

I had never said that to him before.

"No problem, man."

The sound of Louise scoffing as she automatically slapped at his chest — and his consequent yowl, followed me.

I only huffed and balled my hands into fists as I marched off. And in my head, I repeated over and over that even though Jack used such a word that meant precisely as implied, he had not done so maliciously nor was he in any state to understand why I was so pierced by it.

The teenagers stared up at me as I halted before them. Their Daemons appeared to be as relaxed as they were —lounging and wisping in and out of visibility as if these people in particular deserved a night off.

"Uh…can I have some weed?"

I had never interacted with them when we were younger —except for one person. And she looked just as surprised to see me as I was.

"Alex Grahams?" murmured a girl with tiny twin plaits, in cargo pants and a hooded jersey. "Lily-Mae, if you remember. I never thought I'd see you at a Fall bonfire. Or back here. My Mom meant to come over, but…"

I winced. "Just call me Alexander," I forced through my teeth. "I don't shorten my name anymore. You…all kind of ruined it for me."

"Are you still on about that? Loosen up, dude," quipped the boy next to her. The aforementioned Eddie McCarthy —who believed that he was a better skateboarder than he really was according to his social media. He had the classic elitist-family-rebel-for-the-sake-of-it look down; and split-end dirty blond hair cut to frame his narrow, speckled face.

His Daemon stirred to life.

"You can't use '*dude*', you idiot," Lily-Mae hissed, elbowing his side. "I know that none of us were the nicest people to you. We're sorry. Here." She lifted up her own half-finished joint. "Have some of this."

"Uh, thanks," I mumbled.

I tried not to think about the way I should hold it between my fingers, and instead concentrated on smoking it correctly. I didn't cough this time so it could already be considered less embarrassing. I drew a deep breath and watched the end glow before I exhaled.

"Oh, by the way," Eddie started talking again, a smirk playing on his lips. The darkness over his shoulder whipped about with increased vigour. "What's the deal with you and Shane Hyde?"

I nearly choked. "…What do you mean?"

Lily-Mae shook her head. "He just means we've heard you guys have been hanging out. Like, a lot."

"Don't you know about the rumours, Grahams?" Eddie scoffed.

"No."

"Whoa," breathed the boy sitting right on the grass and flipping his hands over. "Guys, I think my hands are on fire. So warm."

"They're not, Pete," Lily-Mae sighed. "Take a break."

Pete's Daemon did not seem bothered with overseeing the festivities, given that his own shadow wasn't there against the trees.

"No one knows much about Shane Hyde. Not even his family," Eddie grunted. "You know that people think the shadow things are his fault?"

My expression hardened. "Is that so?"

"Because he doesn't have one," Lily-Mae elaborated.

"Neither do I. Are they *my* fault, too?"

"What do you mean you don't?" Eddie scoffed, glancing a little ways past me. "It's right behind you."

I stole a glance. I couldn't help myself.

Someone else's Daemon was peering above, over my shoulder. Claws attempted to reach out but they failed to advance far enough to touch me. I tensed, before the frown I could make out evaporated and I was staring at the smoke from the bonfire.

"Others have it worse," Lily-Mae said candidly, turning to the huddle of Carley, Georgia and Laura next to an oak —wrapped up tight in long arms of darkness. "I.e., the Charm Schoolers."

It was not as if they didn't deserve it.

I took another drag and looked at the tepee. A flash of dyed hair caught my eye. Through the haze of smoke and setting marijuana, I realised that the turquoise staring back at me was Shane Hyde's. Those glowing irises did not waver. Not when I stayed precisely where I was, still inhaling. As if daring him to approach. I wanted him to. I was certain that my face was cold and blank, but he had a subtle look of pain. It only lasted for a flicker of a second, before he looked pissed off.

I ostentatiously turned back around.

"Hyde is selective of his friends," I announced as I blew out towards the specks of light I saw heading for the moon.

It was so big, and round.

I let out a soft laugh. "The personification of ice."

"Or a frigid statue," Eddie added.

I laughed again.

"But he's nice, for a closed-off statue," I admitted. And then laughed again, with Lily-Mae and Eddie joining in. Even Pete chuckled —though that might have been about something else. Being high was letting words fall out of my mouth that ordinarily would have been hindered by things like shame, awareness and reason.

"I think *you're* the only one he's nice to," remarked Lily-Mae.

"Ha, no way," I scoffed, flippantly waving my hand. "He's got *such* a winning personality," I spluttered. "And that fucking jawline."

"You're certainly funnier this way," said Eddie.

"It's magic," I giggled.

"That's *exactly* what I said," Pete spoke up. "Great minds."

"The greatest minds." I leaned down, then found my hand connecting with his in a weak high five after stumbling slightly.

My brows suddenly knitted in thought. "Maybe he's afraid to feel," I muttered. "He'll run off at the mere hint of someone caring. He won't let anyone get that close. Which is a shame, 'cause he's a really good —"

Lily-Mae's eyes widened. "Uh, Alexander —" Her finger pointed to the fire behind me as she frantically sliced a hand in front of her neck.

"…Who's the one running, again?"

I whipped around.

Shane Hyde stared back at me from a much closer distance. His eyes still dragged me down, and made me…stop. I was too lost to decipher the look on his perfect visage, but it didn't instil me with anything calm. And then I laughed —right in that face, because the silence was unbearable.

He didn't even blink.

"Hyde," I murmured, aiming for indifference. I lifted my hand to take another drag but his caught mine before it made it to my mouth. My body tensed —but that shock did not last long. It was swiftly overtaken when Shane plucked the diminishing joint from my fingers and brought it to his own mouth. His gaze remained locked.

"Grahams," he returned, before slowly sucking.

And then much like Pete, I was on fire. Shane turned his head to blow out smoke but his eyes still watched mine.

I didn't know what to think. The words were no longer there.

"Man of the hour," Eddie then sneered from somewhere in the blurred background. "What hole did you crawl up out of, Hyde? Hell?"

I wanted to laugh at that.

Shane's eyebrows furrowed in the smallest hint of irritation. "Blow it out your ass, McCarthy," he clipped. His eyes were still not straying.

Then his hand started nearing my face and my lips parted of their own accord, before he gently placed the joint between them. I breathed in. That same ferocity he'd had when he had watched me sipping from the straw was there. He withdrew on my long exhale. His gaze offered me the same challenge that I had given him. If I dared. My eyes lidded.

He leaned in closer —and to the side as an afterthought —to graze his lips against my ear. "Come find me later," he said softly. Then I watched him walk away, unblinking; with poached drugs and all.

Lily-Mae's eyes darted. "…Intense."

"I'd use a different word," muttered Eddie, lighting a new joint.

"There is nothing going on," I immediately reassured, turning back to address them. "I'm way out of his league."

the edge of everything

ALEXANDER

MY EYES BLINKED open to see the side of Shane Hyde's jaw. I frowned and forced my brain to cooperate. My head was on his shoulder. I stirred —before flinching sharply. I was about to ask for how long I had been asleep, when I caught sight of the view.

We were sitting on the end of the lowered back of a truck, overlooking the hub of the town below. Scattered houses and orchards broke apart the surrounding forestry. The river lay west.

A sharp dusting of stars competed with the moon.

From here, it was difficult to tell that something was wrong; that Pine Creek was infested with Daemons. Everything looked normal. Everything looked alive. Shane then turned to glance at me knowingly as he took out an earphone. "You sober now, Grahams?"

I wriggled my fingers. My body was solid again, and the fog that had been in my head had receded. "More so."

Smoke lingered in my senses.

I tried to piece together what had happened between Lily-Mae telling me to take another hit before waking up next to Shane —far enough from the bonfire not to hear any drunken jostling. Jagged bits of memory cut in over each other. Tripping over a log; getting smacked in the face by twigs; declining a game of truth or dare but then participating anyway…

A cold wave of shame washed over my back.

It was only when I glanced aside that I realised Shane had been staring at me intensely throughout the flashback. I cringed and curled my fingers tighter over the edge of a stranger's truck.

His brows then furrowed, even as he turned to frown at his sneakers.

"…Are you mad at me?" I asked.

He had glowered at me through the flames and embers. I had too, but I had been consumed with a righteous indignation.

Like we both owed the other something.

"No," he sighed. "I'm mad at myself. I didn't say what I wanted to, at the bonfire. At first I didn't even know that you were going be there. I…I *couldn't* say anything in the moment, or when I thought I was ready. Shit —I did want to talk to you, Grahams. I *did*. When we would find ourselves alone, of course. But why did you get so out of it?"

Because you looked at me like that.

Because I thought you didn't care.

Because we…maybe we'd done something wrong.

"I…don't know," I murmured, rolling my head to look up at the sky. My entire body was wound tight. "I guess…I got carried away."

Shane let out a sound between a growl and the sucking of his teeth. "I should have been looking out for you."

My mouth twisted into a shape as I glanced down to stare back at him. "You don't need to babysit me, Hyde."

He met my gaze again. The blue of his irises had dulled to a teal once again. "You keep acting like I do."

"What's that supposed mean?"

"When I first met you, you looked like you'd never done anything bad in your life. Now you're going at it to the extreme."

He looked borderline…disappointed. It was kind of disturbing —stoic and frigid in a way that nearly had me tempted to feel guilty.

"I've done things," I insisted, nudging his side for emphasis.

Shane blinked. He didn't lean backwards or avoid my eyes. He held that stare as a smile spread his lips —the sly kind I had learned to be wary of. "Name one," he dared.

I swallowed too loudly.

His nose was very close to mine. It had been two days since the library incident, but we actually hadn't talked about it. I knew it would have been infinitely worse if we hadn't talked at all. Shane's interest in me wasn't something to doubt. I felt it in everything. What didn't make sense to me was his hesitation in giving a name to whatever we were.

Any name at all.

He had to know who I was, since he was the only one who could keep their memories. And although I had not told him that I had just discovered who *he* was, I was not pushing for something —even something official. I was just looking for clarity. Boundaries.

I glanced downwards as I slowly lessened the distance. After a beat of uncertainty, he was moving closer too. That caused my heart rate to spike —then my lips hooked onto his just once; as soft as our first kiss but even slower. More forlorn and forbidden.

I left it at that.

I waited for his response as I then withdrew, this time not embarrassed enough to avert my gaze.

His eyes refracted the light of the moon. The tension of muscles in his face fluctuated between tightening and remaining relaxed.

"You sure this is…okay?" Shane then whispered. Heart-wrenchingly earnest. "We both know what's going to happen soon. What will happen after. You want to spend it this way? With me?"

A silent gasp escaped my lips. "…I don't want to care about what *will* happen," I told him truthfully. "All I know, is that I don't want to not do something today because of the consequences of tomorrow. I want to live exactly how I want while I have the chance. I want…this. You."

"Even though…even though you're good, and I'm…"

"Don't you finish that sentence," I warned, reaching for his cheek. "I finally have an answer to a question you've asked yourself for a very long time. You were created to be a monster. You have done monstrous things. You'll probably keep doing them still. But you need to stop looking at me like I am the hero to your villainy. I'm not that simple. I have no good in me but this: the ability to love what doesn't deserve it."

For the first time, I saw Shane Hyde doing something like crying.

Though I doubted it was the very first time he had.

Lining the bottom of his eyes were glinting pools of feeling. Ones that he might not understand, but that were there, nonetheless.

"Do you see the good in me, Grahams?" he asked.

"Do you have any?"

He flinched. "I…I don't even think my love for you is good."

I struggled to swallow. "Well, who said that love *is* always good? Do you think bad things can be capable of love?"

"Yes," he answered without hesitation.

"Pity. That must mean I'm no good after all. Because I want to love you," I whispered. "And I don't want anything to stop me from doing it."

"That's the thing," he rasped. "Everything will stop you."

I drew a breath.

I was too entangled in the sound of my pounding heart and the smell of the rushing water to voice any semblance of a response. Or maybe there was a way that I could answer which disregarded definition, irrespective of where my conscience was inclined.

The skin of his palm skimmed the side of my face. "…I will stop you," he confessed. "That accident at the massacre…that's *your* death."

"…You killing me isn't exactly news," I murmured.

The tears spilled. "No, but I'd like to stop doing it."

"I can see why. I think that's proof of something."

Then I kissed him again. And he kissed me back —his fingers moving to tangle the hair at the back of my neck as he gently tugged at it.

Fear that he obviously harboured did not creep over him —at least, it did not seem to be working its way into the kiss. No, Shane was shivering with a disbelieving giddiness. Neither of us knew where it might go, but I had no doubt that he also wanted to find out.

He paused for just a moment, and gently lowered my chin to open my mouth. I drew a soft gasp before Shane tilted his head and went at it with a newfound desire —though still patient and thorough. The sensation of that contact was entirely new to me, yet after the initial rationalisation my stomach fluttered with a swarm of eager butterflies.

It was the sort of slow kiss designed to make you warm and insatiable and desirous; therefore reluctant to end it at every hook and bite.

In the moment, I could have continued kissing him forever.

Shane's hand then slipped back down to his side, and he began to pull away hesitantly —because nothing stopped him from pecking my lips a few times before withdrawing completely.

"This is the continuation of a very bad idea," he breathed.

My eyelids fluttered open in a daze.

I couldn't stop thinking about it —for a long while afterwards. But in the immediate aftermath, I went very still.

I started to wonder why he had stopped. It worried me more that this time had been my initiative —but he had overtaken and grabbed the reins once more. I didn't like the feeling of it being…delicate.

Would the hesitation remain?

What if his fears overrode his wants and made him realise that maybe he didn't feel what he thought he did?

No, I consoled myself. He was in love with me.

BUT MAYBE HE DOESN'T WANT *TO BE*.

I couldn't bear the thought.

When we had caught our breath, I readjusted my glasses and pressed my forehead to his as I inhaled the scent of pine. I could feel the stare of his eyes even as mine then focused on the tips of his fingers grazing mine between us. Maybe that was an answer in itself.

"I'm sorry for getting so high," I murmured.

Shane sighed. "You don't need to apologise to me. Just remember to look around you. And don't listen to anything McCarthy has to say."

I let out an uneasy laugh. "Ha, yeah."

His features softened. "If you for whatever reason, *want* to smoke, or if you're running out of shit to do, just come find me."

I bit my lip to keep from grinning like a lunatic. "…Cool."

Shane wiped his cheeks, and then absentmindedly stroked mine. "By the way, you uh…want to go to the diner sometime?"

I shivered, and couldn't tell if it was because of that gesture or that it was growing colder. "Just the two of us?" I asked.

He clenched his jaw tightly. "Yeah."

"Sure. It's a date," I blurted out. My eyes widened in time with his. "I mean! Uh…like it's *confirmed*," I hurriedly amended. "Not that I thought it was —um…like a definite relationship thing or…"

Shane burst out laughing.

It was such a joyous sound.

I had never heard him express such an emotion, either —it had always come out as a chuckle at best. I stared at him in awe as he threw his head back and *laughed*.

As though nothing mattered.

As though it were only the two of us at the edge of everything.

When Shane then sighed, his eyes found mine. I started. They sparkled again; with all of the blue and green of nebula clouds.

He smirked and leaned back on one hand. "So you want to go out?"

My gaze slitted. "Pardon?"

"Milkshakes," Shane mused, glancing up at the starry expanse. "You and me. All that sappy stuff." Then he winked at me. "It's a date."

"Like that time we basically shared a drink?"

"More romantic than that."

I scowled on impulse and hit out at him, but I could not stay angry. I liked the banter —I liked talking to him and hanging out with him and I wanted to snicker at his stupid jokes.

Though not at the ones made at my expense.

"…It would be my first…date," I mumbled.

I expected him to start —or perhaps to laugh again, but he remained perfectly still. "Good. No standards to surpass."

"Hyde!" I exclaimed, offended despite the grin which threatened the integrity of a frown. "My standards in general happen to be *very* high."

And he seemed to meet all of them.

"I think that it's a good thing," he reasoned. "I find it special, anyway. Because *I* get to set a standard."

I didn't want to admit it, but my heart raced at his words. "Holy shit," I said instead. "*That* was certainly a line."

"Do you hate it?" Shane quipped, leaning closer.

I managed a small smile. "I didn't say that."

His eyes searched mine for sincerity, before he reached for my ear and put in his dangling earphone; lingering to brush his fingers through a few stray curls by my temple. His cellphone was playing one of my favourite songs, not his. "Good. Because I only plan on becoming worse."

"I dare you," I encouraged.

We slipped into a relationship like it was an overcoat.

It was an oddly familiar, yet cumbersome fit. It needed tailoring.

If anything, the passage and repetition of time had still allowed us to discover things about each other. Here on Earth, we were not confined by the heat and imprisonment of our previous memories.

And it was beautiful, in its little bubble of delusion. No Daemon and no demon and no God, was going to burst it.

I had never dreamt of having a boyfriend —even now that I had one I acknowledged that the circumstances were not ideal. No one in their right mind would choose to pursue a relationship with someone they knew was about to die or worse, someone who was about to kill them.

Someone they would then see again a while later, without the memory of any of it.

If there was one thing I couldn't understand, it was how Shane did it, cycle after cycle. There must have been instances where he had not even bothered to get to know me for that recurring reason alone.

I wanted to say that I was being selfish, but the truth was we were both selfish by indulging whatever it was; a love rekindled, or a different love completely anew. But we equally wanted that gentle violence. Shane had never been in his right mind, and I had nothing to lose.

I told him as much when we met up in the woods the next morning, and he still had that look of constipated disapproval. He would not meet my eye, and he fidgeted like last night hadn't happened.

"You really should think it over," he insisted. "I'm a beast, Alexander. Death in its most ruthless sense. No matter what, I suppose you are lucky never to carry one cycle to the next. But I'll be even more damned if I let you unknowingly fall to Hell with me."

"I don't think I'll care if you're there."

He crumpled further. "That's not natural."

"*We're* not natural," I countered.

Shane paused in thought.

"…If anything, I'm concerned with how this will affect *you*," I said while reaching for his hand. He let me hold it limply —before he squeezed back in reassurance. "You're the one who will have to go on, knowing."

"I had resolved long ago to spare us from that pain," he admitted. "But having you…*remember* —having you feel again even the smallest part of what you felt before, is making me waver."

"So this is the only cycle so far where I…" I trailed off, squeezing his hand. "I can only imagine how much it hurts —and why you *tried* to stay away from me. I…I can try to understand why you wouldn't want to have this and indulge me, but…have you never wanted to be selfish?"

Shane's face contorted with disbelief.

I dithered, getting the sense that I'd said something foolish. All he had ever done had likely been selfish. The cause of the curse certainly was.

And I knew that there should be some resentment or begrudging after finding out he had doomed the entire town for my sake…yet I could not feel that. It was bizarre, but the only thing that came to mind was a gross flattery. That he could rage so, at the loss of me.

"Every thought I've ever had of you has always been selfish," he told me, leaning in and cupping my cheek. His thumb slowly brushed against my temple. "To beg for you; to distance myself; even to spare or take your life." He gathered the strength to meet my eyes then, no matter what he'd see in them. "…You and I are forever shackled, and neither one of us can run away. It's a part of what keeps me here."

Violet bloomed around his burning irises and I wondered for the first time if it happened often.

I drew a shaky breath and curled inward, but he didn't move. His eyes stayed trained to my own. It was not that I was put off by the intensity of his words. I was a little frightened by the weight of us.

His mouth then found mine in a full, begging way which more greatly resembled surrender —and it finally dawned on me what we really meant. Though the apprehension melted, as I did, when Shane pulled back my head. I shuddered at the heat —but it was over before I could roil in it.

He smirked, knowing precisely what he had done.

"…No fair," I whispered.

"Nothing is," Shane chuckled.

the art of lighting water

LOUISE

SHE HAD INITIALLY felt bad for leaving right at the start and for many succeeding hours; rendering Alexander Grahams defenceless at the Fall bonfire —but after hearing about what had happened afterwards the feeling started slipping.

Louise didn't want the gory details of them and Shane Hyde sneaking off to talk and turn a very odd friendship into something else —something that seemed to have fit them all along.

She was happy for them, so she thought, and tried not to let conflicting ideas cloud that look the two got when they made eye contact.

Like the world was ending but it didn't remotely matter.

Or that they would be the ones to end it.

Louise had never seen a couple look at each other like that. Especially not her parents. So she began to wonder if love really was a choice and if she had had unrealistic expectations all along.

If her mother had been wrong about the social inner workings of the world and the way she conducted her faith, then that opened up endless possibilities on what else she was wrong about.

What of Louise's faith itself?

She had heard more of those rumours at the bonfire —the ones which accused Shane of being directly responsible for the Daemons and every other oddity of Pine Creek. That somehow, it was all his fault —despite also being a human being, because he was the only one without the thing plaguing the residents.

But Alexander didn't have one either. That made even less sense.

"What are you thinking so hard about, Barnes?"

Louise turned to see Jack Branner swaggering towards her on the main street. Her heart skipped a beat and she tucked back a few stray loosening curls, lowering her gaze in that way girls did to show that they were shy.

Her Daemon stifled a laugh.

"Nothing," she mumbled, shuffling on her feet.

She bit back a smile.

They had nearly kissed last night.

He had gotten her talking again after a few more swigs of wine, cosy and close as they leaned against a large tree trunk. She had thought that he would go for it —irrationality that solitude had later scolded her for —and had been disappointed when he had stopped at stroking her cheek and calling her pout cute. Louise should've known that something was wrong after catching Laura Takunda staring at them; brows knitted in a frown.

It had just been nice to think that someone could still want her.

"Good," Jack chuckled. "Wouldn't want you turning into one of those brainy girls who questions everything."

Louise's supressed smile slowly morphed into a frown. "What?"

"Come on —isn't it annoying trying to have a conversation about stuff that doesn't even matter?" he cooed, reaching for her chin. "Stick to that chitter about appearances, sweetheart. Ideally it'd be nice if you could go back to your old style, too, but I can wait. I'm a very patient man."

"Excuse me?"

"You've dragged this whole '*identity crisis*' thing on for too long," he sighed. "We miss the old Louise."

Oh my. Looks like he sees your mother in you, remarked solitude. *You could always prove him wrong if he's incorrect.*

Damn right he was incorrect.

Louise huffed, seeing red. "You mean you miss the Louise who kept her mouth shut and didn't think for herself —so that she would actually go out with losers like you?"

"What," he snapped. "*Losers*?"

"Oh my God," she scoffed, turning sharply to storm off, "I can't even bring myself to pity you, peaking in high school and whatnot. I hope that all of your future divorcées choose not to bear your children!"

"*What —*?"

She was not satisfied with her final words, but she had not been able to stand another second in his presence. And for once, her Daemon was pleased in a way that did not welcome any claws to her skin. Though she could not shake the idea of that result not being a wholly good thing.

The remaining walk to the grocery store was too short.

Her feet made their way to the snack aisle without thought before she snagged a couple of bags of chips and a chocolate bar, and whirled for the front counter. To Hell with it all.

Donatello Ricci glanced up, startled.

He had been there at the bonfire last night. He had seen her pinned to the tree, stupidly giggling with a football player. She had hated the look of scorn and pity he had thrown their way.

Now she felt her face warm with embarrassment.

"…Did you get home okay yesterday?" he asked, ringing up her items and clearly trying not to judge outwardly.

Louise pouted again. "No. It's been really shitty, thanks for asking."

"What, you *didn't* snatch up Jack Branner?"

"I'd rather snatch his throat."

"Ooh," Donatello whistled. "I take it the date didn't work out."

"He's a sexist prick, like my Dad," she sniffed, handing over money. "I was too blinded by the idea of being desirable to see it."

His face fell. "You were drunk."

"That's worse."

"Too true."

He then made that face that indicated that the little cogs in his head were turning. Louise tilted her head and waited, vaguely interested in what he might say next. They had not had a proper conversation in a long time. Of course, they had never been *friends* —his parents knew hers and they had only had each other for company at the small get-togethers in the city.

Even back then they had been as different as chalk and cheese, but at least they had been able to talk about something and play as children. It was when they had hit puberty that they drifted so far apart that they were essentially strangers. At first, it was Louise who had pulled away; acting as if she didn't know him. As though she had become too good for their barely a friendship. That was what her old friends had told her.

Solitude threw it back at her occasionally, and her Daemon enjoyed feeding on that guilt. Eventually, Donatello had given up on trying to talk to her —even at those inane events where no one else would be there to liven the boredom. Even when his family had moved into the town.

But now it had been too many years and it had grown to be too weird

—speak nothing of his very strange attempts at what could be considered flirting. It was horrendous to think that *he*, of all people, could even like her after the monster she had been.

Half of her resistance came from that remaining kernel of something like standards she had and he did not meet; while the other was quite the opposing notion —of her being abominably unworthy of his interest and pursuit. He deserved someone who wasn't…her. And all that came with that. In her frustration she often fanned the flames of hurt and tried to —hopefully —make him hate her. Though she had had no such luck yet.

"…Don't diminish your worth because you keep being told a guy like Jack is all you deserve," Donatello eventually sighed. "Even through our rough patches and journeys to become better people, the perceived worth should never dip down to someone you tolerate but treats you like shit."

Louise blinked, then frowned.

She didn't like that he sometimes had a way with words.

"Whatever," she muttered, taking the filled bag from the counter. "It's got nothing to do with you, anyway."

"Right…Oh, before you go," he went on. "Would you want to —"

"No, Donny."

"I didn't even finish my sentence," he protested.

"Yeah, I know."

She didn't want to feel bad. She *shouldn't* feel bad. There were plenty of damning things for her too agonise over, and bluntly rejecting Donatello Ricci over and over wasn't one of them.

"Why do you keep shutting me down?" he grumbled, ruffling his curly ponytail. "I literally haven't done anything to warrant your dismissal."

Donatello was rather good-looking. He was not otherwise the kind of boy she would have considered in the past due to his creative hobbies, but objectively, if they really had been strangers, she might have…

Louise shook her head. "Ooh, you just did. Talk normal."

"Come on," he pressed.

"It's everything," she blurted. "The way you breathe, even."

"I really thought I had a chance." He sounded hurt.

"Why would you think that?"

"It's just…I mean, you're not out of my league anymore."

Her brown eyebrows shot up. "The *fuck* did you just say?"

Donatello started. "Wait, that came out wrong —"

"*You* came out wrong!"

She stomped past the small freezers towards the exit.

"Louise, please. I'm so sorry. That's not what I meant to say. I *meant*, you are now in a position where that stuff shouldn't matter. It never really should have, but I'd hoped that you breaking away from those horrid girls would change you to somebody I could recognise."

Her feet caught some invisible sticky substance on the tiled floor. He stopped right behind her. She could see his shadow and Daemon cast on the off-white. They engulfed her.

"Do you…do you really hate me?" Donatello murmured.

Her hands balled. "…Don't make me answer that. I'm only indulging this encounter since no one else is here. You talk about me not letting my worth diminish but what are *you* doing by pursuing me? I'm…I'm a bad person, Donny. You should know that."

"*Were* a bad person."

"How are you sure?"

"Because I knew you before. And this Louise is reminiscent of her."

That was probably the sweetest thing that anyone had ever said to her no matter how much she was not inclined to believe it. And it might have given her courage and motivation, if her Daemon wasn't hanging onto his every word to twist and pick apart later.

"I keep trying but I'm just not there yet," breathed Louise.

"And here I wait."

She whipped around, coming up to his chest. He leaned down slightly to meet her eyes. She had forgotten what colour they were truly: a crisp Fall honey that darkened in the shade. All of a sudden, all of those years came flooding back —all the comradery and the connection they had reluctantly fostered. So did the betrayal and terrifying development of…feelings.

For once, she gave him a look of fragile vulnerability instead of shock and horror. "But you shouldn't," she said.

Her voice broke.

Donatello returned her bravery with a tired smile. "…I can do what I want, Louise Barnes," he said softly.

Her cheeks flushed a little. She certainly didn't deserve that.

Mercy, said solitude.

After taking an uneasy breath, Louise regathered her dignity. "You want, maybe…to try being friends? Properly, this time."

He smiled a bit wider. "Okay."

There was a knock on wood.

Louise glanced up from the book she had been reading to gauge any repetition. She wasn't expecting anyone —or that noise on a tree trunk.

She was curled up in her treehouse the next afternoon, getting quality time away from her parents. The knock came again.

The teenager rolled over to lift the latch on the floor which opened a trapdoor. Ruth would never dare to intrude, and she was sure that Henry had forgotten where it was.

"Who is it?" Louise called out, before peering over.

"Hey. Your Dad said I might find you here."
She blinked down at Donatello's tentative smile. He already had both of his hands and feet up several rungs —of course, he had had to in order to knock on the underside of the trapdoor, too.

"Oh. Hm. What brings you here?"

"Day off," he explained. "And I thought we were getting to know each other again now. This is a rare chance to see you."

Her eyes narrowed. "Well, aren't you eager."

Donatello ascended a few more rungs until his head rose through the threshold. Louise hadn't moved, so his face was far closer than it had been before. All she could do was stare; at his freckles and wild curls tied into a bun. He stared back for a moment, and she saw no hint of disgust.

"So…can I come up?"

His lips moved, and she then found the sense to lean back. She cleared her throat, before settling back down on the cushion she had taken from the living room. Donatello had to *crawl* —he was way too tall to extend without hurting his back. His Daemon didn't seem to like the predicament very much either. She couldn't hold in a soft laugh at the sight. Solitude did not mock her for it.

"What have you been up to?" he asked, kneeling on his haunches.

"Reading," Louise answered. "For the first time in years."

His gaze travelled up and down the length of her; from her oversized hooded jersey to her short, loose pyjamas underneath. She hadn't thought of it before, but suddenly she felt all too exposed.

"Can I read something?"

"Sure."

Donatello shuffled over to the shelves to browse. She was half aware of his presence as his finger skimmed along the spines. The small words on the pages swam and wriggled and refused to obey her concentration.

Then he spoke again, and she couldn't get back into it all.

"It's been ages since I was in here. I still remember you trying to push my head back out through the trapdoor."

Louise made a high-pitched noise. "I did that?"

"Yeah. When you turned ten, you said your treehouse was strictly girls only —so you could talk about stuff I wasn't supposed to hear."

"Oh my God," she groaned, burying her face in the pages.

He laughed —and the full sound startled her. She hadn't heard it in a while. She hadn't seen that particular face either —the one that almost lit up and wrinkled his long, narrow nose and creased his eyes.

Something fluttered onto the floor.

The teenagers paused as Donatello picked up a weathered, torn page. Louise's instinctual reaction was visceral. How on earth had she managed to tear book? Upon closer inspection, though, there was something wrong with it. Scrawled over the printed paragraphs in thick permanent marker, was her own handwriting.

Her appal heightened.

Until Donatello's gaze narrowed to read the words. "What *is* this?"

"Let me see."

He handed it over. Her eyes swept the page —and also narrowed, though in confusion. She couldn't make sense of what she was seeing.

Written there in a flurry of urgency and fear, was a passage that read like a prophetic, ominous warning…dated five days into the future.

THE LION MUST NEVER LAY WITH THE LAMB.

IT WILL DEVOUR AND WHISPER.

AND THE LAMB WILL BLEED.

THIS IS THE TRAGEDY THAT CANNOT BE UNDONE.

Louise's mind had no idea what any of it was referring to —but a chill went up her spine as if her body knew. As if it remembered.

Donatello acknowledged the fear he saw in her face, and it slowly set in that it wasn't a prank or joke. Though while it was comforting to have someone there to witness it and be believed, Louise was well aware that she couldn't prove it really had been written in the future. Sure —she did not have any memory of writing it. But there was the possibility that she had been drunk and had blacked out.

Even with the creeping feeling that it was otherworldly.

"Hey, doesn't the bible mention something about a lion laying with a lamb?" Donatello spoke up, brushing back loose curls from his forehead. "Though, not like this. This doesn't sound like…poetry."

"You're right," she whispered. "That verse was somewhat positive. I have a bad feeling about this. We…we have to check if there's more."

the confession

ALEXANDER

SHANE HYDE MADE it difficult to keep anything a secret.

He didn't shy away from displays of affection or not maintaining any space between us. Even in the seclusion of the furthest poorly lit booth at the back of *Straws & Fries*. He assured me that no one would see us here nor care to investigate. So we sat right next to each other; knees to knees and elbows to elbows once again, with chocolate and caramel milkshakes and a platter of crisp, warm syrup-drenched waffles between us.

"This *is* more romantic," I murmured, leaning over to take a sip of his milkshake through its striped paper straw.

"Don't just finish mine," he gasped, retaliating by swiping my cherry. "It might have been a mistake to introduce you to chocolate."

"There was no mistake," I smiled, tearing off a piece of waffle. I was bringing it up to my mouth to eat when I then noticed Shane with his own expectantly open. I scoffed.

The diner was empty apart from a few rowdy teenagers sitting in the booths closer to the front, facing away from where we were.

I swallowed, psyching myself up for the unthinkable, and then placed a piece of the waffle on his tongue.

He made a show of eating it —and gently took hold of my hand before I could withdraw. His tongue poked out, and slowly ran the length of my thumb and forefinger. My breath hitched and my glasses slipped but he didn't look down. That turquoise wouldn't let me go.

And then he did; leaning away as if he had accomplished some great feat, while my hand was suspended there for a good few seconds.

I didn't know whether I wanted to wipe my fingers…or lick them.

"Gross," I whispered unconvincingly, cringing.

"You liked it though," he mused, his back to the leather rest. "I could tell by the look in your eyes."

"Damnit."

Then my smile fell.

Shane tilted his head and folded his arms on the table. "What is it?"

"Should I feel even slightly bad for not properly checking in with my Dad for a number of days? I know he's *alive*, but is that enough?"

"No." He did not even hesitate. "Why should you be obligated to care about that man at all?"

Despite the steep deterioration of our relationship, my father had been ordinarily far easier to get along with. Although it was a '*don't ask, don't tell*' sort of communication, it wasn't as if Hugh had been completely and unapologetically awful to me. I craved a supportive parent, but our views and values were too different and he couldn't always give what I needed. I still had a roof over my head and food on the table —though that detail had changed as of late. I had the roof, but I hated being under it with him. We had the food, but that had abruptly become my responsibility.

There was a limit to my complaints —especially because of Daemons, but one fact remained. I couldn't *breathe* in that house.

"He *did* contribute to bringing me into the world," I mumbled.

Shane's brows furrowed in mock thought. "Hm. Minimum merit."

I feebly slapped his shoulder. "Not helpful."

He let out a soft chuckle and sighed, then reached to swirl the straw in his milkshake. "I'm sure I'm the worst person to ask about due parental affection, you know. I don't *have*…uh, parents. That Hyde family is the closest I'll ever get to such a thing. I was made —for a specific purpose without other intentions. I mean…the one who made me likely expected some reverence. Once, long ago, I think I offered it," he admitted, turning to meet my eye. His expression softened. "But then I fell in love with you. Before you were taken from me."

Resentment soured the sweetness of his words and the warmth of his gaze at the end of his rant. I folded my arms on the table too, leaned over to bump my shoulder into him, and hooked my little finger on his.

"…Maybe we don't owe our makers anything."

The rigidity melted in Shane —I could tell as he then broke a piece of waffle and offered it to me.

My mouth opened.

It was his turn to stiffen and turn a little red as I dared to mirror some of his previous movements, even if he attempted to keep a straight face.

"Damnit," he hissed.

I sheepishly withdrew. He was right —a part of me had liked it. And it made me wonder what else I might like. I had never explored anything to do with sexuality. In fact, for a long time as a younger teenager, I had identified as both asexual and aromantic. That was how it had felt at the time. It had taken one crush to throw a spanner in the works. And it had taken a bit longer for me to realise that I didn't need yet another box, and that there was no rush nor need ever to be completely certain.

I put my head on Shane's denim shoulder. "This is nice."

The corner of his mouth quirked upwards in a smirk as he moved his head a little. "Pleased to hear so."

For a moment, I wondered what it might be like not to keep our new development under the radar. To walk around Pine Creek and do whatever we wanted, without fear of disapproval —or worse.

We had no safety net. That was our reality. So I wondered if we would remain that sort of fantasy, even on Earth.

"…I had another dream last night," I spoke up.

"Yeah? What about?"

"How I got to Hell."

His irises glimmered with curiosity. "The very first time?"

I shook my head. "It's not as clear as the ones I've had, but I remember it. It's such a strange experience. I was just sleeping, when my body felt like it was being pulled apart and broken into pieces before being knitted back together. Then there was…fire. In every direction. I felt the heat of burns but my skin didn't tear and bleed."

"Whoa," breathed Shane. "That's how you got there? But why?"

"I still don't know the answer to that," I sighed. "It cut off as soon as the burning cooled. I doubt it was the first visit. I'd known where to go."

"So…you were stolen away."

"Kidnapped?" I reiterated, taken aback. Though there was no surprise there. Especially given my destination, and the fact that I hadn't died.

"Do you have a timeline yet of when it all started?"

I paused. My eyes widened slightly at the realisation. "It was the night that my Mom's diagnosis worsened to the point of…"

Shane wholly took hold of my hand, intertwining our fingers. I could not get any more words out of my throat, and I could feel my vision blur. How cruel. I wanted to curse whatever entity had taken me —had preyed on my devastation to twist the hurt further like a knife. If God was indeed real that meant I had been abandoned. That was the only way I could see it. If the way I had lived my life did not grant me a place in Heaven and I had been sent to Hell instead…I was no child of God.

Maybe I had never even belonged to Them.

"*Alexander*."

I drew a sharp breath at the sound of Shane's voice; sudden and desperate as if I'd taken air amidst the sea. But it grounded me a little. I leaned into the low murmur, engraining it in my mind.

"Alexander."

The second time was to soothe instead of rescue.

"I…I would never have met you otherwise," I rasped, looking at him earnestly. "I don't like that I was taken against my will, but maybe there was a reason for that, too."

He frowned and squeezed my hand. "I…do not think that I can thank the one responsible, just for that."

"Why —because it was me?" I whispered.

"Perhaps I'm as blindly wicked as it seems."

I lifted my free arm to hold my cheek in my hand. "And I'm into you still. The miracle of irrational and tunnelled disregard."

His forehead pressed to mine. "This is no miracle."

My breath halted again, but now for a different reason. Would he dare to kiss me here, even for one second? He definitely breathed like he was thinking about it. His eyes searched mine, and I watched the little slithers of purple materialise around his pupils. A glimpse of the iron beast.

"May I?" he asked at a volume only I could hear.

The temptation nearly outweighed the fear. *Nearly*.

"…Maybe we should wait until we've left," I answered. "Not because

I don't feel like getting caught for it —but rather that nobody likes seeing people making out in public."

He let out a frustrated sound. "You're killing me, Grahams."

"That'd be a first."

"Low blow," he said through his teeth, leaning back as if it took all of his strength. I held out another piece of waffle and leisurely sipped at his chocolate milkshake. He bit it out of my fingers with stubborn reluctance, then took the tall glass away from me.

"I have an idea," I said. I plucked another striped paper straw from the condiments basket and stuck it in. "Now we can share."

"But what about the one you already ordered?" Shane pointed out.

"We can share that too."

His face scrunched with scepticism. "I'm not really a caramel fan."

"Shame," I quipped, pursing my lips and drinking from his anyway.

"You're so lucky you're cute," he huffed, claiming the other straw.

I hummed in a smug response.

We stared at each other regardless, downing the glass. I could never have imagined that my first date —as far as I was aware —would be such a beautiful cliché, but I was not complaining.

It was difficult to decide whether or not to be surprised in discovering the human experience Shane Hyde had fostered in the reality of the curse. Both willing and unwilling. There were aspects of his personality that had only evolved over so much time versus answers he gave related to newer parts of himself. In a way, he had begun to paint two different portraits of himself —one of a supernatural monster, and the other of an emotionally repressed teenage boy. I knew that he was a mixture of both, but the one that I was seeing in front of me felt the closest and most tangible; literally but just as figuratively. The beast was out of reach beyond Shane's eyes, and his human form was all the softest parts of him.

I liked the sound of his hypnotic voice, but I couldn't help wanting for what he truly sounded like; as I'd heard before. I hadn't dreamt of it since.

In the end, there wasn't much that we could ask each other past basic questions around the lives we were currently living.

Shane knew different facets of me across time.

He was too protective of a vulnerable state for me to dig.

But I understood. Anything deeper than the surface made him slip into anxiety that I couldn't judge because past iterations of myself had caused all sorts of defence mechanisms to lock in place.

And I couldn't undo them in one cycle.

One life.

Or more realistically, a few days.

Strangely, the prospect of knowing when I was going to die did not rattle me as much as I thought it would —or should. Knowing that he was going to be the one to kill me was a pushed back thought, too. I chalked it up to having no control anyway, and that the curse was inescapable. If I wasn't going to remember any of it, then the accidental death was my last concern.

It was a way of thinking that would have had me squinting last month but in the moment, I wanted to explore the dreams and the memories and all that being with Shane in the reality in which we found ourselves could offer. I wanted to understand and live it in that capacity.

"I've got to know something," I announced as we trekked through the woods. "What exactly is it that you like about me?"

From the first word and the smile on his face, I knew that he had had the answer prepared and rehearsed for an unfathomable amount of time. "You are my key to the whole world," he began, glancing at me. "It was you who opened up all the possibilities I never would have experienced; all of the joy and anguish of existing. All of the pain, amidst the triumph. You made me realise that I could *feel*, Alexander."

I blinked at him, dumbstruck. Had I really been that impactful on his life? "I…I really did that?"

"Yes. And sometimes, it's the only motivation I possess."

My surprise morphed into pity. "I suppose I should be happy you view it that way instead of hating me for it."

"Hate could be the other side of it, though," he muttered. "Despite all my gratitude, maybe a speck of me resented that enlightenment."

"Mm. Maybe."

I reached for his swinging hand and clasped it tightly. He threaded our fingers and then stuffed our hands into his denim jacket pocket —forcing me to stick directly to his side. I buried my face in his chest, embarrassed even though we were blissfully alone.

"You don't get tired of telling me every time I ask, do you?" My voice was muffled in the faded blue.

He chuckled lowly. "Nope."

I couldn't understand.

"And what about you?" Shane then asked, making me raise my head. His voice had lowered and softened. "You've…never said it enough to me."

That struck a fissure into my heart. It had never fully occurred that the implication of his terror of being involved with me was steeped in a large number of cycles where I hadn't loved him.

Where I hadn't known him.

"My reasons aren't quite as profound," I warned, meeting his nervous gaze. "I might have opened up the world to you, but for me, I think it was the opposite. I was…suffering. I did not want the world. Then I was taken to meet you, and even though you were a manifestation of unhinged evil, I found a solace in your company. Despite being referred to as a '*monster*' you too were being mistreated by your world. And so we made our own," I smiled. "You *reminded* that I could feel."

His reaction wasn't what I had expected.

Although I knew he hadn't heard all that very often, I hadn't thought that he would stare at me…as if he had never heard *any* of it before. My feet stalled, and he jerked to a stop with me.

"What?" I questioned.

He took a few seconds to reboot —before he shook his head slightly and blinked. "…You've never said *that*. Not as profound, my ass."

I paused. "Never?"

"Yeah. Usually your answer is that you like my face."

"*What*?" I cried. "…I mean, I do, but —"

Shane chuckled softly, which baffled me further. It was absurd that I had only straightforwardly admitted a shallower attraction to him all of those times before, but I quickly got stuck on the fact that I had never told him the more heartfelt reason.

"That was the most beautiful thing I've ever heard," he then remarked, bringing my focus back to the present. "Yes, you've never said that to me, but I'm rather overwhelmed by the honour of hearing it now. Especially because I came close to possibly *never* hearing it."

I pressed my lips into a tight line. I couldn't make the empty promise of perhaps I would say it again. I couldn't break him like that.

"You want to go back?" Shane asked, looking at the darkening sky.

I fidgeted, just *thinking* about what my father would say if he caught me sneaking back inside. "…I don't think I really want to go home."

He frowned, pondering over the refusal. Then a shrug.

"Sleep over."

My brows knitted. "Is that a request or a demand?"

"Which is more likely to get you to agree?"

I thought about it. Despite my joking, there were a few reasons why I would want to sleepover at Shane's. There were good and bad ones —but a bubbling curiosity charged past all the reasons not to.

I looked him dead in the eye and licked along my top lip, sticking my nose up. Something shameless and bold overtook me. "Neither. *Beg*."

One of his dark eyebrows slowly raised in astonishment —before he inhaled sharply and a smile stretched his face. "…I like this side of you, Alexander Grahams."

"That didn't sound like begging."

Those eyes gleamed with mischief. "…Pretty please," he purred; rows of perfect teeth gleaming as he playfully tilted his head.

My knees went a little weak.

I swallowed. "Damnit."

the stars and their moon

ALEXANDER

THE HYDE FAMILY had not met me.

That was an advantage.

They would have only heard distorted accounts —if anything —but they hadn't had the opportunity to see me in person and form an opinion. Shane had warned me of some of their views, however —so we had to exercise caution. Or at least, I wanted to.

Shane seemed intent to piss them off.

"Everyone," he announced as rounded the living room doorway. "This is Alexander, my closest friend. We'll be having a sleepover because the Grahams' house sucks."

Three heads turned.

It was nice to meet a pair of parents who weren't in their pyjamas and dressing gowns. Mr and Mrs Hyde were actually dressed rather formally for a Saturday night —as if they were going to a dinner party. Mrs Hyde stood in front of a large mirror on the wall, pinning and tucking her light brown hair. Her husband sat in an armchair ready to head out of the door in a pinstripe beige suit. And a young boy sat cross-legged on the floor in front of a television that didn't work, with a tablet that did.

Their Daemons billowed on a phantom wind —two of them tall and well-fed, while the smaller third wafted with barely any guilt. All of them plastered against the wall like a shadow.

"Sleepover?" Mrs Hyde repeated. "Shane, you know that we are going out to *Willman's*. It's date night."

Shane's discomfort with that was written all over his face.

"What, I can't babysit with a friend over?" he cut back. "That'll make for more eyes on Ken."

"Lord give me strength," Mr Hyde grumbled.

The little blond boy stood up and ran up to me. "I'm Kendall, but you can call me Ken. I've never seen you before, but I've heard stuff. So wow, you really *don't* have a shadow monster."

"Good observation," his father said.

"Yeah, I guess I don't. But I…I'm around," I defended myself. "I did used to live here as a child."

"Before we came," Shane added.

"Ah," Mrs Hyde quipped, whirling around and causing the skirt of her dress to billow. "Well, I'm sorry Alexander but as tempting as it seems to let more people look after Ken, we have just met you. We haven't even had a conversation with your father." She then gave me a onceover. "You do seem like a good boy, though…I mean *person*."

I winced. The attempt sounded disingenuous.

"Samantha's right," Mr Hyde sighed, heaving to his feet. "You cannot spring something like this on us, boy."

Shane folded his arms and stared his stepfather down, before clicking his tongue. "Oh, I wasn't asking for permission."

My gaze narrowed. "Shane —"

"You can't bring a stranger into the house and then just expect to get away with it," Mr Hyde clipped. "Look, I'm sure that *this* particular friend would not hurt a fly, but that is not a free pass."

"Absolutely true," agreed Samantha. "We may have a reservation and want a break from you and Ken, but this isn't happening."

Shane breathed hard through his nose. Kendall was still staring at me.

"I like Alexander," he stated, turning back to his parents. "It's hard to try sleep when there's shouting. Pretty please can they stay over?"

His parents shared a look, before his mother let out a sigh and leaned down beside him. "…Ken sweetie, you might not understand this, but it's not proper for us to allow someone we don't yet know well, to sleepover. A playdate is a different thing. A safer thing."

"But they can't go back to their house," he whined.

"Until I hear a valid reason, Alexander is not staying," Mrs Hyde said softly, glancing at me. "Not a chance."

I dithered, unsure of how to respond. It all felt too personal to disclose but I knew that they would not consider agreeing until I said something. I looked at Shane, and he offered me sympathy. No one was forcing me. I simply had to decide between staying in that house holding my breath, or if I could bear divulging queerphobia just to take that air.

"Um…it's not…necessary," I assured. "I just…I'm not having a good relationship with my Dad," I tried. "It's really bad, in fact."

The Hydes weren't buying it.

"…Lots of beer," I added, my voice lowering. "I…I'm scared."

Samantha's gaze softened significantly as she hugged her younger son close. She then looked to her husband. He was not as enthusiastic, but his rigidity wavered as he processed my vague reasoning —said that way for

Kendall's sake. He huffed, adjusting his blazer. Like surrender. "…Okay. We're going to be late, Samantha."

She got to her feet and patted Kendall's head. "Shane, you know the rules —even if Alexander will stay here for the night. Do not ignore your brother. That means no locked doors —you need to be able to hear him."

"*Yes*!" hissed the little boy. "…You'll be all right here," he told me. I managed the slightest smile —but inside I was grinning like a lunatic. It all aligned with my resolution: to Hell with consequences and tomorrow, for that matter. It was everything, now.

"Shane, did you hear me?" Samantha checked.

"Got it," he quipped, very smug in his triumph.

She put her hands on her hips. "We *are* going to have a talk about this the first chance we get. This will not happen again."

"Sure," Shane drawled.

"Just to be clear, this is not us caving into your ridiculous whims," Mr Hyde snarled on his way out. "We're simply responding to a dire situation —and we'll be paying Alexander's father a visit tomorrow." He turned to me. "That all right with you, so —uh, kid?"

His effort was unsure and self-conscious but better than his wife's.

Shane Hyde had let on about what life at home with a family that was not his was like, but being amidst them painted a far more vivid picture. I could sense the way that the parents were trying to discipline the child who had grown to be so unruly that they were on the brink of giving up; and an icy reception of that. Neither side was wholly to blame —because neither side focused on a dark reality.

"I can't thank you enough." I was now milking it. "Mr and Mrs Hyde."

"Aw —you can call us Samantha and Jeffery, dear," Mrs Hyde smiled, before patting Shane on the shoulder upon her exit. He let her do it, even though he appeared viscerally uncomfortable.

"We should be back late," Jeffery informed us, pointing importantly. "At a time you *should* be asleep."

"Yessir," Kendall saluted.

"Love you," Samantha told her children. "Oh, Alexander —ask Shane for anything you might need. See you in the morning."

"Thanks, Samantha," I called after her. We all waited for the sound of the door being shut.

Kendall then stared up at us. "I did a good thing, right?"

"Yes," I confirmed. "I am in your debt."

"Ken," Shane spoke up. "I'll pay you five dollars to leave us alone the whole time. We're going to watch movies in my room. Movies *you* can't watch. Disturbance is allowed for emergencies only."

His brother actually deliberated over it; slowly stroking his chin as if it had been a proposition to solve a prestigious crime. "…Okay," he then chirped, before heading back for his patch of carpet.

"Is this…safe?" I whispered to Shane as he then placed a hand on the small of my back to guide me towards the stairs.

"It's standard procedure," he smirked.

There was a working lock on the door, unlike my room.

Shane's bedroom was a clearcut reflection of his outward personality: grounded, unapologetic yet somehow still unspecific enough to leave him a bit of a mystery. The few posters that were taped to the grey walls were generic to the point of being suspicious. As if he did not quite know what he liked, and needed to uphold an image.

The only part that was real in some way was the mess —his bed was unmade and the clothes basket was beginning to overflow.

The window was open, though, letting in a fresh breeze and airing the bland space. I then noticed Shane's stare as I glanced upwards. My fingers fiddled with my cardigan's buttons. All of the nervousness I had not been feeling before flooded my system as reality settled.

We were all alone.

"Not quite what you thought?" Shane quipped.

"Well…" I started. "Where are the instruments of torture?"

I was joking. Probably.

"Is that how you see me?" he smirked, though it was obvious he was a bit offended judging by the knitting of his eyebrows.

"…At first," I admitted, averting my gaze. "But not anymore, I swear. This is *much* better than my terrible imagination —"

He barked a short laugh, before ruffling my hair. "I know it's different from that haunted prehistoric mansion, Grahams, but no need to struggle with compliments."

I half-heartedly shoved at him, appalled. He caught my wrist, bitterly smug as I wriggled in the strength of his grip.

"It's not a mansion. It's not that big," I grumbled.

Shane leaned down to be at eye-level with me, coming close enough for his nose to brush against mine. My glasses tipped with the movement.

And that smile did not falter. "In comparison."

I swallowed, but there was no spit in my mouth. Then my body began to warm up. My eyes narrowed as Shane continued to stare with a wicked amusement glinting in his gaze.

"…I wonder if other parts of you turn red instead," he murmured.

"Oh my God!" I cried —probably like a startled kid despite the fury I was wielding.

He laughed again, before pressing a finger to his lips in a gesture to keep the volume down. I clapped my hands over my mouth, worried that I might have alerted Kendall.

No footsteps came scurrying up the stairs, thankfully. The bribe and tablet were proving to be sufficient enough of a distraction.

"Are you full from earlier? I can get us snacks if not," Shane asked as he fished a laptop from some forgotten corner behind an unsurprisingly untouched and quite orderly desk.

"Yeah —I'm full," I sighed, lowering onto the mattress and pushing my glasses back up. I stared up at the ceiling. I blinked in bewilderment. Stuck up on the plaster in clusters were glow-in-the-dark stars, moons and meteorites. A lone rocket dominated the centre, large and soaring towards the only sun.

I abruptly sat up. Shane threw himself onto the bed beside me, causing me to bounce. "What?" he said.

I pointed to the stickers. "*Those*, are the most unusual things in your room."

He glanced upwards. His eyelashes were lighter in sparse light too —closer to the natural blond of his hair. I stared for a while.

Then his eyes were looking into mine, and I flinched. It would never fail to unnerve whenever he looked at me head-on.

"Not the condoms?" he snorted.

It took me completely out of it. My face contorted as I let out a sigh. "No, even those seem on brand."

He blinked rapidly. "Damn, called out by my own partner."

He finished logging in and opening the downloaded movie files. It still made my heart flutter to hear him refer to me as his partner. It was a small, beautiful solace in the chaotic tangle of my life. Like he understood.

"I'm not shaming you, Hyde," I assured, leaning towards him. "For some reason, it just hadn't crossed my mind that you'd still come with a story —like a real kid. The fact that you left them up there for all of this time…does that mean something to you?"

Shane stiffened, and looked up at the ceiling again. "…Maybe."

He'd never lied to me.

I was grateful that even when we had first met, he had never given me an evasive response, or misled me. He had been honest —not because he was an earnest person, or because it was in his nature. It was a bit ironic, if I thought about it. Even if he had been cold and abrasive initially, he had always ensured that what he said was truthful. When Shane Hyde said the word '*maybe*', it was because he was afraid. It wasn't a no, and it wasn't a yes. But it wasn't confident, and it wasn't strong.

I offered a small smile. "I like them," I told him. "A lot."

He looked back down at me with a much more softened expression. "Then I won't ever take them down."

It felt like there was a deeper meaning to that. But it was one that I couldn't guess, so I inched my hand towards his. This time he flinched at the slight contact of our fingers, before they interlaced with the speed that rivalled a flowering bloom. Because as we would go on, it was all delicate and new.

There was a reason that small things like these felt different with each other. The mundane had become beautifully unfamiliar —now capable of making our hearts race and our palms sweaty in a giddy way that felt like we were going to die from just that.

"Come on," Shane then murmured, shuffling backwards as best as he could manage with one hand under his laptop and the other still adamantly holding mine. "I've picked a romantic one."

"Just for me?" I quipped, leaning in close as we snuggled up against his strewn duvet and pillows.

"Just for you," he confirmed, subtle condescension creasing his smile.

I poked his cheek, and his response was letting go of my hand to snake his arm around my waist instead —making me fit just underneath his chin with my curls tickling his sharp jaw.

It was a movie I had already seen before.

But I hadn't ever watched it with Shane, so he didn't know about the box of tissues I had had beside me and the blanket in which I had wrapped myself —not to mention the mortifying recollection of peeking from that blanket at any of the sexy scenes.

I bit the inside of my cheeks, becoming increasingly aware of where our skin touched. Could he hear my rapidly racing heartbeat?

Feel it?

He was, contrastingly, very serious about it. His gaze was intently on the screen despite his disinterest. I couldn't help but smile.

Just for you.

"I think I'm in love with you," I told him.

Shane's head slowly turned. I thought he might reply with something along the lines of '*congratulations, you are now officially the last person to know*' —but his face was so earnest.

"I need you to know…that I've never felt what I feel for you, before," he admitted. "Warm, nervous and shit. But it's big. Sometimes it feels so big that I might burst."

My lips parted in surprise. "You're good at hiding it."

"That's because I only panic when you're not looking," he chuckled.

"I want to show you the least awful of me."

"Feel free to look like a fool sometimes," I quipped.

"*Wow*, Grahams."

"Just to make it fair."

He paused, then pressed his lips to my cheek. And lingered. "…I've never actually seen you as that kind of foolish, Alexander."

My heart lurched and skipped a beat.

Never?

Had Shane truly never looked at me and seen what I always saw? It was perplexing to think that even when we had met and expressed hostility, all he had seen was the one person who had ever mattered.

Then I *giggled*. It was from pure joy because his statement meant that he had been seeing just another human being: just Alexander. Regardless of what he had once heard, and steeped in the memory of my soul.

And that meant everything.

I turned in his arms, and smoothed my hands along of the sides of his face. His eyes lidded as he leaned into it, in time with me. It was the softest contact. I had gotten better at kissing, and finding the right force to use. But the full sensation of Shane's mouth and the heat of our breaths would forever lighten my stomach and hammer my heart.

He kissed with raw feeling, while I kissed with some kind of desperate agency —despite not being fast. It wasn't that I wanted to get it over with —I *liked* kissing him —it was the phenomenon of storing for a lack in the future that sat in my reasonable mind. The possibility that I wouldn't have this tomorrow, or the next day, and needed to get my fill while it was still being presented to me. There was an unpredictability with all of it.

With Shane. With myself.

Impulse told me I wanted it now.

Reason kept my hands on his face; kept me exactly where I was; and waited for Shane's tongue to brush along my lip in any indication that we could go further.

Confidence and desire trumped reason.

I moved —quickly and without caution. The laptop slid onto the bed, and I slid onto Shane's lap. Like I had been made to fit. I had to pause as I processed where I was —where his legs were, and mine. It was hot and I couldn't breathe. Yet all I wanted was to wrap my arms around his neck and kiss him again.

"Grahams," Shane rasped —in a tone that likely wanted to be firm but came out like a plead. Or a beg.

And the sound gathered heat and weight between my legs —it was an entanglement of nervousness and something far more dangerous.

His hands were on my waist. I went rigid at the realisation, yet could no longer keep still. Every atom that made up my being began to buzz and quiver. His fingers slowly dug into my skin over my t-shirt and cardigan. Then they lowered to my hip.

My spine arched.

Shane let out a soft breath. His skin was warm instead of its usual cool as his fingers wandered underneath my clothes —with enough trepidation to feel out my reaction, and allow me to discover if I wanted it.

"…Is this okay?" he murmured.

Gooseflesh prickled in the wake of his touch. Fire, too.

I *did* want it.

"Yes," I whispered, taking his face in my hands before I kissed him again. Unflinchingly and…suggestively. I licked my lips as I withdrew.

Shane blinked —showed a flicker of surprise and a bit of colour in his cheeks, before I abruptly found myself thudding onto the mattress back-first, sprawled beneath his looming body. I gasped and held that breath, but what flashed through me was not mounting regret. He had flipped us over so suddenly that I just hadn't gotten the time to see and acknowledge the focused intensity of his gaze and the way he shuddered with restraint. So I did; my eyes slowly lidding.

I didn't know where it was going anymore.

But we didn't stop.

I clung to his loosening denim jacket in vicious declaration that he should remain right there, close to me.

With me.

And I almost literally drowned in the next kiss; now deeper to counter any lack of firmness, while still slow and tender. Strange and weightless sensations settled in the pit of my stomach —but I knew what they were and what they meant. I simply couldn't decide whether the development scared or exhilarated me.

It was probably a swirl of both.

Shane's grip on my midsection strengthened and he no longer seemed concerned with not lowering his full weight down on top of me. And as though the action caused the direct release of it, a small moan popped out from my parting lips.

He paused, leaning just far enough away to stare at me with wide eyes. He did not laugh or smile. That turquoise gleamed, and the expression on his face was less of pride and more…

I pressed my lips together.

"Now is not the time to be embarrassed," he murmured.

"I don't think this is embarrassment," I whispered.

His brows rose ever so slightly.

What was I implying?

I did not have answers. All on which my mind could concentrate was our making out and its indefinite duration. So we tentatively leaned back into another kiss —one which turned fierce and needy. The heated change in pace was quickly gotten over though, before our hands began to explore without forethought.

Fingers skidded along curving backs and trembling shoulders as our clothes became half pulled off. Amidst that haze I felt one of his hands slide to squeeze my backside, then slowly wander down along my thigh. I let out another mortifying sound, but this time it was echoed by Shane's own. That did help. It eased the fear that I was feeling it all too much — more than he was —and reassured me that it was mutual.

He wanted me.

It was all blurred and breathless and consuming; violent in a way that almost questioned our initial hesitancy.

My glasses were getting in the way.

Shane seemed to notice precisely when I did, and he carefully plucked them off of my face while barely breaking away.

I then wrapped my arms around his neck and arched upwards into the motion of his hands settling on my hips. He held my body against his as he slowly ground; rigid and rhythmic and pleading —

There was a thumping up the stairs.

Suddenly I was in Shane's bedroom, on the upset bed with his fingers inching under the waistband of my trousers.

The realisation was jarring, like waking from deep sleep. Shane jerked away instantly, his eyes growing wide as violet crescents materialised.

"Uh…Hyde," I breathed. "Your irises —"

He frowned and quickly pressed an entire hand over my mouth, before vigorously shaking his head. I mirrored his expression even as I struggled to retaliate. The purple slithers couldn't dissipate fast enough.

A louder thump startled us again. As though Kendall had run directly into the door.

"Shane!" he cried, rattling the handle as soon as he realised the issue. "Hey. Mom said you're not allowed to have the door locked."

"Shit," Shane growled, before easing off of me, fixing his long sleeved grey t-shirt and trudging over.

I sat up and pulled the laptop towards me —trying to make it seem as though we hadn't been doing anything. But my heart was racing, my face was aflame and my hands were too slippery as I adjusted my cardigan and put my glasses back on.

Oh. Meu. Deus.

Maybe I was finally losing it. Maybe I had decided that a little teenage rebellion, unsupervised tomfoolery and a bit of experimentation were in order. That *had* to be the reason why I'd let Shane go so far.

Why I had disregarded all of my inhibitions.

Otherwise…I had to consider a new possibility: despite all the turmoil writhing within me, I had found a trust in Shane. I trusted him that much —enough to melt into him without a lot of thought.

"What could you possibly want, pipsqueak?" Shane was demanding. "Are you trying to *break* the door?"

Kendall poked his head around to stare at me, completely ignoring his older brother. "I'm hungry," he declared to the both of us, as if the world had to stop spinning as a consequence.

Shane nudged and guided him forcefully back out, into the hallway. "You already *had* dinner."

"But Mom and Dad said you have to take care of me if you ever want 'em to trust you." He pouted and folded his arms importantly.

"So I have to obey your every whim?"

"I'll tell," Kendall threatened. His shadow seemed to smile while it writhed slightly out of shape on the wall.

"You little snitch," Shane hissed between clenched teeth. "What about our deal? You want the five bucks or not?"

"Ice cream," said the boy. "As much as I want."

I was not sure what was giving him the confidence to ask for such a thing. His immature Daemon was *roiling* in the nourishment of breaking the rules. It did not claw at him though. Maybe the creatures drew a line at little children.

"You're an evil genius, Ken," I piped up. And it wasn't a compliment. He flashed a toothy grin at me.

"Don't encourage him," Shane scoffed.

"Oh I'm not," I assured, flopping over onto my back.

I finally let out a breath as I heard the door click closed and two pairs of footsteps retreat. Their absence then allowed me to process just what exactly had occurred in the last fifteen minutes. What bobbed upwards to the surface was the realisation that I had had little to no hesitation. I had been prepared to continue, and that…didn't startle me.

My body wasn't shaking with shock.

I ran a hand down my face and groaned. I wondered if it was going to be especially awkward when Shane returned. My heartbeat warned me of the answer being yes. I wouldn't be able to look at him. Maybe when we were under the safety of the middle of the night, I would have cooled. So I rose and followed downstairs; intending for us to stay there with Kendall until we all had to go to bed.

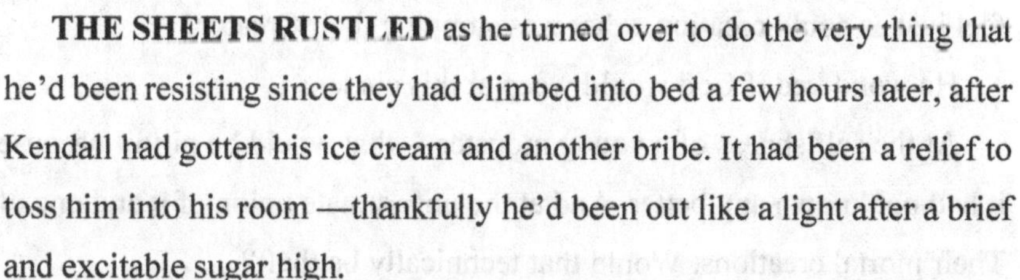

the ruination

SHANE

THE SHEETS RUSTLED as he turned over to do the very thing that he'd been resisting since they had climbed into bed a few hours later, after Kendall had gotten his ice cream and another bribe. It had been a relief to toss him into his room —thankfully he'd been out like a light after a brief and excitable sugar high.

It had been only a little awkward when the two teenagers had entered Shane's room and remembered that they had been planning to share that bed in the corner of it. He had hurriedly asked if they were still okay with the arrangement while skirting around the reason why —and to his delight Alexander had assured it was fine. Very quietly and ostentatiously, but it was still delightful. They had no idea of his selfish thoughts.

Shane observed Alexander's sleeping form; their dark curled hair and the strands that fell over their face. He couldn't see as much as he wanted to in the dark, but he could make out the shape of their nose and cheek — where the cool, still air settled against the skin.

So. Damn. Beautiful.

Life really brought out all the beauty he'd thought he'd seen back in that cell. The flush of the living and the fullness of muscle.

To his dismay and guilt, Shane could not get used to it. Every single time —his breath would catch at every single glimpse. At every reminder that in that moment, the soul was real again.

He wondered if God ever wept.

At the devastation of the world, or even for Their souls. What Lucifer had told him suggested quite the opposite —especially in that book They were so fond of —but Shane did not believe that weeping was so beyond the range of the Supreme. Their Saviour had done it.

Their angels had done it. So had the Fallen.

And if the prized warriors of Heaven and their damned brethren could feel just as could creation, what was stopping their Creator?

He wondered if God would weep at this curse.

At the selfishness of a young monster —that would be pitiful because it had not known any better. And at the unfortunate union of it and one of Their mortal creations. Would that technically be theft?

Shane decided then and there that he was quite fine with that.

His hand reached for Alexander's ear, brushing along its curves. Then he traced their small jaw, before halting at their shoulder.

Brown eyes were suddenly open; staring at him. They held the beast in place; and he was paralysed by the brilliance.

"…Oh," Shane murmured. "You're awake."

Alexander drew a soft breath. "How can I not be?"

"Sorry," whispered Shane. "I…I got carried away."

They fully shifted onto their side to face him. "That's okay. I'm a light sleeper. Why are *you* still awake?"

"Can't sleep. Ken ruined my mood." He frowned, the plaster over his eyebrow piercing pulling and tugging slightly on his skin.

Alexander's mouth curved into a smile —wide and infectious. Before their eyes lowered, as if they could no longer hold Shane's gaze. "…Um. So. We got really into it earlier."

"Yeah."

It all flickered through his memory in rapid succession.

Oh Morningstar —had they really done all of that? As if they had been starved of something…*everything*…and each other?

Shane didn't blush easily nor often. But he had been doing more of it recently —ever since he and Alexander had gotten together.

Even a while before.

"Would you…what would you have done if we hadn't been untimely interrupted?" they whispered shyly.

The two of them hardly ever had this sort of conversation. It was more so a bridge to cross —a topic to be discussed further in each future. Even if those futures were doomed and destined to be short lived.

Shane's throat ran dry. He wondered if he should in fact be honest…or instead choose not to frighten them. But he recalled the feelings of those moments —of the heat and the butterflies and the urge to go much further; times that Alexander didn't remember having gone.

And the confident clumsiness in their movements.

"…I think that I might have wanted…to touch you," Shane confessed. His voice was low and careful. There was a chance that the soul wouldn't actually want it. Not in this life. "And not just imagine it," he added.

He understood that they had some dysphoria around certain aspects of their physical body and identity. It had taken them years to reconcile with their born anatomy, and they had only ever spoken twice about how this kind of scenario would play out. Each individual part and concept of their body carried its own weight, but he knew that it wasn't ever something to be pushed. Alexander didn't owe him or anyone, anything.

"Where?"

Their eyes were wide and curious, fully taking everything in. The urge to hear an answer outweighed hesitation.

Alexander's response made the demon blink. He could not look away from that beautiful warm brown. Their irises didn't refract without light, but he could still see their soul within them. It took Shane several seconds to process the fact that this Alexander was willing to explore that aspect of their relationship.

And they felt safe enough with him to do so.

For a split second that was all that had, and ever would matter in this wretched cursed existence.

Shane shifted on the mattress. "Where do you think?"

Alexander's gaze wandered down from his eyes to his lips. "Oh," they said aloud, absentmindedly. Their attention appeared absorbed in wistful staring. The monster was then sure he had never known patience.

His fingers moved of their own accord and grazed Alexander's parted mouth. Slowly. Desirously. And they indulged the gesture; a warmth self-consciously radiating from their face despite their obvious curiosity. Then before Shane knew what he was doing, his own mouth had replaced those and he was kissing them again.

Feeling exploded at the touch; at his hands sliding down Alexander's hips and slowly riding up their t-shirt as he pulled them in closer; at theirs clutching his flexed shoulders. Their grip was different from what it had been earlier. It skittishly lowered to his bare arms.

Careful and charting.

The exploration was with purpose. They wanted to map out all of the paths of muscle. The two then parted for air —before Alexander fingered the bottom hem of Shane's t-shirt, breathing shallowly.

He inhaled sharply but gave a slight nod when their eyes lifted to ask for permission. And there they stayed. A shiver rippled through him at the splay of their hands flush on his abdomen. At the graze. On his stomach, along his back, and round again. Then the hands skidded downwards.

It was growing dangerous. Shane stiffened in realisation, oh so subtly taking hold of those hands and locking their fingers together. Alexander broke the eye contact in response, curling back. But he gave them a small smile and brought their fingers to his lips. The soul's breath hitched at the soft kiss —and then they let out a hushed laugh.

"You can touch me if you want," the beast murmured. "But you need to understand how it…affects me."

Those dark eyes widened in surprise. "Just from that?"

"Just from you."

Alexander bit their lip as they glanced up at his eyes again. The space between the two of them lessened. And even though each sound that came out of them was stifled in another kiss, the eager movement of the rest of Alexander was telling. The warning did not deter.

Shane had always thought that this was the best bit. That begging — that longing. The proof that it had all happened again. That he had found this fleeting perfection again. That he would never learn any damn lesson.

Legs then began to make audacious advances.

The monster reminded himself to pause, drawing shallow breaths. He knew exactly where this could go. "…Are you sure you want to do this?" he murmured. It would only be touch —they couldn't do more than that.

Not here, and not now.

Alexander nodded slightly. "I haven't really thought about wanting to before. But I think I want to try…with you."

His heart swelled at those words.

Even wrapped within the curse, the soul would still be tethered to him. Whether or not Alexander knew of the time before, the love was constant. That need to be close had carried through every cycle. And Shane would predictably cling to that —viciously.

His fingers slowly moved to the waistband of their —technically his —shorts. "Tell me at any point if you want to stop."

"Okay."

He had feared that it might be awkward the next morning, where no cover of darkness could hide what they had done.

What they had felt.

In the end, Alexander had not stopped him. They had been tentatively uncertain the entire time but it had not actually been, in any way, awkward or uncomfortable. Those soft breaths and gazes had been all the indication to continue. Then they had fallen asleep in his arms afterwards.

Shane couldn't stop fucking smiling.

"…What?" the soul sighed from across the table, idly twirling a spoon around in drowning cornflakes.

They were padding around barefoot in one of Shane's very old t-shirts —a rare thing that actually fit —with curls dishevelled and eyes sleepy in the late morning sun.

"Nothing," Shane answered around a mouthful of his own cereal. He tilted his head to the side after swallowing. "I'm just…happy."

He had never felt it before. Or perhaps, given it a name. It was not the absence of sadness or a joy that left no room for other thoughts. It was the sort of happiness that bloomed in spite of the approaching shadows. And they certainly still slithered near. Nothing would stop them.

"You…you don't mind that I didn't really take anything off, do you?" Alexander whispered. They hadn't been ready for that.

"No," assured Shane. "I could still feel the shape of you, after all. And I like every inch. There is nothing that will make me turn away from you, Grahams. Nothing will make me love you less."

They squirmed in their chair, unsure with what to respond. Then they chewed on their lip, idly lifting and dropping their spoon. "…I can't stop thinking about it. I guess…I really enjoyed it."

Shane grinned slyly. "I could hear as much."

"*Hyde*," they hedged, tightly gritting their teeth and softly kicking his shin underneath the table. Their eyes were wide and serious in warning.

He only laughed.

That was also a constant. Teasing, and its violent and bashful answer. It was like clockwork but instead of becoming a dull pattern, these sorts of conversations were a delight each time, afresh.

Alexander shook their head as they ate another mouthful. While they couldn't recall the previous cycles —which was likely for the best —the beast was grateful that memories of their first experiences together were coming back. Those mattered more.

Shane thought about the time that they had left. It was closing in; the death and ink would start to seep in less than a week. He didn't want it to end. He did not want to think about what might happen after —of a prison from which he still could not escape.

The demon leaned forward slightly.

"Would you just want to stay up in my room all day? I doubt that the conversation between our parents will be over anytime soon."

They dropped their spoon in surprise and it landed in the bowl with a splash. "We can *do* that?"

"We can do whatever we want."

Alexander thought about it.

Shane could provide many reasons. The house was utterly empty. Kendall had left earlier that morning with Samantha and Jeffery, to be dropped off at a friend's house. There was no stopping them.

"…Finish your cereal," they muttered, biting back a smile.

And Shane did, with gusto.

Breakfast turned into a hasty affair; cornflakes shovelled down as quickly as possible so they could go back to pretending that the whole world was quiet. Then the beast took the beauty by the hand, before leading them to the living room.

"What do you want to do here?" Alexander asked.

"Dance," he grinned, tugging on the sofa. He quickly pushed all of the furniture back against their respective walls and fished his cellphone from his pocket. He scrolled through the playlist he had made a few years ago that was exclusively the soul's taste. He picked one seemingly at random.

Their eyes widened at the start of it —with shimmering excitement.

"Shane, I can't believe that you've kept tabs on the songs I like all this time." They gasped when he reached for their hands and took both in his, then spun around the carpet clearing.

It wasn't a song Shane would listen to on his own or without prompt. It was full of magic and poetry —as if someone and bottled wild folklore and used it to write music. It stirred the spirit and quickened the heart.

Music made utterly to be felt.

Alexander was smiling. Their eyes almost lightened to a dark gold in the streams of sun; nearly glowing as the beast's did.

"Of course I have," Shane playfully scoffed, flinging them out before bringing them back in for a twirl. "What else can I possibly do for years on end but pine and obsess over anything that reminded me of you?"

"Oh my God, stop," they chuckled, burying their face in the crook of his neck. He pressed his lips to their temple.

They continued to waltz clumsily in the six step formation —back and forth on the patch of carpet. Each rotation had both pairs of feet barely skimming the floor. All of a sudden, the Made demon recalled what it had been to fly on iron wings.

Prior to the curse, using his wings had been a freeing feeling.

Now he associated them with the darkness and that heavy sticky, thick coating on the lining of his stomach.

But Alexander had never experienced flight like that.

Shane took hold of their slimmer midsection —and lifted the teenager up several inches off of the floor. They let out a cry in surprise, scrambling to push down on his shoulders for balance, before safely touching down.

Their expression did not match his. Shane was snickering, but the soul seemed flabbergasted. Then they took hold of one of his arms and gently squeezed whatever muscle was coiled there.

"You're really strong," they stated. "I'm nearly the same height as you but you held me there for a while."

"…Oh."

Alexander tilted their head to the side and pressed against the monster, tugging on the thin, round collar of his grey t-shirt. "Does my observation surprise you, Hyde?"

"I just didn't expect you to say that."

"What did you think I was going to say?"

"I don't know —maybe I thought you might have decked me for doing that, or something."

"Now…why would I do that?" Alexander mused as they lazily draped both arms over Shane's shoulders. He paused with the brush of their nose against his own, and the feel of their breath. The two swayed from side to side as if they were at a junior prom. "I've always wanted to be swept off of my feet by a tall, very-bad-for-me guy," Alexander smiled. Teased.

Shane felt his own lips stretch. "Is that so?"

His hands acted without prompt and abruptly dipped Alexander down close to the floor, then pulled them back in for a soft stealthy kiss. He felt a smile through it. And wordlessly, the soul pulled him out of the living room and up the stairs. Giddy, hushed laughter then echoed through the halls before the teenagers disappeared into Shane's bedroom; locking the door behind them.

The beast turned around to the soul when silence had overtaken once more and pressed them to the door; paired hands threading and gripping, either side of their head on the wood.

"I am not going to take anything off this time, either," Alexander said candidly. "It's worse in the daylight."

Shane blinked. "You…you want to do it again?" he whispered.

Their lips pressed together in an indignant line. They were not going to admit it out loud. And the Made demon was tempted to laugh a little; not out of maliciousness but because of the irony he saw in Alexander not possessing the nerve to ask for it outright, despite the numerous romances in which they had likely read of it.

"You'll have to take *these* off though," Shane informed them in a purr, glancing downwards at the shorts. "They're one of my favourites."

"I can't steal it?" dared the soul. "That's like, the number one rule of dating. All of your clothes are now mine."

"Uh, I'd like to see you try."

His lips were a breath away from Alexander's.

He paused to gauge their willingness. They stared with an anticipation that therefore drove him to consume —in a kiss which curved their back from the wood. Shane spared no desire; he put all that raged within into the heavy embrace, escalating it into a devouring of reckless passion.

Now that he had gotten this taste again, he was certain he could never be without. Yes it was painful, but he wondered if avoiding Alexander in every cycle was the best thing. His disregard for everything else had won out, and he found himself thinking that in the next reset, he wouldn't stay away —not unless he looked into that bronze and saw clear disdain.

He'd try.

He was lost in that desperate haze as he squeezed their fingers tighter. It was too much and not enough. The door rattled with each move against it —with every push and pull and shudder.

Then he let go of Alexander's hands and held their neck instead, while his other hand raked through their dark hair. They threw back their head and fiercely grabbed the back of Shane's t-shirt; digging into his shoulder blades. The door protested —the heightening sound urging them to have at it somewhere else.

Parting was slow and reluctant.

But the soul grinned; laughed so much that it crinkled the corners of their eyes, and Shane thought that that was the single best thing that had ever happened in all of history.

the shape of a name

ALEXANDER

IF THERE WAS one reason for me to want to live, it would be all of this. Shane Hyde had managed to squeeze in a month's worth of time into a single day —we were not even doing anything special, but being in each other's presence was enough. Just breathing the same air.

We did not spent long in sleepwear as the day progressed. I had two emergency outfits in my tote bag —kept there for runaway situations, in which I couldn't bring all my clothes. I had jumped horrendously at the sight of Shane in a towel emerging from the bathroom after I was done. It had been one thing to run my hands all over him in the dead of night. It was quite another to see that skin bare to my gaze, in the sun.

I wanted to sculpt him. Not because his form was so flawless —almost the opposite. It was a mundane, human body; a pinnacle of normalcy. As if a beast didn't dwell underneath. Or maybe even in spite of it.

All returned to normal when we settled on the bed with another movie, cuddled up in the comforter with all of Shane's pillows behind our backs. We had a plastic bowl of bagged popcorn on our laps, steaming and salty to counter the muddy chill of the outside.

There was a beautiful lull that engulfed me in that ease. We were safe in that cloud of white; in that pocket.

I glanced to the side at Shane. Even at that angle his luminous eyes dazzled brilliantly. My gaze travelled from them to his temple, large nose and the piercing in his brow. I really *did* like his face.

He turned.

"What?" he smirked, hitting the spacebar.

"Nothing," I said. "Just…will I know that it's you, when turn into that iron beast and find me?"

Shane hesitated but it did not look as though it was because he did not want to answer. I held my breath. Of course my question would aggravate a tearing wound left perpetually unstitched.

"…You never have," he answered me, voice tight. "Not until you meet those monstrous eyes."

I was close enough to see those individual muscle fibres of blue again. And the crescent rings of purple as they started shining. That light more so skimmed the surface rather than the turquoise. Like filaments of light, the iridescence came in several embedded strands.

My lips parted. "I don't think I'll run this time."

There was conflict in his expression on how to react. Could it even be considered sweet, or was it just a pitiful tragedy?

"Every time I killed you, a piece of me died alongside," he admitted, dropping my gaze. "Until it had then happened so many times that there was nothing left in me. But that took a very long time. Even then, I would stiffen in those moments; freeze, despite the numbness. Like an automatic response. Then it turned into bitterness —a whirlwind of fury, frustration and despair. Yet I wept…on the inside. For every death."

"But I remember," I reminded him. "Things I never have before; or so we established. I'll know it's you. And I will not be afraid."

"I think that's worse," Shane hissed, reaching for the bowl of popcorn and placing it on his desk as a safety precaution. He shimmied to face me properly. "If I become consumed by my nature, I don't know if I'll know that it's you. At the height of rage, I'm blinded to such an extent that only your eyes pull me back up to the surface. But that moment has never been long nor early enough."

"Then I'll just have to try to make it so."

His hand lifted to cup my cheek and guide me closer, so his forehead brushed against mine. "I hate how you're so…calm about this. The death. The massacre. It's starkly different from all your previous reactions that I don't know how to behave anymore."

If I did not take deep breaths and keep my composure, I would surely burst. I'd break and fall apart amidst the terror that could take hold of me —but I did not, because all of my focus was on my own damn satisfaction and the need to entangle myself with a monster sworn to destroy.

I reached for the side of his face and he leaned into the touch, his eyes fluttering closed as I offered, "Maybe all we can do is live. For now. Did you know that you and death cannot exist at the same time?"

His eyes opened again. "Who said that?"

"Epicurus," I answered. "*When we exist, death is not; and when death exists, we are not*." I felt him stiffen beneath my fingers.

"I am death," said Shane.

And the profound undoing of my point hit me quite hard and suddenly. I was implying that the two of us, could not exist at once. Or even the two halves of him. But I did not want it to be true. Not even a bit.

"Then we must both die," I offered limply.

Shane pressed his lips into a very tight line. "Because it's nothing that we can control." That was the sound of reserved defeat.

"Because it's nothing we are *meant* to control. Too much has already been orchestrated about us. Shouldn't we take every opportunity to focus on just us? *Meu amor*," I murmured, tilting my head.

The skin beneath my hand turned a little pink. "Just us."

I jerked forward to hug him tightly.

"Lie with me," he whispered. I nodded.

We shuffled and lowered to the sheets —bundling within the blankets with our arms around each other. There we settled; breathing steady and slow, listening to our heartbeats. Without the static noise of the movie or the crunch of popcorn, I could hear every tiny sound as the light filtered through the curtains. And for a few minutes, time paused there. I treasured the feel of Shane's body against me; of the brush of skin and fluctuating temperature beneath layers of clothing. It was the kind of familiarity that I hadn't noticed I had been craving for a long time.

His fingers ruffled curls of my hair. "Can I call you…Alex?"

My limbs twitched, before I went rigid. I did not know how to react. The urge to scream wasn't there, thankfully. My stomach churned only a little bit —only in a conditioned response. Maybe he had never known.

"I…I don't actually shorten it like that. My father and all the assholes in this town ruined it."

Shane started. "Forget it, then. I don't want to cause—"

"However," I murmured, turning my head to meet his eye. "I realised that it sounds different when you say it."

That turquoise glimmered in the sun. "When?"

"Just now."

"How did it sound?" he asked.

"…Really cute."

Shane leaned in, before softly capturing my lips. My hand moved for his bleached hair; tangling my fingers in it. He groaned —at the gesture itself rather than at the minimal force I used. And I smiled at the sound. Roiled in it, and offered one in return.

I felt one of his hands inch downwards until it gripped my waist and he withdrew to reintroduce air to his lungs. He looked at me earnestly, so I paused. He thought about it for a moment.

"Please…don't feel obligated to push your boundaries for me. If you hate the shortening of your name and it causes you pain, then you do not have to accommodate just because it's me."

"I don't," I assured, scrambling to roll over on top of him. Then I sat up, over his lap. And he grunted as he heaved upright along with me. "The name itself is not what causes me pain," I explained. "It's people's *intent* when they use it. Even in ignorance, the response became automatic and ingrained. But…I know that you don't mean anything bad by it. So, I want to hear you say it. Say it just for me."

His eyes shone with a wild intensity.

"Alex," he whispered, before the sound was lost in my mouth. "*Alex*," he said again between our next kisses. "Alex…"

I loved it.

I loved how he said it. Felt it. And though not all of the qualms would be dissolved immediately, I did not pull away and I did not feel small.

"Can I draw you?" I blurted.

Shane Hyde glanced up from his laptop.

"Hm?"

We had been hauled up in his bedroom into the late afternoon. If his parents were more seriously talking to my father, then the discussion was taking far longer than anyone had anticipated. Maybe Hugh wasn't letting the Hydes leave, out of anxiety and guilt —or there was more hostility in the ongoing exchange than we'd thought there'd be.

But I was well aware of the impending fall out; and in the present, all I wanted was to relish the quiet before that storm —and its aftermath.

"You want to draw me?" Shane remarked.

"I mean," I started, "I just…It's just that I've never had a live model outside of class. It's just been landscapes, still life and reference photos."

I forcefully suppressed my expectations of a positive response. He had no reason to agree —and the more I thought about it, the more it seemed like a waste of time. Who would be willing to stay still for that long?

Shane blinked. Then stuck his chin in the air. "Okay."

"Oh my God, really?"

I perked up, immediately bouncing to retrieve my bag from the floor and fish for my art supplies.

"Yeah," he answered. "Want me to pose?"

"No," I said, straining over the edge of the bed. "Just sit as you are — naturally."

"Nude? Like a French girl?"

My imagination took off. About what could happen afterwards. And I hit my head on the side table. "Hyde, I swear to *God* —"

"I'm joking," he laughed.

I slumped in giddy relief.

But it was not something to make light of. The reference was humorous, but the sentiment made my ears warm and my toes itch. The fact was, we were still learning about each other's bodies and boundaries. And it was breath-taking —being that comfortable with someone. Though I was just as in need of paced, steady steps.

After grabbing everything I needed, I twisted back upright. I flipped open the sketchbook to a blank page as I crossed my legs.

Shane sat exactly where he was, his line of sight completely focused on me. My fingers stayed as steady as I could manage as I mapped out the structure of him. I had never sketched a portrait. When a model was before a class, there was a sense of professionalism. When only one artist drew one model —the space was small and sacred.

Intimate.

And although I knew that this was only one side of him, there was also something so subtly revealing about a portrait. A willing vulnerability and statement. I wondered what this piece would say.

Perhaps that this was the tender part of him, which was a little more rational; a little more tangible; and a little more feeling.

I wanted to see his true form too, though.

I wished it could be under better circumstances. But no matter what happened to us after the purge, I hoped that we would be together.

In Hell, oblivion —or amidst nothing at all.

And I hoped that we would remember.

Every few seconds when I would glance upwards to see the shape of Shane's face, our gazes would meet and lock in the most heart-stopping way. My breath would catch and my throat would dry. And that twinkle in his too blue eyes would appear as he gave me the slightest smirk.

Like he *knew*.

"What?" I rasped, lifting the sketchbook higher so he couldn't see my face; which had all the evidence apart from colour.

He chuckled softly. "Nothing," he said. "Just…cute."

I bit my lip while tapping the pencil against the top of the page. Then Shane's fingers curled over, and lowered it to my lap.

"What?" he murmured back.

I struggled to string together a sentence. I stared straight at him, taking in every detail. My hand wandered to fiddle with my glasses out of habit. "…You're so beautiful."

The smirk playing on his face spread. He showed those perfect teeth and his eyes crinkled at the corners. Then he leaned in, very slowly, tilting his head to the side. Never looking elsewhere.

My lips parted to receive him. It was just a lingering hook; I felt him smile wider as he pulled back. But it turned into more when I didn't loosen—when I started to expect something which went further. His grin eased with concentration. His body stayed obediently still for several seconds, before he dared to begin encroaching —crawling forward on the bed and guiding me backwards.

I fumbled, pressing back on my hands while he moved in above me. I let go of the sketchbook and let it slide to my side. My arm rose, its hand arrowing for Shane's neck as we then tumbled over onto the mattress and tangled ourselves in the comforter.

His hands went on their own journey.

They guided my hips to curve beneath his body, and draw my legs up to hook over his back. I made a sound in surprise, before kicking the air and clawing at his shirt.

The heat of yesterday came rushing back as my spine curved up off of the mattress. I would never forget the fervent burn of his mouth on my skin, and a pleasure that had taken me somewhere else. Everywhere else.

The giddy discovery that I *liked* it, and that that was okay.

Shane's fingers were gripping into the linen tightly; almost ripping it, as though he was still afraid I might run away. But when he lowered more of himself, I had to snap out of it.

"Hyde," I hissed, gently pushing against his chest. "We…shouldn't. Your parents could come home at any time now."

"Did that stop us before?" he murmured.

My embarrassment was violent. "Uh, well…that was in the morning."

"Your excuses are flimsy," he pointed out, not daring to make a move but lingering on the waistband of my jeans. "The door is locked and you can just pretend it's midnight again, and everyone is asleep."

"…*Caralho*, you're awful."

"Are you just now realising?" he smiled along my jaw.

"Shane," I growled, reluctantly arching away. "What kind of faces do you think your parents will make if they find us like this?"

He paused.

Then made a guttural sound that was a mixture of protest and surrender. He had to have at least some ideas about what his family —real or pretend —would say if they knew what we had done under their roof.

"…Damnit," Shane muttered, before he groaned against my neck as I laughed. It turned into shrieking when he rolled us over, trapping me.

The doorbell rang.

We heard it resonate through the entire house, deafening in the silence so we couldn't question whether or not it had rung. Then the sound echoed again; odd and demanding.

"That can't be your parents," I whispered. "They've got keys."

"An unexpected guest," he concluded.

It rang once more.

Shane grumbled as he quickly freed us from the cocoon he had wrapped us up in, before we fixed our clothes and wandered down the stairs to the front door. He peered through the glass peephole —and started.

"Who is it?" I asked, tensing.

"*Barnes*," he said the name exactly as I had.

I leaned over his shoulder. "Why?"

"She looks…distressed," Shane said flatly, running a hand through his hair. "And she's got a boy with her. Ricci."

My brows furrowed as I met his eye. I saw a similar uncertainty. But I nodded, when he reached forward for the door handle.

Louise Barnes drew a sharp breath as we came into view with the door swinging open. Her mouth was open to say what she had wanted, but she did a double take when she saw me standing next to Shane Hyde. Inside of his house. The establishment of our relationship might not have been a surprise to her, but its development certainly was.

Her arms were shaking, bearing a stack of paperback books —and at her side stood an equally frazzled Donatello Ricci. Their Daemons shared in their dishevelment; flaring and whipping in disorientation, without an odd, maniacal grin in sight.

"You lost?" Shane quipped, a sarcastic smirk pairing up with his glare as he leaned in the doorway on one arm.

Donatello winced at the sight of Shane Hyde. But his fear was paused when he realised that I was there. "…Alexander Grahams?" He returned my pointed glower.

"Yeah, and?" I clipped.

"Listen —we need to talk," Louise cut in, uncharacteristically serious. "Thank God we found you both in the same place. We were going to go knocking at Alexander's after talking to Shane."

"Good thing you didn't," I assured. "Hyde's parents are in the middle of something with my Dad."

"…What exactly *are* you two doing together?" Donatello then asked, his gaze narrowing suspiciously.

I scratched the back of my neck. "Well, technically it's none of —"

"Hanging out," Shane stated, very matter-of-fact.

Donatello was perplexed. "…Why?"

"What do you mean, *why*?" I snapped.

Louise shot him a glare. "Please stop talking."

His eyes travelled the lengths of us. It then hit me. Shane and I likely had a few bruises on our necks and shoulders. I took a small step behind him; pushing my glasses back up my nose.

"Oh." Donatello's eyes widened. "*Oh*."

"Task at hand," Louise ground out, turning back to us. "Donny and I found something that could be related to *The Haunting of Pine Creek*, as Alexander put it. The thing is," her tone then took a solemn dip. "We may have also found stuff…concerning you two."

the barring

ALEXANDER

DONATELLO RICCI DID not like the outdoors.

And none of us were willing to do anything to accommodate him. It was rather entertaining watching him squirm and think twice about sitting on a rock about fifteen minutes later, in the woods. It was mildly cold and the fog swirled at our ankles, but the wind was hardly whistling through the trees and birdsong was scarce. As if it was all empty.

The sun shone through in a thick haze of cloud; only visible as a muted circle of light that still hurt to look at head-on.

Donatello scowled like it had all been made to spite him.

The rest of us were squatting in a circle, pouring over Louise Barnes' cause for paranoia: a notebook's worth of material.

She had compulsively written over numerous pages of her books — which had shocked me initially —but the curious part was that she had no memory of doing so, and that some of the confusing passages were dated certain dates —with the year —which hadn't yet passed.

"Um, this one looks eerily similar to this one," I spoke up, holding up two pages. Shane leaned over to skim read. It told of a red apple that fell from a tree and was then scavenged by a silver fox.

THE BLUSH APPLE FALLS FROM THE TREE.

UNRIPE AND DAMNED.

ONCE WEATHERED AND BRUISED, IT IS ONLY DESIRED

BY A SILVER FOX THAT HAS SINCE LIVED ON BLOOD.

"Make that four," Shane quipped, handing over another set. They all said the same thing, over and over —some of them word-for-word copies while others rearranged and paraphrased. The same greedy creature; but instead, it was a rose that it found or a cluster of red berries —or that the fox had outright stolen the object of its own volution.

"Actually, there are a lot of '*duplicates*'," Louise sighed, gesturing air quotes. "When Donny and I ransacked my treehouse yesterday, we found dozens of repetition in the cautionary tales."

"Is that what you're calling them?" Shane cringed.

Louise levelled at him a highly fed up look. "Do you have a personal vendetta against how I name things, Shane Hyde?"

"Kind of," he admitted. "Since you're making a habit of it."

"Weird," muttered Donatello.

"Got something to share, Ricci?" Shane sneered.

"I think the repetition might mean something," I interjected, growing exasperated. "Aside from the actual words." I elbowed Shane and slowly shook my head —to his dismay and outrage. Maybe he was devastated to discover that I sided with basic civility more often than not.

"I agree," Louise said importantly, sticking up her chin. "Many of the duplicates have the same recurring date, or are around one."

I glanced at Shane. Her words reminded me of something. He held my gaze, acknowledging the meaning behind the gesture. He did not look as enthusiastic to divulge the information we knew about the curse, though. In fact, he looked a bit nauseated.

Even though an explanation needed to be offered, I didn't want to be the one to do it. I could understand why Shane *wouldn't* want to tell other people —there was no telling how they would react to such a disturbance.

To have all of their spoken and unspoken fears confirmed —and then worsened. They were not me, who had been equipped with the necessary memories and context not to freak out about the repetition of a portion of life and the massacre that reset it. Even I didn't know for long it had been going on. The likelihood of Louise and Donatello listening and reaching a calm understanding of the cycles and the events that kept it all running was so low that I started berating myself for even thinking about it.

It's not your secret to tell.

WHAT WOULD THEY DO TO SHANE?

You don't want to be the one who gets him *killed, do you?*

HE WOULD NEVER FORGIVE YOU.

I hated that the thought lingered in my mind. And I hated that I started spiralling because of it. Unsure of the beast's innermost reasoning, it was difficult to predict what he might do —or think —if I inadvertently caused his death; if we twisted the set course.

Though I had no doubt that this cycle had already done plenty of that.

"Why don't we try deciphering these '*tales*' first," I then suggested in a rush. I was desperate to distract myself so I would not think of betrayal and unforgiveness. If I was going to drown in something, then I was going to choose cryptic messages that transcended time.

"Most of them are pretty abstract," Louise said. "But these…these are the ones I had a bad feeling about, and about you."

She handed over a few pages. I read each and offered Shane a glance, ensuring to take my time in figuring out which letters were written there. Louise's scrawl was not that legible, and it only worsened from passage to passage. Either due to her natural handwriting…or something sinister.

THOUGH THE SHADOWS RISE OVER EACH SHOULDER,
THE BEAST AND LAMB HAVE NO DARKNESS.
FOR FROM IT THEY WERE MADE,
AND IN IT WILL THEY BE CONSUMED.

A shiver rattled along my spine and chilled my blood to ice. It did feel targeted. It mentioned only two creatures not plagued by shadows, unlike everyone else. And that a different darkness would overcome them. My eyes automatically searched for reassurance in Shane's. For strength. But all with which I was met was that apprehension he had given in the diner those weeks ago. Like he shared my fear.

WHEN THE LION PROWLS
THE LAMB WILL NOT KNOW.
NOT UNTIL CLAW RIPS FLESH

AND BLUE IS ECLIPSED WITH VIOLET.

The next passage resonated too loudly and solidified a lot of the ideas pushing through my determination to stay distracted. I had a feeling that I knew exactly what it was talking about —too similar to what Shane had already told me about my death. There was no room for anything else: the curse, the iron beast's culpability and now these '*cautionary tales*', were connected by a web of threads that could not be untangled without pulling out other unwanted ends.

But it also read like a violation; as if the most personal parts of us had been revealed to all the world.

Maybe that was why I wanted to be sick.

"Donny and I think you two are the lion and the lamb," Louise spoke gravely, whipping her head back and forth between us. "Based on all the pages using that metaphor and how it matches with you in the real world."

"Matches?" Shane snarled. "You think we're a couple of animals?"

Donatello's mouth opened.

"*Don't*," Louise swiftly commanded, pointing in his direction —to which he threw his own up in defeat. She sighed and fumbled to sit cross legged on the forest floor in her shorts and tights. "Look, it isn't an insult. We didn't want to think it either, but you *are* the only residents in Pine Creek without Daemons. And this one speaks about shadows over the shoulder, but the lion and the lamb being exempt."

"…For something worse," I murmured.

Every pair of eyes met the others before lowering.

No one disputed it based on shenanigans. Deep down, we all believed that Louise had not written the pages for some elaborate joke at ungodly hours of the morning. We could all feel it —on the wind, in the rustle of the trees and with the rush of the river. We knew that the supernatural was real, and among us.

"Do these…Do all of these '*tales*' only talk about Alexander and me, then?" eventually asked Shane. He was reining in an onslaught of emotion judging by the furrow in his brow and slight grinding of his teeth.

"It's the only connection we've made so far," Donatello answered.

I didn't like that.

Shane could tell as much, and so wrapped an arm around my shoulders in overt affection and comfort. I hesitantly leaned into him.

Louise would not meet my gaze. The closer I observed her, the more sleep deprived and frantic she seemed. I wasn't sure if it was because she felt guilty for what she apparently wrote, or for generally where we found ourselves. And at least Donatello stopped scowling long enough to throw an expression of pity.

I thought that Shane would appear to be the picture of cool, but when my head turned his jaw was clenched so tightly that groves that had never been there before threatened to pop out from his skin. That comforted me as all that welled inside of offence.

And a visceral denial of the teenagers' theories.

It reminded me of the bible —though every time that book had spoken of a lion and lamb in had been a positive light to illustrate the wonders of God, and that anything was possible.

What we had read implied precisely what those scribblings had set out to achieve: to paint us as forbidden.

I had already thought that what we had was wrong in the eyes of those who lorded over us, but this cemented it.

"Let's see the others," I said after a while, after clearing my throat and blinking the beads of tears from my eyes. I had faith in something or other, that I could find another subject matter and deflect the sympathy.

We sifted through the piles —with absolutely no help from Donatello of course —and organised them according to mentioned creatures. In the end we were left with four piles in total, with the other two centring a pair of birds and no animal at all.

My focus turned to that. If all the others represented people or beings, maybe the last one pertained to the curse itself.

That would certainly be one way to connect some dots.

Because the pile didn't speak of specific creatures, I had decipher each on its own. Each was different; it had its own riddle though it still abided the parameters of death; and each needed its own attention. I handed one to Shane as I poured over another.

TO DANCE THROUGH RIVERS AND DROWN

IN THEIR WATERS; TAKE HEED OF EACH BLADE AND FLOWER

THESE VISIONS OF NATURE SERVE ONE PURPOSE:

TO REMAIN EVEN WHEN ALL ELSE WITHERS.

I could understand all of the words individually, but not together.

It was about plants and nature, perhaps some existentialism in the last sentence —it didn't quite sound like the curse.

WHITTLE AWAY THROUGH TIME AND FLAME

AND FAN THE FIRE THAT SCORES AND MAIMS;

NONE SHALL ESCAPE THE ENGULF AND TERROR

LEST ONE WITHOUT FEAR SHOULD REMEMBER.

The next described a great fire, that seemed more to do with Hell than the town. And so I perked up, because that was along the lines of what I needed. I showed it to Shane —and his eyebrows knitted together with a curious dread. All that was readily relevant was me remembering.

But I couldn't confirm nor deny possessing absolutely no fear.

Fear of what, was the determining factor.

"Hey Barnes," without lifting his head to address her, Shane frowned with a question. "When might you have written all of these anyway?"

"On the day of the dates, obviously," Donatello muttered.

"Is your name Barnes?" Shane snapped.

"Donny's right though," sighed Louise, tucking back stray strands of her hair. Her Daemon followed suit —but it scraped the curls back more than anything. "It's all the information we have to go on." She scratched the side of her arm like it might distract. "If…if they're from some distant past, then that begs the question of how I knew what to write. I don't have any memory of them or taking a pen to paper —they were just found. Like I said…it wasn't as if I used my treehouse before this."

I shot Shane a look. I wanted to ask if this event had ever happened in the past cycles, but I couldn't in front of Louise and Donatello. Not if he was unable to tell them.

He returned the worried, furrowed brows and tossed the page vaguely towards the pile. "This is frustrating," he stated. "I…I thought that I used to know things about this place. Now it feels like I know nothing."

I reached for his hand, even as he crossed his arms over rising knees. He couldn't offer me a smile of gratitude, but his eyes were still turquoise and not teal. And his statement revealed the answer I was looking for.

"Like nothing makes sense anymore," I murmured.

"Nothing at all has ever made sense," Donatello deadpanned, pushing off of the tree he was leaning against. "Especially with you two."

My gaze narrowed at his self-important face —then drainpipe trousers and bobbled grey sweater. "What are you trying to say?"

"If there's something we should know about," Louise elaborated.

Her expression was no longer grave or one of pain. Her hair billowed in an ever restless breeze, and even her Daemon paused to listen. She did not dare to glare, but the offence and betrayal were there. Donatello halted at her side, hands shoved into his pockets.

And perhaps I had never noticed it before or so blatantly because other members of Pine Creek made a point to mostly mind their own business. But it crushed me now. The othering. The fact that we could not possibly understand the torment that a Daemon inflicted, because their pain was so tangible —that must have meant that we felt nothing.

If we didn't wince; if we could sleep; if we did not parade around the signs of our suffering like a show…then surely it did not exist.

Shane and I were different from them; from everyone else here, and no bubble could shield us from that forever.

"…Maybe your memory isn't so reliable," I cut back at Louise. "You have some nerve to imply we're strange unfeeling freaks of nature when it was *you* who once tormented other human beings."

The girl flinched —even her Daemon looked taken aback. And a flush of colour and shame pinkened her sickly complexion.

Donatello *really* looked as though he wanted to say something in her defence, but he kept his mouth shut for once and levelled a stern glare at me instead. There was nothing that he could say. He knew the truth.

I got to my feet and dusted off my wide-leg jeans. "Even if Shane and I were an apple and a fox; or a lion and a lamb, we are under no obligation to solve some curse —especially if we don't have a hand in it."

I was unabashedly lying, but they didn't know that. It served my point. And suddenly I was glad that we hadn't told them.

Their suspicion was neither unwarranted nor uncalled for. I knew that the only people not afflicted with the one thing everyone had was enough cause for questions. More so when we were frequently regarded as close —and unsubtle about it.

It all still made me angry.

But I couldn't differentiate between it stemming from an odd inkling of guilt, or of simple offence.

"You think we begged to be spared any more than you wish that you had been?" Shane added, taking my lead. His irk was also rooted in show. He towered to my left, moving when I moved; to walk away. "We don't have to sit here and take this."

Then we were storming off out of the woods; huffing and puffing with an anger that was not ours to feel.

They all deserved it, so I had no reason to feel unjustified. And if I did feel that way, then I should embrace that cold malice. At the end of it all, Louise was right: Shane and I *were* responsible for the haunting, and all the death it brought.

And I was beginning to exhibit less and less remorse.

the vow

SHANE

THE SOUL HAD never been so prickly.

Shane's hand to their skin was to that of a cactus —except Alexander was the one who flinched, as if the beast was covered in spines too. Neither of the pair seemed to be able to comfort each other in the wake of epiphany.

In the wake of reality.

They were running out of time and people were growing restless. The curse was adding rules unto itself while gearing to hurtle off its rails. The cycles were no longer the repetition of a wretched mould; but in a twisted way, the Made demon had gotten quite comfortable with that structure.

There had been an order in that cruelty.

A predictable reliance in the mercilessness.

And now Shane was blind, stumbling out into the dark with everyone else. Even though he knew that certain bits and pieces were still going to manifest, it was alarm that reverberated within him.

He had never been so alert.

So afraid.

He thought that maybe that was what Alexander was feeling too. Without the layers of self-righteousness and questionable faith in the beast, there was nothing onto which to fall back. Certainty was crumbling away from under their feet, sweeping them up with the paranoia and chaos.

"Have you, uh…ever been hunted as a witch?" Alexander asked him seriously; arms folded and gaze on their boots. "Like the Salem Trials."

Shane frowned.

The two were huddled in the library, after having had a disapproving exchange with the librarian. They had stomped in there too, muttering and grumbling like children denied. It was still their safest place —as well as the last, where no one would think to look.

The best place for a hushed, panicked conversation as far away from the librarian and her disappearing Daemon as possible.

"I have been hunted for exactly what I am," Shane answered, begging Alexander to turn their head and meet his eye.

They refused.

And then asked another unsettling question. "Do you think…the town would kill you if…if they knew about what was going on?"

He had thought it over many times.

A part of him had even wondered what that might be like —to die. He was incapable of doing so. Maybe in a mortal husk…but his curiosity had always remained just that after a hair-raising encounter that had been too close with the brush of death. Many cycles ago, when the curse had begun to wear itself upon the demon, he had actually tried to get the residents of Pine Creek to rise against him. He had thought they would've had a hard time believing him initially, but it seemed that they had all been searching for a scapegoat since the dawn of the Daemons.

Shane had barely escaped the mob before reverting to Ferream.

He had never made that mistake of self-sacrifice ever again.

"Yes," he answered the soul. "I once tried to turn myself in, but I got away before they could try." He then struggled to voice the next thought from his impulsivity. "Do you…do you want me to tell them?"

Perhaps he would consider human death for them.

Alexander flared, and snapped, "No."

The monster was surprised by that response. At its speed and tone and very choice. Why on earth had they asked those strange questions, then?

Alexander levelled at him a tired glare. "If you die, I'll kill you."

It wasn't funny.

It wasn't remotely funny but Shane then muttered, "That'd be a first," and attempted a soft smile that he hadn't been entirely sure would lighten the mood before making.

It did not.

Which was not a surprise, because it was not funny.

"I don't want you to die," murmured Alexander, still glaring. "I don't want you to leave me here. Alone."

"I'd sooner take you with me to wherever I find myself."

They unravelled a little. "…Wherever?"

"Even if we cease to exist."

And that provided a grotesque comfort: that their story should rather resort to nothing, than be pulled and torn. And that the Made demon was selfish enough to steal them away on instinct.

Shane ran a hand through his hair. Such destruction was second nature to him —but what about Alexander? Were they not softer and susceptible to things like regret and guilt; things the beast was only skimming. Human minds changed constantly. It was quite possible they would not be able to live with one decision forever.

"Maybe we're bad kids," Shane sighed, leaning back on the shelves.

The soul curled into themself again, squeezing their knees up into their chest and hunching over. "I want to stop feeling like I am responsible for my parent's wellbeing. As if I'm obligated to live my life solely to make sure that they don't fall apart."

"If you live to hold the pieces of someone," Shane offered, turning to meet their gaze as Alexander glanced up, "you yourself will buckle."

Their face crumpled as if his answer had confirmed all of their fear. "Even if it's family?"

"*Especially* if it's family."

Lucifer was not '*family*', but he wanted to apply the same logic.

Alexander's knuckles pushed against the delicate skin gripping their jeans. The demon was hit with the sudden panic that it might draw blood. His own hand slid across those fists —cold and firm. The soul still started from the prick of spines, but they did not move away. Their grip loosened noticeably. Then they drew a breath.

Tension eased on its exhale. Relief. Reassurance that they were not a horrible child for wanting a life boat to escape the drowning they had been subjected to since birth; in a sea of inherited problems.

And those issues were not theirs to fix.

"It's all suddenly so clear," Alexander whispered, moving to lean on Shane's shoulder. "My mother was the one holding it all together. Then she broke. And now we can see that shattered foundation in her absence, but while Hugh's clumsily trying to rebuild it, I want out of that house."

"You want to build one with me?" smiled the monster. "It'll be small and made of stone, wrapped in ivy. The foundations are old but they were built with loving hands. It's been knocked once before, but that was only its walls. It's still got good bones."

Alexander lifted their head to look at him. "You handed me materials a while ago. And here we are, planning to move in."

"For how long?"

It was out of his mouth before he could stop it.

The soul blinked, surprised. Which in turn surprised Shane. He hadn't expected them to give him a face that asked what he was on about instead of appal at the notion of keeping them to himself for as long as possible.

As if they had always been captor and captive.

Alexander took hold of one of his hands, brought it between their sides and then linked their little finger with his limp one. Sparks danced within the skin and the gesture; crackling and fizzing with more substance than even their soft embraces.

"Forever."

And Shane believed that.

His parents were finally back when he eventually slunk out of his room. Alexander had braved the night and decided to face their father, and even with Shane's fretting they had gathered all they had brought with them to take back to that house they hated, just to alleviate their conscience.

For the soul's sake, the beast hoped that Mr and Mrs Hyde had gotten to talk some sense into their father.

He would find out soon enough.

Samantha and Jeffery seemed weary as Shane hesitantly rounded the corner to the living room. The house was quiet without Kendall running through it. It felt several sizes too big with just his mother and stepfather.

"Has Alexander gone home?" Samantha asked.

Too hopefully for her son's liking.

“Yes,” he answered flatly. “We went out later in the afternoon.”

“Good,” Jeffery cleared his throat, loosening his collar as he sunk into the armchair. The furniture had been returned to its place when Shane and Alexander had come from the library. “There is no question that last night will not happen again. All children need parents.”

“Hopefully after our little intervention he won’t feel scared of his own home,” added his mother.

“They,” Shane immediately corrected. “Alexander doesn’t use ‘*he* and *him*’ pronouns.”

She dithered, blinking slowly. Her Daemon did not seem too bothered and only ran one claw along the ends of her ponytail; snagging just a few strands. “Right. My mistake,” she breathed. “You know that I’m not used to all of that political correctness, Shaney.”

“Stop it,” he bit, his eyes slitting in caution to the onset of rage. “And don’t make excuses. Just make an effort.”

“Do not speak to your mother that way,” Jeffery interjected, stomping a foot on the carpet. “If you ever have something to say that you think is so important, you say it with respect.”

The Made demon ground his teeth together and weighed out options. There was no use in starting an argument, even though he felt justified. It was also futile to whirl off to his bedroom —they would only corner him later. In order to maintain the façade of surrender and slip through their clutches as soon as possible, Shane had to cooperate. Pretend.

“…Sorry.”

It was cold and empty and for the sake of it, but Samantha cradled the word in her hands like a generous offering to a deity.

“You seem to care for your friend very much,” she smiled. “Which is a refreshing thing, believe me. I now understand why you were pushing for Alexander to spend the night here. I am not saying it was completely acceptable but given the dire circumstances, I would have classified it as a justifiable emergency, I suppose. Mr Grahams…is not an alcoholic. Not as how we would categorise it. He assured us that he simply had a difficult relationship with it, and that the shadows are easier to deal with in…that state," she relayed with some difficulty, glancing aside. "Of course, those reasons are a bad sign. But we tried to be clear in our warning of how that was affecting Alexander. He seemed to understand, then."

"So…he'll stop drinking, and accept his child?" Shane quipped.

"None of it is so straightforward," his mother sighed. "None of it will be easy. But we cannot tell Mr Grahams how to live his life or how to see his own…child."

Jeffery nodded, stiffly. "As a man of God, I can only imagine how any of Alexander's struggles are affecting Hugh just as much."

The monster ground his teeth together.

Both of them were afflicted, but that did not mean that one should take away from the other. Both were human beings who were in need of love and attention. Though Shane, being as biased and one track minded as he was, decided that Alexander's wellbeing was more of a priority.

Personally.

"Now, we also wanted to speak about certain boundaries," Samantha then went on. "Of the house and everyone in it."

Shane grunted to show that he was listening. Pretending.

"You cannot spring things onto us at the last minute, in hopes that we find ourselves with no choice but to concede," Samantha began, adopting that annoying mothering stance. "We could have easily forced Alexander to go home after all. But we reacted like concerned parents and allowed him —*them* to stay in a safe place for a bit. However, it's not your jurisdiction to decide who stays under this roof and when. We have to talk about these things in advance and properly plan. As we do with your brother."

He gave a patronising nod.

Jeffery shifted in his chair, sluggish and top heavy —quite like the tall Daemon perched there at his back. Its claws gripped his shoulders like it would massage them, but instead of rolling, the creature dug deep into the man's flannel shirt. Only taunting.

Samantha's husband did not offer much verbal agreement. Shane had an inkling about why. Perhaps meeting with Hugh Grahams had resonated with him in a bad way, even if the two men were at different stages of life and progress.

Shane was preparing to make a frigid exit to remind the parents of the distance which had not budged, when the doorbell rang. Again. The beast unintentionally glared at the front door, but it was more for the thwarting of his plan than a thought for who might be standing outside.

Though this ring was patient. They did not even press the button twice. So Shane's anger was cooled by an onset of apprehension. He didn't think it was Louise Barnes, even if it was possible.

There was no shadow falling onto the inside of the entrance.

"Are you expecting someone, Jeffery?" Samantha asked.

"No," he grumbled. "And for God's sake —it had better not be another surprise guest." He looked directly at Shane.

The monster raised his eyebrows in a show of claiming innocence.

His mother made her way to the front door. "I'll go see who it is."

The hairs on the back of Shane's neck prickled. His look of ignorance fell into a sceptical frown. If it wasn't Louise and it wasn't Alexander —because they would have milked the doorbell for all it was worth —then it had be someone with enough arrogance and sense of self-importance to be sure that they would be promptly answered.

Power slithered in beneath the door, that only he could see.

That was no mortal.

"Mom," he blurted —because a part of him knew that that was one of the only ways to get her attention. "Let me do it."

His face must have been enough of an indication that the situation was not what it seemed, so she hesitantly retreated and let him pass.

The door handle was as cold as his skin.

There was no need of opening the door slowly, but the polished metal stuck to his palm and fingers like flypaper. He noticed the sunglasses first, then the bright scarlet trousers and blazer.

"You seem almost surprised to see me," said the stranger in red; more feminine than the last. "But that's impossible."

Just what he needed. More barons.

They flicked the sunglass off to reveal two depths of a lifeless black. Those grinning sharpened teeth were a sparkling white, though.

"What are you doing here?" asked Shane, gaze darting back inside.

"Fulfilling a duty," they stated; the amusement easing. "Do not worry. The mortals will not remember. So, it would appear that you did not heed the first warning. You were warned not to tamper with the elements of the retribution and you did not concede. Based on data obtained discreetly, you are still fraternizing with that *soul* —"

"Don't call it that, you lowly demon," ordered the beast, "All that I do with them is out of something you cannot understand."

They sighed. "What —love?"

Shane started. He felt trickles of sweat down along his back. Cold and unnerving. He had not thought that they had even heard of the word.

The baron paused and inclined their head. "What, did you think that I wouldn't know of such a thing? How can I *forget*."

The monster held their ground and dug his fingers into the front door, despite the unfairness of their form being a grown adult and his being an adolescent. The stranger reached for the high collar of their shirt, to reveal a long jagged scar that ran haphazardly across their neck.

It was the type of scar tissue that was left after what essentially would be, a severing.

"This is what love did to me, pet," the stranger in red deadpanned. "I was promised by a conniving witch, something greater than my purpose —something better and purer," they dramatically —and as sarcastically declared, throwing up their hands, "that would outlast all of the evil from which I was forged. And do you know what happened after I succumbed to such naiveté? I gave my *Excumen* and was bound to that hag for nearly two centuries until she was finally caught and executed by some church. This decapitation was a jealous man's handiwork, and it was only healed because of the chains the witch held on my throat."

"Not all mortals desire power," Shane ground through his teeth. "And not all demons are so foolish."

"*Foolish*?" echoed the stranger, slender brows arching over widening dark pools. "I knew nothing of the Earth when I touched down on it. Do you believe that I gave my name, knowing all that would come with that decision? You fucking traitor. The only satisfaction that I have ever tasted is seeing that witch once more in Hell, starved and burning, while I was granted the opportunity to honour my part of the contract: eternal torture. The terror and regret in her eyes are really quite something, young demon. Perhaps I understand your bloodlust."

The beast levelled at them a look of indifference. "I do not care if you have found an amusing pastime," he said flippantly. "These situations in which we find ourselves are not the same. *You* were betrayed by a human who did not truly love you. Not my problem."

The baron's expression soured. "That soul does not love you, Ferream—how could it possibly love a monster?" they hissed. "It will betray you the moment it sees fit. Do not delude yourself into thinking you exist in a balderdash story where you can somehow obtain a life that is not riddled with pain and suffering. Know your place."

"And what of yours?" Shane cut back, eyes slitting as the crescents of violet carved out the rims of his irises. "Does the Morningstar know that you're here, doing as you please?"

The stranger in red regained their poise, and clasped their hands over their blazer hem. "The king was not the one who sent me here."

Shane went very still.

And the baron noticed it. A smile stretched their stiff mouth. "If I was you, I would revaluate what deviating from the set course brings. For the soul. For your sanity. Are you not yet tired?"

"*Nothing* matters more to me," he insisted.

Just as he had reserved all of those years ago at the first threat of being separated. There was absolutely no point in anything without Alexander. Without those memories. Without that exquisite violence.

The stranger shook their head in showing pity as they redonned their sunglasses and turned on their heel. "You were entrapped in this town for a reason, Ferream," they reminded him. "*Yield*. Lest you wish for another illustration of what that is."

The demon stepped into the dark as Shane bared his teeth to the night. "…Never again."

the shift in a truth

ALEXANDER

I WAS DREAMING. I was dreaming, and I was aware of it.

It did not unnerve me but my body coiled into a wound spring; poised to react to anything at all. My surroundings were too shrouded for me to see in any direction, but my feet still shuffled forward. My soles lingered and fully felt out the texture of the ground with each drag.

It was broken and sandy.

And warm.

Too warm.

My throat was cracked in a way that was far past the point of dehydration. Each breath was a fight and harsh wind over a scorched desert. There had never seemed to be a drop of rain here either, from the temperature of the air and how the moisture felt sucked from every part of me.

I could feel a wall to my side.

My crumbling fingers pulled against it for a familiarity, only to be met with rough brick and dirt that cut into them; exposing tenderness beneath to elements I could not see. My eyes were wide open —and saw nothing.

My toes caught the edge of what scraped like a protruding rock, and I was flung to the ground. It now seared like hot coals. I scrambled upright —and in the panic my hands snagged on cloth. Noticeably fine cloth that did not assault the senses.

"…Another wandered in," murmured a disgusted voice; though it was too far from my ears and echoed in a chamber. "I don't think it can see."

The cloth was ripped away, and panic boiled up again.

"*Please…*"

The sickly rasp came from my own mouth. I had wanted to cry out; to be heard and aided, but in truth, I had barely made out the word myself. I wheezed and tried again.

"Ugh, it *speaks*," came the voice again, now more repulsed. "My word —take it to the Lord of the Flies."

More footsteps echoed about me.

And I knew that I was dreaming. My brain whirred in the background for that title —'*Lord of the Flies*'. This place burned like Hell, and I was dry and shrivelled like a sea creature, amidst arduous darkness. *Hell.* The gears clicked into place.

I did not know all demon names, but this one was one of the prominent figures. Lord Beelzebub.

Something with immense strength suddenly lifted me from the awful, rocky ground and derailed my train of thought. A thick arm had wrapped around my midsection; smooth and cool and…glassy. Whatever creature carried me, it was not made of flesh and blood.

It did not do so with care, either.

The wall, I assumed, still came into contact —with my head. I swung back and forth with my holder's lumbering gait and with nearly each other sway, grazed the crudely smoothed structure with my temple.

It felt so unforgivably real for a dream.

I heard Lord Beelzebub before anything other sense.

There was the fierce hum of fly wings which were only more annoying because I couldn't see any. And the important demon let them buzz for a few seconds more before the sound abruptly cut off, and the sweeping of cloth along the ground replaced it.

I was prodded, plucked and flipped over again before being put on my feet. My limbs were shaking.

"It cannot see," sighed the first voice that had found me.

"I believe that to be a fortunate thing," said another —this one deeper and flat. Unbothered. "I will deal with it, Crowley."

My heart wasn't beating.

It should have started racing a while ago but it did not possess a beat.

And I was dreaming.

That reassured the sudden cavity in my chest and allowed me to place the name of '*Crowley*'. Hell. A prominent demon…the Serpent General. His footsteps were light and swift —and retreated rapidly.

My heart might have been involuntarily dormant but it didn't stop my breath from hitching and clawing the insides of my barren throat.

Lord Beelzebub clicked his tongue. "You must be thirsty, little one," he whispered. "Why don't we step into my office, where we can then have a discussion about your journey to a place you do not belong."

We only walked on a few steps —through which a heavy hand guided my shoulder. The floor changed, and my feet felt it out. Metal.

Though I could not see the office, I could certainly *smell* it. Evidently it was indeed fortunate that my eyes had been prevented from witnessing any of the pungent scents hitting my nose. There was the dry, musty smell of old mould; something suspiciously close to mucus; and an underlaying base of rotten meat.

My nose must have wrinkled up, because Lord Beelzebub then let out a soft chuckle. “You mortals are always so entertaining.”

The hand steered me in some direction oriented to my left, before my legs hit some sort of wooden chair. I did not want to think about the soft, squishy moss-like substance coating it as I was lowered without a choice. I then realised that I was wearing sackcloth for a robe —only that, besides what I decided was the generous allowance of underwear.

And even though I was asleep and none of it was happening right there and then, a feeling of both comfort and unease washed over me. Comfort in knowing that it wasn’t a present reality…but unable to quash the dread that it once had been.

Once, long ago, I had not been dreaming.

“…Where am I?” asked the version of myself who hadn’t known.

“I think you know,” Lord Beelzebub answered my whole being. “But what you might not, is how you got here and why.”

“I was in bed,” I rasped. Frowned. “Then I blinked to darkness.”

“You were summoned.”

My body wanted to scoff, even there. “…Humans can get summoned to Hell?” I finally whispered the word aloud. It still tasted wrong; like that word did not belong there.

“They can,” confirmed the demon. A few flies started buzzing again. “More often than not, they slip through small cracks of dormant or active gates. But not you. You were called here.”

“*Why*?” The scratching voice in my throat returned to a desperate and grating escalation. My fingers gripped the edges of the disgusting chair in a moment of absentmindedness. Lord Beelzebub did not offer an answer but he did laugh softly. Perhaps he had delt with many others like me, and had grown bored of that question, and our very real fright.

Whatever the reason, I did not see it as justified.

But this was Hell.

And I was dreaming.

"...Perhaps you will gain the ability to see," the demon then mused. "For now, you will ask no further questions about that in particular. You were brought here because of a violent cry for the smallest slither of respite. Or sweet oblivion. God did not answer you. Someone down below did."

"God has never answered," I breathed, and the sentence scorched the inside of me like blasphemy. "And this is not oblivion."

"No, you have not yet died, little soul," he confirmed. "You can take comfort in that. But you also cannot wander free. Summoning means that you were brought here for a task. As adviser to the Morningstar, it is my duty to oversee incidents such as these. As it happens, I believe I already know what mission you were given."

Nervousness flooded my system, and it was in both versions.

This was the point where the present and my memories blurred.

"You expressed a loneliness," continued Lord Beelzebub. "And so to alleviate that and perhaps help reclaim a zeal for the little life you have left, you have been tasked with keeping some...*thing* company."

"...Reclaim?" I echoed. "I do not think I ever had it."

The demon gave no reply, but I had the feeling that he was looking at me the same way that my mother had. The way my therapist might have. That pitying gaze that held an unchecked amount of disappointment and their own sense of superiority for never having felt that way.

"I find it amusing that I mentioned the basis of your task and all that concerned you was the fact you have stopped wanting to live."

Whatever eye contact I had thought I'd been making then broke. "Do

I have a choice…about any of this?"

"…The short answer is no," he sighed, sincerely enough. "Should you wish not to accept the task, all memory of this encounter will be removed from your mind."

I needlessly blinked in the attempt to digest. "Do you mean '*erased*'?"

"I do not."

No hesitation. There should have been no expectation for the slightest ray of fairness in Hell. Especially because I was a living soul, untethered.

"…What is the long answer?" I dared.

I heard the smile in his voice as he indulged my curious terror. "If you agree to carry out the task, you will form a contract with your assignment —and yes, *that* sort of contract. One of blood. Either way, you might die."

"And if it's…violated?"

Lord Beelzebub cleared his throat in a worrying business-like fashion. "The wake of a broken contract will not be favourable to either of you."

I considered what it was that I had to lose. The version before and the one that was dreaming. What truly tied me to existence, and was leaving all of it behind worth pinning hope onto a stranger —onto a creature that had pointedly not been described as a demon. It was possible that meeting it would be worse than life on Earth.

It could be my Hell.

But in that battle between the past and present, I realised that the little child within me had been that desperate. The fact that I was mulling over it in the first place —part of me already thought the arrangement viable.

Part of me chose whatever awaited. Part of me, ultimately already had.

My fingers then curled in over the edges of the chair again. "Before I accept, can I ask…are you the one who summoned me?"

"Hm. You know what, no one has ever asked me that."

And, the Lord of the Flies did not answer.

Instead a wave of heat ushered me from the chair, backwards and out of the office onto that rough ground. The only guidance he offered after pressing a knife to my hand was to follow the feeling that did not belong, and to run if I felt a presence stronger than his. Otherwise I was invisible.

That, and I would not remember when I woke.

That was what had made it click back then —before. I was asleep, and none of it was really real. Even if I felt the heat in the soles of my feet and slicing edges of rock in the walls and the silence of a heart.

Lord Beelzebub was content with thrusting a blind, starved minor soul out into the bowels of Hell, and toss them only riddles and a blade of gold imbued with ever burning celestial fire.

I tried to supress the panic.

This was what I had chosen.

I curled the fingernails of the knife-holding hand into its palm to keep sharp and ran the other hand along the wall. I didn't feel anything new or different, so I followed the wall and listened to the hum of flies.

After a few minutes the air shifted.

The heat parted and where my body slipped on through, the welcome sensation of ice wafted over me. It began as a shower. Then it coated the outer layer of my skin, before it started to seep. It settled within my bones and muscle; cooling the inside as if I had suddenly become it.

It did not plateau —the iciness continued to gather and guide, until it was all I could think about. I was stumbling after it fast, still without sight. Perhaps I did not need it.

But as the cold intensified and satiated, blurry shapes of light bloomed in the dark. I consciously blinked, fighting for clarification, before objects began to draw themselves into my view. Flaring torches mounted the wall my hand ran against, and the ground was more broken than I had thought. My feet faltered at the abrupt shift. Then I took it all in.

There were no lakes of endless fire. There was no screaming. At least, not where I was. Here, there were prison cells of gritty metal. Many were empty with their detained simple silhouettes. Then I spotted a guard.

I wondered if *it* was a demon, because it did not look anything as the church had speculated. It was not leathery and blinding scarlet —its skin was uncut gemstone in a spectrum of bronze to deep ruby. Its wings were edged stained glass; no horns curved from its head, and eyes were burning pools of white flame. A golden mark branded its forehead. A pentagram. And though it more resembled a work of art than an agent of torture and sin, I still exercised caution. I still felt the welling of fear.

I started as its gaze landed on me. Then lowered to the knife.

After a beat, it turned its attention elsewhere.

I uncoiled.

Good to know that Lord Beelzebub would come to be trusted on occasion. That didn't dampen a flood of relief. My heart should have been pounding unbearably. I should've been gasping for air and struggling to stand.

But I was dreaming.

And I wanted to know from where the ice came.

I shuffled on, now presented with a visual representation of damnation and drew shallow breaths that had since been tunnelling harshly through my throat. But that cold was a balm.

About seven torches on, everything stopped.

The scorching heat evaporated; the ice turned to chilled water; and my fingers unfurled from the knife's handle. My head turned to discover why. It was the very last cell, and its bars seemed to be of a different sort of grit —it appeared and smelled like salt. Not table salt but sodium chloride in its raw, crystalised form. Behind them was a large shadow.

Though the scent of salt was strong, it could not mask a heavy stench of metallic mortal blood.

Streams of light spilled into the cell in rippling flickers. It allowed me to see what was within. But nothing could have prepared me. The creature was hunched over, with distinct horns rising high above its head. It had its wings open but drooping in the rear; hard structures that didn't seem to be made of feather; with the only sound coming from inside being the clinking of linked chains.

CUT YOUR PALM. MAKE THE SEAL. OPEN THE GATE.

My hands moved to obey. Slowly —stupidly so —I pressed the tip of the blade to the base of my forefinger, then dug in. Blood burst from the wound —which was not that alarming. The horror was my body moving without my input, and then raking the golden knife through my left hand. All the way down and across to the opposite border of my wrist.

TAKE THE BLOOD. DRAW FROM THE BEAST.

OPEN THE GATE.

I wanted to scream.

Well, the version of me that was dreaming. Because right then I could feel the searing heat of metal and the tearing of veins and muscle very clearly. The dripping knife clattered to the ground in a soft ricocheting patter as I had to grip my arm and wince. The blade glinted in the torchlight, and my blood sizzled in the red sand —or perhaps it was the celestial fire which burned upon the grains of Hell.

The prisoner lifted its head at the sounds.

My body didn't tense, but I was aware of the instinct to hold my breath as it stirred to life. To be bound by so many chains…I could only assume that it had either done something terrible to be down there —to be the one most heavily guarded —or that it *was* something terrible.

There was a dry and tired rumble within its throat, before the creature heaved upright. The chains clanged and rattled with a resonance closer to that of steel; as dust shifted with the shuffle of knees and legs.

A hand curled around a bar.

A humanoid hand.

My eyes narrowed and adjusted. I might have regained my sight, but my vision was still in need of glasses. The hand was not flesh —that skin was a washed grey. But it was not skin at all. Light hit the sculpted limb like it would hit a machine with lustre. It was all smooth iron apart from long, organic white hair.

Red blood was splattered and dripping from its frame, though. My feet should have backtracked at the realisation. Instead, I didn't move at all. I stood at its bars and stared. My hand became trivial despite the unending flow. But I knew that I was dreaming. And I was fascinated.

Its eyes were not metal either.

Our gazes held for a long time. Assessing. Becoming accustomed. Its irises were a crushing turquoise blue ringed with a crescent of purple light around depthless black pupils. I wondered what it thought of my brown, since they were boring and flat.

Because it did not look away.

The cryptic voice did not order me to draw blood and make a seal. It was quiet, with just me and the iron creature. Wordless. And it was cold.

Fear was not something turning my bones to lead as it once had.

I looked into that brilliant blue —even if its gaze was slitted in anger —and I was not afraid. I withdrew my bloody hand, taking it out of sight. The creature tilted its head slightly. Past the blood and iron, I saw an all too familiar lack of zeal. Had this been the reason for the task? Was I to reveal the world to it…something I hadn't managed to do for myself?

The iron hand retreated. But its eyes did not waver.

I wanted to say something. Maybe that I would not bind it in blood or any other way, because freedom had been ripped from the both of us.

My lips parted.

Then the dungeon melted; running and distorting like water washing away thick walls of old paint. I still saw blue oceans as I was washed away with it —before jerking from pulled, damp sheets as air barrelled to my lungs. It took a few moments for me to take in the dark ceiling of a bedroom, in a house that swallowed.

I hurriedly inspected my hand through a blur of streaming tears. There wasn't any blood, even if my nerves remembered the pain. The individual fingers curled and stiffened as their muscles shook in memoriam.

There had never even been a scar. No inexplicable appearance of a red jagged split across the skin one morning, urging me to think a little more deeply about nightmares I could not recall. Whatever happened in Hell, stayed in Hell.

You were dreaming, I reassured myself as breath refused to come fast enough. As my heart galloped and stumbled. Like it had not been beating.

Maybe the wounds would only show on my soul.

You were dreaming.

My nails still scratched my palm and my body still folded on itself as I trembled through the remembrance. And I hated that I could do nothing.

I hated that I was awake.

III

AFTER

the truck at the end of the world

ALEXANDER

REASON HAD ABANDONED me. I was beginning to wonder if it had ever been with me at all. Because there was no explanation as to why I was standing below Shane Hyde's window, in his back garden, flicking pebbles at the second storey window. On my arms swung my tote bag and a duffle of sheets; with two pillows wedged above, against my sides.

I didn't want to be alone any longer.

Not for another night; another moment; another life.

If the version of me that knew all that it did only had a couple of days left before the massacre, I wanted to spend them with Shane —no matter what was to come of it afterwards.

He opened the window almost immediately, as if he had been unable to sleep. "Grahams?" he hissed, leaning out. "What are you doing here?"

His gaze then caught sight of the bedding.

"Bring a shit-ton of blankets," I said.

"What?" he did a double take. "Are you…are you running away?"

"To the woods," I clarified, pointing to the left, where the town turned into the outskirts of the forest and the upward slopes of mountain began.

"Is it something to do with your Dad or his Daemon?"

"…Not really."

Shane breathed a sigh of relief before disappearing into his room. He was downstairs and trudging towards me within a few minutes. I had no doubt that he had left his bed an upheaved mess to get the comforter he balanced in his arms, with a pile of thick blankets draped atop it.

"I can't believe that you did all of that without question," I whispered as he stood before me, grinning. Awaiting praise.

"Anything for you," he explained. One eyebrow then raised, tugging up its piercing. "And you've done that for me before."

I glanced downwards. "Touché."

"Do I get to ask questions now?" he prompted.

"Not yet."

I beckoned him back around to the driveway before we started the trek to the stranger's pickup truck where we had gone after the bonfire. Shane's curiosity only compounded the closer we got. The expression on his face was that of a kid who had been told to close their eyes for a surprise. I had no gift waiting for him, but I knew that he wouldn't be disappointed with what I had in mind.

He blinked rapidly when we stopped in front of it. The vehicle wasn't weathered beyond the rainfall that had fallen since that night. There had not been any more, so it was sunned and warm to the touch. I got to work laying out a few sheets in the back and only called for the blankets when the entire back had been covered.

"…Oh," said Shane. "We're sleeping here."

"We…don't have to if you don't want to."

"That's not what I meant," he murmured, unceremoniously dumping the large pile in the back. He wandered over and then tentatively brushed his fingers against mine. I felt his shallow breath on my cheek as I flinched involuntarily, but I leaned into him to allude to something else bothering me and not his proximity.

His lips grazed along my temple, then kissed it. "…I'm going to guess that you just want to spend the night with me, regardless of where that is —but neither of our houses are an option."

I managed a slight nod as I put my forehead on his shoulder.

"I'll be there," he told me. "Wherever you are."

I wrapped my arms around his torso and breathed in. After that dream I needed to remind myself that he was real, and this was real. That just as the iron beast had solidified itself in my reality, Shane Hyde needed to be just as reinforced. He was the only form that I had on hand, and I wanted to hold onto it with all I had.

I didn't want to be dreaming.

Shane gently tugged his fingers through my curls. "…So are we going to finish setting up, or…?"

A soft chuckle bubbled up in my throat and I unhurriedly loosened my grip. "I just…I had another dream."

We folded the blankets on top of the sheets; creating a thicker base to avoid the discomfort of the raised metal over where the tyres sat, before I tossed the pillows toward the back window so our feet would dangle over the lowered edge.

"Why don't you tell me about last night," suggested Shane.

We climbed in after kicking off our shoes, then pulling off his jacket and my cardigan. It was warm beneath all of that soft polyester, yet I still pressed myself into Shane's side and burrowed further.

He didn't push for me to start talking. Not about my father, nor about the nightmare. I decided to start off with the most simple thing to unravel.

"My father didn't have much to say," I confessed. "He seemed almost remorseful, as if anything your parents had said had stuck with him. What I was worried about was to what extent would that reproach go. I did not go into a conversation with a lot of expectations. But…he didn't raise his voice or his hand, and he tried not to accuse me of anything even with the knowledge that I had slept over at your place. Yet I saw the venom in his Daemon's eyes, and a hunger it couldn't satiate just from him."

Shane wrapped his outer arm around me, enveloping my body into his within layers. "Was it worse?" he asked. "The silence?"

"No —it was fine," I mumbled. "It gave me room to breathe."

He gently squeezed. "I'm proud of you for braving that."

"Me too."

"You can always come find me right away if you feel in danger, or don't want to be there —like you did today. Even if it's two in the morning."

"Do we even have that much hypothetical time left?"

Shane groaned and held me even tighter. "Don't remind me."

Time would keep slipping through our fingers, and all that I could do was wait and be stripped of memories that would only compound for him.

"I don't want to sleep," I breathed. "Let's stay up all night."

"Are you afraid to have another nightmare?"

"No," I indignantly denied, glaring up at him. I expected to see a smirk but instead I was met with a startling expression of concern. I might have wanted to escape, but he was grounded in it. In all seriousness. "…It gave me context," I eventually murmured. "It felt so real. But I knew that I was dreaming, in the moment. It was like two souls occupying the same space in a setting that was familiar to both, yet strange. And it showed me…all that had taken place for when we met. I met the Lord of the Flies and the

Serpent General —and caught glimpses of demons made of glass. Though most importantly, I now remember why I found you in the first place."

Shane maintained that mastered look of stony interest. "Which is?"

"Apparently Lord Beelzebub knew of a kindred deprivation we shared as beings stumbling through our existences. Maybe, he thought we could benefit one another. I would not be lonely, and you might be tame."

His jaw turned white in a hardening clench. "How reckless. You could have been killed."

"But I wasn't," I pointed out. "I stood and sat outside of your cell for nights upon nights and you did not once try to maul me."

The blue of Shane's eyes flickered as he dropped my gaze. "…Maybe because I saw something in you that I hadn't seen in other mortals. They all have this desire to survive. But when I saw your eyes —even that very first time…I did not see any will. I did not see any life."

"I was simply fascinated," I reassured. "Through the slow process of finding a will, I was captivated by you. For some strange reason."

"One that I can't possibly think of," he admitted. "Have you ever felt the urge to kill? The need for blind rage and the delight in destruction?"

My brows furrowed in wry amusement. "Not particularly," I admitted. "But you know, I think it had less to do with me growing an understanding of that programming, and more so that I would not define you by it. And I know you think I'm a really good person, but I'm not. I've wished death on people. Maybe I would think twice about picking up a knife, but I think I would smile at their demise. Be glad of their bleeding. And I even doubt what I've been taught of faith. I *can't* be good, Shane Hyde."

Conflict chiselled away at the stone, bringing forth critical thinking. "You're certainly still better than me, though."

"I would argue that you have changed too. If only for me."

"*Wow*," Shane sarcastically drawled; bright eyes widening, "you have an awfully high opinion of yourself, Alexander Grahams."

"Well I think I should, considering we're in this mess because you fell too hard and became obsessed with one little soul."

He growled and pulled me flush against him. My cheek pressed to his skin. I could feel his heart beating. I found sense to remove my glasses.

"I *am* obsessed," he grinned. "Unapologetically so. You command my every breath. In fact, if it meant freeing only you from this cursed time loop forever, I would kill every resident again. Without hesitation."

I didn't think about the consequences of such a promise. If that could happen, I would not be the one to stop him. Though I supposed that it was easier to talk about these things rather than experience them, since words had no immediate effect and I could pretend not to feel any trace of what I wanted. I had innate empathy.

But my frighteningly comparable obsession with the iron beast would outweigh it, each time. And I deserved to be so selfish.

"Ferream," I whispered as I turned to look up at the indigo sky through the blurred tops of the red and yellow and evergreen trees.

Shane did not answer for a few seconds. Though I did notice his heart pick up its speed. Then, "…Do you know what it means now?"

"It's your name," I sighed. "I've known that for a while. At first, only belonging to the beast. But when I realised that the two of you were one, I finally understood. It's…it's really bad for you…to have a human know your real name, isn't it? Should I…try to forget about it?"

He drew a tortured breath. "I don't mind that you know my name. You always have, actually. But I trust you. It's all about intent, remember?"

I smiled. Yet another thing we shared.

Mine seemed of a lesser degree in comparison to his, though. I had the power of his name over him —as if we were in a supernatural horror. All that my name could do was cause visceral flashbacks.

His could get him killed.

That seal I had been close to making could have done the same. For a moment I felt awful —that I had ever considered it, though I had had little to no options, and I hadn't known him as I did now. The phantom pain in my palm was a steadfast reminder never to fold, never to '*open the gate*'.

Not when I was so unsure of what it meant.

And I couldn't pluck the courage to ask.

All I could offer was my hand in his, clasped between us under all the blankets, with my thumb idly stroking the outside of his. Then we carried on watching the constellations move across the night sky and the fireflies dance between them. I had not been paying attention to the moon, so now it appeared to be waning. It shone brighter than it did in the city, since there was no pollution in the area to hinder the light. It looked so big and imposing. As if it saw all that we did and all that we were.

Coming to this stranger's truck had been an impulsive thing. I hadn't thought about possible rain or the actual owner. It was one thing to sit in the back of it, casually. It was quite another to camp out.

Then Shane's hand grew a little warm and my shoulders went a little stiff at the brush of his body next to mine in the space that wasn't enough. He was closer than I had initially and willingly desired.

Now it was all still and quiet, and I was growing a little self-conscious. And reason was yet to return. "…Have we ever had sex?"

Shane tilted his head, spilling white waves out onto the pillows. "You mean, gone further than we did yesterday and that night?" he muttered.

I nodded, still staring at the slightly blurry sky.

"Yeah…twice," he said.

"Oh."

I was, at least, genuinely surprised. I had considered the possibility of the answer being '*no*' but the truth confounded me. In all that repeating time, it had occurred more times than *not at all*? Had I truly felt so secure within myself that I had reached across that line of my own volution?

It was a comfort to know that an iteration of me had found that peace. Even if a tiny part of me as I was, wished that it could've been this one.

"It…wasn't so romantic," bit Shane, noticing my frown.

I turned my head to look at him. "Did you want it to be?"

A violent shade of pink coloured his skin. I couldn't tell what emotion widened his eyes—shock? Mortification? *Anger*?

"That doesn't mean what you think it means," I assured, feeling a heat invade my own face. "I…I don't think I'm comfortable exploring it in this cycle. In this lifetime. Especially because you and I are not strangers. We have a history that means a lot more to us than what people might think. And I want to cherish every moment of that, not rush it. To soak it in."

A small smile spread his lips, before he pressed them to my forehead. "I wanted it to be beautiful," he confessed. "I wanted it to *mean* something—to be something that you would never forget. That was why I was happy when we'd then slept together and you got all shy and smiley; saying you couldn't stop thinking about it. That was enough for me. I don't intend to do anything to you in the back of a stranger's pickup."

"That's not what I meant to imply," I hissed, quickly whipping to bury my face in the crumple of blankets. "…Oh God, I just wanted to tell you how I really *felt*."

The words came out muffled and frustrated. But he heard them.

"I know how you feel," Shane assured me. "You told me. I mean a lot more to you than I had previously been believing. And honestly, that was kind of the best day of my entire existence. To hear…that I was loved."

My head slowly re-emerged before I blinked at him, and smoothed a hand along the side of his face. "It shouldn't have to be defined nor limited by how we physically express it," I said softly. "There is no blueprint that says we have to do certain things, or by a certain time. We can lay here in the back of some person's truck and look at the stars."

"That sounds pretty beautiful."

"Doesn't it?"

So we did. We laid there, content with the softest grazes of lips, and gazed at the sky. I pulled my glasses back on to see clearer and held onto Shane as tightly as I wanted to. This would be the last moment of peace I would experience with the consciousness that I had, and I refused to waste it.

I didn't want to forget.

"Hey, I have something for you," Shane spoke up. "Since the world is going to end, and all."

"Okay…"

He shifted around in the blankets, reached into the pocket of his jeans — and for a moment I thought he might produce a packet of cigarettes and a lighter —but I was just as surprised by the small glass bottle in his fingers instead. Sparkly black liquid moved within.

"Is that…nail polish?"

"Yeah. Apparently I raided my mother's dresser a couple of years ago and now I've had a few of them in some of my drawers in every iteration." His turquoise eyes flicked to my brown. "Want to paint yours?"

My body lightened. "What? Really?"

We shuffled around to sit up and then lean back on the window, with the pillows cushioning our spines. Shane grinned as he unscrewed the cap. I was mesmerised by the bottled galaxy. My heart began to race and rattle, and I began to wonder why I seemed physically unprepared for something I had always wanted to do.

It would all be meaningless soon. Even Hugh would not be able to do anything about it. But in that moment, it was everything.

“Alex, your hands are shaking,” Shane said gently. He had taken hold of one and brushed his thumb along my knuckles. And he was right —my hand trembled in a mixture of excitement and trepidation. I glanced down at it, and at his. His fingers were so much stronger and shapely than mine —like unflawed, carved marble. They held mine steady and soothed that panicked movement as I dared to look back at his face.

“I…I don’t know why I’m nervous,” I laughed uneasily. “I’ve always wanted to do nails. It was on my list of things to do to affirm myself when I move out and far away.”

“It’s all right to be unsure of something new,” he assured as he dipped the brush into the bottle. “But you have to be honest about wanting this.”

“I do.” I nodded vigorously. “I want it. Paint them.”

“Okay.”

I concluded that it was giddy exhilaration that prevented my emotions from being calm. I followed the fluid movement of Shane sweeping the brush along each short nail, coating it in starry black.

And it was magic.

Every brushstroke that put the swirl of colour to the beds of pale pink sent something along my nerves that gave the feeling of the most startling euphoria —the most exquisite happiness. And if simply doing up my nails brought me that much joy, I wondered what else might complete me.

A sniffle cut through the soft laughter.

Shane paused immediately, peering at my face. “Hey, what’s wrong?” he asked. “Is it too much. Do you want to do something else?”

I gasped and shook my head, frowning slightly. I blinked as I realised that tears had gathered in my eyes and a few had slipped to drip onto the blankets. "These are happy tears," I breathed, before smiling. "I'm *happy* right now."

Like I doubted I ever quite would be again.

"I think I underestimated how much this would mean to you," Shane chuckled. "I love it when you smile like that."

"Cheesy," I taunted. But I only smiled all the more.

"It's true," he insisted, softly blowing on his masterpiece. He cradled my hands in his, becoming lost in thought. "…I'm going to miss this."

I planted a kiss on his cheek. "Me too."

Shane scoffed, meeting my gaze as I withdrew. Purple slithers seared across the bottom edge of the rings of blue. "I'm going to need more than that to preserve to memory, my dear Alexander. From where else might I be able to draw comfort when we're ripped apart once more and the only warmth I feel is that of my own?"

My face contorted. "Getting cringey —"

He laughed and carefully pulled me towards him. "You love it."

"I love *you*," I whispered, eyes lidding as my line of sight gravitated to his mouth. And I felt him smile into a kiss so deep with longing.

the hunt

LOUISE

SHANE HYDE AND Alexander Grahams knew something that she didn't. And it was starting to piss Louise off.

It was a brisk and biting morning; though fog had mostly lifted, it did not instil any good feeling nor put her at ease. If anything, it felt like the most ominous warning not to become comfortable.

So she took it as such —the past day where she had not caught a single glimpse of the pair since they had stormed away, Louise had kept herself occupied scouring the books in her treehouse, the shelves in her room and theorising about the haunting. The temperature had kept slipping close to thirty-two degrees, and she wasn't about to dismiss that detail either.

It could just mean a colder Fall, but there was no longer a margin for error. Winter was charging and she needed to know why.

Why the wind howled like a prowling creature.

Why the river spilled a little beyond its banks.

Why the clouds and their rain had come so low to the ground, and why the moon had grown larger at night.

And Donatello Ricci was not as much of a help as he thought. He was definitely trying to be a better friend —but Louise Barnes was so focused on deciphering the curse that she couldn't return the sentiment. It seemed like a chore to hold conversation with him beyond short response. Despite that deflated look on his face Louise knew all too well, she did not feel as bad as she should. She was not evolving as well as she'd hoped.

The one thing that had changed though: she was willing to express it —albeit in a roundabout, metaphorical fashion.

"Have you ever been hunting, Donny?" she asked, cross legged on the floor of the treehouse. "Where you have to be so still and precise without any distractions?"

"I can't say that I have," he admitted. His brows furrowed uncertainly, as if he were unsure of which answer was acceptable.

Fortunately or unfortunately, it wouldn't matter.

"Well I'm hunting right now, Donny," she sternly clarified, eyes wide for emphasis. "And at the moment, you are the crunch beneath shoes and the clicking of the safety on a shotgun."

Donatello paused as he digested her riddle. "…*I'm* a distraction?"

"This town cannot take it anymore, Ricci," sighed Louise. "They need answers. *I* need answers. And I believe that those can be found in these." She held up a fistful of those scribbled cautionary tales.

The boy's mouth twisted into a shape. He looked as though he might take offence but something worse overtook that instinct. *Pity*. He looked at her and he thought that he understood why her words were so biting —and frankly, that was something which she loathed.

She would rather he got angry.

She would still rather that he hate her.

And maybe she had just exposed a slip of that tender truth on her face then, because his expression softened and he shuffled a little closer toward her. His close proximity made her want to cry, or curl up and disappear.

Her Daemon lapped it up like an exhausted animal to water; its claws a promise of later when she was entrapped in the exposure of her bedroom with nothing but it and solitude.

"…Who made it your responsibility to solve all this?" Donatello asked in a gentle voice. A hammer to her glass state. "Will the world crumble if you don't figure it all out?"

Louise's shoulders heaved in a strained, silent sob. "I feel like it will."

"It won't."

She stared at him in disbelief. "How do you *know* that?" The question was ground out, as she blinked away beads of tears. "I feel this tug within me, egging me on; urging me forward. Sometimes it feels like a threat. I *have* to sort this out. If I don't…then who will? Do you want to keep being tormented by these fucking monsters —?"

"—Hey, hey," he interjected, "Shh, it'll be okay. Nobody wants these to stick around. I'm just saying it's absurd that you think it's your mission alone. Like you can't have any help."

She'd told him.

Louise had told Donatello all that she had discovered before and after Alexander's return. They both knew that something important was being omitted. And Shane Hyde was at the centre.

In fact, she was fairly certain that Alexander themself played a very crucial role in it all, seeing as they were as Daemon-less as Shane and had somehow tamed the wild beast of Pine Creek. Before them, getting Shane to talk was like coaxing a wall of opaque ice. There was something about the quiet, half Portuguese teenager that had Shane utterly wrapped around their little finger.

And Louise doubted that it was sex.

What charged between them ran deeper —more sinister, if those pages were to be believed. An apple and a fox. A lion and a lamb. One of them was to be devoured, but she could not tell which was which.

But it mentioned a darkness consuming them both.

There was no outright or even veiled implication that the two were in fact directly responsible for all that was happening in Pine Creek. Louise didn't even really think so. But she *did* think Shane Hyde had brought on those Daemons, and that Alexander Grahams knew how.

"I can't…I don't want to do this alone," the girl finally admitted. Her voice was a breathless whisper, nothing more than a breeze through hair. "But I've never really asked for help before."

"That's okay too," Donatello reassured. "It takes practice."

Louise pressed her lips into a line so tight, her skin blanched further. It had felt as though she had been withering away into the shadows of her Daemon and becoming it. And she was sure that it was a fate she deserved and had not dared to question.

A person like her did not truly get to be selfish; did not get to want for something that would be of benefit to her and her alone. All that she did, was done to atone. Her body coiled up in a spring.

Realisation sunk in like muck.

Was she chasing to free the town for some kind of forgiveness? Was that her motivation —had she developed a heroic complex?

"Do I…do I *have* to save anyone?" Louise asked aloud. Asked the boy in front of her. His opinion mattered, somehow.

He didn't have an answer for her.

"…Does it make me a worse person?" she followed up.

Donatello sighed and offered her an apologetic smile. "You look like you went through the type of change that opens people up to the real world around them. It's still your decision if you want to help those people you think might be disillusioned, though."

"I'm not better than them," insisted Louise, hugging her jean-covered knees into her chest.

"I think that admitting that goes a long way in showing that you might be," he chuckled lightly.

"That's not funny."

She levelled at him a stern glare, curling her bottom lip in a surly pout. His Daemon wavered over his shoulder, unsure of how to react to the kind gesture. It jerked —almost as if it were repulsed by the very notion, then distorted in anger. The black smoke dissipated into the shadows between the filtered streams of sunlight.

There was something that was bothering her. Like an itch beneath the skin; a small thing that lingered and refused to go away; she was trying to interpret a page that hadn't fit with any other pile. A page which had sent chills down her spine and frozen her limbs.

For starters, there were drops of blood on it, like ink.

No —she had *written* it in blood. At least in part. Though even if it'd been a few letters or the entire thing, the fact remained that there was dry human blood on that particular page; on that particular message. It scared her. What could have frightened her so much that she resorted to that?

If it was more of a prophecy then what would happen to fulfil it?

She also knew that it was for her, personally.

She didn't understand how she was a cat, but her gut told her that she was the creature that watched, swatted at an apple, and knew of the things that others did not. There was an ominous feel; beyond the blood, distress and beneath in the layers of text. It wasn't a threat, but Louise was being told to do something. And quickly.

The hours of daylight were growing shorter.

"I'm sorry for how I treated you," she finally whispered. "I don't think that I've ever apologised for it, even though you seemed to forgive me."

"Well, I certainly don't rationalise it," he quipped as his auburn brows knitted together. "It was a shitty thing to do, and I believe that you treated other people much worse. I don't excuse it, but people can change. I think you can change. And I see it happening right in front of me."

Louise wiped her cheeks with long, dark green sleeves. "Thanks."

Though that page didn't seem to think so. It implied that she was just as sly and conniving as she once had been —more so from a distance, but still with that overseeing self-importance.

And she didn't want that.

Donatello's gaze fell to the pile before her on the floor, and narrowed in on one in particular. "Hey, you know how we've been focused on pages that are dated in the future? What about the ones from the past?"

"What does that one say?" Louise got up to crouch on her haunches.

"…It's the shortest. '*The day the darkness opened its jaws*.' That's all it says in the middle of *A Christmas Carol*."

She blinked rapidly. Then she scrambled for that dreadful page —and shoved it in Donatello's face. "The dark swallows," she deadpanned.

Understandably, his expression morphed into one of confusion. Until she put the pages side by side, and his eyes flicked between the two. They widened slightly.

"These dates definitely track," he confirmed. "The '*jaws*' open before they '*swallow*'. Could it be in relation to the Daemons?"

"That's possible. Maybe there's a cohesive timeline."

"Want to check?"

She nodded, rising to her knees.

The task of reorganising all of those piles into chronological order was daunting. It also brought her back to that exchange in the woods. Could it be that Alexander had a point? While she didn't accuse them of something fully dreadful, she could not shake the feeling that their involvement went beyond an apple and a carnivorous fox. Beyond them succumbing to that dark along with the rest of the town.

Louise shook her head.

Don't split focus.

Her gaze skimmed her handwriting as the letters swirled upon others; over similar phrases and similar dates. She kept a specific lookout for the dates in the past as well as the future —until she saw that day's date.

THE TREES HIDE ALL THAT LIVES.

THE FOG COVERS ALL THAT DIES.

THE CAT AND THE SPARROW WILL

DISCOVER ALL THAT DEVOURS.

That familiar iciness slid down her back as she read the last two lines. If she was the cat, she had the suspicion that Donatello was the sparrow. His hair matched the feathers —that reddish brown was close to the same shade. That was not the part which unnerved her. It was the odd promise that the two of them would find some new kind of monster.

It wasn't threatening, but it certainly wasn't a suggestion.

It was inevitable. Likely today.

Louise pulled her sleeves over her fists and gathered the pages at her feet, before stuffing them into her backpack. After slinging the straps over her shoulders she moved towards the trapdoor. She then looked back, to offer Donatello an expectant look.

"Hey Donny," she quipped. "Want to go hunting?"

Although Louise Barnes detested the fact that her father had been an avid hunter, she failed to see the irony of her doing something similar —even if it was arguably more ethical and she didn't have killing in mind.

She didn't have a rifle; only her wits.

And the tall boy next to her. Donatello blocked out the sun when she looked at him from the side, and the rays reached out like a halo. He had tied up his hair into a ponytail —a feat of which she was a little jealous.

She absentmindedly twirled a lock of hers between her fingers.

"It's kind of cute when you do that," Donatello suddenly remarked.

"What," she blurted.

"When you twirl your hair," he clarified, staring ahead.

She consciously did it again. "You don't…find it *annoying*?"

"No," he said seriously. "But, I think that it's only cute when you do it. Your eyebrows furrow and your lips curl in a hint of a smile, and then sometimes you bite your lip."

Louise Barnes was quite sure that her face was a pale pink.

She didn't know what to think. She knew that Donatello actually liked her in that way she craved, but they had agreed to be friends. She had not removed the possibility of more. However, she had not given the notion the go-ahead. A part of her still felt unworthy, but a bigger one was more concerned about rounding herself before she invested in another person.

Any future partners deserved that much.

The colour in her face did not fade immediately. Was he naturally this way? It'd been a while since they'd had the semblance of a conversation, so in truth she barely knew him. But he knew her. Enough to be sure that the person Louise had been the past few years wasn't really her.

A small smile tugged at the corners of her mouth.

The snapping of several twigs caused her to jump.

Her head went in the direction of the sound, and her heart leapt to her throat. Was this how they would die?

Donatello tensed, whipping around with her.

But the following scampering of hooves put her fear at momentary ease. It appeared to be a deer, a few clusters of conifer away. The whistle of the wind through tired branches rose above the taut silence.

"If I get mauled by a bear," Louise quipped, "I'm blaming you."

"This was entirely *your* dangerous idea."

"And yet here you are. Come on Ricci," she scoffed. "Where are those protective instincts? I'm the girl here."

"Fuck off," he chuckled with disbelief, shaking his head and moving to continue along the path.

He was reasonable. She liked that. Despite whatever feelings he had, he wouldn't force them upon her, and he wasn't self-sacrificing. And that meant everything to her. If the two were ever meant to be anything more, it would stem from a friendship she desperately needed.

Someone who believed that she could be better —and that being their priority. Someone to remind her that she was growing.

Her Daemon dragged its claws down the side of her arm, tugging the oversized jacket draping her withering frame. It dampened the flicker of hope and loveliness but she supposed that her attention was redirected.

Louise ran the words over in her head.

The cat knows the dark swallows.

The cat and the sparrow will discover all that devours.

The hair at the back of her neck prickled as her whole body shivered. The version of her from the past was right —though there were two types of darkness which consumed. The literal dark; the thing over her shoulder, and the darkness within. Within her, and within all.

Her Daemon let out a wry chuckle at her acknowledgment. She could feel herself getting weaker and weaker ever since the creatures had taken form. Everyone was a little more tired, a little more unwilling, and a little less alive. The Daemons were taking from them —that was evident.

But there was no sign as to why —aside from her observation of hers finding pleasure in her misery.

Or keep her in check.

Louise and Donatello then paused in a clearing in Kindling Acre. The dry tree branches reached out like the thin crooked arms of the teenagers' shadows. But that wasn't the thing which unsettled Louise.

"Is that a grave?" Donatello voiced the question.

Under a lone, lopsided sprout of a tree, there was a waterlogged cross made of cardboard. It had been wrapped in clear tape but it hadn't stopped the rain from soaking through. The words were still legible.

Louise padded over and gingerly lowered before the cross, sliding her hands underneath her grey plaid skirt as she did so.

"…Good Omen," she read. "Taken too soon."

"Is that a…paw?"

"Surprisingly well drawn," murmured Louise, before grunting as she heaved back to her feet. "I'm guessing this is a pet's grave."

"Who would bury their pet *here*?"

"I don't think it's as weird as it seems," she assured. "I heard that the Hydes' cat passed away just two weeks ago—"

She stopped short, realising something.

"Oh that's sad," Donatello winced.

Shane Hyde had buried his family cat in the middle of nowhere in the Kindling Acre and Louise could feel the temperature drop; both internally and externally. It wasn't the commemoration. She had absolutely nothing against wanting to care for a pet's death.

But why here? Why like that, with a washed up bunch of cardboard?

"It looks like something out of a horror movie."

"I don't know." Donatello twisted his mouth into a shape and shoved his hands into his pockets. "Seems pretty on brand to me."

"I know Hyde is dangerous and secretive," admitted Louise, "but that doesn't mean he would automatically do something like this. He's dating *Alexander Grahams*, for Christ's sake. That's got to have changed at least his ability to interact civilly with the general population."

"Still can't believe *that*," he muttered. "Though…he does seem more chatty. And he doesn't get violently angry. So in that same vein, what if this was entirely innocent? What if Shane just held a funeral?"

She pressed her lips together and indignantly folded her arms as if she was cold. She could not shake the feeling that it wasn't.

"…Whatever," she grumbled, turning away. "This doesn't necessarily mean anything, anyway."

Yet as they then trudged out of the clearing, Louise's gaze strayed to that leaning sodden cross and would not waver until it was entirely out of sight. She'd heard her own words. It did not mean that she believed them.

The woods grew thicker and leafy as they neared the ends of the Acre and approached the high hills banking the Youngs River.

The stretch of it wasn't wild, but the water certainly flowed down and crashed against the scattering of rocks. It still made sound —a warning of its dangers. Louise and Donatello did not dare to cross. The tributary was narrow enough to attempt it but neither were experts nor had the unbridled recklessness to try.

They stuck to the path alongside it, peering between the gaps of trunks on the opposite bank. And although the girl could not make anything out of the darkness there, her Daemon fabricated images of distorted faces in the undergrowth and in the twist of the branches. Horrible creatures in the likeness of people she knew. And they all seemed to be reaching outwards for her, desperate to devour —

"Uh, what exactly are we looking for?" Donatello's sigh dispelled the spiral of thought. Her hair fluttered from the catch of a protruding twig. Or her Daemon.

"I don't know," Louise revealed. "The only solid clue that I have is a deadline. We could very well be chasing something abstract."

"Based on what has happened in this town, I wouldn't put it past your cautionary tales to be talking about a very tangible monster."

"I agree."

Sweat trickled down into the back of her shirt despite the chill of the air. She wasn't sure which form was worse. That dread only compounded as the two wandered towards the cliffs that overlooked the town. Once, it had been the go to spot for indecent activity. Now that no one went very far anywhere, it was still and prowled only by wild animals.

Or so Louise thought.

She herself hadn't been up there in a couple of years. There was a new thing: a blue pick up truck parked overhead. It had been there for a while

—probably as long as the signal and vehicles had been down. Maybe even longer than that.

Aside from its presence, there was something else out of place. White sheets and a comforter hung over the truck's sides; haphazard and in the middle of either being lain or removed. And by an all too familiar boulder was the silhouette of something that Louise and Donatello shouldn't have seen. Not that it was unusual. They were simply, suddenly intruding.

It was two teenagers making out in the woods.

It was Shane Hyde and Alexander Grahams.

Louise started. They broke apart immediately before whipping around at the vocal accompaniment of Donatello's surprise.

"What the fuck," Shane hissed —more disappointed in the abrupt end of what they had been doing than being caught.

"I assure you, this is *not* what I expected from this morning," clipped Donatello, pivoting on his heel. "PDA is a no for me."

"It wasn't exactly public until you showed up," Alexander pointed out in a muffled grumble.

"Are you two stalking us?" Shane followed up, baring his teeth.

"No," Louise said firmly, raising her hands. "We were doing our own thing and happened to stumble across…that."

"A likely story," Shane spat.

Alexander looked as though they could not decide between glaring in righteous fury and hiding behind Shane's frame in mortification.

"Look, it's not that important in the grand scheme of things," Louise went on. "I think that we only have a few days left at best, until '*the dark swallows*', and we still don't even know what that means."

Alexander and Shane shared a look.

It was a long look —a silent back and forth over something quite often discussed. Several furrows of eyebrows and darting glances.

Theirs resembled apprehension. His was not much to go on at all. But then he turned to Donatello and Louise, and drew a breath. That turquoise gleamed in the hazy sunlight, and struck her with a very familiar wariness. The hair at the back of her neck rose again. For the first time, solitude was silent and her Daemon was pulling her *away*.

The reaction she was sure she'd show when they found what devours.

"We know what it means," Shane confessed.

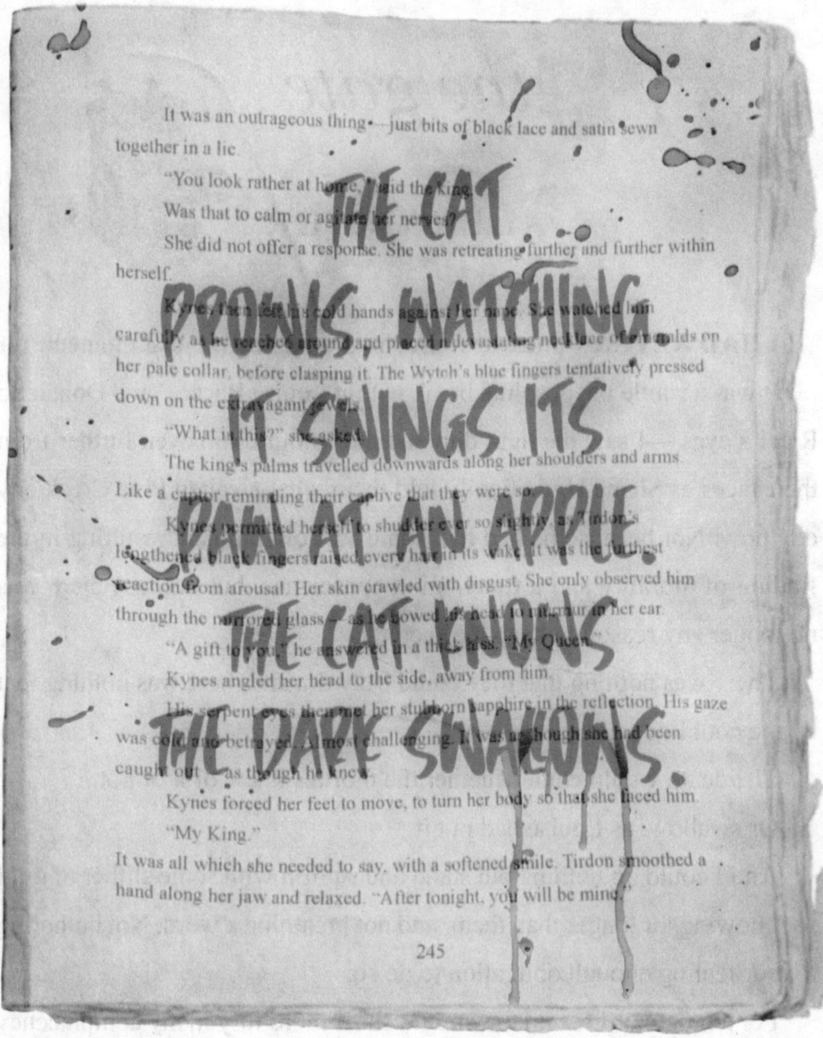

It was an outrageous thing—just bits of black lace and satin sewn together in a lie.

"You look rather at home," said the king.

Was that to calm or agitate her nerves?

She did not offer a response. She was retreating further and further within herself.

Kynes then felt his cold hands against her nape. She watched him carefully as he reached around and placed a devastating necklace of emeralds on her pale collar, before clasping it. The Wytch's blue fingers tentatively pressed down on the extravagant jewels.

"What is this?" she asked.

The king's palms travelled downwards along her shoulders and arms. Like a captor reminding their captive that they were so.

Kynes permitted herself to shudder ever so slightly, as Tirdon's lengthened black fingers raised every hair in its wake. It was the furthest reaction from arousal. Her skin crawled with disgust. She only observed him through the mirrored glass — as he bowed his head to murmur in her ear.

"A gift to you," he answered in a thick hiss. "My Queen."

Kynes angled her head to the side, away from him.

His serpent eyes then met her stubborn sapphire in the reflection. His gaze was cold, and betrayed... Almost challenging. It was as though she had been caught out — as though he knew.

Kynes forced her feet to move, to turn her body so that she faced him.

"My King."

It was all which she needed to say, with a softened smile. Tirdon smoothed a hand along her jaw and relaxed. "After tonight, you will be mine."

245

THE CAT
PROWLS, WATCHING.
IT SWINGS ITS
PAW AT AN APPLE.
THE CAT KNOWS
THE DARK SWALLOWS.

the gate

ALEXANDER

I HAD NEVER witnessed worlds imploding before that moment.

It was a subtle but absolute break within Louise Barnes' and Donatello Ricci's eyes —I saw the light dim and the colour drain even further from their faces as Shane Hyde finally told them what awaited Pine Creek any day now. Not because he had had some sort of epiphany resulting in the finding of morality and a functioning conscience, but because there was no longer any reason to keep it a secret.

There was nothing that they could truly do, and there was nothing that Shane could do to stop it.

The death would come whether the mortals knew of it or not.

Or swallow, as Louise had put it.

And I could do nothing but stand and squirm with some slither of guilt for knowing far longer than them, and not breathing a word. Not bothering to, nor feeling enough obligation to do so.

For a moment, I feared they might show more fury in my complacency than Shane's complete omission. But they were more stunned that angry. At first. The shock and disbelief turned to scepticism and deep frowning a few seconds after Shane's stumble through a recount. What counted as an appropriate reaction? Violence? Everything would be justified in their eyes, but not entirely in mine.

And I was aware that was completely selfish.

"*You're* all that devours," Louise eventually murmured; monotonous and matter-of-fact. Her face was contorted with betrayal, and I understood it. I had never seen her blue eyes so dark and empty. They were not alight with conviction. That was defeated acceptance.

Another awful thing to add to an already awful life.

Even if the revelation made all she had accomplished meaningless.

And for some reason, that sparked something within me. Not for her sake alone, and certainly not to aid her growth —though that was for the betterment of all humanity —but for the sake of life itself. The idea of it carrying on. The idea of time being corrected.

I didn't want to live through this yet again, to my knowledge or not.

I knew that the mortals before me wouldn't, either.

But I could think of nothing to do differently to destroy the curse and free them. Most things were unfolding as planned.

Shane didn't deny Louise's statement.

We all knew it was rooted a perceived truth. Only I had known that it was fundamental. His head hung —in a way that was difficult to tell if it was for show or genuine —and his hand was frigid as I held it. And Louise honed in on the gesture. I braced myself. Now she would tear into me.

"You knew about this?"

It didn't come out as an accusation. She was actually surprised. And I tensed, overcome with uncertainty. There was no right thing to say, even if there was a morally correct one.

"I did," I admitted. "But…it wasn't my place to say anything."

"Does he kill you too, in his little spree?" Donatello clipped. "Or are you the love he spares?"

"He does kill me," I answered tightly. No matter how much I wished that it wasn't true. No matter how much I wished that I could change it. I could no longer look anyone in the eye.

Why had I run at that moment, after voicing that I had fallen in love? Why had I not stayed?

"And you're *okay* with it?" asked Louise, dumbfounded.

"There…there's nothing I can do," I forced, retreating further. Though I did not want to release Shane's hand. It was stubborn in his lifeless icy hold. But he didn't move away either. "It'll all reset soon."

"This is batshit," Donatello bit, taking a step backwards. "I would yell and call you a liar, but these things are proof of supernatural forces." He pointed at the darkness over his shoulder. It flared with his anger. And it did not hurt him for it. "Doesn't mean it's not crazy."

"I agree," chimed Louise. "I would say that this is a betrayal, but you never had any loyalty to this town in the first place. To our lives. We mean nothing to you —only Alexander does."

Her words pierced me like a spear, and pinned me to an invisible wall. My chest began to constrict. I could not breathe. All I could think of was to run. Just as my father had insinuated.

And it sounded disgusting, but I couldn't help saying in defence, "You don't know him like I do."

Louise and Donatello gaped at me.

"…Wow." That was all she managed, while Donatello could not even get a word out. I flinched at the flurry of outrage and flabbergast billowing in his darkening eyes.

I was betraying them, in a way. If that's what they believed.

"Don't you feel any guilt?" Louise then berated.

"No," I whispered. "No I don't." Perhaps the more I said it, the more true it would become. "I barely have an attachment to this wretched place, and I understand what Shane did. I am not saying I am on any moral high ground —on the contrary, I am almost as bad as him. You can hate me, if you want. It will not save you and I don't think…I will, either."

Each word reinforced my conviction; turned my muscles to iron from jelly. It grounded me —that horrible, corrupt promise.

The girl's horror turned into hurt —a hurt that she had no right to feel. But she showed it anyway, in hopes that I might waver. That I might see reason. An absurd laugh threatened to burst from my lips.

Reason had abandoned me.

That fact seemed to sink in as Shane's grip on my hand strengthened and he then pulled me into his side, like I was the only anchor that he had to the world. It was a statement —they had no choice but to acknowledge if not reluctantly accept.

"Have you…always been like this?" Louise had to ask. "Back then — when we were kids?"

She had turned away in body language; half back towards Donatello, with her arms wrapped around herself in unease rather than attitude. She was afraid of this, of us. Of death. And I did not blame her.

I dwelled on her question and its phrasing.

"Back when you were a monster?" I deadpanned.

She winced.

I enjoyed the feeling of my counter slicing into her —as I was sure that her Daemon did as well.

"…To be honest," I mused, "I think I've known Shane collectively for longer than I've known you."

"Why…*why* after what he did?"

"He did it because of me, not to me," I clarified.

Donatello scoffed. "This is absolutely unforgivable. You're choosing a supernatural war criminal over the entirety of a civilian town!"

"So what," I snapped, feeling the silent protest in Shane's squeeze. "I never said that I was better than you. And I am certainly *not* choosing the humans who ruined my life, over an overwhelming love I've never felt in my existence before."

"Before," echoed Donatello. "Precisely. Do you think that this…*thing* is your '*one and only*'?" He looked at Shane with visceral repulsion. And Shane took it, remaining still and expressionless.

"Thing?" I ground out between my teeth. "He's not a *thing*, you prick. And yes, I do think that. Why? Because of the fact that this curse exists at all. We mean something…preternatural, to each other. You don't know what either of us have done to get here. What we would do again."

"At our expense." Louise sucked on her teeth, bringing back a flicker of the past. "I…I don't think I can take this conversation anymore."

She turned fully to storm off.

Donatello shot us one more disapproving glance before following suit. And I watched them go, Shane's hand being the only reassurance that I'd done a terrible thing but I didn't have to feel terrible about it.

Not anymore.

There was a nagging feeling in the back of my mind, by the base of my neck. While I had no obligation to save Pine Creek, what of my own life?

Unbeknownst to me, I had become absentminded after our encounter with Louise Barnes and her cautionary tales. Those words still lengthened my spine and sent a quiver along it, but I was trying to suppress.

If I didn't think about it, they couldn't become something.

Something else.

Nothing was fine…but it didn't need to be worse.

"Alex," Shane said gently, in the musty library. We had come straight from the woods having left our bundles of sheets and blankets —deeming neither of our houses worth the time. Time that we did not have, and time we would rather spend together. He reached over to hook his little finger on mine. His voice and my name within it snapped me out of a haze I had been lost inside. "You don't have to care."

That was true. I had a choice.

"…I don't want to feel like this," I whispered hoarsely.

His face fell a little. "Feel like what?"

"Human."

"But…it's one of the things I love about you," he murmured, the corners of his lips lifting in the softest smile. It made me melt.

I didn't want to melt.

I wanted to be sharp and cutting; I wanted to be felt and leave an awful taste that lingered. I wanted to break, not be broken.

"Damnit." The hiss was out from between my teeth in something that closer resembled a reluctant surrender than bitterness. My fingers did not move. His remained tied down to mine, in the most gentle promise.

It weighed a ton and pressed down on my ribcage. But I had to remind myself that he had never believed it before then —that I could be serious about the thing that bound us, and actually be in love with him.

"…I wish I could stop it from happening," I muttered. "Forever."

I pressed my head against his denim shoulder.

"Me too."

"I…once had the thought that me remembering could have an impact on the curse. Like that one page said —about no one being able to escape unless one without fear should remember. We already know that I am not afraid. But nothing has come of me having access to those memories."

Shane paused in thought. "What about the nightmares? Have you ever found a clue in any of them?"

My muscles locked, and in turn, I felt him acknowledge the reaction. "The only clue I can think of is that my body remembers the jarring shock after waking, and the sadness from parting."

"…Yeah, I don't know how that would help."

But his question oiled the gears in my mind.

If my memories themselves held no hint of stopping the cycles, then perhaps it wasn't so straightforward. The solution could be more abstract and metaphorical. Instead of specific elements guiding the investigation, there could be merit in the broader narrative; or the reason itself as to why I was having the dreams.

I dwelled on the one of a few hours ago.

Though I had nothing but speculation with which to work, I started to wonder what would've happened if I *had* made that seal and opened that gate. What might that binding have achieved? Maybe I wouldn't have run, and Pine Creek would not have been caught up in the middle of that rage. Or, maybe I would have then been apprehended by the very creature I had instinctively avoided in the dungeons.

I had not paused to contemplate that thread. What if I had managed to escape the jaws of real death?

"Hyde, what's a seal?" I finally blurted. "Or…or a gate?"

I expected him to stare blankly with no real answer, but instead he was haunted. I lifted my head and blinked at the colour draining from his face. My brows knitted together in confusion. "…Shane?"

The display of panic and dread lasted only for a few seconds. Then he became that familiar icy stone. He didn't avoid my gaze though.

"No way," I murmured. "You know what they are."

"Of course I do," he deadpanned. "I am from Hell —made and raised. Even I know what a seal is. And gates are basic knowledge."

The light had fizzled out from not only his luminous irises, but where it should have hit in a reflection in his pupils.

My hands shot out to his shoulders. "Don't do that," I pleaded, "don't shut down. It's all right to *feel*, Shane. Especially if it's just us. Please feel with me. Like before."

The muscles in his face tightened as his jaw clenched.

It was painful to broaden that spectrum, and allowing those thoughts to fester and submerge in things that had never been through your system prior. I knew that. I wanted him to know I was so proud of him for feeling it all anyway. For feeling it for me.

Colour seeped back slowly —in time with Shane's shallow breathing. His rigid shoulders loosened in my grip. Then purple crescents ringed the turquoise and my own breath hitched.

"Seals are…usually blood contracts," he choked out, curling his hands into fists. "There is no greater bind than that of mixed bloods. It lasts till death. Usually beyond, especially if all parties are immortal. They are not to be used for any old agreement. It's the sort you can't ever escape. And gates…those are the hungry mouths of Hell."

My eyes flicked downwards. "…Louise called you '*all that devours*'. Is there a chance she should've been referring to a *gate*, instead?"

Shane noticeably started, as if the suggestion itself was preposterous.

"I am not aware of any gates in Pine Creek," he insisted. "And I know the town inside and out."

"Oh."

It wasn't disappointment that flooded my expression, but helplessness and defeat. If he had no ideas, then it was a dead end.

"However," Shane mused, "if there was a gate right beneath our noses, it must be locked, seeing as nothing has ever slipped through before. But it's also possible that the gap might only be large enough for the smallest animals to burrow through. It still wouldn't explain everything."

"Why would Hell even imprison you in the town if it had the potential to let you escape?" I quipped.

"They might not have known," Shane bit. "They were simply working to make the punishment fit the crime, after all. That, or…somebody was awfully confident it wouldn't be found."

I met his calculating gaze. "Or opened."

His frown morphed into a glare as he bent his head.

I then tilted mine slightly, attempting to meet his eye again. "Hey — why did you stop feeling just to say that? We haven't…" I trailed off, my eyes widening. "You saw, didn't you? When I first came to your cell, you saw the blood."

Shane swallowed. "…I smelled it," he stated flatly. "The knife falling gave it away."

"You never mentioned it after."

"There was nothing to mention."

It was dismissive.

"Hyde," I said firmly. He didn't react. My hands balled. "*Ferream.*"

He flinched, before matching my glare. "I didn't say anything because I was grateful that you had changed your mind. Why would I ever mention it again? Seals are permanent, terrible things. I didn't want to accidentally persuade you to make one anyway."

I ground my teeth together but I couldn't fully fault that logic. I could be angry that he had not explained them in the first place, but he had had good reason to ignore it entirely.

"I have never lied to you, Alex," he then reminded me. "I swear."

"I…I know," I mumbled limply.

He had only left things out.

The silence that settled over us strained over our individual bitterness and was louder than any scream. This was the first disagreement we had ever had. I half marvelled at, half looked on in disbelief that we hadn't fought before. In all of the years that we had known one another, was this truly the only thing that had ever snagged the fabric of our tapestry?

It did not feel healthy.

Had he always bent to me?

Or had I, to him?

I growled and held my head in my hands. It startled Shane, who dithered beside me before stroking the side of my face with his knuckles. I let out a soft breath before shivering at the contact.

"I am not fragile," I told him.

He chuckled. "I'm realising that." He then slowly leaned inwards, to press his forehead to mine. All I could see were those shimmering pools of blue as his hand gripped my chin and tilted my head. "Something like me doesn't deserve someone like you."

My face grew warm at every whispered word. It caressed like his hand and burrowed beneath my skin.

"I think that's why it's called love."

"Mm. Love."

I didn't care about the librarian as his mouth grazed my own; or when his teeth nipped my lips and his tongue traced along the scar on the bottom one. I shuddered, something electric shooting within my veins at the touch and tease. Then Shane paused, still moving his lips —before my shoulders shot up at the sound of an uneasily cleared throat.

I whipped around, hearing the echo of my heartbeat in my temples.

An uncertain librarian stood there. She was not flustered with disgust. It seemed that she was uncomfortable with the general act of kissing here. Her fingers fiddled with the ribbon tie around her neck, while the heels of the polished *Mary Janes* over her tights did not budge apart.

"Got something to say?" Shane grunted.

I shot him a brief look.

"Please refrain from…escalated behaviour," she put delicately. "This is a place of learning and solace foremost, thank you. I can…*hear* you."

Shane raised an eyebrow and his piercing caught the sun. "The library is quite appropriate for such a rendezvous," he countered. "Have you got any idea how many teenagers use the bookcases like a cheap motel?"

She was actually taken aback. "Excuse me?"

"Hyde, this is why no one talks to you," I bit.

"But I'm making a point," he grumbled.

"Well stop it," I commanded. I turned to the librarian. "I am *so* sorry. We won't do it again."

"I never said the library conducts itself like a monastery." She met my averting gaze as she walked back, and offered something suspiciously like understanding. And *amusement*. "…But show some consideration and be a little more quiet."

Shane stared at my mouth. "So she basically just gave us a go-ahead. Do you think you could moan less?"

I wanted the ground to unhinge its jaws and take me to an early grave.

"*Puta merda*," I hissed, "that did *not* just happen."

"We're going to keep being interrupted as long as we're out in public, Grahams. Making out is frowned upon within view of salads."

"You're not helping," I clipped, sharply hitting at his chest.

He smirked like he was proud. "I never do."

My cheeks and the back of my neck were burning. It didn't help when Shane leaned over, to blow on the skin. I jolted and my spine straightened —resulting in the exact opposite reaction needed.

"…Minus thirty," I warned through clenched teeth.

"Whoa, your nape goes a little red," Shane murmured.

"*Hyde* —!"

A loud shush caught the end of my exclaim —and only compounded the embarrassment. He just snickered like it was funny.

"The world as you know it is about to end, Grahams," he sighed. "Live a little." I hadn't realised when the violet had faded.

All I could think of was how he wouldn't be included in the sentiment. How he was cursed with living —to live too much and indefinitely. And that death would separate us once more, leaving behind a slew of scattered memories along my footprints in the sand.

"I don't want to do anything without you," I then whispered, turning to face him. "To live or die. Feel or exist numbly. I just want to stay right by your side."

Shane drew a deep breath and became stone once more. "Next to me is the most dangerous place to be," he warned, leaning back in the chair. His eyes almost seemed warm. "But also the most appreciated."

My hand reached for his jaw. He started leaning in again, which made me smile. I did not let him get far, however. When I could feel his shallow breath I turned, missing the action. I went for his ear and felt him tense at the touch. "You can't kiss me like you did and expect me to be quiet."

His eyes ignited as they slowly widened with intrigue. "And *you* can't say that and expect me to be normal about it."

My foot tapped rhythmically beneath us. "How will you be about it?"

His lips ripped back in a snarl. "Repressed."

I couldn't fight off the grin that spread in precedence of laughter. "So find a place out of view of salads."

"…Fine."

There could not be more than a day until the end of our present reality and Shane Hyde's priority was getting as much of me as he could manage — the me who remembered. His solution to the interruption problem was to sneak into the empty high school; a feat only complete with a pair of bolt cutters and several bobby pins. Thank God for the broken alarm system.

I mentally added breaking and entering with vandalism to the endless list of mass murder and assault.

I saw a determination within him that roused and perplexed me.

But then the escapade started to get a little fun and exciting —so crime drifted further and further over the horizon of relevancy. All there was in the grand scheme of things was Shane, me and the lack of air. And hands in the darkness; though I didn't dwell *on what* exactly we did that.

In most aspects I didn't blame him. I clawed just as viciously. He had told me that he struggled with containing his attraction and desire. And he held me as though he would never be able to ever again. With our track record, that was unfortunately entirely possible.

So…why would he not fight to *keep* this reality?

We were lying on the carpet of the teachers' lounge; side by side, but each pair of feet facing opposite walls. We'd since caught our breath and tugged clothing back into place, and the ceiling had this intricate engraved pattern I had not noticed before. It was rotating like something from a far off dimension, out of a movie.

Sex was sort of ethereal when high.

Instead of two people in motion, we became extensions of each other. I did not know where Shane's hands ended and mine began. His skin had been burning hot, scorching everything that it touched. And my red nape was still tingling from his teeth in my neck when he had sat me up on the History teacher's desk.

"Damnit," I drawled, fighting the urge to laugh. Even though I could.

"Damn what?"

Shane leisurely blew a plume directly towards the smoke detector that wasn't working, before passing the joint over to me. I breathed in, holding it in my lungs for a moment longer than usual. I breathed in until it filled and became me —until my fingers turned translucent and misty like those wisps of grey escaping my parting lips.

My eyebrows furrowed. "Do you think that Louise and Donatello will tell everyone?"

"It will be too late by the time word reaches ears that matter," he stated frankly. "Everything will be inky black and running red."

"I'm going to see you ripping into them," I mused aloud. "And I think I will be happy."

"You deserve to be."

"Thank you."

Shane *did* laugh.

"And when you do kill me," I continued, "I will look upon your face, and burn it into my memory."

His fingers lingered when I handed the joint back. Mine slipped right through, curling around in a way smoke did not obey gravity. Yet I could feel the sensation of touch as well, as if I were still solid.

"You know you won't remember," Shane murmured softly.

"But I drew you," I pouted. "After all those dreams. What you actually look like. Iron and bloody, with those beautiful wings."

I felt his shoulder tense against me. "Paper isn't immortal, Alex."

"But you are."

"Mm."

I turned my head, my cheek pressing to the carpet. He mirrored the action, unblinking as he took a drag. He blew out slowly and vaguely as if simply breathing so that the smoke barely wafted out, and rose instead. But I still opened my mouth, like all those weeks ago. Shane shifted slightly to peck the tip of my nose.

His irises had turned into real topaz refracting in the pillars of sunlight. There was no violet in sight and his eyes were lidded, numbly. There was no slither of feeling because he was in fact blocking all of those out.

"I've been thinking," I told him.

"Yeah?"

My gaze wandered over his face. "What if…we *could* break free from the curse? What if we can keep this cycle?"

Shane's eyebrows twitched. As if he wanted to frown but the muscles wouldn't fully cooperate. "What do you mean?"

I reached for his fingers, still seeing through grey and flesh and bone. "Don't you want to preserve this version of me? The one that knows who you are, and loves you still?"

"They're *all* you," he sighed. "Like fragments of a stained glass mural. And, even though I hadn't thought much of it before, I don't know if your memories change anything. Not enough to break the loop."

"What if they're just a tool and not the final product?" I suggested.

"Like…a key that unlocks something more?"

I plucked the diminishing joint from his idle hand and inhaled. "Yeah. We need to think of what we can do differently. What…what would show that we want to stop reliving all of this?"

"I have to, you know —learn a lesson," he grumbled, moving to sit up and lean back on his hands. He pursed his lips expectantly. I smirked and brought the little roll of paper to his mouth after rising from the floor like a zombie. He hummed and then released his grip, blowing up towards the smoke detector again. He took hold of my free hand as I polished off the last of the joint, and pressed his mouth to the palm.

I wondered if he knew it was the hand I'd cut.

"Well," I breathed. "Have you learned anything?"

"Aside from the fact that I could not possibly love you more? No." He glanced up with his eyes only, beneath dark brows. I swallowed, shivering as his lips kissed my hand with vigour. My teeth ground together.

"I'm hungry," I stated.

"Me too," Shane mumbled. He kissed the skin once more, then moved to get to his feet. "Come on, let's get to the diner or something."

"Actually, I think it might be better if we go to my house," I countered. "We can't count on not getting mobbed in public."

His mouth twisted into a shape. "…Fine."

We were sure to leave a minimal trace of our patronage before heading around towards my neighbourhood through the woods.

Nothing was moving that was not supposed to. The leaves rustled, the river ran and the breeze billowed. But the clouds raced across the sky. As grey as they were, they didn't seem to hold much water. The air was heavy with a promise of rain, but remained dry and suffocating.

Like someone holding back tears.

My hand flew to Shane's side and grabbed at his fingers. He chuckled and laced them with mine, then pulled them into the pocket of his jacket. I leaned into his shoulder. I didn't want to part from this. From him. Why did it feel like he didn't want to consider the same?

"…Have you resigned to giving up?" I eventually murmured.

I could see the strain in his jaw as he clenched it. "I have never wanted to get my hopes up, Grahams. In the past, there had been cycles that would give anyone in my position that glimmer of hope; to think that maybe this time, this time we'll break it." He turned to look at me. His gaze glistened. "And I don't want to feel that pain again."

I understood.

Or so I thought. I could understand why he would not want to explore the possibility of failure. Why he would not want to rip open that wound. But it was that terror which kept him from realising another possibility: this could be our only chance to escape. The dreams meant something. I had no doubt that it was a sign glaring us in the face.

"But what do we have to lose?" I asked genuinely.

"More than you think," Shane answered with equal sincerity.

"I find it difficult to believe that you would rather enjoy this cycle for what it is and let the next one begin without trying anything."

"If I expect nothing, then I'll regret nothing," he hissed.

"For God's sake Hyde, take a look around. We have a chance this time and you sound like you're letting it pass. I know you are afraid. But you'll never know if you do not try at all. You *will* see me again, in the end. We just have the opportunity to shorten that time between, and remember."

Shane stopped walking.

I skidded to a halt in time, breathing shallowly. I was still intoxicated and it was starting to feel bad. My heartbeat pounded in my temples and I had no control over what I was saying. But I knew that it was honest.

"Don't you think I want you to remember?" Shane whispered. "Don't you think I've entertained this idea? Of course I want to break free and be with you again…but every time that I think about what could happen, I'm standing on the edge of a cliff, inches from falling. And there's just this length of rope tied around me and on the other side, dictating whether I slip or stay. Do you know who holds that rope?" he asked me.

I shook my head, frowning deeply.

"It's not you," he clarified. "You and I are not the masters of this story or any story, for that matter. The one who holds the rope is my creator — the Lord of Darkness; the Destroyer; the Devil. And they have never had any intention of letting go."

A shiver shot along my spine like a lightning strike. I understood all of those words separately. It took a moment to process exactly what it was that he was saying. His fingers tightened on mine inside his pocket despite the harsh expression on this face. In the end, I was all that he wanted.

I was all he had ever truly wanted.

"Then I'll untie it," I declared. "I'll even stand at the bottom of by the rocks and catch you."

He turned his head. His eyes speared right through to the centre of me —to my very soul, as if he could see it. Then I realised that he likely *could* see it, under layers of mortal humanity and innocence.

"Alexander," he breathed. His eyebrows smoothed out as he appeared to weaken. "Goddamnit."

My other hand rose to his cheek. There was a thought in the forefront of my mind. "What if when you kill me again, I…*want* to die?"

Shane started violently. The purple fizzled to life, arcing the blue and shining with such an intensity that the strength in my knees wavered.

"What," he rasped. "What did you say?"

I frowned. "What…what's the big deal? I have already died countless times. Isn't it all beyond our control anyway?"

He cursed; letting go of my hand and jerking away. Then he let out a growl, and covered his face with his hands. He dropped to his haunches —and I could have sworn I heard the choked echo of a sob.

"…It's not about controlling the situation," he viciously bit. "It should be about…oh Christ. How can you just *say* that? I mean —I've heard you say something similar. But I…didn't know what it meant back then. I did not know that it might mean…this."

I froze. That thought had not crossed my mind. "Oh."

It was all that I could manage.

"How can you even think I might feel nothing at the idea of you…of the look on your face when I…"

He couldn't finish the thought. The damning consequences. That even if we broke the curse, we wouldn't be permitted to stay together.

"I want to do this with the hope of ending up in Hell," I said hurriedly, lowering before him. "With you."

Shane paused. His head lifted slowly, and I was greeted with the most gut wrenching sight. Tears were streaming down his face. Those blue eyes had turned into waterfalls off of the edges of oceans. And my bottom lip trembled as I lowered to be at face level with him.

"Why…why would you want that?" he whispered. "You don't…you

don't belong there."

My gaze softened. "Because it's where you are. I belong with you."

A shudder rippled through him. "That's unbelievably foolish."

"Isn't it?" I forced a soft chuckle.

"Love," Shane sighed, tasting it on his tongue again like it had become mundane. "Love is terrible…if it would make you want to die. Especially like this, with some sort of purpose."

"It destroys," I murmured. "Didn't I tell you that?"

"I know," he said flatly. "I know. I know. I *fucking know*."

"I love you, dear monster."

"And I love you, my sweet mortal," he whispered. "Though we shouldn't, Grahams. We…really shouldn't."

I didn't care. I took his damp face in my hands, swiped my thumbs on the lines of tears still falling, and kissed him —so softly that it was barely anything. But Shane clung to it desperately and shakily dragged it out, as if he would never feel the sensation again.

He panted erratically when we parted slightly, still within distance to press our noses together. The purple did not fade but the gradient of it was a beautiful blend from which I could not look away.

I felt tears well up in my own eyes, lodging any words I wanted to say in my throat. There was something I needed to know; something that felt important to a distant part of me than the present. "…If I stopped coming to you, would you mourn?"

"Yes," said Shane. "Bitterly."

the king's foot soldiers

ALEXANDER

HUGH GRAHAMS DID not ask a single question when Shane Hyde and I wandered in through the front door.

I was surprised to see him on his feet —though not that much by the bottle in his hand.

He only glanced at us briefly, the light dim in his eyes, before turning away to the living room. And he did not say a word when I pulled Shane to the kitchen, not bothering with holding onto his forearm instead of his hand. Not bothering to cover the nail polish. I knew that he could tell how red both of our eyes were. And I knew that he knew exactly why.

Shane stared at me from the marble island as I aggressively prepared ham and lettuce and tomato sandwiches. He didn't say anything for a long while, but I did not mind his silence. I respected it.

Then he held his chin in his hand and cleared his throat. "I've thought about your suggestion," he said. "But I think we need a different solution —I do not think your intentions will change the fact that I still kill you."

"Of course," I said tightly.

"So…there is something that I need to tell you."

I braced myself, butter knife in hand.

"Another baron came to warn me, a couple of nights ago," he began. "I didn't think much of it, as usual, but they told me of a love which had been their end. They were tricked into giving their true name by a witch. Upon the witch's death, the demon was put in charge of their torture."

I shivered. I was sobering up, and I understood his words all together. It was such a terrible thing, to be betrayed by the one you loved. I would never use Ferream's name against him. So why was he telling me?

"…Let's make that seal."

My hand slipped and the slightly grated knife's edge caught the top of my finger. "*Merda*!" I yelped, letting it clatter to the floor. "…Ow."

Shane was next to me in an instant, holding up the wrist to assess the damage. "I really didn't mean to startle you. It's not that deep, thankfully. Where do you keep your Band-Aids?"

"*Ow*. …Upstairs."

"Come on."

We abandoned the food and ran up the stairs to the bathroom. I could only bite my lip as Shane rinsed and dabbed, before stretching a Band-Aid to the top of my left pointer finger. The nick ran the side of the nail, searing and stinging. It felt better as he cradled it in his hands.

Then his eyes flicked up to my face. "Does it hurt?"

"What?" I rasped. "…Oh, no. No, it's not that."

He let out an uneasy breath, then ran a hand through his tangled hair. "I know what I said about seals. But you are not that witch."

"But…*torture*?" I hissed. "Do you really think I'd be up for that?"

He almost looked like he would laugh. "Oh, Alexander, what do you think happens to mortals who end up in Hell? It's not about surviving. If you end up in Hell after death, it can only be for one thing."

I had been afraid that he might say that. I glanced aside.

"…I'm not forcing you into anything," Shane assured. "I just thought that since you had your sights set on Hell anyway, I would offer an option where it was guaranteed we would see each other."

I rubbed the side of my arm. "You…you wouldn't be pulled from your old duties?"

"I do not know," he answered honestly. "I am no ordinary demon," he sighed. "However, if the law stands for every instance, then Lucifer would have no choice. I would have to be your…torturer."

"I am not a masochist," I bluntly stated.

Shane's face finally crumpled and he burst out laughing. It made me jump, before I rolled my shoulders and felt the sound warm up my insides and alleviate some of my fear.

His hand brushed along the side of my cheek after he caught his breath and took a step closer. "I would never actually hurt you, Alex. Even when the pain is not quite real, and even if it is demanded of me. The seal would ensure that only I could touch you —that the punishment would be at my sole discretion, and no power would be able to take that from us."

It was the most gentle whisper.

I could feel his breath on my lips —then his stare. And then his finger as it softly grazed that scar. A shudder reverberated up my spine.

And even though the promise was of safety and reassurance, I had an adverse response. My lower stomach knotted and my lungs constricted in the onslaught of…

"What…would you do to me instead?" I murmured.

Shane noticeably swallowed. "Hypothetically," he mused, "I might do something quite forbidden. But I really shouldn't tell you."

I was staring at his mouth too. "Is it bad?"

I knew that it was.

Words were just filling up the silence. His forehead pressed to mine.

"Absolutely."

I was still unsure about the eternal torture, but he'd given me good reasons for binding ourselves together ahead of the massacre. If going to Hell was inevitable, perhaps I would brave the seal just to end up in the palm of the monster's hand. Because he was the only one who would not harm me.

My eyes lidded. "Let's pull down the stars and align them ourselves."

"Oh. Are we going to make that seal, then?"

"I'll get a knife."

I ran down the stairs and grabbed a chef's knife from its slot. I didn't stop to think. Then I halted in front of Hugh headed for the kitchen again.

With a large knife in my hand.

"What are you doing, son?" he asked.

I bit my tongue. "…Witchcraft."

He held the bridge of his nose, drawing a sharp breath. "What the hell are you playing at, Alexander?"

"I am finally taking charge of my life," I informed him. "I don't expect you to understand, but I need you not to stop me. This…*could* help you."

My father had become pale.

He had always been that light shade; susceptible to burning in the sun and tinging blue in the cold. But his Daemon —of which I was still wary —was draining even the little melanin he possessed. It loomed over him now, eyeing me with an interest that had me viscerally leaning back. The voids of depthless despair didn't waver, and for the first time in my entire existence I felt sorry for Hugh. I really did.

"Is that the Hyde boy?" he muttered. "Is he in on your witchcraft?"

"I…I love him."

My father started. "Excuse me?"

I held the knife tighter. "I'm in love with a truly terrible creature, but I would rather be damned with him for all of eternity than spend a single season with you."

"What? I did not raise you to—"

"You don't get to say that," I cut him off. "Do you think that existing in the same house for seventeen and a half years counts as '*raising*'? Until Mom died, you couldn't even have a conversation with me. And now you think that anything you have to say holds weight?"

He balled his hands into fists. "I regret letting your mother have all of that free rein over you. Maybe…if I had been more involved, you would not have turned out this way. *Look* at those nails."

Breath went in and out of my nose in harsh pants. "Are you serious?" I snapped. "Are you *actually* serious? It is truly astounding that the only thought that pops into your head after confronting your only teenage child wielding a giant *knife*…is that they're not straight."

Hugh pressed his lips together—so much so that his mouth basically disappeared. I could see the conflict in his eyes as they attempted to come back to life. But his Daemon clutched his shoulder and smiled at me, like it was some sick game.

Like I had asked for my father's pain.

"You don't get to comment about anything I do anymore." I held firm. "I learned that recently. I can be grateful that you met my basic physical needs as a child, but that's where it ends. And it's entirely your fault."

"*Alexander*—!" he thundered…or tried to. The sound got stuck inside his throat and he choked on that last syllable. His Daemon dug its claws into that tough dry skin, scraping with a ferocity that seemed just for show and just for me. But I…did not feel as much for it as I had before.

And the creature seemed to notice —by the lack of my response, even as Hugh clutched at his chest like he couldn't breathe.

I still saw very little life flickering there in his gaze.

I would rather he hate Shane for what he really was than him being a boy. At least in the way we all knew him as a mortal.

"I'm sorry," I told him. And I meant it. "I'm sorry that you're too late. I hope that if you live on, you can love a little better."

I didn't wait around to see what face he made in response.

I furiously wiped my cardigan sleeve across my cheeks as I ran up the stairs. Shane didn't ask why I was crying when I opened the door. But he did wipe the tears that kept falling, and carefully take the knife from me.

"Are you still up for this?" he asked. "That…didn't sound good."

I nodded. "Let's do it now, before Hugh tries to climb the stairs."

We barred the door with my dresser, before standing in the middle of my rug without thought for the consequences of dripping blood onto it.

"Wait, in my dream I was given a special knife," I spoke up.

"That was for me," Shane explained, pointing the stainless steel to his palm. "No ordinary blade would have pierced that iron skin."

"So you *do* bleed," I quipped.

"Not easily. My real blood is pure flame."

"Whoa." I then glanced at our feet. "And we…don't have to draw any symbols on the floor?"

He let out a short chortle. "Uh, this isn't a summoning."

"…Right."

"Try to relax," he advised, pressing the edge into his skin. "Making a seal is not as complicated as it sounds. Though it is irrevocable. All we need," he then grunted as the blade pierced and slashed downward, "…is to mix our blood and recite a few words. I'll do that part."

"It really is witchcraft," I gasped.

Shane frowned in offence. "Please do not ever say that again. Witches have their own rules to which they are bound. This is pure demon casting and anyone who tells you otherwise simply gives Lilith credit for all that she learned from Hell."

"Okay, okay," I chuckled, gripping the knife's handle as he handed it over. It was heavier in my hand than it had been downstairs. I felt the full weight of what we were about to do, and was given the chance to retreat if I so wished.

There's a bad feeling about all of this…

MAKE THE SEAL. YOU KNOW YOU WANT TO SPEND FOREVER WITH HIM.

When the louder voice in my head repeated the words '*make the seal*', it didn't sound nearly as sinister. And it did not instil me with confidence to hear them out of sync. I looked at the bandages Shane had brought for our hands when we were done. He was prepared —not only for this very moment but for what came after.

I had already cut my hand once before.

I was not prepared. Not for the pain, the blood nor the bond.

But I would have courage, because all I wanted was the iron beast in front of me, holding his wrist and wincing slightly as the air hit the open wound. This blood was red. I looked back at the gleaming knife. This was the answer to that. This was the thing we could do differently.

Every muscle in my body tensed as I cut into my left hand. It was not as meticulous and painful as the first time, but I still dug my other fingers into my wrist in an attempt to alleviate the sensation.

Shane held out his cut hand, beckoning me. I hesitantly stepped closer and met his palm with my own. It felt very strange. But we held our hands there together as the violet burned along inside of his irises, and he began to speak.

I didn't understand any of the words.

They were in a language that I had never heard —likely one so ancient that it was possible it had once been the tongue of angels and Heaven. As he spoke, the burn and sting turned into something stronger and heavy — as though our hands were being forged into one.

Curls of black smoke then licked along our rigid fingers, circling our fists as it seeped from the cuts and into the air around us. It caused me to shiver but my feet remained planted beneath me.

"Breathe," Shane reminded, in English.

MAKE THE SEAL. OPEN THE GATE.

The voice was back but it was a whisper at my ear. It had been a little difficult to place in that memory but now I was awake and I could tell that there was something distinct about it. It rumbled and commanded armies and parted seas. Even at that volume, at that nudge.

THE GATE WILL OPEN. THE SEAL WILL BE MADE.

THE ASH POURETH.

YOU HAVE BEEN FOUND.

Shane met my gaze as the smoke engulfed our hands. That blue anchored me there. And I was once again tumbling within it and slithers of flaring purple; utterly lost and with no desire to be rescued.

Something strange then happened at the point of contact. A heat burst amidst the hurt. Tongues of near-white fire flickered over skin with all of the heat of a candle, before I realised that it was Ferream's blood. The red burned away but did not cauterise the slashes themselves. The fire's only purpose seemed to be activating the seal. My eyes went back to his. The crescents had almost outshone the turquoise completely.

Flame and smoke swirled between us at increasing speed, and I felt it knit the invisible threads of our beings. Then the light began to die, along with the billowing warmth.

YOU HAVE BEEN FOUND.

And the darkness retreated, drawing back to the centres of our palms —before burrowing its way within, turning the corresponding arms' veins inky black. They were raised and defined, as though actually filled with something solid. I marvelled at it for a moment. Whether it could be called magic or if that name was too generous and misleading from a true horror, I didn't mind. It was simply the proof of tying myself to the iron beast.

Red dripped onto my rug.

"Oh, we're still bleeding," I pointed out.

Shane had to catch his breath. As the violet light faded from his eyes, I bent to retrieve the rolls of bandages and tape. I wrapped his hand first, slowly and with tentative pressure.

"It needs to be tighter than that," he warned, flexing his forearm.

I blinked. I pulled the bandages tighter, gritting my teeth in effort as I attempted to keep my gaze from that muscle —and the darkened veins.

Once I had tucked the tied ends and applied the strips of tape, he eased that hand in and out of a loose fist. "Not bad, Grahams," he smirked.

"I've never had to do that before," I admitted.

"Me neither. Let me know if it's too much."

I flinched at the first wrap; still fully aware of that open cut and all the air rushing to it. But as it became thicker the pain dulled to a manageable ache, and I was able to loosen my stance. Shane kept razor focus with his tending. A small smile tugged at my lips.

"We really did that," I breathed when he was done. He didn't drop my hand. He kept it open in his hold, as if he could still see the jagged opening beneath all of that cream.

He glanced up at my expression of apprehensive relief.

"Now we wait," he sighed. "Wait to see if this is what we should have done all that time ago."

"I'd hate to see a lord of Hell be so *right*, though," I chuckled.

Shane's gaze softened. "Fair point."

Hard, desperate pounding rattled the front door.

It shook the walls and rocked the dresser against my own. We shared a look, frowning with uncertainty. The sound only continued, growing in volume and force —until my father likely opened it, and two voices yelled from down the stairs.

"...They shouldn't be here together!"

"Something's happening, and it's *their* fault!"

Shane wandered to the window and looked up to the sky. No darkness covered it, though. It wasn't the end yet, but Louise Barnes and Donatello Ricci were screaming that it had already started.

That commanding echo from my first memory had not disappeared. It rose again, stirring within my head. Though quiet, it drowned out all other sound and hissed with the hollowness of a breath down my neck.

THE GATE IS OPEN.

Louise Barnes was noticeably more petrified than livid.

She and Donatello both were. I didn't know what to think after they'd burst into my house, but their manic panic put me on edge.

Her wide eyes met mine as Shane and I descended the stairs to assess the commotion. Then her gaze fell to our veined arms, and she started.

Another strange thing happened. At the sight of these bloodied hands, all of the Daemons recoiled; curled away and hissed like the seal repelled.

"What have you done?" Louise fearfully demanded.

"What did you let them do, Mr Grahams?" Donatello asked Hugh.

My father dithered, because he had no idea. When he began to eye us the way the teenagers were —like we did not belong, I became angry.

"What are you talking about?" I clipped.

"We cracked another page," Louise admitted. "And it's worse than all the others. *Blood and fire will tear stone; the fox will cower in the light of the King's soldiers. The dark is poised to bite, but the shadows will part. The jaws will close, for the last time.*" She recited it word for word, barely glancing at the crumpled paper in her hand.

My fingernails dug into my uninjured palm. The words from the voice echoed; haunting the foggy state of my mind. It swept the blanket of grey and stirred the muddle of thoughts. Dread followed in its wake.

The gate was open and we had been found.

I almost drew blood from my other hand. I didn't like not knowing.

"You two did something," Donatello accused. "And set something in motion —something to do with the darkness swallowing."

Shane and I shared a sceptical look, before his eyebrows raised as if he'd realised the meaning.

"What did you do?" Hugh rasped, pointedly at me.

I looked back at Shane. He didn't look guilty. In fact, fear had seemed to seep into him, too. I audibly swallowed.

"…I think we opened a gate," I said —and watched every single other person drain of the colour they had left.

The girl looked to Shane. "What does that *mean*, exactly?"

He eyed my father, who looked weaker by the second. "…We should not be talking about it here," he instructed.

"Then where the *fu* —," Donatello started.

"Outside," I cut him off.

We scrambled past Hugh and spilled out of the front door. It was only when Shane had confirmed that not a spill of ink blotted the grey sky that he dared to divulge the specifics of what we had done.

"Alexander and I made a seal," he explained. "A contract that tethers our souls or essences together beyond death —which is inescapable."

Donatello made a face, while Louise narrowed her eyes as if it was all common knowledge. "And the gate?"

Shane turned to me. They all did.

I drew a sharp breath.

No one would believe me. That was what my gut told me. Never mind Shane's blind faith and Louise's deep rooted guilt —Donatello likely only harboured hate for me —it would be hard to take what I had experienced as truth; something that replayed like a horrid fog of air and poison.

It didn't help that in the end, it all felt like dreaming.

But I told the story of falling to Hell. And no one interrupted.

The consequent silence was thick enough to slice. It seemed as though nobody wanted the first word. No one wanted to be the first to dismiss it. Then again, the roaring voice which had compelled me was all we had to go on for an understanding of what '*opening a gate*' meant. That, and the definition Shane had given me.

I spoke after another beat.

"…I think '*all that devours*' might be a gate. But even if it isn't, Hyde and I have caused a mouth of Hell to open."

Louise stuck her nose in the air. “That might explain *this*.”

She jerked her thumb over her shoulder, at her Daemon. There was a new sort of hunger in its stance; in its hollow eyes. One that didn’t seem satiable. The form of smoke lashed in and out of visibility as if its fabric of being was being pulled apart in different simultaneous directions. Like strange, wispy elastic.

Donatello’s had seen the sense to dissolve into his shadow —but even it was being snatched out from the edges of the silhouette.

The ghostly, bereft expression on Shane’s face was indication enough that he had never seen this before and that it unnerved him.

“They started doing this just after we had found the last page,” Louise said gravely. “And my guess would be, at the exact time *you* two risked a disease by shaking bloody hands.”

“We didn’t mean to open it,” I insisted. “I didn’t even think we would until we were in the middle of it, and that voice started saying all that.”

“What else did it tell you?” asked the girl, folding her arms.

“That we had been found.”

“By what?” snapped Donatello.

“I…I don’t know,” I answered limply. “It didn’t say.”

“That just makes it more ominous,” Shane muttered.

Donatello’s eyes set. “Or you’re lying about not knowing.”

“Donny…” sighed Louise, half-heartedly smacking her shaking head. Something had happened between our last confrontation and the present. Something that put Donatello’s bias into perspective —or heightened her fear of what was to come. And it minimised the need for animosity.

“*What* did you say?” Shane ground out through gritted teeth.

“Why should we believe you when you’ve left things out before?” he countered. “Why should we —”

Nothing tangible cut him off. He stopped short because all our gazes snagged to a spark in the air; like the lighting of a kiddie sparkler. It then fizzled out as soon as it had pierced the gloom, but there couldn't be any denial. We had all seen the same thing.

Then another burst from nothing —and another, and another. They all grew bigger and brighter and violent, before sprinkling in a shower. Until they no longer disappeared and began to spiral. Suddenly they had turned into carnival fireworks.

And they dared to encroach, inching closer and closer until they halted in front of our semicircle. We all took several cautious steps backwards.

The spirals then converged into a singular explosion —and when we had blinked to regain our sight, three people stood towering within height of Donatello. One like a young woman, another as a man, and the third a greyed unimpressed grandfather.

Quite like the strangers in red, yet not.

These wore gold.

And they didn't hide their eyes —which actually would have been just as appreciated, because unlike the wells of nothing, these were glazed bits of white; no irises and no pupils or veins. I didn't try to hide my disgust.

Shane visibly stiffened beside me, as if their arrival triggered his fight or flight response. And that set my mind racing.

The pulling darkness behind Louise and Donatello had streaked away out of sight in the burst; as if shadow could no longer exist.

That led to the other defining feature: how the light bent around each of them. It wasn't so much a halo than it was the sunlight repelling around their forms, bouncing from the satin of their three-piece suits and spearing outward. My mind skidded to a halt.

Were these of the other side —were they…*angels*?

"Oh," Louise breathed. "*They* found us."

"Do not be afraid!" boomed the feminine stranger, those soulless eyes widening in proportion with a very unsettling smile.

Their male counterparts heaved disappointed sighs.

And that voice…I shuddered at the realisation that it sounded all too much like the one in Hell. But it could not possibly mean anything. Most demons had been angels, once.

"I've been dying to say that again," admitted the stranger, giggling as their short bob of shimmering chestnut bounced with the movement.

"*Michael*, this is not that kind of situation," hissed the other younger angel. "We're in human guises."

"Don't suck the joy out of this," Michael cut back.

"Joy?" the oldest grumbled and scowled, stuffing their hands into their fitted pockets. "Need I remind you that we're on a mission, and you two are being an embarrassment."

The flanking angels pouted sourly. Then turned back to us.

"Um, excuse me," Donatello was the first to overcome astonishment, and narrow his eyes in bewilderment. "What the hell is going on?"

Michael made a face. "Oh no, don't say that. It is such an awful little expression. I know for a fact a demon started it."

"Uh, okay," Donatello appeared to take them a little seriously. "Then how about, *what in heaven's name*?"

"Better," they brightly chirped. "And appropriate —"

"*Michael*." The grandfather was at their wits' end. It was all that they needed to snap to make the angel shut up, though. The attention returned to the teenagers. "…Children," they started, eyes slitting with stern. "I am the Archangel Gabriel. And you," their words then arrowed specifically to me and Shane, "are in a realm of trouble."

"Archangel?" echoed Louise, her head whipping back and forth. "So it's…all real, then?" She only paled further at the prospect.

"Sure," the stranger at Gabriel's other side scoffed, folding their arms. "And you're on the naughty list."

The poor girl was about to fall over.

"Ha! And you keep telling everyone that you aren't funny, Raphael," Michael chuckled, hitting out at their arm.

I took a step forward as Donatello caught hold of a stumbling Louise. "Did you come here just for us?" I demanded. Shane was still frozen, that expression permanently etched to stone. He looked like he might be sick.

Gabriel raised a silver brow. "Whatever could you mean by '*just*' for you? You have been found, child. We have been searching for a long time —and that imbecilic seal led us straight here, to this…" they glanced to the treetops and distant mountains, "little town."

"This little town had been doing quite well for a long time, thank you very much," Donatello bit.

"Yes, I'm sure it did. But that was before the demons decided to make it their own personal plaything. And we cannot have that," Raphael spoke up. "Hell was not authorised to carry this sort of procedure."

"Beast," quipped Michael. Shane flinched violently, but refocused his eyes to narrow at the Archangel. "We are aware that you answer to your, uh…'*king*', but we unfortunately hold more power than little old Luci, so we have the right to kick you out of —"

"Michael, you are spinning again," Gabriel frowned, dismissing their rambling. "Messages are not Michael's forte," they sighed. "And no, we don't have the right. But what we *do* have, is the warrant to detain you."

"Says who?" I drawled.

"Says God," Michael grinned.

"What —God cares about this sort of thing?" I sneered.

"God cares about everything," Raphael scowled. "How dare you think otherwise. This matter was under my jurisdiction, and even after Hell told me some stupid excuse, I chose not to believe them. I knew that there was something abhorrently wrong with this backwater town. Especially when it then disappeared off of world maps entirely. Of course, it did take us a while to notice, but you can blame your small size in that regard."

"Stop insulting our town," Louise Barnes found her voice again. She glared at the three celestial beings with the ferocity they likely associated with confronting demons. "You barge in here unannounced and then talk as though you can do whatever you want with it. You're just Archangels. You can't fool us into thinking you are that anything more than glorified foot soldiers and messenger boys!"

The angels blinked with an unfamiliar shock.

In the face of a common annoyance, Pine Creek was *our* town, and all crimes were forgotten.

"Oh, now you're definitely going to Hell," Michael muttered.

"Speaking the truth in defence is a sin?" snapped Louise. "You are not anything like the bible described!"

Michael blew on their nails. "Yeah, well, the progression of time will do that. It's the twenty-first century, dear."

She let out a little scream, before Donatello held her back from a very impulsive and violent response.

Archangel Gabriel's eyebrows knitted together in thought. "Why *are* you children not frightened? We are supernatural. Something you do not see every day. Yet here you stand, firmly planted to the earth."

"Mortals usually fall to their knees," Raphael remarked.

"It's the twenty-first century," Louise childishly mocked.

"The demon told us all about it," Donatello grumbled, tightening his grip on the girl and nodding at Shane.

Gabriel's eyes lidded. "Of course it did."

"Did you force the soul to forge that seal, monster?" Raphael then shot Shane a dirty look. I reached for his unbandaged hand, clutching it tightly. His gaze fell to mine, and warmed a little. Then blazed.

"Oh God," Michael blurted.

Of the three, Raphael had not even *loosened*, let alone cracked a smile. They stood exemplary: without a crease or a long marbled dreadlock out of place, as the pinned back up-do framed their warm brown forehead.

But when their line of sight fell to clasped hands and the stare beyond friends, that rigidity cracked like the splitting of a boulder.

"This is blasphemous," they declared as much. "The last time demons freely ravaged the human population, giants roamed the Earth. You know not what you do."

My fingers squeezed. "We're going to Hell together."

Shane squeezed back, and a bit of colour came back to his face.

Michael sucked in a breath. "They know exactly what they're doing."

"If you came to dissuade me, it was too late several years ago," I told them. "I've been in love with him long since I was last down there."

"You cannot love an abomination," the Archangel Gabriel clipped.

"Why does everyone keep saying that?" I muttered.

"*Well*," Donatello winced, rolling his eyes as Louise resigned herself to be limp in his arms, "that was our same reaction when you told us. We don't get it either, Alexander. To us, he's the creature who decimated our home without remorse or even a second thought. He *kills* you, too."

"Well, I *know* he's more than that," I ground out.

"He is the incarnation of evil, Alexander Grahams," Raphael huffed.

"I do not think you are aware of all he is truly capable."

Once again, it wasn't our town. We didn't belong.

My face screwed up in frustration. I wasn't going to cry. I was going to roar. I heard all of the words they said, but I would absorb none of them and adhere to their demands. What did it truly matter, in the grand scheme of things, if the monster of Hell had someone to love?

"He's the *villain*," Michael drove the point further in. "While we, are the good guys. Your trust should be in the Lord your God."

Shane hung his head, still poised to run.

I shook my head in disbelief. "Have any of you stopped to think that maybe I don't actually want to be rescued or reasoned with? That maybe I *do* know how wrong it is, and that I'm doing it anyway?"

Gabriel floundered. "You what."

"I made the seal with him," I said clearly —and loudly. "I chose this. I *choose* this, and I will keeping choosing it. Just because he's the villain, doesn't mean that I'm the hero. Maybe I'm just the character on the side."

"So you choose to be destroyed along with him." Gabriel's tone took a dark turn. Even their eyes seemed to dim. And they towered over us, to the point where I felt compelled to shrink back and try to heed Michael's initial words of greeting.

I clenched my wrapped hand into a loose fist, ignoring the scream of shooting pain which followed up my veins. "If that is what it will take."

Shane moved; he shifted on his feet and decided that talking back to Archangels wouldn't kill him. He took a step forward beside me, putting out an arm as a shield. I blinked at him. His fury was directed ahead. The only reassurance I received was the conviction in our gripped hands.

"I have never wanted anything for myself in my entire existence, but this. Every deed has been of duty or instinctual impulse —but Alexander was the first selfish thought I ever had." He was almost growling with the rage welling up closer to the surface. I had been the one to defend us until then. It filled me with something sweetly giddy to hear him voice his own opinions. "It's irrational. But no one is going to take that away from me."

"And what gives you that right?" Michael countered. "To be selfish?"

"There is no right," Shane admitted. "But I will not stand by if you try to tear us apart, or take them. Not after what we've done to stay reunited. I will be selfish, and damnit —I'll even fight a war for them."

Archangel Raphael let out a muffled grumble, before turning toward the road. Gabriel ran a hand down their face and hissed something along the lines of a waste of time as they followed, but I wasn't listening.

I put a hand on Shane's shoulder and peered over as he paused to look back at me. He smiled a smile that made me want to reach for his face — but then I saw the look on Donatello's face and bit my lip instead.

Michael cleared their throat, their smile also vanishing. "Neither side is going to be pleased about this."

"Why should we care?" Shane shot back; his arm around my waist.

"I did not think that God even knew my name," I added, curling into him. "If They so desperately wanted me to have nothing to do with Shane then They should have been there when I needed it."

Out of the corner of my vision I saw Louise Barnes cast me a pitying glance. In fact, there might have been the semblance of empathy. But then she lowered her head and withdrew, as if found unworthy.

"*This* is when you need it most," Michael insisted, pointing downward at their polished shoes.

My eyes widened in alarm. "Are you joking? Where was God when a little kid cried themself to sleep at night, afraid to go anywhere outside? Where were They when that child thought they would *die*!"

"No being can question the Almighty," Michael clipped. "Everything happens for a purpose. They work in —"

"Mysterious ways," I drawled. "So I've heard. I have no need of Them now. Just because it's about the destination of my *soul*? You should have thought of that back when it mattered."

Their mouth pressed into a tight line. "I see you are not inclined to be obedient and heed warning. The consequences are yours to bear."

"Nothing new," I said briskly.

We watched them regroup with the other angels; muttering something between themselves before sparing us one last look —and bursting into a flash of that blinding light, though this time we shielded our eyes.

"You cowered before the light, fox," accusingly spat Louise.

"What else did you think he was going to do?" I snarled back.

She had nothing to say in retort. Just the lingering thought that the last page was coming to fruition, and it was growing closer and closer to the ominous last two clauses.

My father was dithering in the doorway, biting at his nails. His eyes asked a million questions, but his voice wouldn't cooperate. His Daemon mirrored his cower, scratching at the posts to hold him back. He forced his way from the front steps and breathed fresh air for likely the first time in a week.

"How much time do we have left?" Donatello asked Louise —finally letting go of her middle. Her cheeks flushed a little only then, as she ran a hand through the ends of her hair to smooth it out.

"Any minute," she sighed, looking at Shane.

He didn't meet her eye, but kept his grip on my hand. He didn't deny her hypothesis. Ferream could tear through his skin right before us.

"Who were those…people?" Hugh eventually choked out. I had seen him in baggy sweatpants and an old, knitted sweater numerous times but somehow it was an embarrassment in front of those my own age, outside of the house.

"Archangels," I answered him. "Looks like you were right, Dad."

He didn't *look* like someone who found out they had been right. There was no smug smirk in acceptance; no declaration of him having told me so. Realisation for him, was a confirmation of his worst terror.

I wondered if he could continue with that knowledge. Hugh Grahams feared God, and not in the way of reverence.

And it was another thing that did not surprise me.

"It might be safer if you're inside," I lied. Half lied. It would only buy him some time.

I felt Shane flinch at the words. I felt his guilt. Even though he didn't like my father and thought him unworthy of much respect, he was still a human being. And I had a feeling that now meant something to him.

"Bye," I offered as my father hobbled back to the front door.

It was the last word I might offer him. I thought it sufficient.

Louise and Donatello did not. They stared harshly at me, expecting more. And when I didn't give anything or run after him in one last embrace —not that we had hugged very much at all —it made them hesitate. It only hit harder, the fact that I was ready to throw away life here. Life on Earth.

"Do you think it'll be different this time?" I asked no one in particular and had little hope of getting an answer.

Even Shane…no. *Especially* Shane, didn't dare to open his mouth.

But I could see the fragile hope on their faces; placed entirely within the scorching seal in our palms and ink in our veins; even if none of them had the strength to voice it and give it horrible weight.

the witch from out of the ground

ALEXANDER

"WE NEED TO find that gate." Louise Barnes tried to be firm. "We have to see if anything…is escaping from it."

She clutched the straps of her little leather backpack so tightly that her knuckles turned ghostly white. But that was where she decided to cap her fear. Her gaze was controlled, the blue flat and faded, and no makeup was smeared to her skin at all. It was as if she had made peace with the end.

Though she had nothing to panic over, really.

She wouldn't remember.

No one would.

Her plan was for Donatello and me to venture into the woods with her, with me as a guide since I knew what Hell felt like. Shane Hyde wouldn't be coming with us.

I didn't want to leave Shane alone —especially today, but for the sake of the mission it was best to split up and ensure that Ferream found us at the last possible moment. I bit my lip about closing the gate being a waste of time and unimportant in regards to the loop, because Shane had never mentioned a gate or it opening up before.

Which meant he had the slightest inclination to think that it might be worth it. I would take that gamble with him.

He drew me into his arms and held me there for too long and not long enough. We weren't interrupted. Despite all that we were and all that we wanted, love remained glorified on its pedestal.

My mind drifted to all of the books I would leave behind. All of those stories had stayed with me. After wistful daydreaming of a romance that would sweep me off of my feet, I finally had the agency to make it reality. I had that love. It was darker and more twisted than a younger version of me would have thought, but it was mine.

He was mine.

And my body began to tremble as I thought of what the day meant and what might await after death. I had not lied to the Archangels. What held my fear was every moment I would not have Shane with me; through the death I might remember and the impending imprisonment before he could join me. I might burn without him in that realm.

"Do not be afraid," Shane whispered into my ear as his fingers tugged at my curls. "Either you will forget, or we will find ourselves together."

I tightened my arms around his neck and nuzzled into the crook of it. "Come find me later," I murmured against his skin.

He pressed his lips to my temple, before tentatively withdrawing.

"I will always find you. Just as you once found me," he breathed, his hand lingering in the hold of mine.

Donatello Ricci had to reluctantly pull me away as Louise took it upon herself to front the crusade and start walking before Shane had even left the front yard. I stared down at my hand. There was nothing to see on the blood. No strange symbol to mark it —or even a sensation different from pain. It was simply the cut of a knife. My veins remained filled.

But it reminded me of him.

That would give me strength.

"He'll be fine," Donatello sighed as we wandered after Louise. "He's done it so many times before."

I shot him a look. "That's not funny. Do you think he would just stop feeling anything? In the end, he has no choice. None of us do."

He huffed, breathing through his nose, but offered no argument.

I blinked.

Neither teenager seemed to have their Daemon. Their shadows cast on the ground, but the glitching darkness seemed to have perished in the angels' light. Their absence must have still felt fresh.

Louise was very quiet. Maybe if she opened her mouth an unstoppable flood would break. Her hands were balled and her breath was harsh, but she made no complaint and shed no tears.

And then she stopped, looked about her with a sceptical frown, before turning around to us. "…The voice is gone," she rasped.

"The what." Donatello mirrored her expression.

"My Daemon."

He whipped around as if to find it a few paces behind him. "Holy shit, it's gone," he gushed. He rubbed his eyes in disbelief.

"Those angels were good for one thing," grumbled Louise, sticking to her fed up, tired local guide gimmick.

"Wait," Donatello cut in. "Your Daemon spoke to you?"

The girl tensed, backtracking into a defensive position and flushing a still sickly shade of pink.

A sudden shiver up my spine served as a distraction. They both looked at me with wide, questioning eyes. I swallowed and rubbed the side of my arm, regretful of my two layers. But, that did heighten the abrupt wave of heat which crashed into my side.

"That way," I mumbled, pointing right of the tree ahead of us. "I can feel the heat."

Louise wasted no time, leaving Donatello and me to straggle.

Even though I was the guide and their only hope in finding the gate in time, I had no desire to be at the forefront. I was content navigating from the rear, steering out of the way of Louise's stomp and edging away when Donatello wandered too close to the path of my feet.

He saw it for what it was —uneasy but respectful avoidance.

Yet he sighed heavily like it was still another nuisance. A red herring, it would seem, as he decided to strike up a conversation.

"I won't lie," he started without actually looking at me. "I think you're incredibly stupid."

I didn't know what to say to that.

Then he admitted, "I've never been in love. I don't know what it feels like to want to do anything for someone; to have all reality revolve around them. To kill for them. To die for them. As you said, you and Shane Hyde have known each other longer than the rest of us think. I *still* think this is a lot. What do we know of the world? What do we know about anything?"

My mouth twisted into a shape.

His head turned to glance down at my face and discern what he found there. The results were inconclusive.

"…If I explained love to be the most wonderful thing in the world, I'd be lying." I paused to point to the left as Louise peered over her shoulder for direction. "It's exquisite —slow and spiralling from a connection until you can't call it anything else but. It burns bright. Depending on what sort of fuel you are, it can burn forever. Not a lot do."

Donatello softened. "So what makes you certain that yours will?"

"The roar of the flame," I answered simply, clapping my hands before stretching out my arms. "We…we're a part of one another. I know that it sounds crazy and outrageous, but I really think we complete each other. Not in the sense that we can't live without, but that we *fit*. Like two pieces of a puzzle. Made for it."

Donatello blinked rapidly. "…Wild."

"I'm not denying that."

"And what of pain?" he went on. "Love is pain."

"It is," I sighed, pointing Louise around a pine, "it is the most awful, breaking pain." A smile tugged my lips upwards slightly. "…And I would never not want to feel it."

He stared at me, in a way that suggested he had understood in part, for the first time. Like he understood a part of me.

"By the way," I then mused, lowering my voice and staring off at the horizon. "If the loop closes and you survive, could you bury me with roses afterwards? Just a sentiment."

"What," Donatello blurted.

Louise halted, right in the middle of a path. She turned around slowly and levelled at me a look of scorn. "Alexander Grahams. How can you be so ready for death? How…how are you not scared?"

I fiddled with the stray grey wool at the edges of my cardigan sleeves. "Because I know what comes after it."

"Even though that would be Hell?" she frowned.

"I've already been."

She pressed on. "And you'd willingly go back?"

"Because *he's* there."

Donatello drew a sharp breath, idly scratching the back of his neck. "I don't get it Barnes, but apparently they would do anything for love."

"I would do anything for Shane," I corrected.

"Why him?" Louise questioned.

I didn't have to think too hard about it. I had always known. "He was the only one who listened, apart from my Mom. He didn't judge, he didn't minimise, and I extended that same curtesy. I…I fell for him first. He did not know what '*to love*' was, in the beginning."

This was news.

"You fell in love with the Devil's spawn, without expecting anything from him in return?"

I nodded. "Though he was made —not related."

"That's worse," she said candidly. "You know that, right? If he was a son then you could justify it by saying he doesn't have to be like his Dad, like you. But because he was moulded that way; created to destroy and be an absolute menace, there is no redemption. There is no justice."

All monsters are made.

That was what she was alluding to. But in its literal sense only, not in the way that Shane had meant; that they could be born and made and both could be true, separate or at once.

"Well, what about you, Louise?" I flipped it back on her. "Were you born or made? Because according to you, it's one or the other."

She started.

"Alexander," Donatello interjected, shaking his head.

I shot back a glare. "If she can't answer, then she can't accuse."

Pink flooded her face again. And she could wonder for the rest of her life if I would always hold that part of her over her head.

I would.

"What…what's Hell like?" Louise shuffled around and mumbled. Her demeanour had shifted. "You know…since I disrespected some angels."

Instead of some misplaced sort of pride, her eyes brimmed with more of that very real existential dread. I might not be afraid, but she certainly was. Her fingers twirled a thread hanging from the hem of her plaid skirt. And maybe it was because I could tell how much nerve it had taken to ask or because I would've wanted someone to help me too, that I answered.

Although, I doubted that I would want to know at all if I didn't know what I did, or was uninvolved in an iron beast's revelation.

So while I didn't want to spare any empathy, I extended a hand in pity with only the slightest hint of spite.

"Hell is where hope dies," I told her flatly. "Life and time do not exist, and every unnecessary breath burns like a scorching desert. Nothing about you is well, nothing about you is glad. Emotion is a luxury. Agony is free. And every surface either burns, or scars."

I watched the flicker of light that had been in that blue disappear.

Donatello paled in turn, before taking a step away from me, as if I too was a monster. "Why would you *want* that?"

"Because Shane is not bound to that experience. And with him, I feel."

The two shared a lengthy and uncertain look, but decided not to push for further explanation.

Louise took a step backwards, turning towards the path again. "…You must really love him, to be so beyond reason."

"There is nothing reasonable about us," I reminded her. "Also, turn to the left. It's getting stronger."

Her gaze lingered for an uncomfortable amount of seconds before she sprung down the fork in the dirt, her skirt bouncing and heels striking the leaves in a rustle. What did she want me to say? That I wanted to stay on Earth; bitter and vengeful simply because we were all human beings, and that *that* should make me feel something?

Perhaps I would have wavered if Pine Creek had been kind to me. Or if I had been rescued sooner. That little child was still curled up within a boundless chasm, shivering in the dark. And being a martyr for the town's sake alone would not heal them, and lay them to rest.

They needed a love that thinking of others could not provide.

The heat was now slamming into me in waves upon a shore. I was but a bed of sand, slowly being dragged yonder grain by grain, until more and more of me wore away. I could almost see those pieces flying, wafting to the gate to where they belonged.

My lips parted at that conclusion.

Was that truly where I belonged? I recalled Kay Isotton's words, about a home not necessarily being the same one into which you were born. But that then meant that Hell was that home.

My already chipping black fingernails dug into skin and bandage alike and I bit back the yelp of pain as I pressed against the slash. I didn't want to believe it. I didn't want to think it —even though if the loop broke and the town returned to wider society, Hell would be where I spent eternity.

I had hardly pondered Heaven. At a young age, I had questioned why mortals were rewarded or punished based only on performance and being friends with Jesus. According to Sunday School, we were all born flawed anyway. What we did mattered a little less than worshipping a God Who we couldn't see or with Whom we couldn't have a real-time conversation. So why did we do anything at all?

Why did the world still spin, and what was the point of starting when it was all going to go up in flames? Surely it would be simpler to make us immortal again, but without intent to kill or to harm one another. Free will was well and good, but with all the infinite power, there had to be a middle where people could make decisions while not ruining their reality.

That was the sort of thinking at which my father would have started huffing and puffing. He wouldn't call it a solution like I had, of course —to him it was blasphemy and the corruption of evil. Sometimes it was the corruption of man too —as if he was better than his fellow human beings because he carried around a possibly mistranslated book and used God as a scapegoat —and on occasion, bodyguard.

I thought that we were *all* born broken.

I thought we had all been made.

Even those angels.

Apparently, God didn't like questions.

And I was full of them.

I kicked a pebble from the uneven path as my mind drifted to Shane.

The sky was still clear. He hadn't yet changed. He hadn't yet mauled. But he would, and feel it all over again; inescapable torture of now doing something against his will. That was what was driving him to a brink each time. The fact that he didn't have the choice, and that it no longer signified something cathartic and triumphant.

I could only imagine the bounds of his sanity after so many cycles.

Quite abruptly, I stumbled into a tree.

My body rammed into the rough bark and my breathing shallowed to pants. I tugged at my cardigan. It was growing too hot. My vision spun.

"Alexander?" Donatello stopped beside me, hesitantly raising a hand to steady my shoulder. "Louise, wait!"

She pivoted. Her eyes widened at the sight, before she wandered back to crouch at my other side.

"It…it feels like the dream I had last," I rasped. "My throat…it's hard to breathe. I need water. It must be…right up ahead."

That seemed to be the last concern, as Louise rummaged through her backpack for an unopened bottle and unscrewed the lid. I gulped it down gratefully; spilling a little as my hand trembled and its grip weakened. But at least it soothed that dryness. Then I had to remove my outer layers, and bask in the brisk Fall wind.

"Wait, I think I *see* something," Louise announced, squinting through the gaps between the trees. It looked like someone had dumped a number of boulders into a small clearing; they all lay somewhat flat but they jutted out haphazardly with little walkway between them.

The ground beneath us shuddered.

A crack, large enough to be the foundational width of a house split in the ground around the rock. As it widened, the earth collapsed and caved inward to accommodate its size. It opened up like a mouth unhurried and yawning, wide and hungry.

The heat which hit me came in more aggressive crashes, and rendered my knees weak and useless. But I raised my head, narrowing my gaze at the unfolding phenomenon.

We then watched a woman burst from the crack; adorned with tattoos which decorated skin a shade like mine, a strapped black corseted gown —and a pair of luminous silver eyes which arrowed straight to us. Hair as dark as coal billowed in a draft, loosely pinned back as dirt scattered and flew. She wore no scowl —simply a look of grave determination.

The ground stabilised, trembling to a soft rumble before it stilled.

Without breaking eye contact, which seemed to hold us all among the leaves where we were, she rose to bare feet and began to walk. The skirt of the gown dragged through the drying muck, snagging on stick and rock alike. But her focus was three teenagers balking at her arrival.

Louise leaned away, unable to shuffle anywhere or straighten; pulling me with her. Donatello braced himself at my side, eyes widening.

I then became aware of a panic inducing feeling. Lord Beelzebub had warned me of presences greater than his own. And the intensity emanating from this stranger…she led with heaviness.

She was more than a demon.

The woman's tattoos ranged from a Chinese dragon to stalks of thorns wrapping her forearms and legs. A snake wound from beneath her corset while an eye marked her left shoulder. And spanning from her right cheek to the base of her neck, was a thin crescent moon.

She was tall.

Tall in the way that most people found to be intimidating. Tall in the way that commanded terror. When she reached the threshold of the line of trees, she assessed us; her glowing gaze slowly roving from one mortal to another. Louise Barnes tried to be brave. She offered a levelled stare in returned scrutiny. It did not go unnoticed.

Then the woman spoke.

"I take it the foot soldiers have left?"

Her voice rumbled through the trees themselves —though she spoke with an out of place gentleness. Her expression might have been that of a harbinger, but there was a motherly warmth in her eyes.

I blinked. "…Do you mean the Archangels?"

"Foot soldiers," she reiterated. "Those above must have been *so* busy, that there was no one else available to send. Typical."

"Who *are* you?" demanded Louise, putting an arm in front of me that would do nothing, but was a surprising sentiment.

"…I see a struggling fire within you, Louise Margret Esther," said the woman from the ground. "Why do you douse your own flames?"

The girl violently started, flushing red. "*What*?"

This stranger knew both of her middle names. Hardly anybody knew Louise's middle names.

I grunted in the effort to alleviate the weight of my body from my left arm. "Did you come from the gate?" I asked.

She glanced back at the large, jagged hole. "Ah," she acknowledged. "I did. I came through as soon as it was spotted. I had forgotten that you mortals are unaccustomed to such occurrences."

"Who are you," Louise prompted again; this time with some bite.

Her silver eyes twinkled. "I am Lilith. Mother of demons and The First Wife. I have come to counsel."

Donatello's jaw dropped. Louise pressed her lips together in disbelief. And I looked upon the creator of witchcraft with awe.

"You," Lilith directly addressed me. Those eyes also picked me apart; as if all of the creatures of Hell always saw far more than there was to see. "The one without fear. The apple that fed the fox. You forged a seal and welcomed the dark."

I swallowed. All I could do was agree. Though she did not look angry. There was no understanding, which I got, but she was from Hell. She had knowledge of the consequences.

Louise inhaled sharply. "How…how do you know about '*the fox*'?"

Her gaze slid to the girl. "Because I told you of it. Long ago."

It seemed to dawn on Louise fully, as a shiver jolted up her spine, that we had all been living this for an egregious time. She turned to Donatello, who had become just as pale.

"So…you came before, from a gate, and told me of all I wrote?" asked Louise. There was a disappointment on her face —as though she'd wanted all the agency due to some then, mysterious occult reason.

"There has never been a gate," Lilith stated. "I couldn't come without a physical form in the previous cycles, so I entered your dreams."

Louise frowned. "My…dreams…"

"You did not remember," Lilith explained. "No one ever does."

My head hung. Just as I had never remembered mine.

"What about the page in blood?" then pressed Louise, now able to let go of me. "Did I hear to write it like that from my dreams?"

Lilith shook her head. "Only the words, Louise Margret Esther. Blood leads to power. Power leads to greed. You must have felt desperation."

The girl viscerally cringed. "I hate those names."

A strange smile tugged the corners of her dark painted lips. "You will not always. Guard your nightmares. Only grant *me* permission."

I lifted my head as Lilith then turned back to me and crouched down in front of my knees. She reached for my chin, before tilting it upwards.

"So this isn't some kind of paradox?" I asked uneasily.

"No child," she murmured. "But that means something, doesn't it? As we speak, the beast lies in wait, waiting for the sky to turn. But you were right to come to the gate. You were fortunate it was me who entered, and not a demon or worse —our king, Lucifer."

My muscles locked and all of the heat immediately rushed outward. I was hit with the brunt of the wind, at that title. *Our king, Lucifer*. Besides what I had always known from faith, the Devil had always struck fear. It had to be that way, because everything was intended to be so starkly black and white. But I knew that no matter what my learned opinions of them, the response that I had had was something closer to having been readily and physically exposed to all the power at the king's beckoning.

I remembered the feeling of their presence.

That was why I had run.

"Are you also here to tell me that I have made a mistake?" I then went on. "I don't want anything but Shane. And I don't care where or how."

Lilith chuckled. "Oh, I'm aware. I said that I was here to counsel. But I didn't say who, did I?"

My chest tightened. Donatello's hand had still not been allowed to let go of my shoulder. For some reason, I didn't want her speaking to Shane. It wasn't that I feared he might change his mind. I was confident in all of his love and selfish wants. No —I feared *for* him. This unholy witch could do something awful to him and I knew that I wouldn't be able to stop her.

My brows knitted in an ounce of anger. "Don't hurt him."

"He is not mine to play with," she clarified candidly. "So I cannot do anything without repercussions. And the Morningstar doesn't take kindly to those who touch their things."

I shuddered. I was one of those. Aside from the gross categorising of the iron beast, I supposed that blame lay with me on leading him astray. Although I wanted to laugh at the thought of a mere human mortal leading a demon anywhere, for that matter.

It was wildly amazing that I had managed to invoke *the* Devil's wrath as a nameless soul without purpose or rank.

"He really is like their son," Louise then remarked —more to herself, in a low mutter. "You'd think Shane is the antichrist or something."

"Unfortunately," Lilith stood again, brushing straying strands of hair aside, "the relationship is more of a pet and owner. An owner who doesn't see that pet as a living being."

My teeth grated together. "That's despicable. Why —"

"—What did you expect, exactly?" the witch rightfully cut me off.

And so my humanity would flicker again; how could I act so morally superior in light —or lack thereof —of all the decisions I had made before in self-satisfaction? Yet at least I thought of the beast as its own entity.

At least I treated it as if it were alive.

Louise's remark rang in my head. *Antichrist*. Upon further thought, it was not a bizarre connection. While untrue, it turned the gears within my mind. I looked back on the time when I had wanted to rid Pine Creek of its curse. All before I learned of why it existed in the first place, and how Shane had been driven to it.

All, for the sake of one.

That was what he had once told me. How he had once justified it. And so, if it had begun that way, then there was only one way for it to end.

There was indeed something in the cycles that we could do differently.

"*I*…need to die," I then mused, frowning at my shoes.

Louise and Donatello did a double take.

"I have to be the person he kills," I reiterated, meeting Lilith's gaze. "I have to be the only one, instead."

She stared at me, unblinking. It was neither denial nor confirmation.

It was Louise Barnes who displayed the most outrage. "What are you talking about, Grahams? You *don't* have to do that."

"I have always been ready for death," I told her, turning my head. "For him. I was meant to die anyway. It will be one, for the sake of many."

Her own mind whirred. "I'm pretty sure Jesus already did that."

"Yeah, but he did *for* you," I corrected. "I'm doing it selfishly."

"Wait, wait," Donatello interjected, glaring at me. "So you would be the only victim in his spree? What, just because he knows you from a time before. How can you be so sure that it will end with you?"

"I…can't," I admitted. "I can only try. And neither one of you can be there with me. You will only serve as temptation."

"You had better try quickly," warned Lilith, glancing upward. "I can smell ink on the wind."

the eclipse

SHANE

HE KNEW IT was Lilith before he had even caught sight of her inked skin and sculpting gown. Her silver eyes still held the history of the mortal world; still filled with all the scorn and wisdom she had honed.

She used to smile as though everything was a game to her.

She wasn't smiling now.

The teenagers had definitely found the gate. Shane Hyde had felt when it had opened. He knew precisely where it was, and how wide it had grown. Thankfully, no demon would willingly follow where the witch had gone. Alexander stood at her side, shivering like the temperature had now taken them by surprise. Shane didn't like the nervousness there within their eye—which refused to meet his.

From the moment that they had been separated, his skin had prickled in the tell-tale sign of the monster stirring. He had not wanted it to happen in front of the soul.

Sure, they had expressed wanting to glimpse his true form within their mortal life —but in the end, he still worried Alexander would not like all they saw once it stood before them once more.

"Ferream," Lilith greeted.

The First Wife did not even don the depraved grin she usually grinned when she was up to no good. That didn't absolve her from mischief.

She had no regard for whether or not Alexander already knew Shane's *Excumen*. The witch would be content in getting a rise from him. So when she didn't, the sparkle in her eye waned in disappointment.

"I think I know how we can end it," Alexander spoke up, rubbing the side of their darkened arm. "You won't like it, though."

Shane tensed, clutching at his own arm but for a far different reason. The demon was beginning to push through. He could feel the crescents of purple in his eyes flickering to life.

But he might try anything, now that time was slipping.

"Okay," he said slowly, glancing at Lilith. She gave nothing away.

Alexander's head hung. "…I need to be the only person who you kill this time. The first and last."

Shane pressed his lips into a tight line. He didn't want to get angry. It was difficult to maintain his composure when the beast inside was just a mass of rage with no room for anything else.

"I know it'll be hard," continued the soul, trying harder. "But I thought that maybe if Ferream experiences that devastation before anything else, they will stop —just as they did when it happened at the end."

Lilith folded her arms as she shifted her weight onto one hip. Her chin raised but she said nothing. She was enjoying this.

The Made demon gritted his teeth.

He hated that their logic was sound.

That it was plausible.

But the real fear of failure gnawed at him as did the fangs of the monster; digging in deeper and deeper until all that he could feel was pain. He did not want to slaughter them at all —even though he knew that had never been an option. Alexander had to die; and perhaps realistically, the demon could only decide on when. Shane's gaze slid to Lilith.

"Did you convince them of this?"

"I am just as surprised as you are," she assured, rhythmically tapping her nails on her forearm. "I did not persuade them in anything."

"Then why are you *here*?" he bit.

"To ensure that *you* are aware of what you are doing," said the witch. "I hope you have given this thought, little monster. Will that seal save you from the Morningstar? From the consequences of learning nothing?"

"I can lie," Shane sneered, his fingers curling in harder. The soul took notice. "It's what we're all so good at."

"And what will you say?" pressed Lilith.

He had to pause to think about it. "…That I can now discern the right time and place for carnage."

"And how will you say you learned that?"

His lips ripped back in a snarl. "Through the relentless destruction that I carried out against my will. How I hated having no choice."

The witch smiled then; unable to contain her amusement any longer. "I doubt that it will come to that. I doubt Lucifer will grant you the chance to explain yourself —nor the presence of this mortal soul. In fact, they'll likely rage over the seal. As if you have been stolen."

"I don't want to be owned," growled a little bit of the iron beast. "I do not want to be chained and tied down to someone who only sees me as a tool. I want…I want to be valuable. I want to be equal."

Lilith's gaze softened slightly.

Alexander took half a step forward. Their eyes were finally steady and locking on Shane's —no matter of how wild they were becoming.

"Would they take you away from me?" the soul asked. "*Could* they?"

The monster swallowed. He had considered it, albeit reluctantly. As a topic over which he wanted to avoid spiralling, he had pushed it all the way to the furthest recesses of his mind. Until it had nearly disappeared.

It was Shane's turn to glance aside.

That was all the answer he could manage.

And even though he could tell that it made Alexander droop further, he also knew that voicing it would worsen the feeling.

"That seal only ensures *your* safety, little mortal," Lilith clarified. "A demon will have no protection. Especially one that never knew Heaven."

"You…you did that, *knowing* that you might still be in danger…even after binding?" pushed the soul. "Did you do it for me?"

Shane forced himself to look somewhat normal as he glanced upward, though it probably ended up manifesting as a menacing stare. "Anything for you." The ripping pain was spiking towards his shoulder.

Alexander's face screwed up as a film of tears welled in the bottom of their eyes. "Then let me do something in exchange," they rasped. "Let me save us. Save everything."

"I…I don't know if it will be enough," admitted the beast.

"What is this I am hearing?" quipped the Mother of demons. "Do you doubt yourself, Ferream? If you love this soul, their willing offering must be enough."

He bared his teeth at her. "Do not question what I feel," he warned. "I am hesitant only *because* I love them."

She scoffed. "And so the feral beast fell in love," she mocked. "Irony in its most indigestible form. I cannot believe I am wasting my time with a pair of foolish teenagers who think they know all there is to know about love —enough to stake their lives upon it. Love is not your salvation, dear children," she declared, looking between them, "It will destroy. You may not see that effect yet; for a long time. Or, perhaps you will see it as soon as your time here is over."

"Stop being cryptic for once," Shane hissed. "Why can you never just say something precisely the way it is?"

Lilith then levelled at him a harsh glare; those silver eyes narrowing as their light intensified. "And where is the fun in that?" she deadpanned. "It is all which brings me joy."

Alexander visibly stiffened at the sentence —to Shane's utter dismay. The Archangel Michael had coined that first; finding entertainment in the wake of others' torment and terror.

Shane's grip on his arm tightened. He did not actually have the time to think. He raised his head to the sky. It was a dark grey, promising rain. At least, that was what it *had* promised.

Now the ink would run and seep.

"You must choose," Lilith didn't miss a beat, shifting to her other hip. "Before the dark swallows."

Shane cast Alexander a look of desperation. The soul, however quiet and unconfident, wasn't budging. They truly thought this the best course of action. They truly thought that inside the fog of initial confusion, they could stand before the iron beast and calm it with one soft motion of their hand or risk being sliced in an ever consistent moment of blindness —or worse, both things could happen in combination.

What if Ferream gazed into loving bronze, wept as tears gathered there in theirs too…and still ran its claws straight through them?

What if Alexander *did not mind*?

What if their lips curved in a smile at the monster, believing that in a few moments the two would be reunited? As if they did not blame it at all.

But Ferream would carry that guilt.

Shane blinked.

Guilt.

That was the sticky, thick substance coating the inner wall of his stomach. That was that which plagued him cycle to cycle; massacre after massacre.

The Made demon *felt bad.* Not to be confused with remorse —Shane would do it all again for Alexander. To find them each time.

But there was now this epiphany that most human beings cared about other ones, unfathomably so. And with it, he had to consider how the soul felt about them too —how far they would go for them.

Even if he came first.

That made the guilt impossibly thicker. Heavier. Sickening.

"Alex…ander," he struggled, feeling the sudden loss of the limb in his hold. It stiffly writhed, as if possessed. "…No matter what happens, know that…you are everything to me. Ferream…must know this, too."

"*Shane.*" They darted forward, uncaring of any watching eyes in their vicinity, and seized him by the collar. The feeling of their mouth was all and nothing; a fierce and indiscernible goodbye, damp with tears that had previously been too much to cry.

Neither could breathe.

Neither cared.

And when Alexander finally forced themself from him, Shane had almost forgotten the pain. Almost forgotten the impending disaster, and the larger one to come. "I have already seen the worst of you," they whispered, hand grazing the demon's cheek. "You will not surprise me."

"Yeah, Grahams —that's the *last* thing I'd want to do."

A chuckle burst amidst the weeping. "I will see you on the other side, Hyde," they promised. "Wait for me…one last time."

"I…I want to be that wishful," he admitted.

"I hate to break up this very touching moment," Lilith reminded them both of her presence, "but the ash poureth."

Alexander started, whirling away. "You…it was *you* —"

The witch held a finger to her lips before glancing skyward.

The clouds had stopped being such, and instead, night spilled onto the blank stretch of grey. One of Shane's hands lifted, on its own, to smooth over Alexander's curls. Shane flinched at the sight of iron, with sharpened nails. Here it came once again.

A boy looked on with wide, terrified eyes like the soul had never seen, before more pieces of Shane Hyde fell away.

There had come to be a dominant fear in the monster.

It was afraid that one day, it would wake to find itself back in that cell —but with a significant lacking of its sweet mortal. As if they had never come, never taught them the yearn for freedom. As if it had never known love. Though love was such an unbearable burden, the beast had wanted to bear it. Always.

So as the creature lost its grip on a teenage boy with bleached hair and a sweet tooth, it hoped that it would not lose that speck of mortality, too.

+

ALEXANDER

THOUGH HE WASN'T fully Ferream, he wasn't Shane anymore.

That skin had hardened and greyed in places, and one wing jutted from his right shoulder blade. All the grey was cracked and chipping like some kind of ancient statue. That wing —even with its counterpart —surely did not possess the structural integrity to lift him from the ground.

His erratic breaths came in pants; heavy and taxing as the monster was straining to burst from beneath the flesh but the boy supressed it as much as he could. He wanted to give the people a chance, on the possibility that the loop would sever and they could carry on.

I did not run.

Lilith stood with me, even as the darkness began to prevent any sight. But between, as little slithers amidst unstitched shadow, I glimpsed more and more of Ferream; his glaring eyes the only piercing light. I wondered how much would be visible beneath the shroud.

What if he would not be able to tell…not because it was difficult in that raging state, but simply because he *couldn't* see?

But then I thought back to his ordinary stare —called that only due to the human face from which it arrowed. That look had always been intense and unnatural. I was then almost sure that he could see through the dark.

The last billowing partings within it allowed me to see all that the iron beast truly was. And even though it was cut up in intermittent ribbons, it was different than what I remembered of my dreams.

I could take it all in now —feel the surface of him with a real sense of touch and hear his voice with anxious ears.

Completely aware and alive.

My breath caught at the curving horns and rippling, broad shoulders. It was nice not to see any blood splattered on him which was not his. His wings, stretched upwards, pointed in at one another; extended bend flush against extended bend.

And even though he was covered in cracks, he was not broken.

The iron showed signs of wear but it more resembled marks of growth than scarring. I marvelled at what I saw —until neighbours began to pour into the street. So I only heard. Ferream shifted in demeanour.

Like a child who'd lost sight of their parent, his head darted back and forth. In turn, those wings and horns ripped through the air; creating their own brief gust of wind and echoing a low, troubled growl.

I followed it, taking an undaunted step forward.

My hand hit freezing muscle. He hadn't been very far.

Ferream paused at the contact, stilling though the rough sound did not leave his throat. The iron rose and fell under my palm with uneven breath. Mine went still. It was a strange thing to witness.

The skin was cold —a clue which I realised had always been there in Shane. But I was used to it, and it did not deter the consequent exploration of what stood before me. For a very few short seconds the monster let me. Maybe a part of Shane lingered there.

Then he was wholly gone —

Ferream took hold of my wrist; the very one wrapped in bandages. In the haze, the ink in my veins wasn't visible. And his had not transformed along with him. If a cut remained I couldn't feel any blood from his palm.

But it must have embedded deep, because I could feel a heat.

As if the fire coursing through him remembered.

Even if he didn't.

The grip he now held fast on me was all the indication that he *didn't* know. Another growl rippled through the unseen.

I tried not to panic. I should have seen it coming —I should have been better prepared to handle the beast's disorientation.

Instead of bolting, I impulsively reached for his face. My hand grazed his temple and horns, having gone too high, before lowering to his jaw.

My lips parted.

You could have just spoken from the beginning, idiot.

CALL HIS NAME.

"Ferream," I said. Pleaded. "Ferream, it's me."

Lilith drew a breath somewhere from behind me. Her slender fingers curled into my shoulder as her shallow breath neared my ear. "See you," whispered the witch, then all which was left of her was a laugh on the air.

I didn't get the chance to decipher to what she was referring.

The monster's hand tightened to the point of pain.

"Love has abandoned me," he said, speaking not only to me but to all those who stood around us. "And now, so has your God. Only my wrath lies before you." His voice…I felt bad for thinking how lulling it was.

His grip fluctuated in strength, bringing me to my senses.

If things within him were still fighting, I needed to further disrupt the events of the past cycles. It was as if he were reading a script. We needed the opportunity to improvise.

A sudden scream curdled my blood, causing me to start.

Mrs Keller —the mother of Lincoln's father —cried at the top of her lungs that the Devil had arrived to seek retribution, and that that was the glow of turquoise and purple which they all saw.

"Don't listen to her," I blurted, grabbing his arm with my other hand. It was so solid and large that I couldn't maintain a hold.

"I am the messenger," answered Ferream. "And I have no master."

"*Ferream*, please!"

I was growing desperate. I recognised the words from when he had told me about the loop —these were his last words before slaughter. And that he would go for his mother and brother after the first victim.

The first person to die had always been Lincoln Keller.

As the Hydes' next door neighbour, the Keller family had apparently spilled out at the grandmother's accusation. And the son was the one too inquisitive for his own good. Even when the possibility of him actually coming face to face with the Devil was very real.

I didn't know where Lincoln might be, so I had to keep Ferream right in front of me. I had to take his place.

There was nothing in particular Keller had done to become marked as the first casualty. The fact that he had been the closest had seemed enough reason. But there had to be more to it, since my closer proximity wasn't changing anything.

"Look at me," I demanded, gritting my teeth.

The iron beast's gaze moved slowly back towards me. I could not see anything beyond those eyes. And even though I told myself that I had no fear, my heart was beating rather wildly at the prospect of being blind to a multitude of differing outcomes.

All of them death, of course.

But I hadn't really wanted to go out unaware.

Was that the apprehension, then? It was not that I cowered in the face of death —I simply wanted to see it as it happened. Not knowing —being caught unaware…that frightened me.

I had to breathe.

I had to recall how it had felt as I wondered the halls of Hell before my sight had been restored. I had been frightened then too, but the feel of my surroundings had calmed a heart that hadn't needed to beat.

Ferream was losing his patience. The rage was boiling over.

What could I say to reach him? For him to realise that it was me, even without the light which had revealed it since the beginning?

"…Ferream," I said firmly. "You don't have to do this anymore. The soul isn't gone. They didn't run from you. They ran from something else."

The monster grunted, shrugging my hand off of him. He did not let go of my wrist though. But he didn't growl, and he didn't rear his wings. All was quiet, giving people a chance to run back inside of their homes.

Now the street was secluded and no one knew that I stood before the object of their terror; knowing how he looked and how he raged.

When he spoke again, my heart thundered with the hope that we had managed to alter the cycle.

"My sweet mortal is gone." His voice had dropped in volume. He was only talking to me. There was only this. "They were *stolen* from me."

"I am right here," I told him, running a hand up his forearm.

He flinched at the caress, trying to place it.

It took him a moment.

"…I know this touch," he murmured.

His altered voice was mesmerising. I supposed that that was precisely what Lucifer had wanted. It was a siren to a tired sailor's ears.

"You can see them again," I went on.

"How," he demanded with a return of bite. His grip tightened again.

I reached for his other arm and clumsily took his hand. I brought it to my chest, pressing the sharpened nails to the skin below my collar bones.

"Pierce," I instructed.

I actually felt him flinch. I felt a pronounced hesitation which he had never before expressed. No one had probably asked him for death.

Amidst memories of the begging to spare, this was new. Strange.

Suspicious.

"I love you," I whispered, staring at the glow of his eyes. "Still."

For a moment I wondered if what I had said would affect him so much so that he wouldn't dare raise a finger against me. That words alone could reach through and satiate him.

Reality was claws abruptly tearing into my chest.

I had thought that I would have screamed. Yet all that escaped me was a soft gasp, like an odd relief.

It hurt.

It was obviously the most excruciating pain I had ever felt, but those eyes did something that made me look past the sensation. They slitted in a way that implied emotion along the lines of hurt, anger or unease. It was possible that he felt all of them. But no sound indicated which.

My fingers reached for his face for the last time, even though the twist resulting in the sharp movement made me wince. His claws did not slow nor pause. And I was surprised to find something warm near my fingers, where his cheek was —more so untouchably hot.

It was just a blur of soft light in the darkness.

It was fire.

Fire slid down by his temple, flickering and burning even as it spilled like tears. I predictably softened, even through all of the agony and uncertainty around whether or not this could mean what we wanted it to.

People say that as you die, your life flashes before your eyes like some kind of strip of film running through a projector.

That you see all of your accomplishments and all of your regrets, and remember all which you had held near or pushed aside when alive. It was supposedly beautiful and profound.

As the life slipped from me, I didn't see all that had come before.

I didn't see my childhood; I didn't see my parents —I didn't even see the godforsaken town. There was nothing of pain, no echo of it, nor faces of tormentors past.

I didn't see *anyone*.

When I died, slow and thorough, spots of darkness encroached on the edges of my vision before devouring completely. That was all there was.

Nothing.

As if I had never lived at all.

Thank goodness I had managed to say something of a goodbye to the ones I had wanted to. Louise Barnes had stared hard at me with no right to cry. There had appeared to be a myriad of things unspoken upon the tip of her tongue, but she had bitten it. There had not been enough time nor enough forgiveness.

I would not have even had the opportunity to treat her with a little less hostility in the next cycle.

But I hoped that she lived.

I hoped that she could one day look in the mirror, and not see the husk of a monster. I hoped that Donatello Ricci would be less judgemental, and win Louise over. I hoped that the Hydes could heal and live the way they had before, without Shane.

I hoped that Kay Isotton would continue giving away flowers.

And I hoped that Hugh Grahams would someday find the courage to detach from that urn, to scatter his late wife's ashes. And his child's. Then perhaps start another family and love them in the way they needed.

So I used those last few seconds of consciousness to visualise others, and thought that maybe I hadn't seen my own life because I hadn't wanted to. I was allowed see what I truly wanted, and it not be myself.

I could let go.

My eyes were closing. The defined circles of light were growing dim and abstract with the lightening of my head. I think the monster continued to weep. And I think that it spoke again as I fell further and further outside of my body into the depths of a cold, murky ocean.

"A…Alexander?"

It was too far and I was too weak. But I smiled and disappeared.

the closing jaws

IN THE GLEAM OF GOLD

+

FERREAM HAD NEVER cried.

Shane Hyde had —only in fabricated memory prior to doing it in front of the soul, but not the iron beast.

To cry; the very concept of it, had always been weakness. A weakness that the monster did not have —a weakness unbefitting of Hell's worst.

So when his unbloody hand rose to the heat on his cheek, he knew that something had happened. Fire streaked iron, burning it slightly red.

The demon looked upwards. The ink in the sky was starting to recede. That had never occurred before. The reset, though never immediate, had always sparked upon the soul's death. Scarlet blood would soak into the ground, deep and darkening —all the blood would pool and turn the earth red. And once that awful sight had rendered all of Pine Creek a prophetic hellscape of the End Times, only then would the torture come to a close. Then a teenage boy would be driven from deep sleep with a gasp which was the echo of a scream; clawing at his sheets and knowing that he had not been dreaming.

The ink was *receding*.

Ferream looked down at the body in his arms.

"Alexander," he said again. He knew that they were gone. But at least he had *known*. The dark had worked against the anchors of their eyes, and it was thanks to quick thinking that the soul had spoken instead.

Their voice and even light touch had been enough.

Even if the creature had forced its way out and splintered what made him human…some part had recognised Alexander.

Some part had obeyed them without question.

"Psst! Over here."

Louise Barnes was beckoning the monster, freshly stained and unsure of how to proceed. A thread of the plan had ultimately worked: Alexander becoming the first victim had translated to them being the last. He felt no urge to kill. The devastation was too much on its own for him to feel.

But Ferream was still on Earth.

The soul was alone.

His wings quivered and knocked together as they folded. He had to calm and reassure himself that the death had been wanted this time. That it had been necessary.

The words whirled within his mind; present but finding no traction.

His left palm seared.

"*Shane*," Louise tried.

There was no Shane Hyde left within the Made demon. But he listened to the words she formed, hushed and panicked, urging him to escape. He was simply knelt there with a dying vessel. Once the shadows had fully dispersed, everyone would see. He would be responsible, and they might take up arms to hunt him.

Part of him was all right with that. It was what he deserved.

The part which won out needed to be with Alexander all the more.

"Go to the gate," Louise suggested, far closer than before. "Take their body with you." As if she was standing right next to him. She had no fear in her own way —Ferream towered higher over her than the others, yet she dared approach without caution. But her concern sounded genuine.

"…See you in many, many years, witchlet," offered the monster in his last and parting words.

All he saw as he gathered the body within his arms and reared the iron wings was the glare of absolute offence.

Ferream pushed off of the ground and shot towards the pull of heat. It wasn't easy to fly with a passenger. Even so, Alexander's body felt lighter without them in it. He tried not to think of it as his eyes narrowed on the aforementioned gate —an enormous crack through the forest floor amidst a small clearing.

Blood resumed dripping when the beast touched down. There was still an urge to reach for those dark curls and slowly run his knuckles along a warm cheek. Though this wasn't them, Ferream recognised that this was the face he had been seeing for unquantified years.

And that meant something.

Perhaps in all of that time, the monster and the boy had come together in ways that neither part had anticipated.

He wanted to lay the mortal vessel down in a gentle propping against a tree. Unfortunately, that wouldn't aid in the narrative which Louise had implied that he spin; that Alexander had been mauled by a wild animal.

The marks of his claws did indeed resemble a struggle with a bear, or even a wolf. There was bruising on their wrist from where the demon had grabbed them. *That* didn't look like the work of an animal.

Ferream thought on his feet. He reached for it again —and snapped it. The crack of bone made him flinch. He was not sure if it was because of who he held, or because he no longer liked the sound.

Regardless, he had to cast the body aside unceremoniously. He hoped that the soul would forgive him.

As he pulled the doors of the gate apart and dove inside, he realised that Alexander would never know what it was to fly in his arms.

Lilith was there to greet the iron beast —and he did not know how he felt about it. As did all creatures of Hell but himself, she appeared slightly different here. Her gown remained the same; her hair unchanged. In Hell, the Mistress of the Council had eyes of wholly silver like glowing moons. Her tattoos also emitted light, and moved in ways corresponding to their depiction. The dragon coiled; the eye blinked; the moon rotated; the snake slithered about her midsection. Kohl streaked her cheeks —like Louise's mascara but thicker and purposeful.

Ferream frowned. There was no need to think of mortals anymore.

The Mother of demons leaned against the opposite wall, like she had just been waiting ever since returning. Her disappointment at his apparent success was not lost upon him.

Had she anticipated his capture as the darkness parted for a light? Had she known that this would be the outcome?

"Where are they," Ferream snarled, tucking in his tired wings.

Lilith smiled. "The soul is indeed in Hell. You got precisely what you wanted. However, I do not know the exact circle. Not my department."

This was the witch he was used to; a stirrer of trouble who enjoyed all the misery of men and those she handpicked to suffer.

And though she was of minimal help, he could not help wondering for what reason she was there, greeting him at the gate. Like she had known the minute he would climb through.

"Here they come," Lilith sighed, rolling her head. She was somewhat uninterested. "The Morningstar is sure to be pleased."

The iron beast did not get the chance to ask what that meant.

Four glass demons came to a halt a foot away just as the witch melted through the wall. They parted down the middle to reveal the presence that had made Ferream tense a second prior.

The beast had not seen Lucifer in a long time.

They had not changed —save for several new cracks in their marble. Those eyes still held Ferream there, immovable and unfree. And he hated it. The king of Hell strode forward as though they had caught a traitor.

"You learned nothing," they stated.

There was no question.

No chance for defence, just as Lilith had speculated.

The demon did not answer.

Lucifer frowned. "Do you not feel like begging for forgiveness? How unlike you. Has the mortal realm broken you with arrogance?"

Ferream's eyes narrowed in challenge.

"...Bind him," ordered the Morningstar.

The Fallen Angels moved to comply, threading white chains from the air with the motion of their fingers and a few words of casting. And the beast gave no resistance. He only cared for one thing.

The demons ushered him down the tunnels towards the lower rings — and then Lucifer's golden palace. Ferream stared up at seemingly infinite spires and turrets and wondered what horrors laid within.

He was still splattered red. For the first time in his existence, he cared nothing for getting blood where the king wouldn't want it.

Lucifer seemed to observe as much. They lounged on a rigid piece of furniture the same shade of gold as the ceiling and floors. Then they rose, slowly flapping their marble wings to alleviate the stiffness.

Ferream was made to kneel before Lucifer, salt around his ankles and wrists. As though he posed as a threat worth detaining.

"What is that expression on your face?" the Fallen Angel asked, brows knitting together. "Since when did you know of indifference?"

The beast refused to answer.

Yet to his quick surprise, the king of Hell scoffed and smiled a smile that had it remembering what it was to fear.

"Did you enjoy the gift in the end, little one?" they whispered, sliding a finger underneath the demon's iron chin and tilting it upwards. His rigid muscles strained with confusion. "Did you like experiencing all of those new emotions? It must have been effective, for it to lead to defying me so openly. Those Archangels are right up my backside about it," they sighed —then struck the monster's burned cheek before they straightened. "Too much of a good thing, so they say."

Ferream paused, startled by the unsought discipline, and dared to raise his hands to the hurt. The harsh sensation of marble on iron was not what he'd previously imagined.

Lucifer belted out a laugh. "Did you feel pain, my little beast? Do not despair. Perhaps this will teach you to tantrum sparingly, until the world is finally in need of you."

They had never looked at Ferream like that.

The demon had beheld nothing but fear and unease from others —not scorn. The king had only ever expressed a frustration inward; directed at themself in the past. It had never been the beast's fault.

"I…I do not understand," Ferream spoke up.

"Of course you don't," chuckled the Fallen Angel. "I can explain it in the most simple of terms. I had an upgrade I needed to install. You made things difficult with your latest stunt. I had to get creative. So I recruited a human soul so desperate for a connection that it didn't mind slumming it with an abomination. All that it had to do, was help unlock something that only its kind and you, as you were Made, are capable of possessing. The ability to feel empathy. To feel pain. To limit you."

No. That could not be the truth. The Devil could lie, too.

And the monster's experience had been deeper than that.

Apparently Ferream's shock was quite amusing, because Lucifer only laughed again. "Oh, do tell me all that you felt," they quipped. "Are you forlorn because the soul seemed to have interest in conversations? Did it make you feel important?"

"No."

It was denial, spite and protection all in one. The last thing the monster needed was ammunition to be used against him.

The Morningstar wasn't buying it.

"Oh but you must be," they countered, "if you dared to mar your skin with a seal. Tell me all for which you hoped, Ferream. Did you dream of solace, here? Did you hope for a reward? You stupid, *stupid* demon. You truly are like a child."

"*No*."

He wanted Lucifer to be wrong —he wanted it all to be another cruel lesson or trick, stemming from wild, irrational jealousy. That he had only been treated this way only to ensure a tighter hold on his neck.

"Let us say you felt too much," the king mused, pacing back and forth. "What do you think the soul thought? I think that it pitied you. I think that it took one look at your pouting visage, and decided that it must ruin you. I would have done the same."

"*No*."

Alexander was not like that. They did not dream of conquer and ends, like Lucifer did. All which they cared about pooled within the monster.

Ferream wasn't about to forget that.

"Why are you clinging?" Lucifer questioned. "You got out of the loop on your own. You left that town behind. Why are you vehemently denying my involvement?"

"Because you speak lies!"

He could not stop himself then. The adamant opposition demanded to be heard. And the Morningstar stared back with a mixture of surprise and intrigue. A display of raw emotion was not quite something that they had wanted. Maybe they had hoped for a more controlled conduct.

"You *have* felt too much," they muttered.

Now their interest turned to irritation. Flippant reveals of exactly what was inside, was the sort of thing that could crumble their vision.

The very function of Hell.

Emotion was for humans.

"I *wanted* to feel it," Ferream insisted. "I needed to. And I don't regret it. Even if that soul had felt *nothing*, I…I still —"

Marble struck his face again. Though this time, the expression of the king was not anger. It was cold, rampant disgust.

"You dare start something with a mortal? I thought I made sure that every demon was aware of the agreement we have with those above. We are not permitted to lay with them. So who the fuck do you think you are, when you are so below in status even to that of a baron?"

Their voice hissed —another facet of the serpent.

The Made creature was indignant. That last slap had stung horribly in the wake of his still healing skin.

"The Council will hear about this," promised Lucifer. "And you might be destroyed. Such a shame. And to think, I was considering making you the antichrist. But those humans taught you to be so disobedient."

Panic clanged through him. "I wouldn't have agreed."

The Fallen Angel cast him a glance over their shoulder as they turned away. "You would not have had the choice."

Lucifer flicked their hand in dismissal. The salt chains tugged of their own accord, burning where they pulled.

"*Luci…*" Lilith's voice then echoed through the room. The movement of the monster's chains stopped as the king's concentration was abruptly interrupted. The witch was nowhere to be seen, though her essence hung noticeably in the air. She was definitely in there.

"You know…that rule was only for demons laying with maidens," she continued. The sound carried in different corners of the ornate lounge. It comforted Ferream momentarily, as she had taken Lucifer's focus.

"What are you implying, witch?" snarled the Morningstar.

"The soul —aptly so —is no longer a mortal. They have in fact, *died*, for the final time. That was the consequence of your pet's breaking of the curse. Besides —that child was never the type of human who could bear offspring. Your little experiment has not violated any agreement."

"What," Lucifer whipped around, their wings shakily unfurling. "The summoned human was not a girl? I thought I had told Beelzebub —"

They stopped short, realising where their plan had unravelled. It only stoked the fire in their eyes and widened the fissures along their frame.

"…If you do not wish to continue work on Ferream any longer, Luci, I would be more than happy to take it off of your hands."

"I never said anything of the sort," the king grumbled. They stomped to the window, robes swishing behind them. "I need to think. Just get the damn creature out of here for now."

They had never been able to make decisions in the demon's presence. There was something about his mere face that riled the Fallen Angel. It made him wonder why he had even been created. Why they exerted such force over it, like he was important to them.

Because Ferream had known from the first seconds of consciousness that he could be abandoned at any moment.

Long ago, he had tried to prevent that fate.

Now he wanted it. He needed to be left behind in order to escape their fast grasp.

Lilith laughed and shimmered into solid form by the door Ferream had been dragged through. She grabbed hold of the end of the chains and tilted her head. "Come along, little thing."

He hadn't in fact traded one master for another.

Lilith folded as soon as they set foot on the circles' spiral staircase. A burst of laughter echoed about the narrowing chamber as she flicked her hair over her shoulder. "Do not worry. I have no interest in you, Ferream," the witch assured. "You just needed to get out of there."

The beast swallowed with some difficulty. "Will I not be destroyed?"

All he could think of was Alexander, alone somewhere in the fiery pit, waiting indefinitely for the demon to come find them.

And he knew that they would, as nothing else would matter.

The monster simply wanted to see the soul before anything else could happen. Before he would be the one who was taken from them.

"The Morningstar can destroy you if they so wish," Lilith sighed. "But they would not be able to justify it with your relationship with Alexander. It would only be accepted as a decision on a whim."

That didn't reassure him.

The First Wife drew a breath and tapped his chains three times, which then unlocked and clattered. He stared at her, wondering if not a transfer in ownership, what her true intentions might be.

"You found something, Ferream —a thing rare and incomprehensible to beings who have never tried to understand love. Angels are led by blind devotion. Demons are led by duty and sin. Neither are truly free —not in the way that you could be. When an angel falls, it has no choice. There is only Hell —it cannot even want for the Earth." This came as news to the Made demon. "Sure, it can disguise itself to live among the mortals…but at the end of the day, it cannot die," Lilith explained. "It must continue to exist and wreak whatever havoc king one or King two dictate."

The beast frowned. What did all of that have to do with him?

"*This* is the curse which needs to be broken," she clarified. "And it is creations like you who will accomplish this feat." Her animation promptly diffused as she glanced down at her skirts. "But not you, specifically. You will know of respite in this time. You will know of love."

He tried to smile; to show gratitude. "Where are they," Ferream asked again. Softer, with more hope.

Her lips curled upwards. "You will find them where they found you."

the last tale

IN THE ASHES

+

A FORLORN SOUL sat in the middle of a cell, starving.

They did not know why they were sad. They could not recall. Memory of Earth and all of the life upon it had not been carried with them across the threshold of death. They remembered the vague sensation of stabbing, but this new burning and hunger was overtaking all else. They had never suffered through anything like it.

There were ashes on the floor, around the soul's feet.

Ashes.

There had been something about that, somewhere. Once. Long ago. They dipped their bare toes in the dark and warm layer on the floor, writing in it. The soul didn't know what it wrote but it recognised the curve of some letters and pieced together the semblance of a name.

It wasn't their own. They could tell that much.

They were quite unsure if *they* had a name.

They must have, in the past, when they had been alive. For a moment they wondered what that meant —to be alive. If this state was not alive, what could the difference be?

A hand rose to their chest —and they were alarmed to find a deep gash in the middle of their palm. Though it did not bleed, it radiated some sort of magic. It was unnatural.

The soul then wondered what that word meant, too.

There was no thumping in their chest, which somehow felt wrong. But maybe there never had been or wasn't supposed to be. They weren't sure.

All that they knew was that it was dark, it was hot, and they were very hungry. And it was quiet.

If there were others wherever they were, there was no evidence of it. Their gaze slid to bars of metal. It was still dark, but a flickering light fell on them to give them shape. Each was very straight and very solid —upon the soul's touch, they did not sing. It didn't strike them, of course, but not even a mere scratch pierced the silence.

It was then they came to the conclusion that they had been detained.

Something reprehensible had happened and it had been their fault.

Though, it would be very lonely. They were not a stranger to solitude but the darkness was not friendly.

Was the soul so terrible that it been denied company?

There was the colour red, and the colour silver.

In a story that they had never read, where a small fox wandered about with red dripping from its snout, an apple had fallen from a tree. It hadn't been its time to be picked. The ground was rough and unforgiving. It had bruised its delicate skin. No one would want it then.

But the silver fox then happened upon the apple tree. It looked up at the ones not yet ripe. They were far too high. But the apple at its feet was laying there unattended, possibly forgotten.

It batted it about for a moment, never having seen such a thing though knowing that it was food. It rolled from side to side, passive and unafraid even in the face of a creature much large than itself with blood around its mouth and staining its gleaming teeth.

The fox then laid down on the ground —tired from its usual hunt, and nudged the apple with its paw. It stayed there a while, idle and soaking in the sun. But when the hunger returned the fox began to wonder what the apple tasted like.

The fruit was not something with which it interacted. It was soft and unfamiliar, providing an odd sense of comfort in its solitary existence. In the heat of the moment, the fox gave the apple a lick —then another when nothing came of it, and another. Then its teeth sunk into the flesh, bursting the small fruit into smaller pieces.

It was delicious.

Never mind that it had first fallen from the tree —never mind that the birds had scoffed at it. The silver fox ate up every bit and cleaned its fur. And when it was done, the taste of blood had gone.

The need for it was no more.

The metal bars suddenly sang.

The soul looked upwards between the gaps to a large figure the colour of fresh, light grey ash. It was breathing erratically; short of breath that they themself did not seem to need. The creature beyond fell to its knees, hands sliding downward to where the soul had curled theirs.

Something electric shot through the soul when it felt the cold skin of the visitor. They glanced at their face, trying to place it. Its structure was something which they knew —they *knew* this face but the question was, from where. The soul frowned at the scorched lines running from its eyes down towards its jaw.

"I found you," it spoke, and it was beautiful.

The soul blinked. "…You are very cold. I need that."

The cold thing had wings in its back and horns curving from its head. It didn't look like an angel, but it didn't look like a demon. None of this bothered the soul.

It could be its own thing if it wished.

"Do you not remember?" it asked, frowning as well.

The soul tilted their head. "I can't seem to remember a lot." Even so, the grey figure seemed important somehow. Like a puzzle piece that was integral to the image, but didn't obviously fit with the ones given.

In response, the visitor tensed —and scrambled to hold their fingers. There was that sensation again, like lightning. They started, catching blue eyes ringed with crescents of violet.

Pain blossomed in their hollow chest.

Then the creature moved —it gripped the bars and pulled, grunting in effort. They slowly bent apart to a gap large enough for it to slip through. The soul stiffened. Apprehension prickled its skin as the great thing knelt before them. It didn't look like it meant them harm.

"Please," begged the cold stranger. "*Alex*…"

"Don't call me that," snapped the soul, jerking backwards on the ash floor. "There is only one person who can use that…Only…"

They trailed off, unsure of the words coming from their mouth; words they could not appear to control. Suddenly the soul rose to its knees and reached out towards that grey face. They brought it closer, examining the streaks of burning that resembled the stains of tears, before those eyes of eerie ease and warmth.

A rush of feeling flooded a lacking space; filling in the blanks.

"…Ferream."

With that single word, the world splintered once again.

Alexander knew everything about anything —and that they had done it. They had made it. Only when brown met blue would they know who the beast was. Only at death. Until the two of them had broken that rule with memory of a time laced in dreaming.

Alexander inhaled sharply at their awful momentary unawareness, but the demon was already past that with a smile and the threat of more tears.

"My dear monster," they whispered, pressing their forehead to the iron beast's. Ferream then leaned into the touch of their thumb along the marks left from the weeping of flame.

"My sweet mortal," the demon returned, reaching for the side of their head. His hand gently brushed over the curls and burning skin, to cool it. "You had me frightened. How fragile humans are."

He neared, pressing a welcome, freezing kiss to their parted lips. Their eyelids fluttered as the two paused to stare and graze with their fingertips; to ensure that the other was truly there.

"Would you have mourned?" Alexander murmured. Ferream brushed his thumb along their scar.

"Yes. Endlessly."

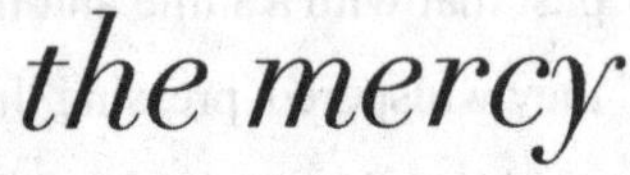

the mercy

IN THE WAKE

+

SOLITUDE NEVER LEFT, though it did talk less. Without Louise Barnes' manifestation of guilt with which to argue, it had resorted to lighter commentary on how she was coming to neglect it. Life was not the same as it had been weeks prior —Louise had a friend, a light and a reason to get up in the mornings.

She also had a thorny branch tattooed to the skin of her shoulder and neck which had appeared the night after the darkness, but she didn't want to think about that. She didn't want to think about the Mother of demons.

There was too much chaos within her at the realisation that while Pine Creek had reappeared on the map, there had been a blip in time. She had lived through Fall. Everyone else was just beginning to don an extra layer.

Louise decided that the strangest thing to come out of the last month was the fact that she *remembered* what had happened. She remembered a boy who seemed to have never existed. She remembered the monster who had killed Alexander Grahams —and she remembered why. Even the visit of Heavenly Hosts and a witch from out of the ground.

Donatello Ricci did not remember.

He did not remember them agreeing to be friends, or all that they had been through afterwards. Their relationship had reset along with the rest of the town and she…didn't like it.

It was a revelation that tore apart her insides more so than any feeling of displacement —more so than the end of her investigations and the start of something far more complicated.

Shane Hyde was gone.

The Daemons were gone.

No —it was as if they had never been there to begin with. Louise had spent a solid ten minutes convinced that it might have all been one horrid dream. That was until she found the body in the woods with marks unlike any animal's she had ever seen.

That proved it had been real.

And since time was moving and cars could start, that meant the loop was broken. Alexander had gotten all for which they had hoped.

Louise was stuck here —with family tearing down the middle and an inexplicable sense of dread.

She didn't resent them. She couldn't. She might hate the love they had found and exalted above all else, but it had been important to them. And that had to matter. If nothing else and of all the crumbling left in their departure, Louise knew that she had no right to judge and no right to rage.

The girl could be angry with the world and at God.

Not Alexander Grahams.

She tried to remember that as she stood by the casket. In fact, she had no right to be here either. A lot of Pine Creek was there; frigid and hollow in the awkward fashion that guests at a funeral stood, as if uninvited. They *were* invited. But they hadn't known Alexander.

Yet they all still had greater reasons to be in attendance.

Irrationally, Louise felt every eye on her person. Maybe the borrowed, collared black dress was too short now. Maybe she shouldn't have worn fraying boots. Maybe she shouldn't have cut her hair shorter off of her shoulders —this time at the hairdressers —but she had pinned two little sections back with small black ribbons.

No matter how rigid her spine and clenched her fingers, she could not shake the looks. Of all of the people who had made life Hell for Alexander when they were all younger, she was the one who had been the worst. She didn't belong here.

Carley Vasquez, Laura Takunda and Georgia Grande stood opposite, in a neat row and plaid grey. Though makeup was scarce, Louise did not miss the dark circles achieved with eye shadow. How remorseless.

There were those who were sad and there were those who didn't know what to say. The town had abruptly been caught up in a death of a person whose very name set off pangs of guilt. In the end, despite any acceptance or denial about who Alexander was, they were now dead.

And most people had respect for the dead.

Donatello Ricci had hoped that he and Louise Barnes would have become friends under better circumstances.

It was a whirlwind of occurrences —of Alexander Grahams moving back to Pine Creek, of the sky darkening with the thickest rain clouds in all of history, and of Alexander's death. Somewhere in between, and just before the funeral, Louise had approached him first to talk. She had asked weird questions about shadows and a monster made of iron, but it had all paled in comparison to her asking if they could repair whatever was left of their relationship.

And even though Donatello was elated with the development, he did not miss the vacancy in her gaze; the far-off emptiness in that ice blue as if she had been —and in that moment, *was* —in another place. In another time. He didn't know how to bring it up, but it felt even more so as though Louise Barnes had fallen out of step with the world.

She was there, but a part of her had unravelled.

When she wasn't staring at something that he could not see, her deeply forlorn exterior hardened like the iron she'd spoken of. She scowled like her milk was sour and she might hiss like a cat bothered in a nap.

It was different at Alexander Grahams' funeral.

As if she had crudely tied up those billowing loose ends, she stood tall and upright and pretended that nothing was amiss. But he could still see her blanching knuckles and every bite of her chapped lips. She might run if he didn't hold her there.

He would have chalked it up to gnawing guilt if Louise had not asked all of those questions like there was something he'd forgotten. She looked at the dead with sorrow and envy.

Donatello Ricci had never spoken a word to Alexander, but as he saw their still face in a bed of blinding white lace and satin, he could not help but think that maybe they had exchanged words, long ago.

Though that had never happened.

There had been a tug however, when the funeral had been organised, to bring a bouquet of roses. Flowers often brought to these tragedies; with the colours each meaning something different.

Donatello held white.

Louise clutched dark crimson.

The woman who owned the little flower shop, *The Honeysuckle*, had arranged baskets of soft red and white, with bursts of yellow. The yellow seemed most out of place —that warmth was for friends of the deceased. But as far as Donatello knew, Alexander hadn't had any friends back here —they had left them in Albuquerque. Those friends hadn't known of the death until a couple of days ago.

Only one of them had made it: Sebastian Paul.

He stared at Louise and Donatello as if they should be the ones in the casket. And he'd be justified in half of that judgement. Louise Barnes had been the cruellest monster of them all.

How could she dare to attend Alexander's funeral with ribbons in her hair and rose thorns in her skin, pretending that those past years had not happened, and that she was invited?

Louise's pale hand reached for the edge of Donatello's dark blazer.

"I can't do this," she murmured when he'd leaned down.

Strands of his ginger hair fell forward over his brow, straying from a bun. His fingers grazed her own. "Yes you can. You're not that little girl any more. You're allowed to be here. You can mourn."

She pressed her lips into a tight line.

Once upon a time, this could have been her doing. Instead of that seal and promise and the wounds of iron claws, Alexander Grahams could've been eleven and poisoned. And certainly not just by words.

Louise could have been a killer —arguably on par with the iron beast, even though her count would have been one while his was infinite. He'd killed because it was within him. He had been made that way. She would have done it of her own volition. And the only question that she could've asked was, what sort of monster was *that*?

Could she blame her parents or herself? She doubted that her instincts were anything like his, but would that translate to no evil residing there? Just as Alexander had asked the question she had been unable to answer: had she been born or made?

Donatello turned bold and laced his fingers with the girl's, holding on tightly like that strength would be enough to keep what was left of her by his side. He didn't mind that he had lost a piece of her somewhere —even if she never found it again, he would strive to ensure that she lost no more.

Louise squeezed his hand as Alexander's favourite song began to play on the speakers. A soft, lulling song that drew more tears from onlookers and reminded her of a boy no one knew.

The firm fingers in her hold tensed in slight surprise. She did not dare to glance upwards at Donatello's face; to guess what his reaction was even though she knew how he felt. He didn't let go.

Her gaze was straight ahead, across the cemetery grounds at the other side of the horseshoe of guests. Sebastian Paul's eyes were bloodshot and puffy. In his arms, he bore bushels of velvet yellow blooms.

Louise was glad that she remembered for only one reason.

So Alexander could be buried with roses.

They were going to be cremated, like their mother.

Louise Barnes had seen it in Alexander Grahams' diary. There'd been a confirmation in her suspicion that while no resident remembered that Fall, written accounts from that period of time would be preserved.

Just as hers had, through the loops.

Alexander's writings and drawings on '*The Haunting of Pine Creek*' were all intact and unaltered —down to the dates.

Louise was sure their father wouldn't know what to do with it all, so she had asked for the materials. Hugh Grahams had been distracted and absentminded; unaware of what Louise Barnes had done in the past and never having been privy to *any* of Alexander's diaries.

The books sat heavy, like a burden tenfold of physical weight, inside of her leather backpack. They were safest with her, but she could barely bring herself to *actually* read them. Each was a glimpse into their mind. It felt invasive. But she had peeked, only for reassurance that she wasn't crazy and that the thorns on her neck *meant* something.

She had had no dreams of Lilith yet.

Donatello Ricci didn't find it strange. He didn't have much opinion of it at all, but he hadn't looked at her with contempt or anger when she had shown him. And Louise had shivered at the graze of his fingertips along the stark lines, as if he could feel something there other than skin.

She was on her way across town to see him now. They would do that from then on —hang out and talk and listen. Sometimes of the past. Other times of the future. And rarely, though never dismissed, she would talk *at* him about a month that had never happened. Louise was never sure how much of her ramblings he actually believed, but she appreciated that he never shut her down or interrupted.

Donatello sat in a booth in *Straws & Fries*, picking at a plate of fried chicken. His face lit up at the sight of Louise, wandering over draped in a familiar tan jacket trimmed with black wool.

He blinked. "You're wearing it," he remarked.

"It's a nice jacket," she quipped, sliding onto the opposite seat.

"That doesn't change that you stole it."

Louise wasn't having it. "You said it was a gift, in the end."

"Yeah, well…I just hadn't thought you would…*accept* it." Donatello turned bashful —as bashful as a boy of his size could be, while still being considered endearing. His hair was loose and unruly, fanning out in curls like a small mane. Louise wanted to tug her fingers through it.

"Do you want to know the last thing that Alexander Grahams wrote?" she asked quickly, averting her gaze.

"Mm?"

"Just a word. Verisimilitude. All scrawled and hasty."

"What does that mean?"

"Something appearing to be real," Louise murmured, folding her arms over the table. "…I think they wanted something to be real."

"I think you might want the same thing," tactfully remarked Donatello as he set aside an eaten wing. "From what you've told me."

"Hm," she huffed, glancing down at the wood. "But the difference is, they actually found it. It was real for them."

His hand reached across the table for one of hers. And she smiled only in part, without her eyes. He wouldn't understand. With all the knowledge of those cycles and the witness of their hopeful end, Louise would be the sole inheritor of a piece of history forever lost.

Aside from immortal words and sketches.

And Louise couldn't help thinking that the curse had not been broken, so much as passed onto her.

"Yeah, well... I just didn't think you would accept it," Donatello seemed bashful—as bashful as a boy of his size could be, while still being considered outstanding. His hair was loose and firmly forming natural curls like a small mane. Louise wanted to dig her fingers through it.

"Do you want to know the last thing that Alexander Graham wrote?" she asked quickly, averting her gaze.

"Mm?"

"Just a word. 'Verisimilitude,'" Louise [illegible].

"What does that mean?"

"Something appearing to be real," Louise murmured, [illegible] her arm over the table. "I think they wanted something to be real."

"I think you might want the same thing," tactfully remarked Donatello as he set aside an [illegible]. "From what you've told me."

"Hm," she huffed, glancing down at the board. "But the difference is they actually found it. It was real for them."

His hand reached across the table for one of hers. And she smiled, only in part, without her eyes. He wouldn't understand. With all the knowledge of these cycles and the witness of their tragic end, Louise would be the sole inheritor of a piece of history forever lost.

Aside from the journal's words and sketches.

And Louise couldn't help thinking that the cursed had not been broken as much as it passed onto her.

ACKNOWLEDGEMENT

'*Ashes to Ashes*' for a long time was something in the distant future. I had to rewrite and revisit it so many times, but the prospect of having out for those who needed it was what kept me going. This story is very near to my heart and was sparked from just a few lines of dialogue in a prompt. I am beyond happy with how it has evolved and become its own work —its own message and love letter in a time when I may no longer be the one who needs it, but many people will. I hope that they will laugh and cry and question, and feel the love and torment in every word.

So thank you, reader, for living through this.

Thank you to every single one of my Street Team members, early readers and eager enthusiasts who rushed for the premise and never let go —for supporting me every step of the way.

www.ingramcontent.com/pod-product-compliance
Lightning Source LLC
Chambersburg PA
CBHW010446310726
48979CB00018B/2828/J

* 9 7 8 1 8 3 8 3 9 8 3 8 5 *